IMMORTAL

Meet the mild-mannered little runt who won a
killer's reputation because his aim was bad • the
temptress who conquered the richest, rowdiest
town in the West • the surgeon-turned-outlaw
who invented the art of sticking up stagecoaches
• the kid who grew up to love corn liquor and
women, but whose first love was scalping Indians • the murdering Mexican who offered a
$10,000 reward to anyone who could take him,
dead or alive • the incredible prisoner of Yuma
who started—and stopped—the West's wildest
jailbreak • the crackpot who invented the revolving gun that altered the course of world history • the young Apache brave whose wild
rampage of revenge made him the most feared
warrior of the old West • the wildest hell-raiser
of them all who lived with a gun in his hand and
died with a rope around his neck!

**CLAIR HUFFAKER'S PROFILES OF
THE AMERICAN WEST**
is an original POCKET BOOK edition.

Books by Clair Huffaker

Badge for a Gunfighter
Badman
Clair Huffaker's Profiles of the American West
Cowboy
The Cowboy and the Cossack
Flaming Lance
Guns from Thunder Mountain
Guns of Rio Conchos
One Time, I Saw Morning Come Home
Posse from Hell
Rider from Thunder Mountain
Seven Ways from Sundown
The War Wagon

Published by POCKET BOOKS

CLAIR HUFFAKER'S
Profiles of
the American West

by Clair Huffaker

PUBLISHED BY POCKET BOOKS NEW YORK

CLAIR HUFFAKER'S PROFILES OF THE
AMERICAN WEST

POCKET BOOK edition published September, 1976

This original POCKET BOOK edition is printed from brand-new
plates made from newly set, clear, easy-to-read type.
POCKET BOOK editions are published by
POCKET BOOKS,
a division of Simon & Schuster, Inc.,
A GULF+WESTERN COMPANY
630 Fifth Avenue,
New York, N.Y. 10020.
Trademarks registered in the United States
and other countries.

Contents

CLAIR HUFFAKER'S

Profiles of
the American West

SILVER DOLLAR
AND HIS BABY DOE

Everyone said she was after Haw's money, but she
stuck with him to the end, even after his mines had
burned out and there wasn't anything to eat.

It happened one night in the elegant Saddle Rock
Restaurant. Haw Tabor, the Silver King whose wealth had
made him famous around the world, was dining in solitary
splendor at his special table in Colorado's most luxurious
eatery. He was dressed in a $300 suit and was wearing
diamond-studded cufflinks worth more than most men earn
in a lifetime.

But a subject as mundane as money held no interest for
Haw this warm evening of 1882. His attention was held
by a girl seated alone at a table opposite his across the
room. She was a honey blonde girl with huge blue eyes
and a figure that was almost too much for a man to
stand.

Haw raised his finger about an inch, and the headwaiter
sprinted to his table. "Yes sir, Mr. Tabor. Is everything
satisfactory? Is there anything I can do for you?"

"Who's that young lady sitting by herself?"

"I'm afraid I don't know, sir. I've never seen her here
before. But I can find out."

1

"Don't bother. Just ask her if she'd care to join me for dinner." Haw stuck a $50 bill in the headwaiter's hand.

"Yes, sir!"

Haw watched while his envoy crossed the dimly lit room and bowed from the waist at the beautiful girl's table. The blonde listened, her stunning eyes flicking at Haw briefly. Then she got up and followed the headwaiter back across the room. Haw could hardly believe his good luck; she was going to accept!

He stumbled to his feet awkwardly as they approached him. The headwaiter said discreetly, "Mr. Tabor—Miss Elizabeth McCourt."

Miss McCourt saw before her a middle-aged man with a thickset body and kind eyes. She also saw before her roughly $100 million on the hoof. "I'd be delighted to join you, Mr. Tabor," she said in a voice that tinkled softly like small golden bells.

"Why—it's sure my pleasure, Miss."

When they were seated, Haw said with simple honesty, "You're the purtiest girl I ever saw, Miss McCourt."

She smiled at the compliment. "Thank you, Mr. Tabor. But my friends call be Baby Doe."

"My friends call me Haw."

"I know. I know all about you. I guess everybody does."

Haw blushed. "Well then, let's talk about you—Baby Doe. You new to Colorado?"

"No. I've been here a few months. I came here from Oshkosh."

During dinner Haw learned that Baby Doe had come to the Rockies with her husband, Harvey Doe, who had deserted her a few weeks before. Since that time, she told him, she had worked at any job that would pay her enough to live on. It didn't occur to the Silver King that a girl so short on cash should hardly be dining in the Saddle Rock, or that it was quite a coincidence that she should be seated directly across from him at precisely the time he usually had dinner. "Well," he said gently as they sipped an 1877 champagne, "things must be kinda tough for a little girl like you makin' her way all alone."

"It's not too easy," she admitted, a shining tear edging the bottom of each lovely blue eye. "Sometimes I just don't know what to do."

Haw pulled tenderly at his ear. "I guess you have quite a few debts piled up here and there."

"Yes. I made good money at the Gem Dance Hall for

2

a while, but that's not a nice sort of work to be doing, so I quit. I guess I must have about—oh, almost $1,000 owed to people right now."

Haw took a checkbook from his pocket and wrote swiftly for a few seconds. Then he handed her the folded check. "Maybe this will help a little."

"Oh, I couldn't!" Baby Doe insisted. "I hardly know you. It's awfully nice of you, but—"

"I wouldn't be able to sleep a wink all night thinkin' about you worried with those debts," Haw explained. "For my sake, you've just got to take it."

"Well, I'll certainly want to pay you back every cent. And it's awfully nice of you, Haw."

They parted a little later. Baby Doe waited until she was alone before she looked at the check he'd given her; it was made out for $10,000.

That was the beginning of the gaudy, ardent love affair of the greatest of all the Silver Kings and a strikingly beautiful girl who was considered, by most, to be the best gold digger who ever drew breath in a mining camp.

Horace Austin Warner Tabor was born near Holland, Vermont, in 1830. He was a dreamer who disliked school and broke the Sabbath with swimming and wrestling. His folks tried to make him properly serious by taking him out of school after a year or two and giving him a man's work to do on the farm. But he stubbornly refused to recognize that life was grim and earnest. He grew into a jovial young man with tremendous shoulders, a broad grin and a hunger—never fulfilled at home—to be friends with everyone in the world.

At 17 Horace struck out into the world and became a stonecutter. One of his first bosses watched him sign his name in the paybook and squinted at the signature: H. A. W. Tabor.

"Say, Tabor," he said. "You ever notice, your initials spell out 'Haw'?"

He was Haw Tabor from then on.

At 23 Haw went to work for a man named Pierce in Augusta, Maine. Pierce had a daughter named after that town, who was thinking it was about time she got married. Augusta, a strong-willed, strait-laced young lady, set her matrimonial sights on Tabor. Overwhelmed by her advances, Haw was an easy mark.

3

"First, though," he told Augusta, "I'd like to go out West and set us up on a government grant of land."

"Why? You can work in father's business, and you'll own it some day."

"Well, I'd rather be on my own."

The newspapers were full of talk about booming opportunities in the West. Kansas was particularly wide open. It was only a matter of time until the territory would become a state. So Haw Tabor joined a caravan and headed West. In Manhattan, Kansas, he claimed 160 acres of rattlesnakes and sagebrush. After clearing some land and putting up a cabin, he returned to Maine, married Augusta and traveled back to Kansas with his bride.

A son, Maxcy, was born to the Tabors, and a few months later Haw was elected to the Kansas Territory Free State Legislature. Meanwhile, across the lonely plains to the West, events were taking place that would soon take Haw's mind off politics and eventually carve his name forever into frontier history.

H. Green Russel and a dozen boys had pushed up along the Platte in Kansas Territory (now Colorado) in search of gold. Though they took less than $1,000 in nuggets out of the hills after working through the summer, news of a rich strike came echoing down into eastern Kansas and sped swiftly through the nation. Jack Easton rode his mule up to Haw's cabin one morning before sunup. He hailed Tabor and said, "Hear about the gold?"

Haw buttoned his shirt while standing on his doorstep. "Gold? No. Step down and come in for breakfast."

"Can't. No time. Goin' into Fort Riley for supplies. Goin' west to Pike's Peak. They hit gold out there. Couple of fellas panned $10,000 there in a week. They say nuggets are layin' around on the bare ground up there."

"Where around Pike's Peak?"

"Someplace around there. Someplace on the Platte. Seems to me a fella said somethin' about a creek. Cherry Creek or Apple Creek. Somethin' like that. Well, so long."

The story got wilder and better, until by the time it got back East, it sounded as though Pike's Peak was solid gold under a few inches of dirt on the surface. On foot, on horses and mules and in every conceivable kind of rig and wagon, the money-hungry Argonauts came hurrying through Kansas. Many of them had painted, "Pike's Peak or Bust!" boldly across the canvas tops or wood slats of

4

their wagons. Within the year many of them would cross out that brave message, write, "Busted by God!" underneath it and turn wearily home.

Haw was soon as excited as the others, but he didn't go off half-cocked. The farm hadn't been paying anything, so he went to Fort Riley to work at his old trade of stone-cutting until he had earned enough to outfit himself fairly well. In '59, he loaded Augusta and Maxcy into a wagon brimming over with supplies and headed west into the gold rush country, along with some 30,000 others. They stopped briefly in Denver to find out what the news was.

"Why hell," an old prospector told Haw, "fellas named Gregory and Jackson have both hit it rich. And Old Burney hit a pocket so good he's got six men workin' for him. He sits on a rock up above them with a loaded shotgun to see they don't slip the stuff in their pockets."

The Tabors, with two friends, pushed into the hills beyond Denver. After a backbreaking summer and an idle winter which netted them exactly nothing, the Tabors headed for California Gulch on the Arkansas River, where a prospector named Abe Lee had made a big strike.

Lee and his men were glad to see the wagon load of supplies, and Augusta Tabor added a homey, female touch to the camp. They all pitched in and put up a rough cabin for her and the youngster. Augusta spent the summer nursing men with various and sundry ailments while Haw panned the yellow metal. Lee had given Haw his choice of three claims in a row to work. Haw had chosen the middle one. He washed out about $4,500 before the season was out. The man below him panned $80,000. The man above him took over $100,000.

It just wasn't Haw's year.

Because of Augusta, the Tabors had to go back to Denver for the winter once more. When springtime filled the hills again, Haw outfitted himself with an old Concord coach and lumbered up the thinly worn trails with a couple of tons of provisions. He added an extension to his cabin there and opened the first store in the Gulch. So many people filled the Gulch that several new cabins were erected, and the folks got together to christen the growing camp, Oro City. Since Haw owned the store, he was given the postmastership of the town. Augusta tended the store and passed out letters while Haw went back to his claim.

5

That year Haw's pans were often coated with a thin layer of yellow. He took nearly $10,000.

"This is the goldurndest business I ever saw," he told Augusta jubilantly. "I'll make us rich yet! And when I do I'm going to buy you everything you want. You just name it and it's yours! You'll see!"

"Now don't go on like that, Horace," Augusta said dryly. "You're past 30 now, and it's time you stopped running around through the mountains looking for gold and settled down. You ought to start up a nice business."

"Augusta," Haw said, "when I was a boy I used to think of what I'd do when I grew up. And I didn't know. But now I do. Prospecting and mining is in my blood. Besides, we've already got a steady business in the store."

Augusta sniffed. "You never pay any attention to it! You're always out looking for gold instead of minding the books and taking care of the mail."

At last Augusta's nagging wore down Haw; he stopped searching for gold and worked full time as a storekeeper and postmaster. But he was always good for a grubstake, as countless hard-pressed gold seekers could vouch for during the years ahead.

For 18 years Haw was a storekeeper and postmaster. When paydirt ran out at Oro, they moved to Buckskin Joe where old Joe Higginbottom had struck a rich vein. By the time Haw got to the town of Buckskin Joe to set up his store and transfer his postmastership, it was a sprawling tent city.

A man Haw had staked to $50 worth of supplies came to the store one day when Augusta was there alone.

"I'm movin' on, Mrs. Tabor, and I figure I'd like to pay your husband the $50 I owe him. Would he accept the claim on my diggings as payment?"

"He would but I won't," Augusta said sharply. "I want the cash."

Haw had never intended to be repaid, unless the man hit gold, but he would certainly have accepted the claim. The man wandered out of the store, sold the claim to two men in a nearby bar and gave the money to Mrs. Tabor.

Within a month the two buyers had hauled $85,000 out of the claim.

Haw shook his head and grinned. "Well, Augusta, you saved us the $50, anyway."

After the Tabors had spent six years in Buckskin Joe, the town was inconsiderate enough to run out of gold.

Haw took Augusta and Maxcy back to Oro once more, where a small but permanent group still held out, carefully going over old claims and finding enough overlooked gold to make a living.

Then a man named Stevens came to town. He planned to sluice the gravel of the Gulch for any gold that might have been missed by those before him. His plan was not unusual, nor were his complaints after working his sluices. "Haw," he told Tabor one night, "some black, gritty stuff is clogging my sluices. Making it damn near impossible to wash for gold."

"Lot of fellas have had that trouble," Haw said. "It's a terrible nuisance."

"My partner's been going crazy with the stuff, too. He must have gone plain loco finally. Sent some of the rocks to be assayed today."

Word came back: "Silver. High grade. Assay out at $500 a ton."

This was the rumble of thunder in Haw's destiny. The thunder that is heard before the bolt of lightning strikes.

Oro was soon booming as never before. Smelters were going up. New frame houses and even brick buildings began to rear their heads above the log cabins. Money talk —and action—was fantastic. Oro was renamed Leadville, in honor of those amazing carbonates of lead, and Horace Austin Warner Tabor was elected Leadville's first mayor.

Haw rushed home and told Augusta the joyful news. Her only comment was: "Hmph! Fine mayor you'll make." She had long since ceased to be an inspiration and a delight.

On a sunny day, while Haw was playing stud poker with three friends in the store, two old, ragged German prospectors shuffled into the place.

"Mister, Mayor Tabor?" one of them asked apologetically.

Haw looked up from the game, and the man was reassured by the open, friendly gaze. "Mayor Tabor," he went on, "my name's Rische. And this here's my partner Hook. We wondered if you'd let us have credit for some provisions to go do some prospecting."

Haw made a sweeping gesture at the merchandise in the store. "Help yourselves."

Rische stuttered his thanks, and the two of them began filling a sack with goods while Haw turned back to his

7

hand. When the two had everything they wanted, the tally was about $60. Haw slipped in a jug of whiskey without putting it on the bill. "Gets cold in the hills at night," he said.

"You're a third partner in this, you know," Rische assured him.

"Sure. Good luck." Haw was unimpressed.

Rische and Hook got a mile or so into the mountains before the blazing sun forced them to sit down in the shade of a big tree. Seeking refreshments in their sack, they found the whiskey bottle on top, and quenched their thirst in a leisurely manner. It was dark soon, and they slept under the tree. In the morning they agreed that since they had no idea how to search for silver logically, they might as well dig right where they were.

And pretty quick they were digging up shovelsful of silver. The ground underneath them was worth nearly $1,000 a ton. They named the strike the Little Pittsburgh and went running down the mountain to tell Tabor. "Well I'll be damned," Haw said. Shortly after that the mine was producing $20,000 a week. He started to sell the store and was worth half a million dollars before he could get the details ironed out on the sale of the store's $1,500 stock. He bought out Hook for $100,000. Soon after, on a hunch, he sold his own interest in the Little Pittsburgh for $1,000,000. He bought stock in the Little Pittsburgh Consolidated, formed by the new owners, then sold when shares skyrocketed from $5 to $35 on the Mining Exchange. Haw Tabor was now worth close to $3 million.

Leadville and Haw Tabor became world famous overnight. Everything Haw touched turned instantly into a sparkling cascade of silver. And, indeed, Leadville itself seemed to have been touched by his magic. Every day fortunes were won and lost on the signing of a paper, the turning of a card, a whispered word.

Riding high, wide and handsome on the very crest of the huge wave of silver, Haw was quickly gaining a reputation as a man who did things in a big way. He and his family were living in the fanciest quarters Leadville could offer—and as Leadville was now the largest producer of silver in the world, those quarters were plush indeed.

The only blot on Haw's happiness these days was Augusta. There wasn't much for Mrs. Tabor to nag him about now, so she didn't say anything at all. She almost seemed disappointed at their prosperity.

8

Haw was bewildered and hurt. "I just don't understand you, Augusta. When we was poor, I never blamed you for feeling bitter and stand-offish toward me. I know how hard it must have been for you coming from a good home to settle in this rough country, doing your own housework and chores and all. But that's all behind us now. We're rich. And I aim to make it all up to you, believe me. Jewels, furs, anything you can think of, they're yours."

Augusta stared at him contemptuously. "Horace, why must you always be so uncouth? So ostentatious? You are just like a child let loose in a candy store with a dollar bill. Spend, spend, spend, that's all you can think of."

Haw blinked. "What's wrong with spending money? That's what it's for. What would you want me to do, let it get moldy in a bank vault?"

"Oh, you're impossible, Horace. Don't you have any breeding at all? Nice people just don't make a show of their wealth."

Haw lowered his eyes. "All right, Augusta, anything you say," he said quietly. "I just want you to be happy. Believe me, I want that more than anything in the world."

"Oh sure! When did you ever concern yourself with my feelings?"

Haw fidgeted nervously with his stickpin. "That's not fair, Augusta. I love you." He hesitated. "All I want is for you to love me a little. Nothing means much without that. The only reason I ever wanted all this was for you; for you and the boy." He grinned shyly. "Kind of a shame we don't have a few more kids to share in it, ain't it? Maybe . . . hell, we ain't too old, you know. We—"

"Horace Tabor!" She cut him off sharply. "Watch your language. You're not down in the corner saloon."

"Augusta, please. All I meant . . ." Something inside of him twisted and died as she turned and walked swiftly from the room.

After that Haw tried to forget his unhappiness in work.

Aside from his mining deals, he was, possibly, the most amazing mayor in the history of politics. At a meeting of the town council it was decided that Leadville should have a town hall.

"That's a good idea," Haw agreed.

"But there is a question," a councilman said thoughtfully. "There's no money in the city treasury."

"That doesn't matter." Haw waved his hand in a short arc to dismiss the problem. "I'll pay for it."

Thus Leadville's "Wigwam," a fine, new city hall came into being. A wave of Haw's hand or a nod of his head was worth a certified check drawn on any bank in the country.

Fire was a serious threat to Leadville. Take a thousand flimsy wooden buildings jumbled together under a scorching summer sun, add kerosene lamps and open fireplaces, and mix well with all-night orgies, drunken brawls, riots and general hell raising—and you have one mammoth firetrap. Tabor discussed this with a friend, Billy Bush, over pressed duck at the Saddle Rock Restaurant.

"No matter how you look at it, Leadville needs a fire company," Haw said.

"I've always thought it would be great to lead a fire company," Billy said, taking a sip of 15-year-old brandy.

"All right. We'll set up two fire companies. One for you and one for me," Haw grinned. The Tabor Hose Company and the W. H. Bush Hose Company sprang into potential existence over the dinner table, and within a few weeks they were full blown realities, with handsomely uniformed, well-equipped fire brigades and crane-necked, nickel-plated fire engines of the most up-to-date style.

As a final measure of safety, Haw formed a fire insurance company. From fire insurance he branched out into numerous other businesses, aside from mining. He bought lumber companies, railroads, gas companies, water companies, real estate and opened the Tabor Bank.

When they started to call him "Silver Dollar Tabor," Haw got the idea of putting up a huge dollar on top of his elegant, two-story, brick bank as a trademark. He hired a penniless carpenter, Winfield Scott Stratton, to make the giant dollar for him. Stratton constructed a six-foot, metal disk, engraved it carefully, painted it silver and installed it prominently on the bank

"Damn fine job," Haw said, admiring the finished work. "What's your bill?"

Stratton figured a minute in his head and said, "Oh, I guess $50 would about cover it."

Haw pulled out a wad of bills and peeled off five one-hundreds. "Good workmanship is hard to come by these days. It's worth ten times as much as slipshod work."

"That's sure generous of you," Stratton said. "I won't forget it."

"Ahh!" Haw clapped him on the back. "You did a good job."

Politics, bigger and better than ever, had been sneaking up on Haw. The "Mountain Midas" was snapped up by fawning politicians in Colorado, plied with flattery, attention and lavish compliments and, eventually, made lieutenant governor of the young state.

Because Denver was now firmly established as the most important city of Colorado—and also because his lieutenant governorship required his presence there—Haw bought a mansion in that town and moved his family into it.

Haw was now at the peak of his financial career. He owned operating mines in Colorado, Utah, Arizona, Texas and New Mexico. His income from these mines alone was estimated at $4,000,000 a year. Aside from dozens of companies in Colorado, he owned the Tabor Investment Company, with offices all around the world, and controlled the Calumet and Chicago Canal and Dock Company. With such holdings as half a million acres in southeastern Colorado and 500 square miles of land in Honduras, he was believed to be the largest private land owner in the world. At a time when two-bits bought a fair meal, Haw figured he was worth roughly $100,000,000.

It was about time for a pretty girl to come along and take every cent he had away from him, and Elizabeth Bonduel McCourt, better known as Baby Doe, looked like just the girl to do it.

Haw had never played the girls before, but meeting Baby Doe made him realize it wasn't particularly pleasant being married to a fence post. He met Baby Doe again at the Saddle Rock, and within a few days he hunted her out in the apartment she was renting, far down on the poor side of town.

"I'd like for you to come along with me," he said. "Got a little surprise for you."

"Oh, Haw! How exciting!" Baby Doe hurried to get her hat and coat while Haw stood nervously waiting for her, twisting his hat in his hands.

They took Haw's carriage uptown to the Clarendon, the ritziest hotel in Leadville. At the entrance to the apartment which took up the entire top floor, Haw handed Baby Doe a key and said, "Go ahead. You try 'er."

The huge apartment was magnificent, with ankle-deep carpeting, huge crystal chandeliers and exquisite mirrors and furniture which were beautifully, if somewhat ornately, designed and arranged throughout all the rooms.

11

"It's for you," Haw said, struggling with the words. "I'd like for you to live here. That's all. I'd like for you to be happy more than anything I can think of." He dropped his eyes to the floor. "I know what folks about here are sayin' and thinkin', and I hope you don't care about foolish talk. I just want for you to be happy, Baby Doe, and I ain't askin' for nothin'—like—you know. I'll just stop by and talk to you sometimes, if it's all right with you."

Baby Doe stretched up and kissed him and said, "I know what they're saying. And I don't care. I don't care either, Haw, if what they're saying comes true, about my being your mistress." She in turn dropped her eyes to the floor. Then she looked up at him and said, "I think I'd like it—beginning right now!"

The $100,000 Haw spent fixing up that apartment in the Clarendon was possibly the best investment he ever made in his life.

But Haw was so happy with Baby Doe that he didn't realize he was being too generous in his other activities. He'd given about a million dollars to the Republican Fund in Colorado, and it was a mistake. The guilt-ridden party leaders, trying to do something for the man who was supporting them, promised Haw a seat in the United States Senate as a reward for his "good work."

Completely crazy about Baby Doe now, and wanting to impress her in every way he could, Haw got all excited over the prospect of being a senator. He tossed another $200,000 into the Republican treasure chest and gave Denver a chunk of ground worth $70,000 as a site for a new post office.

But the party had no intention of making Haw a senator. After he had crossed their palms with silver, the party bosses informed him that he couldn't be a senator for a full six-year term. To console him they decided to let him be a senator for 30 days—to fill in a brief vacancy left by one of Colorado's senators who had been named to President Arthur's cabinet.

Haw could see at this point that politics was not his meat. But what better way was there to impress his loving young Baby Doe than by making her the wife of an honest-to-God senator, maybe marry her in the Capital of the United States?

Augusta made a big fuss about the divorce. Why she did, it is hard to say. She received about $1,000,000 in

12

settlement, and kept the Denver mansion. Also, her son Maxcy stayed with her, so she had no real complaint. The best guess is that she just plain hated to see Haw get any real pleasure out of life. However, the divorce was granted about three weeks before Haw became a 30-day senatorial wonder.

Haw left for Washington, a bitter man. Augusta had turned his son against him and his party had broken its promise. He was determined to make his 30 days in office a month to remember. He started off by taking a private train to Washington. He tipped the cabbie who took him to his hotel in the capital $100. When he began his tenure of office, he was spending around $10,000 a day.

When he first appeared on the Senate floor he was wearing cufflinks the size of silver dollars, checkered with huge diamonds and a tiepin made up of a solitaire diamond about the size of a walnut. Naturally, and sadly, he was ridiculous.

Actually, Haw Tabor might have made a good lawmaker. In his short career he introduced two bills; one for a military establishment in western Colorado; the other to protect the national forests. He also tried, unsuccessfully, to talk up a "preposterous" plan to put criminals to work on farms or in factories owned and operated by the government. Part of the money the state earned in this way was to be paid to support whatever poverty-stricken dependents the criminals might have. He was at least half a century ahead of his time with that plan.

When Baby Doe arrived in Washington, she and Haw were married at the Willard in an elaborate ceremony attended by President Arthur and other dignitaries. The wedding reception set Haw back about $50,000 and may have been worth it.

Through a few short, gloriously happy years, Haw and Baby Doe lived in an incredible wonderland of wealth and luxury, backed by what seemed to be a never-ending waterfall of glittering, dazzling silver. Baby Doe saw the first pair of peacocks in the Colorado Zoo and was enraptured by them. With a snap of his fingers, Haw sent a messenger full speed back East to round up 100 of the colorful birds to decorate the Tabor estate. Baby Doe had carriages, horses, dresses and jewelry that all matched. Her favorite outfit was a white dress with light blue trim; with it went her ivory-inlaid, white coach pulled by matching, pure white mares, and driven by a coachman in white uniform.

Baby Doe had two baby daughters in these years, each of whom was born into a fairyland that could match any European princess'. Haw and his wife named the first girl Elizabeth Pearl. They couldn't quite hit on two satisfactory names for the next daughter, so she was called Rosemary Silver Dollar Echo Honeymoon—Silver Dollar for short. Haw spent thousands of dollars outfitting the children. On their birthdays he had photograph albums of the children made up to send to his friends. Bound in gold, they cost him close to $50,000 every year.

When Haw wasn't home doting on his wife or daughters, he was swinging multimillion-dollar deals, running half-heartedly for governor at the insistence of friends, or greeting famous visitors to Colorado. He had, of course, the reputation of being a fabulous host, and his guests included everyone from Oscar Wilde and William Jennings Bryan to ex-President Grant and soon-to-be President Harrison.

Haw was on top of the world when, after seven wonderful years, he was about to close a land deal that required him to put up $1,000,000. For some obscure reason, he had trouble raising the money.

"Funny darned thing happened," he told Baby Doe later. "Thought I had a million or over in half a dozen banks around. But there wasn't as much as I'd thought."

"You should keep better track of your holdings, darling," Baby Doe told him.

Haw promised her he would. Two or three times within the next couple of months he found it difficult to raise large amounts of money with a snap of his fingers. And then one day he needed $1,200,000 to buy a mine in Arizona and he just couldn't rake it up. Frantically he searched through the small mountain of deeds, stocks and bonds that he had accumulated. He'd given away millions of dollars and invested other millions unwisely, over the years. Now he discovered that he only had one solid, regularly paying property. That was the old reliable Matchless, which was still bringing in $2,000 every day. To Tabor, however, that was pocket money. He started juggling his properties, selling vast blocks of real estate and companies to bring up his holdings in silver. But the harder he tried, the worse the results were. He sank barrels of money into what appeared to be a sure-fire silver

14

lode, only to have it run dry the next day. Lady Luck had turned her back on Haw, and, now, he was as incredibly unlucky as he had been lucky before. He could have pulled out of business altogether at this time, and retired with a large fortune, but Haw was a fighter. He was still fighting grimly with every card in the deck stacked against him in '93. That was the year the joker was dealt.

Congress repealed the Sherman Silver Act, which meant that silver was virtually worthless. Its value dropped from $1.30 to 50¢ an ounce. It cost about 50¢ an ounce to mine it.

It took Haw some time to straighten out his affairs after the Sherman Act was repealed. When he finally figured out how he stood, he found he wasn't just broke—he was over $1,000,000 in the hole.

Baby Doe saw that things weren't right when Haw didn't grab for his wallet or checkbook at the first mention of something she wanted. One morning she came to him in the master bedroom and said, "Horace, some men are downstairs." Her voice was tight and worried. "They say they're going to take away the furniture."

"You—you'll have to let them do it. It's not ours anymore." Haw suddenly realized he was an old man, and he sat up in bed and started to cry. "I don't know how it happened," he mumbled. "But we ain't got any more money, Baby Doe. We just ain't got any more! I don't know where it went."

Within a few weeks, Haw, Baby Doe and the two children moved into a $27-a-month apartment.

After they had moved in, Baby Doe said, "Do you have ten dollars for me to do some grocery shopping with?"

Haw searched through his pockets and said, "Will six dollars do?"

Baby Doe nodded at her 63-year-old husband and said, "That will be fine."

Haw breathed deeply and turned his head to the wall. "I'm sorry."

"Don't worry. Don't feel bad. We'll get along somehow."

But what was the gold-digging, beautiful Baby Doe really thinking now that her glorious, Cinderella life with Haw was finished? Why Baby Doe, as lovely as ever and

15

just past thirty, stuck with him the same as she had before.

By selling the few personal effects they had left—a spare pair of cufflinks, a bracelet—they got together enough money to support Baby Doe and the girls frugally for a few months. Rummaging through an old trunk, Haw found a valid claim to some land in Boulder that had once been vaguely suspected of having gold underneath it. He bought a used pick and shovel, hiked to Boulder and started to dig. He hit dirt, sand, mud and slate rock, but no gold.

By the time Haw got back to Denver, Baby Doe had spent her last few pennies. There was no money for food. There was no money for the due rent. And little Silver Dollar was ill.

Gritting his teeth, Haw walked to the Brown Palace Hotel, a plush hangout where he had often spent a casual, free-spending evening in the old days.

A beaten, timid old man in poor clothes, Haw walked uneasily into the lobby. Having struck it rich in gold and hung on to his holdings, Winfield Scott Stratton, the man Haw paid $500 for making the huge silver dollar he put up over his bank in Leadville, was sitting in a big leather chair reading a paper.

Haw hesitated. Then he said, "I wonder if you could loan me a hundred, Mr. Stratton?"

Still not looking up, Stratton said, "No."

Haw straightened and walked out of the lobby.

Stratton put his paper aside as a bellboy walked by. "Say," he asked the bellhop, "did you notice who that fella was who just talked to me?"

The boy said, "Yessir. It was Mr. Haw Tabor."

"What!" Stratton leaped up from the chair. "Good God!" He raced to the door and saw the lonely figure walking slowly down the street in the dark. He went after him and caught Tabor by the shoulder. "Wait," he panted. "I didn't know who you were. Forgive me." He fumbled in his wallet and handed Haw five one-hundred-dollar bills. "Here, for a starter."

"Why—thanks a lot," Haw whispered. "It means a lot just now."

"Look, Mr. Tabor, I've got my office in the Brown for the time being. Come see me tomorrow. Let's have a talk."

"All right." Haw couldn't say any more.

The next day Stratton gave Tabor $15,000 to try to revitalize the Matchless, which Haw still owned, but which did not produce enough silver to mine profitably. When that failed, Stratton and some of his friends wangled Haw the job of postmaster for Denver; postmaster in the building which stood on the $70,000 lot he'd given the city.

Haw worked quietly and efficiently at the $3,500 a year job until 1899. On April 10th of that year, he had an attack of appendicitis. He lived long enough for Baby Doe to get to him and to lay her head on the bed, weeping.

In a sense Haw's death was merciful, for he would never know the tragedy that would befall his beloved family. A few years after he died, Baby Doe's mind began to wander. She went up to an abandoned shack near the Matchless and spent the rest of her life, 37 long years, scraping and scratching at the mine in a futile attempt to find one more rich vein of silver. She became a pitiful old woman, alone and destitute, a pathetic, half-legendary figure.

It was a good thing, too, Haw would never know that one of his daughters would disown her mother, and that the intense, dramatic Silver Dollar would wander away to die mysteriously in a red-light district of Chicago; that Baby Doe would be so impoverished, she would have to walk five miles through the snow to the public library so she could read her daughter's obituary in a three-cent newspaper.

It was too bad, though, that Haw could not know his funeral was the biggest, splashiest funeral Denver had ever seen, with flags across the state flown at half-mast. Headlines and stories over the nation announced: "Silver Dollar Tabor Dies"; "The Greatest Silver King Passes Away." They called him: "The most colorful mining man of all time"; "The most fabulous spender in the country."

Chances are that as Haw lay dying, the only thing he was aware of was the sobbing of his darling Baby Doe. And chances are he was thinking that her love was worth more than all the wealth on the face of the earth. She had stuck by him when he was destitute, old and broken. What more could a man ask of a beautiful girl, or of life?

17

PAT GARRETT
The Man Who Killed Billy the Kid

The cocky little badman and the easygoing sheriff kicked off a legend that made the Kid famous and, unjustly, cast the lawman as the biggest traitor since Brutus.

There once was a cocky, tough little undersized cowboy who turned to horse stealing and was for a while a resounding success in that hazardous occupation. At the same time and in the same locality there was a long-legged, soft-spoken, oversized cowboy who turned to sheriffing and was for a while conspicuously successful in that dangerous calling. Between the two of them, they kicked off a legend that made the short cowpoke more famous than most Presidents of the United States. His name was William H. Bonney, but he is better known in song and story as Billy the Kid.

The law-enforcing wrangler, who was six feet, four inches tall and was named Patrick Floyd Garrett, got the short end of the legend, despite his exceptional length. While Billy has come down through the years as a clear-eyed, hot-tempered, adventuresome little scrapper, Pat usually has been described as a Judas, a coward or a snake-eyed, battle-wise gunslinger who killed Billy by

18

taking advantage of the Kid's personal regard for him. But the truth is that Pat never betrayed anybody and was every bit as brave as Billy even though he had done only about one-twentieth as much gunfighting as the Kid when they finally went for each other.

Furthermore, in tracking down and killing Billy, Pat was only doing his sworn duty—and a mighty painful duty it was, too, since he and the Kid had spent many happy hours together, playing cards, punishing the jug, swapping yarns and swaggering around town side by side, if not shoulder to shoulder. It was a curious friendship, this one between the law-abiding citizen and the trigger-happy outlaw. When you take everything into account, about the only explanation you can find for the strong attachment between them is that each must have seen in the other the kind of man he sometimes wished he could be. It wasn't an altogether unique bond, though. Another celebrated case that comes to mind was the close friendship of Wyatt Earp and Doc Holliday. But Wyatt got a better break than Pat Garrett. He wasn't forced to kill Doc Holliday.

Pat's life commenced one warm night in June of 1850. On the Alabama farm where he was born, and later in Louisiana, he spent a pleasant, generally peaceful boyhood with his family. They do say, though, that at ten he tracked a 13-year-old bully through five miles of snow to give him a punch in the nose. Just what the older boy had done to merit the punishment is not clear—but the incident is significant. When Pat Garrett took on a job, he saw it through.

At 19, Pat decided to go out into the world to make his fortune. He said "so long" to his mother and father and struck out for the magic, golden land called Texas. The Lone Star State turned out to be neither magic nor golden, and Pat didn't make his fortune the way he had planned. But he had a lot of good times and he learned considerable about riding, roping and shooting. For six carefree years he worked as a cowpuncher around Lancaster and as far north as the Red River.

Then, wanting a change of pace, Pat ranged the southern plains of Texas hunting for buffalo. In the winter of '76, toward the beginning of his hunting career, Pat joined a civilian expedition aimed at cracking down on warring Comanches who had been shooting buffalo hunters with disturbing regularity. He distinguished himself as a fighting man in skirmishes with the Indians. He also built a reputation as a man who thought some about the thing called justice. As one member of the expedition said, "Pat had the softest, slowest drawl ever you heard. And he was one of the youngest men in the outfit, something under 26. But for all his quiet manners and his youth, when he said something, everybody listened. And once he started out to accomplish something, it got done come hell or high water. But I remember Pat best because he was one of the few men who regretted fighting the Indians. He figured it wasn't fair, that actually they had first call on the buffalo, and naturally they were peeved that white men were shooting them. If the Comanches hadn't been a threat to the families in the section, I doubt if Pat would have gone along with us."

Garrett didn't go hog-wild killing buffalo the way most of the hunters did, and consequently he didn't make any money to speak of. In 1878 he felt the urge to move on farther to the west, and with a few dollars from the sale of hides in his pocket, he rode toward New Mexico.

Late in the fall the tall young rider was in the Pecos Valley. Near Fort Sumner he rode up to Pete Maxwell's big ranch. Pete himself was sitting on the porch of the ranch house. His practiced eye swept over the threadbare stranger as they exchanged brief salutations. "You lookin' for work?"

"I wouldn't mind a job," Pat admitted.

"It so happens there's a rack in the bunkhouse that'll accommodate that long frame of yours. Step down. Cooky just started out back to ring the dinner bell."

On his first payday, Pat finished branding a few calves in the early evening, went to Maxwell to draw his roll and saddled up to go into Fort Sumner. Another cowhand on the Maxwell spread, Charlie Bowdre, called from the barn, "Ridin' to town?"

"Yes."

"Hold on. I'll go along with you."

On the way Charlie said, "Bill Bonney'll be in Sumner. He's a friend of mine. Maybe you can meet him."

"Fine. Who's he?"

"You don't know?" Charlie was part amazed and part indignant. "He's had a lot of write-ups in the papers around here. They call him Billy the Kid. He rustles steers and mules and horses for a livin'. I've worked on a couple of ranches with him when he wasn't nothin' but a cowboy," Charlie said proudly. And, in a conspiratorial tone, he added, "I still take a ride with Billy sometimes."

Then he filled Pat in on some of the Kid's gunslinging exploits and wound up by saying: "He's like lightning on the draw. I sure would hate to have to face him myself."

At Fort Sumner they swung down at the hitching rail before a saloon and went through the batwing door, taking themselves a table in the back of the barroom. They were polishing off their second shot when five men came pushing through the door and took possession of the bar.

"There he is now," Charlie said, and raising his voice, he called out: "Hey there, Billy! Come over here. I want you to meet a friend of mine, Pat Garrett."

Billy tossed off his drink, wiped his mouth on the back of his hand and grinned. "Sure," he said, swaggering toward the table. "Why not? I got nothing to lose by it."

They were a typical bunch of cowboys, Pat figured, living recklessly from day to day. This Billy Bonney, heading toward the table, was evidently the acknowledged leader, in spite of his youth, since he had been in the most trouble and the largest number of shooting scrapes. Without changing expression, Pat took in Billy from top to bottom. No great shakes of a man at first glance, he was small and slender. His most prominent feature was his buck teeth, which gave him a kind of perpetual smile that set well with his aggressive air of self-confidence.

Acknowledging Bowdre's introduction with a wave of his hand, the Kid swung a chair around and plunked himself down. "Mind if I take the load off my feet?"

"Proud to have you with us," Pat replied, in his slow Southern drawl.

Billy eyed him closely. "Where you from?" he asked.

"Alabama, to start with."

"That's a long ways off," Billy said. "Well, seeing as I'm from a long ways off, too—me and you, we might just as well be friendly."

"Always better to start out being friendly," Pat smiled. "Today being payday, I'm good for a setup."

Bonney laughed, although there didn't seem to be anything particular to laugh about. Then he winked at Bowdre and said: "I just got back with the boys from taking in some mules and horses. So I'm good for a few rounds, too."

That's the way it started, with easygoing, law-abiding

21

Pat and the lawless Kid hitting it off right from the start, each evidently catching a glimpse of something in the other to admire. There's no doubt that the Kid suffered from a nagging, desperate need to be admired by men like Pat. He wanted to be held in high esteem as a fearless man with an iron will who always had a good excuse for being quicker on the draw than the other guy. Just the same, he was continually plagued by the thought that some of his gunslinging wasn't entirely justifiable, even by the liberal code of the tolerant frontier. Time after time, when he was mulling over the details of his various gun fights, he would keep on insisting: "I had to kill him. There wasn't any way out of it. Can't you see that? He had it coming to him. He was asking for it."

As he sat there now, sizing up Pat Garrett's steel-steady, conscience-free manner, he wondered how much Pat had heard about some of those killings and how he would have behaved under similar circumstances. As for Pat, there was something about Billy that put him in a speculative mood, too. Chuckling at this bantam rooster's cocky, comical way of expressing himself, and at the same time calmly taking the Kid's measure, Pat wondered how he himself would behave if something forced him to unleash all the wild impulses he kept so tightly bound up deep inside himself.

Brushing aside that disturbing thought, Pat called for another round of drinks. He and this edgy half-pint were going to like each other more than a little. That was clear enough. It was in the cards. They were going to be friends.

The next payday it was Pat who suggested to Bowdre that they go to town together and this time they found Billy and his three favorite henchmen—Tom Foliard, Tom Pickett and Billy Wilson—in the back of the saloon warming up to what looked like the beginnings of a marathon poker session.

"Well," Billy said, looking up from his tightly held cards, "if it ain't the tall drink of good old well water! How 'bout you? You know anything about poker?"

"Enough to get by," Pat said, pulling up a chair. "You just playing table stakes, or no limit?"

"Now here's a man after my own heart," Billy kidded. "Kind of man my daddy must of had in mind when he got down to business."

Five hours later it was obvious enough that Pat did

know something about poker; more, in fact, than anybody else sitting at the table. At any rate, when the long, fierce session finally ended, he had cleaned them all out, raking in the last sweet pot with a pair of measly tens, back to back. "You can't make money out of poker," he said, "unless you know how to coax the bum hands into paying off as well as the good ones."

Billy drummed his agile fingers on the table. But he wasn't sore. Far from it.

"There's plenty more where that came from," he said, as he watched Pat pocket his winnings. "I've got to hand it to you, Pat. When you set out to pull something off, you don't let up until you settle it once and for all. You do everything the same way you play poker?"

"Could be," Pat conceded. "Like to try me out on blackjack or faro?"

"Not right away," Billy replied. "You'll have to hold your horses until I put over a little deal I got in mind."

Billy shot a quick glance around the table, winding up with Bowdre. "Charlie," he asked, "how good is this here pardner of yours in a saddle?"

"None better," Bowdre said.

"Think he might like to take a little ride with us down the Pecos?"

"Why don't you ask him?"

"Hell fire, that's what I'm doing." Billy looked straight at Pat. "We're going to bring back some disgruntled cows that feel the need of a change. Big boodle in it. Want to go along with us?"

Pat shook his head. "No, thanks."

"How come? Don't tell me you're feather-legged?"

"I wouldn't say that. It's just that I like the job I'm doing."

"You're passing up a good bet."

"I don't think so."

Instead of turning Billy against him, though, this flat refusal to join the gang only made the Kid like Pat more than ever. They began to spend more and more time together, gambling, drinking and sitting around. When one of them ran out of money, the other would loan him some cash to recoup. Folks in the town even made up a little joke about them. When Pat and the Kid were seen approaching, they would say, "Well, here comes the long and the short of it." They were careful never to say it so

23

Billy would hear because, after all, Bonney had the reputation of being the meanest badman around.

From Pat Garrett's point of view, he found a number of things about the Kid that he liked. In the book he later wrote about him, he described Billy as "bold, daring and reckless, but open-handed, generous-hearted and frank." And Pat saw even deeper into the Kid's personality. "He had a lurking devil in him. It was a good-humored, jovial imp, or a cruel and bloodthirsty fiend, as circumstances prompted."

For two years Pat worked up and down the Pecos River as a cowhand while Billy went from bad to considerably worse. Eventually, as the Kid's name as a rustler and gunman became better known, folks forgot that he ever had been a cowboy at all.

In the meantime, Pat was getting to know most of the people in that part of the Southwest. He made friends with John Chisum, top cattleman in the territory whose Long Rail and Jingle Bob brand often included as many as 80,000 head of prime beef ranging from Fort Sumner clear down over the Texas border. Garrett made hundreds of friends among the poorer people and the newcomers to the country who were just getting started. One of his closest comrades was a young blacksmith named Jim Carlyle, a powerfully built, happy-go-lucky newcomer to New Mexico. In his own easygoing fashion, Pat managed to be on good terms with just about everyone he met.

Early during Pat's first couple of years in the territory, one tragedy marred his life. At Fort Sumner, where he and his friends spent most of their free time, he met a beautiful girl named Juanita Martinez. He escorted her to a few Mexican dances, and in no time fell in love with her. They were married in the church at Sumner. Then, only a few weeks after their wedding, Juanita became suddenly ill. Pat got the best medical help available for his bride, but it was no use. She died within a few days.

Pat was lonely and unhappy for many months. Finally, nearly two years later, Pat married for the second time. His new wife was Polinaria Gutierrez, a girlhood friend of Juanita. That year, 1880, was a high spot in Pat's life. Polly was a fine woman. Garrett, now in his thirtieth year, began to think of buying his own ranch and raising a family. But then, later in the year, John Chisum

24

and George Curry, who was later to become governor, paid him an unexpected visit. "Pat," John told him, "George and me represent damn near every decent person in the territory. We've been talking this over between ourselves and with everybody we know, for a long time now."

"Talking what over?"

"Short and simple, we'd like you to run for sheriff of Lincoln County. We'll all back you to the hilt."

"Why me?" Pat asked. "I wouldn't know how to run a sheriff's office. Never even been inside one."

"You can learn," Curry said.

Chisum, in his brusque way, said, "Damn it, Garrett, the number one problem around here, as you well know, is Billy the Kid and his gang. They're stealing us all blind. And as long as the Kid keeps at it there's a hundred other punks willing to take a try at imitating him.

"There's been no law in the land for more than two years, not since Brady was murdered. Kimbreel, Peppin—as sheriffs they would have made fair bartenders. But you're different. Besides, Billy respects you. Chances are you could handle him."

The thought of being a law officer had never occurred to Pat. "I don't know. I'll have to think it over."

"That's right," John agreed. "You ought to think it over. No one wants to rawhide you into a job like that. Everybody knows it'll be a tough nut to crack."

"While you're thinking of it," Curry said, "remember one thing, Pat. You'll be bringing up a bunch of kids in this territory, like the rest of us. You have to decide what kind of a place you want them to grow up in. Now, we think you're the man to bring in the law for once and for all. If you think you're up to it, you let us know."

Two months later, in October, Pat Garrett was elected sheriff of Lincoln County on a reform ticket by an overwhelming majority. During his first days in office he paid a purely social call on Billy the Kid. "Billy," Pat told him, "I'm still a friend of yours as of right now. But I'm going to do my level best to stop the stealing and killing in the county. I hope you don't cross me. But if you do, I'll be looking for you."

"If it comes to that, don't try to take me alive," the Kid said. And he meant it, and Pat knew it.

Early in November, Billy stole a herd of fine horses from the Grzelachowski ranch. Within a few days he was raiding near White Oaks. On the night of November 23, which was the Kid's birthday, he and the gang celebrated by riding into White Oaks and making a drunken, senseless attempt to kill Jim Redmond, who happened to be the only man in sight. Pat got word that the Kid was in Bosque Grande. Quickly forming a posse, he rode to Roswell, then up the Rio Pecos to Bosque Grande in a vain attempt to catch his quarry.

The posse did manage to round up one member of the gang, but since there was no sign of Billy, Pat finally decided to turn back. The tired riders finally arrived in Fort Sumner on November 27, 1880. There Pat got word that Billy had been back at White Oaks. A posse led by Deputy J .W. Bell had closed in on the gang, and after a sizable gun battle the outlaws had split up, some of them taking refuge in a nearby ranch house. Carrying a flag of truce, Pat's young blacksmith friend, Jim Carlyle, went to the ranch house and told Billy the place was surrounded and he had better surrender if he knew what was good for him. That kind of talk didn't sit well with the Kid and he refused to let Jim return to the posse, apparently intending to hold him as a hostage. At any rate, after some wrangling back and forth, Carlyle suddenly decided to make a break for it, and jumped out of a window, taking the sash and the pane with him. Billy must have had his eye on Jim all the time because he managed to whip his gun out quick enough to shoot the blacksmith in the back before he hit the ground.

When Pat heard that Billy had killed Jim Carlyle, he didn't say anything for a long time. He just sat in his chair, gripping the arms with both hands, tapping one foot on the floor and staring into space. Pat had a lot of friends. Pretty nearly everybody in Lincoln County was his friend, by now. But sometimes a man who has a raft of friends hates to lose one worse than a man who doesn't have very many. Shooting Jim Carlyle like that, it just didn't make any sense. Jim never harmed anybody. However you looked at it, it was ugly. No matter what the Kid had to say now, no matter how much he argued, he never would be able to come up with an honest-to-God excuse this time. Jim was gone, and Billy was going to have to go, too.

Pat summoned the members of his posse and hit the trail again. When last seen after making their escape from the ranch house near White Oaks, Billy's gang had been headed south toward a ranch called Las Canaditas. The only members left in the gang now were Billy himself, Tom Foliard, Dave Rudabaugh, Billy Wilson, Tom Pickett and Charlie Bowdre. Many a night Pat had spent playing cards and drinking red liquor with those fellows, every one of them, and it was no pleasure to be out gunning for them now.

After stoking up on all the grub they could hold, Pat and his posse left Fort Sumner and moved along at an easy lope toward Las Canaditas. Half way to their destination they caught sight of a man on horseback, stock still on a ridge and silhouetted against the sky, evidently surveying the countryside. He was too far away to be recognized with the naked eye, but Pat managed to identify him through a pair of strong field glasses. "It's Tom Foliard," he announced, a note of excitement in his usually calm voice. "He's on that bay stallion of his— one of the fastest horses around these parts. He's got field glasses, too, and he's looking this way."

Before Pat finished speaking, Tom had recognized the posse. The next instant he spurred his big bay around and lunged into a mad gallop, quickly dropping out of sight beyond the horizon.

"We haven't got a Chinaman's chance of catching up to him, not with him on that horse," Pat said. "But come on, let's see how good we can do."

They thundered up the rise toward the ridge—but their mounts weren't quite fast enough. By the time they reached the ridge, Tom had passed on over the next hill and they never got a glimpse of him again—not on that wild ride. When they got to Las Canaditas, Billy and his gang had vanished. "He tipped 'em off all right," Pat said, as he dismounted to make a close scrutiny of the fresh hoofprints around the ranch house. "I'd say he beat us here by close on to half an hour."

After a few minutes, Pat remounted and pointed toward the higher hills in the distance. "That's the way they went. They're heading for Los Portales."

Los Portales was Billy's hide-out, deep in the hills. The newspapers had been referring to the place as "Billy the Kid's Castle," but when Pat and his men got there they soon saw that "castle" was nothing but a highfaluting newspaper exaggeration. What the place turned out to be was nothing more than a cave dug into a rocky hillside with a post sunk into the ground beside the entrance. The cave was empty and there was no sign anywhere around of Billy and his henchmen.

It was obvious, though, that the Kid was feeling Pat's breath hot on the back of his neck. On their way back to Fort Sumner, the posse stopped off at the Wilcox ranch, about 12 miles from town. While they were there, Wilcox's partner, an easygoing fellow named Brazil, showed up and said he had some interesting news for Pat. "Charlie Bowdre got in touch with me," he said, "and he wants to know if you're willing to have a little personal talk with him, just for old times' sake."

"Sure," Pat said. "I'm game. But no monkey business. I ain't aiming to let those mavericks dry-gulch me."

"Oh, no—none of that!" Brazil hastened to explain. "Charlie's on the level, far as I can figure, and he's plenty scared. He wants to meet you tomorrow afternoon at that spot where the road forks off about two miles outside of Sumner. I'll ride along with him a piece of the way so you can have your confab without anybody listening to you."

"Okay," Pat agreed. "But keep your eyes peeled while I'm talking to him."

The next afternoon Pat rode up the dusty route alone and saw Charlie sitting on his horse where the path branched out in two directions. "Howdy, Charlie," he said. "What's on your mind?"

Bowdre was nervous and frightened. "What'll you do for me, Pat, if I come in and give myself up?"

"I can't promise you anything, Charlie. But I'll tell you this. If you come in on your own, I'll do everything I can to get you released on bail and to help you get started back on the inside of the law."

Charlie couldn't make up his mind. He kept glancing at the hills as though he thought he was being watched. At last he said, "I don't know. How 'bout if I promise I won't ride with the Kid no more?"

"You're in too deep to get off that easy. You were with the gang when they were rustling up at White Oaks. You were in on the shooting of Carlyle. I wish you'd surrender to me, Charlie. If you don't, chances are you'll be captured or killed."

Bowdre said he would think about it. Then he turned his horse and rode on back to rejoin Brazil.

Soon after that, bad weather set in and trying to find the Kid turned from difficult to downright impossible.

Billy still had enough friends to confuse his whereabouts with lies, and he knew nearly every hiding place in New Mexico. Frank Stewart, an agent hired by some Panhandle stockmen who had been missing considerable livestock, joined Pat in the search. But there was no break in the manhunt until mid-December when a message came that the Kid was again hanging around Fort Sumner.

Pat arrived at the Fort during the night with 13 men. He left Frank Stewart and 11 men in hiding when morning came and went out onto the streets with only one man. Soon he met Iginio Garcia, a relative of Billy's friend, Manuel Garcia.

"I hear Billy's around here," Pat said.

"I haven't seen him," Garcia muttered.

"No matter. I don't care to meet Billy and his gang with only one man. I'm leaving town as soon as I take care of a few things."

Within a few minutes Pat saw Garcia galloping out of Sumner. Billy would soon be hearing from Garcia that Pat was in town with one lone deputy, which was just what Pat wanted.

It began to snow heavily. Darkness came early as a thickening blanket of white covered the ground. Pat and his men waited patiently for the Kid and his bunch to show up. About eight o'clock they were just starting a game of blackjack to pass the time when a guard came to the door and whispered, "Pat! Some riders are coming!"

"Get your guns, boys," Pat said. "Nobody but the men we're looking for would be out on this kind of night."

Billy the Kid, with Tom Foliard on his right, was moving into Fort Sumner at the head of his gang. As the riders came closer to the lights of the town that could be seen dimly through the falling snow, Billy had a premonition that something was wrong. Turning to Foliard, the Kid said, "I want a good chew of tobacco, Tom. Wilson's got some." He swung his horse out of line until Wilson, bringing up the rear of the group, was abreast of him. With Billy riding at the tail end of the line now, the gang entered Sumner.

Pat recognized Foliard as the lead horse came up to the building where the posse was waiting. "Halt!" the sheriff commanded. Foliard made the fatal mistake of going for his gun; a bullet from Pat's Winchester crashed through him. The rest of the outlaws, taking advantage of the confusion and the heavy snow, whirled and galloped away as the guns of the posse roared and bullets sang around their ears. Pat tried for a shot at Pickett, next in line, but the man standing beside him threw up his gun for a wild shot that knocked Pat's aim off.

Foliard had managed to escape with the others, but after he had gone a few yards into the protecting snow he wheeled his horse around and rode slowly back toward the lawmen now grouped in the street. "Don't shoot me, Pat!" he called out. "I'm killed."

"Put up your hands, Tom!"

"I—I can't."

They carried Tom inside out of the cold, and very soon he was dead.

Pat took out after the Kid as soon as Tom had died. But the trail was covered with fresh snow and the posse finally returned to Sumner.

The next morning Brazil showed up in Fort Sumner with some more news for Pat—news that was more to the point this time. "Billy and his bunch moved in on me and Wilcox last night," he said. "The Kid put the bite on me to ride over here and sniff out the lay of the land for him." He hesitated a second as he looked Pat straight in the eye. "But when it comes to a showdown, you know which side I'm on."

"Sure I do," Pat said.

"That's what I figured. That's how come I'm laying it on the line. You got 'em guessing, Pat. The way you suckered 'em into Sumner and got Tom Foliard, they can't dope out what you'll be up to next. They're all of them as jumpy as jackrabbits and fighting among themselves. All of 'em, that is, except the Kid. He's as cool as a morning breeze. All he wants for a Christmas present is a chance to blow your brains out. That's how he feels about you now."

"Can't say as I blame him," Pat said. "That's understandable."

"He's got it up his sleeve to come riding in on you here in Sumner from some other direction and either polish you off or drive you down the Pecos."

"Look," Pat said, "here's what you do. You go right on back to your place and tell the Kid you found me here in Sumner with only Mason and three Mexicans. Maybe that will sucker him in again."

It didn't though, and when the night passed without the Kid and his gang riding into Sumner from any direction, Pat and his posse rode out to the Wilcox ranch, deploying when they got in sight of it so as to make a cautious approach while keeping the place surrounded. But when Pat got to the house, he found that the Kid and his men had pulled out during the night without anybody getting a chance to see which way they went. Pat studied the situation awhile and then announced that, sure as shooting, they had headed for Stinking Springs. "There's an old deserted cabin up there," he said, slapping his lanky thigh, "and that's where I'm going to bring this thing to a head. That's the only cover anywhere around, and even the Kid ain't staying outdoors this kind of weather any longer than he has to."

Pausing just long enough at the Wilcox ranch to stow away a good hot meal, the posse took to the saddle again and reached the vicinity of Stinking Springs an hour or so before sunup. Sure now that they were moving in for the kill, they stopped about half a mile from the old adobe shack and sat for a long time listening and looking around in every direction. It was bitter cold, in fact just a little short of unbearably cold. There was no moon, but the sky had cleared and was brilliant with stars. "All right," Pat said, "we'll hobble the horses here. Don't want any of them giving us away by snorting. And remember, I want all you men to keep your lips buttoned up tight. This is for keeps."

When they were about 400 yards from the shack, Pat stopped the posse again and divided it into two parties. There were 13 men in all, and he kept six of them with him. He put Stewart in charge of the other five men and sent them circling around one side of the cabin where he led his party around the other way. Pat hadn't gone far before he came upon a dry arroyo, which was just right for his purpose. Leading his men down the bed of the arroyo, he was able to get around close to the front of the house under perfect protection. When he was about 50 feet from the front of the shack, he came to a stop. In the dim light that preceded dawn, they could see the shack clearly. It didn't have any windows and it had only one doorway, which was wide open to the elements now, the wooden door and most of the frame having rotted away long ago. There were three horses in front of the doorway, tethered to the projecting rafters.

Counting Billy, there must be five men in that cabin. So it figured they must have taken two of their horses inside to help keep themselves warm. After studying the three tethered horses, Pat speculated in a soft whisper that one of the horses inside the cabin was undoubtedly Billy's famous gray mare, a splendid animal later described by Pat in his book about the Kid as being "celebrated for her speed, bottom and beauty." The fact that Billy had that fine, fast horse inside the cabin with him put an entirely different complexion on the situation. If the Kid once got wind of the posse's presence, it was a cinch he would come riding out of there like a bat out of hell, and maybe give them the slip again.

After a whispered conference, Pat sent a man around to tell Stewart to bring his men to the arroyo, so they could all sneak up together to the doorway and flush out the gang. But Stewart sent back word that he was against such a plan and insisted they wait until dawn.

Pat made no comment when he got Stewart's message. He just nodded and twisted himself around so that he could lie flat against the sloping bank of the arroyo, with his head up above the rim just high enough to keep his eyes fixed on the cabin doorway. For quite a while he lay there like that, silently brooding. This was it. This was what it had come to. Him and the Kid would be shooting it out now, as soon as there was light enough to get going.

Just when the other men in Pat's party were beginning to wonder if the sheriff had fallen off to sleep, he stirred slightly and wriggled around until he was in the midst of his men. "Look," he whispered, "I don't know what you fellows been thinking, lying here freezing like this. You all know how I used to feel about the Kid. But if you figure I'm liable to let that make me cave in when we get down to business, you're dead wrong. I'm here to get the Kid. I know exactly how he's dressed. I got Brazil to give it to me down to the last detail. The second he comes through that doorway, I'm letting him have it. I'm going to get in the first shot. You keep your eyes on me, all of you, from now on. Get yourself in position and keep your eyes on me. When you see me raise my rifle to my shoulder, you bring up your guns, too, and fire away. But remember! The first shot is mine!"

He stopped all of a sudden and caught his breath, as if somebody had kicked him in the groin and he didn't want to let on how much it hurt. Then he twisted himself back around into his previous position and riveted his eyes on the doorway again.

After a while a shadowy figure appeared in the doorway carrying a feed bag. With Billy's gray mare inside that cabin, it didn't seem likely that the Kid himself would be coming outside to feed the other fellows' horses. But Pat must have been too keyed-up to waste any time cogitating over a point like that. The instant he saw the figure in the doorway there flashed through his mind a clear-cut image of the Kid, and for a second he was tricked into thinking this was the Kid. He raised his Winchester to his shoulder and fired. A second later, six other shots rang out and the figure in the doorway spun around and reeled back into the cabin.

A tumultuous commotion broke out in the cabin. For a second, all that Pat and his men could hear was a lot of loud and spectacular cursing, the sum and substance of it being a full and bitter expression of the outlaws' fury over the discovery that they were trapped for fair. Then Billy's voice cracked out over the general tumult like a sudden clap of summer thunder, slashing across a windstorm: "You goddamn bastards, you got Charlie Bowdre! He's done for!"

Charlie Bowdre! Out of the corner of their eyes, the men closest to Pat saw him stiffen a second, then sort of loosen up as he raised one foot a little and gave the wall of the arroyo a vicious kick. He had hoped it was the Kid.

"Garrett!" It was Rudabaugh's voice now, rising above the confusion. "Bowdre's bad hit. He wants to come out and surrender."

"Okay," Pat shouted. "Tell him to come ahead, but with his hands up!"

What went on in the cabin right after that was carried out with such stealth that the men on the outside didn't catch onto it. But when Pat heard about it later, it made him feel a little better about how everything finally turned out.

"Here," Billy had said in a grim whisper as he jerked Bowdre around toward the door and shifted the mortally wounded man's gun belt so his revolver was in front of him and in easy reach of his gun hand. "You're done for, Charlie. Go out there and kill some of those sons-of-bitches before you die." Then he gave Charlie a rough shove toward the door. But as Bowdre came staggering out toward Pat, he kept his hands up, making no attempt to pull his gun. Maybe he didn't want to. Maybe he was too far gone to give a damn. At any rate, he just stood there a few seconds, teetering on the edge of the arroyo, as he looked down at the man he used to pal around with. Choking from the blood that was welling up inside of him, he waved his arm back toward the cabin and mumbled: "I wish—I wish—"

No one will ever know what Charlie wished with his last breath. He died on his feet and toppled over into the arroyo beside Pat Garrett. *Another old friend gone.* Pat drew in a deep, long breath and let it blow back through his clenched teeth, turning into a little white cloud as it hit the freezing air. Then he pulled poor Charlie's body over and stretched it out on his own blanket, folding the blanket over to cover him up. It was a good thing to do, any way you looked at it, for Charlie surely wasn't a pleasant sight right then, not after what those seven slugs had done to him, point-blank at 50 feet.

It was broad daylight shortly after that, and pretty soon Pat noticed a slight movement of the rope on which one of the horses outside the cabin was tethered. He figured the men inside the cabin wanted to get their horses inside so they could make a run for it and he was right. His first notion was to shoot the rope in two, but it was shaking so much he was afraid he might miss it. He waited until the horse was in front of the doorway and then killed it instantly. The dead animal lying there would, he reflected grimly, make it hard for the horses inside to get out. Just to be on the safe side, he shot away the ropes holding the other mounts and they trotted quickly away from the disagreeable noise of gunfire.

It looked now as if the men in the arroyo were going to have to settle down for a good long siege, so to while away the time Pat decided to open up a conversation with the Kid.

"How you fellows fixed in there?" he called out.

"Pretty well," the Kid shouted back, in his usual bantering tone of voice. "But there's no wood to cook breakfast."

"Come on out and get some. Might as well be a little sociable."

"Can't do it, Pat," Billy replied. "Business is too confining. No time to run around."

Things being the way they were, Pat figured this was

a good time to twit the Kid a little about sending Brazil into Sumner to spy on him. "Say," he said, "didn't you fellows forget your program yesterday? The way I got it, you were supposed to come sneaking in on us at Sumner from some other direction, give us a square fight, set us afoot and drive us down the Pecos."

When he heard that, Billy knew that he had been betrayed by Brazil. He clammed up tight and nothing the men in the arroyo said to him could get another word out of him.

Pat and his men hadn't had anything to eat now for quite a spell, so he divided the posse into two sections so they could take turns going back to the Wilcox ranch for breakfast. While Pat himself was at the ranch, looking exceedingly solemn and not joining in the conversation to any extent, Brazil came over to him.

"I see you're taking the Bowdre thing right hard," he said.

"Can't help it," Pat said tiredly. "I killed the very man I didn't want to."

"Look, Pat," Brazil said. "You shouldn't feel that way about it. You know what Charlie said to me when we were riding away from the crossroads that day I brought him to see you? He said to me, 'I wish you'd get that long-legged sonofabitch out to meet me just once more. I'd kill him and end all this trouble for good.'"

Just the same, Pat didn't seem to be any more cheerful when he got back to the arroyo and took up his part in the siege again. Nobody had any idea how long the outlaws would be able to hold out, so as the day wore on, Pat sent some of his men to the Wilcox ranch to bring a load of firewood, forage and grub. About two o'clock in the afternoon, Billy turned loose the two horses in the cabin and drove them out, but he had a little trouble doing it because the horses didn't like passing the dead carcass at the doorway. About four o'clock, the wagon from the ranch showed up with the supplies.

When the men started to build a fire to cook the grub, Pat told them to wait a minute while he studied the direction the wind was blowing. Then he had them start the fire in a spot where the smell of the cooking food would be carried straight through the cabin door. "That'll fix 'em," he said, and it did.

Over a roaring fire, Pat's men roasted several sides of prime beef. The delicious smell of the beef, reinforced

35

by the aroma of hot coffee, was too much for the starving men inside the cabin. Their bellies rebelled. A long stick came poking out of the doorway with a white rag tied to it. After the stick had been shaken around for a minute or so, to attract attention, Dave Rudabaugh came stepping out gingerly, carrying the stick with its flag of truce in front of him. Halfway to the arroyo, he stopped and said: "If we surrender, will you guarantee that no one'll shoot us, Pat?"

"I'll guarantee none of us here shoots you. But I got no control over what might happen further on."

"I know that," Rudabaugh growled, "but will you agree to do your best to get us into some safe place where we can be sure of a fair trial?"

"Look, Dave," Pat replied, a trifle impatiently. "I'm the sheriff. That's my business. That's what I'm here for. Now, if you fellows really aim to surrender, all right, come on out, one at a time, with your hands up. But no monkey business. And I want Billy to come out first. Go on back and tell him that."

Rudabaugh went back into the cabin, and while the conference between him and Billy was going on in there, every man in the arroyo kept his gun trained on the doorway. There was one thing about Billy you had to remember if you knew what was good for you. In any situation, he was utterly unpredictable. So while Pat and his men waited, the tension got so thick you could stir it with a long-handled spoon. Then Billy finally came swaggering out, as cocky as ever, his hands shoulder-high. Pat raised himself up out of the arroyo in a crouched position, steadying himself on one knee, his Winchester trained straight at Billy.

"Stewart," he said, "you step over and get his gun."

After Billy had been disarmed, Rudabaugh, Pickett and Wilson came out, one by one, and were also relieved of their weapons. Then the four outlaws were allowed to come in close to the hot fire and warm themselves while they tore into chunks of rare beef. "Best Christmas dinner I ever et," Billy said, as cheerful as you please. And what he said made some sense, at that, because the day was December 25, 1880. Then he grinned at Pat and announced: "You know, Pat, if we had got the horses inside, we'd have made a break for it. Matter of fact, I had my mare saddled and set for a try all by myself when you killed the horse in front of the door. I knew my mare wouldn't try to pass a dead horse like that. Or if she did, soon as she saw it she was liable to rear up and knock my head clean off on top of the doorway."

On the way back from Stinking Springs, Pat had his hands full keeping his word that he would do his best to prevent his prisoners from gettting hurt. He dropped Picket off at Las Vegas where the man was wanted on several charges. Then he took the other three to Deputy United States Marshal Conklin at Santa Fe, making the last leg of the journey by train. At several points, mobs of hostile citizens had the idea they would like to string Billy up personally. Usually a mild word of warning from the tall sheriff was enough to discourage direct action. Once when a crowd was particularly stubborn, Pat told them he would sure hate to do it, but if they pushed in any closer he would hand a six-shooter to Billy. That sent the crowds scattering in every direction remarkably fast.

At Santa Fe, Rudabaugh was convicted of robbery. Bill Wilson was arraigned twice for passing counterfeit money. The Kid was taken to Mesilla where he was tried before Judge Ira Leonard and found guilty of the murder of Sheriff William Brady. The judge sentenced Billy to hang on the 13th day of May, 1881, at Lincoln, the county seat of Lincoln County.

Lincoln had no jail capable of holding a halfway healthy calf, let alone a dangerous bandit like Billy. With the Kid once more on his hands, Pat locked him in a room on the second floor of a building the county had recently bought, and placed two guards on duty to keep him from straying. Since Billy was in irons, it looked as though he ought to stay put.

But on the evening of April 28th, when Pat was in White Oaks, one of the most famous jailbreaks in the history of the West took place. On the 29th, Pat got a message from John Delaney in Lincoln. It said that Billy had escaped and that both of the guards, Bob Olinger and J. W. Bell, had been murdered. Later in the day, Deputy Bill Nickey arrived in White Oaks on a sweating horse to give Pat the details—at least what few details were known.

During the normal course of events, Olinger had left Billy with Bell on the second floor while he went across the street to have dinner. No one knew exactly what happened next, but suddenly there had been a shot from the county building. Olinger jumped up and hurried out of the restaurant to find out what was wrong. Larry Clements, who was also eating in the restaurant, got outside in time to see Olinger stop just inside the gate across the street that led up to the door of the county building. An old man named Geiss shouted from the corral gate beyond the corner of the building, "Bob, the Kid has killed Bell!"

At the same time a pleasant voice came down from the second-floor balcony above. "Hello, old boy." The Kid was leaning casually out over the railing looking down at Olinger. What stopped Olinger cold in his tracks was the fact that Billy was pointing the deputy's own double-barreled shotgun at him. Olinger had loaded it only that morning and he knew there were 18 buckshot in each barrel. He had remarked as he loaded the gun that the man who got hit with that would never be the same again. Olinger had but a split second to appreciate the irony of it all. The scattergun went off with a sound like two locomotives ramming head-on, and the deputy's body was thrown hard against the ground.

Still the Kid wasn't satisfied. He hated Olinger, a sadistically inclined man who had taken great pleasure in taunting the manacled, chained Kid. He pulled the other trigger and the guard's lifeless body bounced under the impact of the second charge. Then Billy broke the gun over the railing and threw the pieces down at the mangled corpse. "Take it, God damn you," he yelled, and then added this classic understatement: "You'll never follow me again with that gun!"

Billy filed off his chains and rode out of Lincoln armed with a rifle and two revolvers. Nobody stopped him.

After the Kid's spectacular escape, Pat played a waiting game for a while. He hoped Billy would gain confidence and show himself. The plan worked. In a short time Pat got word from the rancher Brazil that Billy had been seen around Pete Maxwell's place near Sumner. To confuse Billy's friends, who acted as spies for the Kid, Pat and two of his men headed toward Roswell as though they were intent on going south. At Roswell, under the cover of darkness, they swung back up north along the Pecos River. For three days they stuck to the hills, following unused trails and traveling as much as they could by night. Finally, on the third night, they arrived at the mouth of the Tayban Arroyo, five miles south of Fort Sumner.

Pat decided the best thing to do would be to go and have a talk with his old boss, Pete Maxwell. Pete was known and liked by almost everyone and he would know, if anyone did, whether the Kid was hiding out nearby.

The three men set up a temporary camp a short distance from Pete's ranch. Then, in the darkness, they made their way quietly to an orchard which led to Pete's main house. When they reached the orchard they heard voices in the night only a few yards away. The voices, speaking in Spanish, carried to them in low tones. Then, by the dim light of the stars, they saw a figure rise up from the ground. The man moved to a fence that bordered the orchard, jumped over it and disappeared into the night.

Pat could not know that the dim figure he had seen was Billy the Kid. Billy, who spoke fluent Spanish, had been talking to some friends. Now he went to the shack of a Mexican companion who worked for Maxwell. He pulled off his hat and his boots and flopped onto the bed alongside his sleeping friend to read a newspaper. A little later, Billy slapped his friend on the rump to wake him up. "Start some coffee and get me a butcher knife," he said. "I'm hungry. I'll go up to Pete's house and get some beef."

In a few seconds Billy was headed toward Pete's place up the hill, with a knife in his hand and only his stockings on his feet.

Pat Garrett was approaching the house at the same time, but he had a slight head start. When he and his two friends arrived at the corner of Pete's long front porch, Pat whispered, "Wait for me here. I'll go in and have a powwow with Maxwell."

Almost tripping over a porch stair in the black shadows, Pete made his way into Pete's large, one-room house. He had been there many times and he knew exactly where Pete's bed was. Walking across the floor to the bed, he said, "How are you, Pete? I'm looking for the Kid. Have you seen him around here?"

"Yes. He's been around for a while," Pete answered as Pat sat on the edge of the bed. "I don't know if he's here right now or not."

At that moment Pat looked up and saw someone come to the doorway. The visitor glanced through the shadows to where Pat's two deputies stood outside the house and said in Spanish, "Who comes there?" There was no reply from the men near the corner of the building and the man came on in. Pat thought he recognized Billy's voice but he could not be sure. As the man entered through the doorway, Pat could make out that he held a knife in one hand and a revolver in the other.

As the dark figure started across the room, silent as a phantom, Pat leaned toward Pete and whispered, "Who is it?"

Maxwell didn't reply and Pat wondered fleetingly if it might be Pete's brother-in-law. The unrecognizable figure that was in fact Billy the Kid came directly to where Pat was sitting on the edge of the bed. Billy leaned down so close that the knife in his hand brushed Pat's knee. "Who're those men out there, Pete?" he demanded in a low tone.

At last Pete got enough breath in his tight chest to talk. He had a choice of two loyalties and he chose Pat. He whispered brokenly to Garrett, "That's him!"

The Kid raised his revolver within a foot of Pat's chest, realizing for the first time that there was another man with Maxwell. He demanded, *"Quien es? Quien es?"* as he backed swiftly across the room.

Maxwell rolled off one side of the bed, taking his blankets with him, as Pat sprang from the other side, drawing his gun and firing about a fifth of a second before the Kid got off his own shot. Pat fired at the Kid once more, but the second shot was a waste of time. His first bullet had gone straight into Billy's heart. Billy never spoke again. He was dead before his body fell on the floor.

Exactly where the last bullet Billy ever fired went, was never discovered. The hammer of his .41 self-cocker was resting on a spent shell. Every man present heard three shots fired. But no one could find where the Kid's slug went. From the sharp angle it was fired, it was inconceivable that it could have gone out one of the two small windows in the room. It seemed to have disappeared into thin air.

After the Kid's death, Pat went back to sheriffing. But within a few months he figured he had a final job to do on Billy. At least eight "yellowbacks"—sensational magazines of the time—had made up their own histories of the Kid, and their stories were for the most pure fiction.

Some of them made Billy a 14-karat, sugar-coated Robin Hood of the plains who did nothing but pay off mortgages for helpless old ladies and dispose of black-hearted villains. Others made him out to be the most cold-blooded killer the world had ever known.

To squelch all such absurdities, and to put the true story—as he knew it—on the record, Garrett wrote *The Authentic Life Of Billy The Kid, The Noted Desperado Of The Southwest,* which was first published in 1882, and is the source of a great deal of what is known about the Kid.

Pat put in his book all the things the Kid had told him back in the old days when they had tipped the bottle and played cards together—and the Kid seems to have had a fine imagination. For example, he told Pat that as a boy of 12 he had killed a drunken loafer who had insulted his mother. Although this sounds like whiskey talk, it was included prominently in Pat's story of the Kid. More than that, it served as the inspiring cornerstone upon which the entire Billy the Kid legend was based—the legend that made him into a western Robin Hood.

Pat Garrett went on to become a rancher after he finished his term as sheriff of Lincoln County. Later on, in the 1880s, he put on a star once more as a captain in the Texas Rangers. He was in charge of a company of Rangers in the Panhandle working at putting down rustling there. Although he saw no more notable action in defending the law he went on to serve one final term as sheriff in New Mexico after his stint with the Rangers.

The years wore on, and pretty soon Pat had five grown kids and a gray-haired wife and it was the turn of the century.

Over these later years of his life, Pat was well known and respected by people in high places. He loved to ride and gamble and hunt, and among his friends were John Nance Garner, who became Vice-President in 1932, the author Emerson Hough, and even President Teddy Roosevelt. In 1901, it was Roosevelt who appointed Pat the Collector of Customs in El Paso, and in 1905, when the Rough Riders had their reunion in San Antonio, Pat was invited as a special guest of the President.

After serving as Collector of Customs for a few years, Pat retired to his ranch in the Mesilla Valley and led a quiet life raising horses for a living.

On February 29, 1908, Pat left his ranch to drive

through the Organ Mountains to Las Cruces. He was driving a wagon, and a friend, Carl Adamson, was sitting beside him on the seat. Pat never made it to Las Cruces. Somewhere along the lonely route, somebody held a gun behind Pat's head and pulled the trigger. Pat obviously never had a chance. His gun hand was gloved. His revolver had never left its holster.

Pat Garrett's murderer was never discovered. There was a lot of hard feeling over the killing because Pat was one of the best-liked men in New Mexico. But for all the hullabaloo, no one was ever convicted of the crime. Carl Adamson said he and Pat had stopped the buckboard to take a stretch. That's when Pat was shot. But from there on, his testimony was meaningless. Wayne Brazil, a tenant on Pat's ranch, later confessed to the killing and was brought to trial but was found not guilty. Still later, a hired gunman by the name of Jim Miller talked freely about how he had killed Pat Garrett but he was never arrested. Many people were convinced that Carl Adamson was the murderer. They were sure that only someone Pat trusted could have sneaked behind him and put a bullet in him without warning.

All that is really known is one thing. Pat left his ranch driving a wagon and came back to the ranch lying dead in the back of the rig with a bullet hole through his head.

Even more perplexing than the question of who killed Pat is the question, why? One thought that comes to the romantic mind is that the fingers of Billy the Kid somehow stretched up out of the grave, after 27 long years, and brought a vengeful death to Pat. This fanciful theory argues that some friend or relative of Billy waited patiently for more than a quarter of a century to pull the trigger that would send a lead slug crashing into Pat's brain and even the old, old score.

That seems highly unlikely. But, of course, both Pat Garrett and Billy the Kid lived highly unlikely lives.

LUKE SHORT

The Undertaker's Joy

*He was a mild-mannered, soft-spoken little runt with
a cool head and plenty of courage. But he won his
grim nickname and a feared reputation in the Old
West because his aim was bad.*

After his third round of forty-rod, the tall Colorado
cowboy had a pleasant inspiration. Banging his shotglass
on the bar top, he turned his gaze happily from the customers ranging the bar to the busy gambling tables on the
other side of the room.

"Let's take this saloon," he suggested to his three husky
saddle-partners, "and tear it apart."

"Okay," another agreed, recognizing the need for
moral as well as liquid refreshment after four months on
the range. "Where do we start?"

"You crazy?" a bearded puncher grunted, glancing
nervously over his shoulder. "Know who's dealing faro in
the corner?"

"Never saw the little gent before," the tall one laughed.
"But if he's supposed to be tough, let's start with him."

The three inspired wranglers turned away from the bar.

"That's Luke Short," their bearded friend said quietly.

43

The fun-loving cowpokes snapped to a halt as sharply as if they had run into the side of a barn. Moving quickly back to the bar, the tall one whispered incredulously, "That harmless lookin' fellow is *Luke Short?*"

"Are you sure?" one of the others mumbled under his breath.

"Sure I'm sure. I saw him when he downed Ike Brown. Cool? Fast?" The whiskered cowboy whistled low. "I swear he was back at his game before Ike hit the floor."

"Hear tell he's the top gunman in the state," the fourth muttered.

"Well, hell," the tall man grumbled. "I still feel like tearin' the saloon apart. But I ain't interested in committin' suicide."

"They got a nice saloon across the way." The bearded one tossed off his drink.

The four philosophers crossed Leadville's main street. Ten minutes later, the pounding roars of Colts and the clear, happy warwhoops of stampeding cowmen were mixed with the crashing racket of smashed tables and chairs and breaking glass.

The top gunman in Colorado looked up quietly from his faro game as the noise from the other saloon shattered the air. "Quite a ruckus," he commented.

"Good thing they went across the street," one of the players said.

"I guess," the deadly Luke Short allowed, nodding toward a man at a nearby blackjack table, "they must have noticed the sheriff was here."

Luke Short could never quite understand that he was one of the most feared gunfighters in the West. Had anyone intimated that the four rambunctious cowboys had left because of his presence, he would have considered it a joke. He would have smiled wryly. And looking at that wry smile, every faro player at the table would have thought he was watching an expression of quiet self-confidence on the face of a highly skilled gunman, a killer so thorough and competent that he was spoken of in awed whispers as "The Undertaker's Joy."

Born in Arkansas in 1854, Luke was a thoroughly inconspicuous youngster both in size and temperament. When he had done all the growing he felt like doing, he still lacked seven inches of standing six feet tall, and he weighed only 140 pounds. He was mild-mannered and soft-spoken at all times.

When Luke was in his 20s, he came to the conclusion that he didn't particularly care for hard work and dull routine. So he left his father's farm and moved west in the late 1870s to find out if there was any truth to the tales of quick, easy money being made there.

In Texas he discovered, as did countless others before and after him, that working as a cowpuncher is not necessarily the road to riches. Twenty-five a month and board for a ten- to 16-hour day was even worse than working on a farm.

With a couple of partners, he finally swung a deal whereby a small trading post was opened in Nebraska and Luke was made proprietor. He was popular with the Indians. Every Sioux within a radius of 100 miles quickly learned that fire-water was available at Short's place and availed himself with ill-concealed enthusiasm. The U. S. Government became suspicious that someone was running an unofficial grogshop when it became loudly evident that half of the redskins in the territory were spending two-thirds of their time gloriously drunk. A cavalry platoon tracked a long line of deliriously happy Sioux straight to the door of Luke's trading post.

Luke denied that he was selling whiskey but admitted, after further questioning, that he did happen to have a sizable stock of 90-proof Old Pine Top stomach-ache cure. Ignoring the humanitarian aspects of Luke's business, the Army placed him under arrest. Luckily for Luke, his guards decided to test the medicinal values of Old Pine Top, and when they were satisfactorily inebriated, he escaped, making his way across the Colorado border and eventually to Leadville.

In this hell-for-leather mining town, he sat down and thought things over quietly. Being a farmer or cowboy was too much work for a sensitive man. Selling liquor to the Indians, even though it was a first-class stomach-ache cure, led to involvement and complications. What he needed was a profitable, enjoyable occupation which did not require an absurd amount of physical effort and which was inside the law. Since Short loved nothing more dearly than a good game of stud, faro or keno, the answer wasn't hard to find. He decided to become a professional gambler and promptly began to master the art.

Gambling was a respectable and highly lucrative business in those days, considered by some to be on a level with banking, and by others to be a notch above it. The only trouble with the profession was that too many gamblers were prone to wind up dead after friendly discussions over what had happened to the other two aces. Since upon occasion it was necessary to tactfully or forcefully handle all comers, from tough miners and cowmen to local barbers and blacksmiths right on down the line to thin-eyed characters who had plenty of cash and no obvious means of support, you had to have a steady eye and no nervous system at all to stay in the business long.

It turned out that there was an awful lot of backbone crammed into Luke Short's narrow little frame. His disposition was invariably peaceful and quiet, and he was, in truth, a lousy shot as well as being miserably slow on the draw with a gun. But he wouldn't back down from anyone or anything on the face of the earth, and he had such rocksteady courage that the best gunfighters got rattled in arguments with him.

Although Luke played a straight game, it wasn't long before a Leadville tough by the name of Ike Brown started Luke's gunfighter reputation rolling after losing his shirt at faro. As Luke pulled in Brown's few remaining white chips, Brown slammed his gigantic paw on the table.

"You're a cheat!" he bawled at the top of his voice.

The gambling room became grimly silent. The rustling of shuffled cards and the clicking of chips were stilled. Voices stopped and even the chattering roulette ball ducked quickly for cover in the nearest slot. In the hushed room, all eyes turned to the chunky gambler who had shouted the angry accusation.

Since Brown was a loudmouthed bully by nature, and since he didn't know he was going to be dead in two minutes, he was enjoying himself. He shifted his gun belt so the butt of his .45 was within easy reach and repeated his charge.

"I say you're a cheat!" he snarled at Luke across the faro board. "You're running a goddamned crooked table."

Luke was never much for talking. He considered the charge briefly, raised his cool gray eyes indifferently to meet the hulking man's glare, and replied with neither malice nor excitement, "No, I'm not."

Convinced that his statement had settled the matter satisfactorily, he casually continued dealing to the other players.

Ike Brown was painfully nonplussed. In his wide experience at terrorizing and occasionally murdering Leadville citizens, he had faced men who cringed away, men who laughed feebly and tried to buy him a drink, and highstrung men who went straight for their guns, but he had never met a man who calmly ignored him. Realizing this was the greatest possible insult, and consciously aware that everyone in the house was on the verge of laughing at him, he roared furiously, "I called you a cheat! And when I call a man a cheat, something happens!"

Luke Short flipped the last card over and observed, "Deuce wins."

Beside himself, Brown shook his fist under Luke's nose and thundered, "By God! I'm talking to you!"

"Place your bets," Luke suggested. Then, looking at Brown with that indifferent stare in his level eyes, he added, "If you're not betting, you'll have to vacate that chair."

Brown exploded to his feet, the chair in question crashing to the floor behind him. He bellowed a frustrated, incoherent oath and clawed wildly for his revolver. Facing the undersized chunk of granite before him, though, his reactions were pathetically bad.

Without rising from his chair, Luke fumbled under his coat for the .44 Smith and Wesson at his waist, aimed carefully for Brown's chest, and shot him squarely between the eyes.

Absolutely certain that the matter was settled, Luke picked up his cards and continued dealing.

When they had swept poor Ike Brown up, an impressed bystander gasped to a friend, "Holy smoke! That big fella never knew what hit him!"

"Brown was damned fast," a bartender observed over a glass of tangleleg. "But Short's the fastest I've seen."

"Didn't even mess up the body no wise," a stud dealer said to the players around him. "The undertaker'll just have to dab a little talcum powder on Brown's forehead, fold his arms over his chest, and he'll have as purty a corpse as you ever seen."

Thus Luke Short, his inclinations and abilities to the contrary, was given the foreboding title of "The Undertaker's Joy," or more simply, "The Undertaker's Friend." As is often the case, the story of the battle grew and expanded with the telling, until Luke was reckoned as a deadly killer who could put six slugs through a bolt of lightning without interrupting his deal, and who never, under any circumstances, shot a man any place except neatly betwixt the eyes.

Since Luke never boasted, or talked much at all for that matter, he had what it takes to become a silent, legendary character whose mere presence inspired respect and fear. Men pointed him out cautiously on the streets of Leadville and whispered about him to strangers in the town, putting him in the same dreadful class as Clay Allison, Billy the Kid and John Wesley Hardin. Some of the whispers were ominous.

"Don't stare, you damn fool, just take a quick squint. He'd as leave blow your head off as look at you."

"He's only kilt one man in Leadville—so far. But before he come here, I hear tell he shot hisself a dozen or so in Abilene and Wichita."

And all the while, peaceful little Luke Short just wanted to be left alone to enjoy his quiet game of faro, keno or poker.

Around 1880, Luke broke the hearts of Leadville hero-worshippers by moving to Dodge City where he met the famous gunman Bat Masterson, who was at the time also a member of the sporting fraternity.

One pleasant evening, after Luke had been in Dodge a few months, a big, square-built man with an air of wealth about him sat at the faro table and bucked the tiger for a while. When the other players drifted away, he said, "My name's Lou Rickabaugh. You're Mr. Luke Short, they tell me."

"That's right."

"I've heard you know how, and when, to use a gun."

"You have?"

"I own the Oriental Saloon in Tombstone. Looking for a couple of good men. Men who can handle cards smart and straight, and who'd sooner forget their britches than their hardware when they come to work."

"Yes?"

"Figured on trying to get you and Bat Masterson down there in Tombstone with me. I don't care what you're making here. I guarantee it'll be at least double working for me."

Bat and Luke both agreed to hire out to Rickabaugh, and in so doing, they became members of what was probably the toughest coterie ever assembled under one frontier roof. Rickabaugh had a good thing in the Oriental.

Miners in the Tough Nut and Lucky Cuss mines of Tombstone were shoveling out more high-grade ore than had been seen outside of a government mint, some of it assaying at a phenomenal $15,000 a ton. With this mighty silver lode in its back yard, Tombstone was wallowing in ready cash and, since the Oriental was a plum, located right in the middle of town, certain people were interested in giving Rickabaugh his walking papers. Rickabaugh, an astute psychologist, gave Wyatt Earp a quarter share of his emporium. This meant that the powerful Earp brothers and their flashy, sinister chum, the tubercular Doc Holliday, were lined up on his side. He hired Buckskin Frank Leslie, another master triggerman, as head bartender. Then, when he imported Masterson and Short as dealers, he had the most impressive array of gunslingers that was ever on hand to insure a customer a pleasurable and relaxed evening of drinking and gambling.

Things went smoothly until late February of 1881 when little Luke Short, the weak link in the chain of iron men from any point of view except courage, was the man fate picked to preserve the peace of the Oriental against the assault of one Charlie Storms.

Storms, a very bad man from Deadwood, was a member of the team of gamblers who wanted to take over the saloon. A legitimately lethal gunman, he had conscientiously practiced shooting at unfortunate human beings and tomato cans all his life. He figured that knocking off Luke Short would not only scare the Oriental owners, but would also add considerably to his shooting rep.

Storms slammed through the swinging doors on the morning of the 28th with a friend at his elbow and a fair load under his belt. Luke was quietly dealing faro when Charlie busted into the place. Bat was working at a blackjack table near him. Storms swaggered across the room, jabbed his crony with an elbow, pointed at Luke and roared, "That little one there? A fighter?" Then bellowing with good-humored laughter, he strode across the room to the bar and bought a drink.

Luke looked after him with a sad expression on his face. Some fellows just didn't have the knack of being genteel. Bat, who may have suspected his friend's gunhand was highly overrated, took the time to whisper, "Don't fight Storms, Luke. That's just what he wants you to do."

Tossing off his drink, Charlie wandered back to the faro table. Facing Luke squarely, he snarled, "I never yet seen a Rickabaugh gambler who wouldn't cheat his own grandmother."

Luke calmly finished his deal and said nothing.

Irritated, Storms added belligerently, "And on top of being a cheat, any gambler who'll take that kind of talk is yellow!"

Luke took a blue stack off a ten spot and carefully set it in the rack.

"By God!" Storms thundered, confusion replacing his arrogant confidence. "Are you too scared to talk?"

Luke paid off on a trey and gave Storms that coolly indifferent glance which, if Charlie had been Ike Brown, he would have realized was the prelude to a funeral. Storms could not, though, have been expected to profit by Brown's experience. He didn't. He shrilled illogically, "Damn you, Short! You're asking for it!"

A couple of the Earp boys wandered in, and Bat Masterson, recognizing his chance, walked over to Storms. "Come on, Charlie," he said soothingly, "no one wants any trouble here." Under Bat's persuasion, and not wanting a gun battle while surrounded by enemies, the nerve-racked killer allowed himself to be taken outside.

Later, when Short had left the Oriental for lunch, Storms took a stand outside the saloon and waited for Luke to come back along Allen Street. He didn't have long to wait.

Watching the small figure approaching quietly along the sidewalk, Storms must have had some nice, optimistic thoughts, how Luke would probably stop and stare at him waiting there, how the little man would stumble in his walk, or maybe duck in terror down an alley or into a doorway.

As Luke continued at an unhurried pace toward Storms, the waiting gunman's emotions switched from elation to chagrin to stark disbelief. Charlie's high blood-pressure nearly blew his hat off as he realized Luke Short had already seen him and was calmly and completely ignoring him.

As the silent little man came closer to where he stood, Storms felt the same near-frenzy he'd felt that morning mounting in him. Suddenly, he understood what the real trouble was. Luke Short wasn't afraid of him. He was scared of Luke Short. Stepping forward, he tried to con-

50

vince himself he wasn't afraid by blustering at the top of his voice, "I'll give you first shot," which, as it turned out, was a lie.

He then did the one thing that was bound to cause fireworks by starting to unholster his revolver. It was a regrettable mistake, for Charlie was excited something terrible by the time metal and leather parted company, and his bullets snarled harmlessly past Short.

In the meantime, Luke, who had contributed not one word to the argument, placidly unlimbered his own weapon and shot Storms three times to the best of his limited ability. All three shots connected and Storms promptly quit living. Since one of the slugs walloped Charlie under the collar bone, only 15 inches from his forehead, the old myth gathered new force even as The Undertaker's Joy went quietly back to his faro game.

No one in Tombstone ever bothered him again. He was later tried in Tucson for killing Storms, but it was self-evident by just looking at the gentle, moderate man on trial that he couldn't have started the shooting. They acquitted him almost apologetically.

Luke saved a fair amount of money during his stay in Tombstone and thought it would be a fine thing to go into business for himself. Consequently, he went back to Dodge City and bought controlling interest in the Long Branch Saloon, which he figured could be a top gambling house with the benefit of a little administrative imagination.

He fixed the place up fancy and as a real kicker hired a pretty girl who played the piano and sang. This was a novelty in Dodge City. Paying customers discovered that it was much less painful to drop a month's salary or get roaring drunk to the tune of a good-looking gal entertaining them with *Turkey In The Straw* or *I Dream of Jeannie*. Business boomed at the Long Branch, and, of course, slowed down comparably at other emporiums in the town.

Dodge City may have had an honest mayor from time to time in the '80s, but Luke wasn't lucky enough to hit one of those rare birds. A party named Abner Webster was the town's top politico. Not only was he as crooked as a corkscrew, but he owned the Alamo Saloon right next door to the Long Branch. As he watched the boys hurry past his place on the way to spend their money at Luke's place, it occurred to him that music must be the work of the devil. With this pious thought in mind, he addressed the next meeting of the City Council. In his forthright manner, he told the assembly that while it was certainly within reason for a citizen to get blind drunk on tarantula juice in a saloon, and while it was obviously a man's inalienable right to lose his roll at keno if he was so minded, the malicious use of an attractive songstress in a saloon was downright disgusting. It was highly immoral, degrading and revolting because it lulled a fellow into a false sense of enjoying himself.

The City Council, swayed by Webster's keen logic and righteous concern for his townsmen, agreed that this was so. A law was passed making it thenceforth illegal to poison the minds of the innocent Dodge City citizenry with any form of music in any saloon.

Luke, always one to cooperate, let the girl and her piano go.

Next Saturday night, Dodge City was rocking to the gay, unmistakable sound of said girl and said piano whooping it up in Mayor Abner Webster's Alamo.

Shocked at Webster's total lack of principle and sportsmanship, Luke promptly hired a four-piece band which did its damndest to drown out the melodious racket issuing from the Alamo. He furthermore swore that if Webster or his puppet sheriff, Prairie Dog Dave, tried to stop him, he would most likely lose his temper for the first time in his life.

While Luke was in the Long Branch, no one dared to lock it up, but the first night he wasn't there, the sheriff and his deputies swooped down on the saloon, booted everyone out and slapped a huge padlock on the door. When Luke returned and found the Long Branch in this unhappy condition, he was, as he had prophesied, annoyed no end.

Striding down the lonely street toward the sheriff's office, he spied that lawman 50 feet away stepping out on the board sidewalk. By the bright light of the moon, they faced each other and Luke reached for his revolver. As his gun roared, the sheriff sprawled into the gutter and Luke, pleased with his improving marksmanship, stalked on by to hunt down the mayor.

Webster was nowhere to be found, and Short finally went back to his hotel. When he emerged from his room the next morning there was a small army of deputies ranged around the door holding cocked rifles, scatterguns and revolvers, all aimed nervously at Luke's small body.

"I didn't murder him," Luke frowned. "It was a fair fight."

"Murder who?" a member of the posse asked.

"The sheriff."

"The sheriff?"

Prairie Dog Dave, it developed, was still among the living. Luke's bullet hadn't come near him, but seeing The Undertaker's Joy reach for his gun, that staunch defender of the people had passed out cold. He'd later been hauled out of the gutter and revived by a few slaps on the face.

At noon, the posse took Luke to the railroad station where they were met by Webster and the ashen-faced sheriff. The leading citizen of Dodge made a short speech to the effect that at 12 o'clock there was one train going east, and another going west. He gave Luke the magnanimous choice of taking either one.

Luke went east, but dropped off at the first stop and wired Bat Masterson, telling Bat that Luke and Dodge City were feuding. Masterson wired Wyatt Earp in Tombstone. Wyatt rounded up Charlie Basset, Texas Jack Vermillion, Dan Tipton and John Green.

All six of the feared gunmen converged on Dodge City to take that metropolis over, mayor, sheriff, deputies and all, and very nearly started a second civil war.

Wyatt Earp was the first of the boys to swing down from the train at the Dodge City station. Prairie Dog Dave was standing near the tracks and almost passed out again when he saw Earp walking toward him.

"Dave," Wyatt said, "there may be some trouble around here soon. I have some friends on this train, and we wouldn't want to be outside the law, so why don't you swear us in as temporary peace officers?"

Suspecting, but smart enough not to question who Earp's friends were, Dave gulpingly complied on the spot. This lent a bizarre legality to everything that everyone did in the next few days.

The Long Branch was soon the scene of gay activity, and one and all agreed that the four-piece band was enhanced no end by Webster's ex-thrush singing with it.

In a democratic crusade to clean up Dodge, Luke and his friends next organized an eight-man Peace Commission, consisting principally of themselves, to oust the majority of political crooks in the city. They tossed out practically everyone but the mayor, sparing him in all probability because it was kind of fun to watch him going crazy. First Webster tried to organize a posse to combat the so-far peaceful Peace Commission. Since the population of Dodge City at that time was only a few thousand, he didn't stand a chance of getting enough men together.

Second, as a desperate measure, the mayor called on Governor Glick, demanding that he send troops to Dodge to "meet the emergency."

At this point, there could have been war, for Luke and his self-appointed helpers were not men to back down and they were popular enough to have raised a husky fighting corps in no time flat. Had the governor sent the troops requested, there would have been a battle which would have taken up a good-sized chapter in any history of the Old West.

Such a chapter was never written due to the fact that the governor, knowing the eight men and valuing his troops, flatly refused.

The *Ford County Globe* reported succinctly, "Luke Short has come to stay."

Now that things were settled to everyone's satisfaction except Mayor Webster's, Wyatt and Charlie Basset went back to Tombstone with their two sidekicks. It wasn't long before Bat Masterson drifted away, eventually moving back east to New York where he successfully settled down to the improbable profession of sports writing.

Luke stayed on at Dodge, and especially since the mayor himself finally went out of business, did well with the Long Branch. As 1885 drew near, however, time began to hang heavy on Luke's hands. In his quiet way, he enjoyed moving about from time to time, seeing new places and people. So when one Jake Johnson proposed going partners in a saloon and gambling house in Fort Worth, Luke made a liar of the *Ford County Globe* by selling out his interest in the Long Branch and going to Texas.

A sprawling, fast-growing cowtown, Fort Worth boasted a good railroad and was coming into its own as a major shipping and packing center. Luke and Jake took over the White Elephant, a huge joint at 606 Main Street which did not in the least live up to its facetious handle. Selling two slugs of whiskey for two bits over the forty-foot bar, and operating square games, they began raking in mountains of money from well-heeled cattlemen and a constant army of thirsty, card-loving cowboys who saved up their back pay for wild splurges in the town that marked the end of their cattle drives.

Luke, as senior partner of the White Elephant enterprise, was soon sporting a rope-thick, pure gold watch chain and the finest collection of out-sized diamond stickpins that ever put the finishing touch to a fancy silk cravat.

But as Luke had noticed before, it was a sorrowful comment on human nature that wherever honest folks are doing nicely financially, greed, dishonesty and coercion rear their ugly heads.

These three heads all appeared together in Fort Worth in the single, lion-maned head of Longhair Jim Courtright. Longhair Jim was rated by many professors of triggerology as the absolutely top gunman ever produced by the West. He was one of the few men who, after discounting tall tales and exaggerations, could actually blast six holes through a playing card at thirty paces. He could do this within three seconds after making a draw so fast that his hand was blurred like the head of a striking rattler.

Setting the pace for innumerable modern racketeers who would follow in his grim footsteps, Courtright opened the T.I.C. Detective Agency in Fort Worth. Ostensibly, this detective agency was created with the high-minded purpose of protecting various businesses of the town from crooks and fraudulent dealings. The T.I.C.'s real purpose was to protect these same businesses from the T.I.C., and shake them down for plenty along the way. All Longhair had to do was show up and suggest that an outfit needed some looking after, and any owner in his right mind would nearly break an arm signing on the dotted line, paying no heed to the cost of the contract. In due course of selling his humanitarian protection, Longhair approached Short.

"You're doing mighty swell here," he said, taking in the elaborate fixtures, the crowded bar and the busy gambling tables.

"No room for complaint," Luke replied.

"This is a pretty mean town. Lot of fellas 're probably figuring ways of movin' in on the White Elephant and taking their cut."

"Wouldn't be surprised."

"You're lucky that I'm here to see to it you get a fair

deal. My T.I.C. Detective Agency, I guess you know, guards your boys and your place against any roughhousing or dirty dealing."

"Not interested."

Courtright was profoundly shocked. "Look, Short. Sometimes it happens that even the proprietors get shot. I'm telling you, you need protection."

"Not me," Luke said softly. "Thanks for dropping by all the same."

Longhair stalked out of the White Elephant muttering under his breath. Short's reputation as a man whom undertakers appreciated was well known to him, and even more than the rep, he found the casual confidence in Luke's gray eyes unnerving. One thing was sure. He would have to collect from the stubborn little man or kill him. If one man had the grit to hold out on the T.I.C., it would start others thinking they could do the same thing. Right now, every citizen of Fort Worth was in the habit of trembling when Jim walked by with his .45 hanging lightly in its cut-down holster. He'd worked hard building his rep, killing an estimated two dozen men along the way. If Short's courage were contagious, it would mean the end of Jim's career of spreading sweetness and light. The more Longhair pondered upon Luke's exasperating and unreasonable attitude, the madder he got. And the more the vision of Luke's unruffled composure haunted him, the uneasier he got.

Courtright paid a few more calls to the White Elephant, becoming increasingly aggravated and upset with each visit. Finally, he delivered the ultimate threat. If Luke didn't come across in the near future, he would cease to need protection from anybody except the Almighty.

"Go to hell," Luke told him quietly.

On the night of February 8, 1887, Courtright waited in front of the White Elephant for Short. Jake Johnson came out and talked briefly with Longhair. Then, terrified, Jake hurried back into the saloon to where Luke was having his boots blacked.

"What's the matter?" Short asked, seeing his partner's frightened face.

"Courtright's outside," Jake blurted.

"What's he want?" Luke inquired, adding to the boot-black, "You missed a spot on the heel there, son."

"He just says he wants to see you."

Outside, Luke said, "Nice evening, Jim."

56

Jake fell behind as the two men started to stroll down the street together.

In front of Ella Blackwell's shooting gallery, Courtright turned and faced Short. "You know why I'm here," he grunted tersely.

"I won't pay," Luke said gently.

"This is your last chance," Courtright informed him, his voice tight.

"I told you to go to hell," Luke replied, hooking his hands in the V of his vest.

"You needn't be getting out a gun," Courtright frowned.

"I'm not carrying a gun here, Jim," Luke said mildly, raising his vest to prove it.

As Short dropped his hands from his vest, Courtright suddenly snatched desperately for his Colt. He had his gun out before Luke had started for his, but marvelous gunman that he was, he was badly shaken by Luke's incredible, fearless calm, and his shots went wild.

Short coolly trundled out his Smith & Wesson and fired three times, hitting Longhair in various and sundry places, the sum total of which killed him.

The stunning news flashed through Fort Worth even as the echoes of the roaring guns faded out on the streets. Little Luke Short had downed their all-time champion gunslinger. And if The Undertaker's Joy had departed from his monotonous routine of shooting adversaries nicely between the eyes, it might have been because he didn't want to ruin the strikingly fine expression of hurt surprise on Longhair's face.

Luke paid no attention to the rapidly gathering crowd. He quietly stepped over Longhair's still body on the sidewalk and went casually back to the White Elephant to see if everything was going smoothly in the saloon.

After Courtright's demise, Luke was regarded as being definitely bulletproof, an invincible gunfighter, and in all probability somewhat immortal. If he had lived to be 100, probably no one would have been fool enough to bother him again. But he was destined to die only six years later at the age of 39.

Through those last six years, Luke lived as he believed life should ideally be lived, in a relaxed and tranquil manner. A man who loved refinement and reserve, he appreciated the absence of noisy gunfire, and except for the occasional mention of the name, "The Undertaker's Joy," which always caused him to wince, the peace and quiet of his existence was interrupted by only two occurrences. The first was when he was married; the second was when a doctor told him he had Bright's disease.

On a trip to Geuda Springs, Kansas, in 1893, Luke told his wife he was feeling a little tired, and went up to his room at the Gilbert Hotel early.

There, on that pleasant evening of September 8th, death came softly to pay its respects to the little man of large courage.

Luke Short died quietly, in bed, as was only fitting and proper for an easygoing, soft-spoken gentleman of mild habits.

DEADWOOD DICK'S
MASQUERADE

An entire nation acclaimed his deeds; he even got to meet the President. But the truth was, Dick Clarke was handier with a pitchfork than a sixgun.

The line between fact and fancy was a fine one in the Old West. With few official records and conflicting "eyewitnesses"—who could give every detail of a gunfight dozens of years later—the school of Eastern dime-novel writers who glorified legendary figures like Buffalo Bill, General Custer, Wild Bill Hickok and Deadwood Dick could take considerable liberties in their portrayals. Consider the following:

"Of course I've heard of Deadwood Dick, as who has not?" said the beautiful blonde young girl with lovely lips like two fresh, dewy rose petals. "I have heard that he is a brave, fearless, reckless Bedouin of The Plains with manners as gracious as those to be observed in the most elegant New York drawing room. Certainly an innocent young damsel such as I would have nought to fear in his presence! My life and honor would be safe in his hands!"

"Ah, be not too sure!" ejaculated her old aunt, who

was serving as her traveling companion on the swiftly moving stagecoach, even now bound for the wicked city of Deadwood. "He is bold and fearless without doubt. But the dear Lord in Heaven above only knows how many men have drawn their last breath while gazing into his stern visage and trying to—as they say out here in the Great Open Spaces—beat him to the draw!"

The old woman's speech was rudely interrupted by the sudden sound of gunshots from without the stagecoach, and the driver shouted in a voice quavering with fear, "It's none other than that black-hearted fiend, Boston Bill. We can expect no mercy from him!"

In a trice the stagecoach was brought to a halt and an evil, leering face appeared at the window. "Climb outa that afore I perforates the coach with m' hoglaig!" cried Boston Bill.

The two passengers paled at these words.

"Alas!" sobbed the fair young maiden. "What is to become of us?"

Boston Bill snatched open the door and pulled the struggling woman out onto the hot desert floor.

"Unhand me, foul villain!" she cried, her innocent young face pleading more eloquently than any words.

Boston Bill laughed heartlessly at her tender pleas, and in an instant was galloping away with his fair captive.

"Woe is me!" her aged aunt wailed with tears of grief flowing down her face. "All is lost!"

"Hark!" said the stagecoach driver, turning his ear to the distant hills. "I hear hoofbeats!" Suddenly his face lighted up and he cried, "Fear not, madam, for all is not lost! There is but one man in all the West who rides a great white stallion such as the one that approaches so swiftly! It is Deadwood Dick to the rescue!"

Needless to say, our fearless hero got there in the very nick of time, saved the girl with nary a scratch, and chastised the villain by placing a lead slug precisely equidistant between his evil eyes.

But, believe it or not, Deadwood Dick was only a character in a series of paperback books written in the late 1800s. He was never anything else.

"Hah!" some of you may say. "This foul villain of a writer has been at the opium pipe again. Why my grandpap swapped tales with Deadwood Dick! My Dad saw him a couple of times. Matter of fact, old Dick flew to

Washington to shake the hand of President Coolidge back in '27. And when Deadwood passed to his reward in the early '40s, most of the papers in the country wrote sad stories about him."

That's absolutely true; still, Deadwood Dick never existed. And therein lies a story.

In 1876, a New Yorker named Edward L. Wheeler decided to write some books and make some money. Though the one does not necessarily follow the other, in Ed's case it did. He made a pretty fair pile writing a series of books about a character named Deadwood Dick. Wheeler, as far as anybody knows, was never west of the old West End Bar & Grill on the outer edge of Manhattan, but he had been hearing a lot about a big strike out West. Gold had been found on a Sioux reservation in what is now South Dakota, and white men were flooding into the area. Prospectors, adventurers, killers, gamblers and painted ladies were busy making a new boom town. Since a fire had charred the trees on one side of the town, it was called, appropriately, Deadwood.

The town had captured the imagination of the nation, and writer Wheeler decided to take advantage of the situation. Staring at a cool glass of beer on the bar before him, he came up with a lulu of an idea—Deadwood Dick of Deadwood. Thus was Dick born in beer foam, and he battled and rescued his way through 64 books during the next 15 years. Outlaw, marshal, hunter, frontiersman, soldier of fortune, plainsman, Indian fighter, cowboy and gambler, Dick took his turn at everything that was romantic and adventurous. When he was bad, he was a Western Robin Hood and when he was good he made Sir Galahad look like a bum. He could shoot, ride and fight better than anybody in the Great Open Spaces, and he was always a perfect gentleman.

If Wheeler had been contemplating that glass of brew at earlier or later dates, he might have come up with Tombstone Tom, California Carl, Virginia City Vic or Leadville Louie. For almost all of Wheeler's characters had neatly alliterative monickers, such as Kentucky Kit, Boston Bill, Sierra Sam and Bessie Burt. (Presumably, Bessie couldn't recall where she hailed from.)

About the same time that Wheeler's brainchild was born, into the Black Hills of gold-rush fame came one Dick Clarke, a good-natured 20-year-old whose only ambition in life was to get a job as a stablehand someplace.

Chances are that Dick walked or hitched a ride on a freight wagon, for he was flat broke and could not afford the luxury of horse and saddle.

Dick got a job swamping stalls at Crook City, not far from Deadwood, at $15 a month and board. At this point, Clarke figured he had the world by the tail. He got three square meals a day and could occasionally go out and get drunk with the boys. Who could ask for more?

And now we will try the difficult task of telling two stories at once. One will trace the development of young Dick Clarke, the man. The other will follow the career of Deadwood Dick, the Western superman conceived by Ed Wheeler.

Eight o'clock came and Dick jammed his pitchfork into a bale of hay. It was time to quit for the night.

"Cuppa coffee, Hank?" he asked his partner.

"Yeah." The other stablehand yawned. "Let's go."

Ma Hollis' place was just across the street, and she poured two steaming mugs for them. "Ol' Smitty come by a while ago," Ma said. "His cousin Al was on the Deadwood stage last week an' it got stopped by some fellas. They got a watch an' seven dollars off Al."

"Cryin' shame," Hank grunted. "Somebody ought t' do somethin'."

"Damn right!" Dick nodded and put down his coffee. "Think I'll take one of them crullers, too, Ma."

She put one on the counter. "Talk has it, some fella named Sam Bass did it."

"No, Ma. Not that kind. The other kind up there with sugar on it." Dick pointed. "That's right. Thanks."

"This is utter falsehood," cried the authoritative voice of the female eccentric Sure-Pop. "I am a United States detective and the witness who brings the charges, Commodore Burt, is my aide. The man in the prisoner's box is the famous outlaw, known to many of you as—Deadwood Dick!"

Had a bomb exploded in the camp it would not have created more astonishment than the sudden declaration of Sure-Pop.

"Deadwood Dick!" ejaculated Commodore Burt.

"Deadwood Dick!" cried several others. "Deadwood Dick, the daredevil road agent!"

"Ay, Deadwood Dick, the outlaw with a dozen aliases!" Sure-Pop replied triumphantly.

"Lynch him! Lynch Deadwood Dick! String him up from the nearest tree!" the crowd cried as one.

Suiting words to action they swarmed about the man in the prisoner's box. *"A rope! A rope!"* they cried. Screaming bloodthirsty cries, they dragged the seemingly helpless man to the nearest cottonwood, and only when the body was dangling high on a rope suspended from a limb was their maniacal fury abated.

"Now thar's the way t'handle 'em road agents!" someone gloated. *"A good ol'-fashioned necktie party!"*

Suddenly Sure-Pop stared incredulously at the hanging man's twisted face. *"There's been a terrible mistake!"* she cried. *"That man is not Deadwood Dick!"*

"What!" the crowd cried. *"Not Deadwood Dick? The wrong man strung up? Deadwood Dick has escaped again!"*

Hank came running into the wide corridor between the stalls. He saw Dick currying a horse and stopped, panting. "Jesus! You hear about them Sioux yet?"

"Uh-uh."

"Man just came in from Deadwood, horse 'bout to drop under 'im! Says the Redskins're up in arms all over the countryside! Some prospector kilt a brave and cut his head off an' the Injuns are fit to be tied!"

Dick dropped the curry comb. "What in hell we gonna do?"

"Stay in close to town, fur one thing. And keep a gun handy. That's what they're tellin' everybody to do!"

"But, Hank, you know I ain't got no gun!"

"I'm gonna git my old Defender out an' carry it in my belt." Hank started digging through his private belongings in an old crate that was nailed to the wall. " 'Nother thing," he said. "News come at the same time. They shot that Wild Bill Hickok right smack in the back of the head." The stablehand found his Defender under a pair of long winter underwear. "Here it is!"

"Listen, Hank," Dick said. "How about the loan of that gun when you ain't usin' it?"

"To hell with that," Hank grumbled. "I bought it to defend yours truly. Besides, you don't even know how to shoot the damned thing."

"Leastwise, leave me take it when I go to the outhouse

63

after dark," Dick said. "They tell me that's a favorite waitin' spot for them savages tryin' to catch some fella all by himself!"

"Never in all the history of The West, has there been a truer, more undying friendship than the one between Wild Bill Hickok and Deadwood Dick," said Bessie Burt. "Either one of them would gladly lay down his life for the other at a moment's notice."

"But how can this be?" Kentucky Kit wished to know. "Hickok has always been on the side of the just and the right. He has devoted his life to upholding law and order. While Deadwood Dick is a daring road agent who scoffs at officers of the law."

"Ah, little do you know, Kit, of the true heart that beats in Deadwood Dick's chest. Many is the time he has ridden side by side with Wild Bill Hickok to bring justice to the poor and oppressed, and to mete out stern, swift punishment to the villains responsible for foul deeds!"

"If only they knew of our miserable plight now," Kentucky Kit wept. "If only they knew that we are being held by those merciless, heartless brigands outside, for what we can bring in ransom!"

There was a wild flurry of shots without, and Bessie Burt hurried to the window of the cabin. "Our prayers have been answered! Yonder come the very two bold, fearless men of whom we just spoke! Now the pitiless wretches who hold us captive will pay for their actions with their very lives!"

The dusty Deadwood street was sleepy and quiet in the heat of straight-up noon. Walking casually along the street with Hank at his side, Dick said, "Glad I decided to come into Deadwood with you. A fella should broaden hisself some, see the sights."

Hank studied a grimy piece of paper in his hand. "Now, how in hell many hoofpicks did the boss want us to get at the hardware store here? This list is all blurred up from sweat."

Dick glanced at the paper. "Looks like a dozen hoofpicks. Twelve. Didn't he want the cavalry kind, with pick an' curry all in one?"

"Yeah, I guess so." Hank scratched his head and returned the paper to his pocket. "Damned hot. We better git us a drink first off, then tend to business."

They were a few feet from the door of the Green Front Saloon, when a booming voice inside roared, "Git your goddamned hands offa me! You little —, I kin whip you any day in the week!"

There was the sound of an approaching battle of some sort, and Hank and Dick backed away from the door. It burst open after a moment, and two barmen shoved out a fat, furious person dressed in filthy buckskins and swearing blue blazes.

"M' God, it's a woman!" Dick whispered.

There was a fair amount of muscle on the indignant female, and she almost got back in despite the human barricade the two barmen formed at the batwing doors.

Finally, giving up in disgust, she threw her crumpled hat onto the sidewalk and stomped on it. "Watch out who you're pushin' around!" she bellowed. "Who the hell says I'm drunk? I'll break his head for him! I've drunk better whiskey outa cans, anyhow! You lousy bunch of —— ——!" Nearly falling, she stooped down and grabbed the beaten hat and crammed it down over her snarled, unkempt hair. "There's lots better places in this damned town than your stinkin', lousy, dirty, cheatin', goddamned hellhole of a dive, anyhow." Spitting at the barmen she blundered up the street, muttering darkly to herself.

The barmen watched her go, and when she was a safe distance away, they went back in. Hank and Bill followed them. At the bar Hank asked, "Who in hell is she?"

The closer barman shrugged. "Thought everybody knew Calamity Jane."

"Not us. We don't git over to Deadwood much."

"She's a kind of celebrity. Don't know exactly why. Claims to been Wild Bill Hickok's wife or girl or somethin' like that. She's the biggest liar ever was."

"We'll take a couple beers," Dick said.

Putting the glasses down before them, the barman chuckled. "Buffalo Bill Cody come by Deadwood one time to hire Calamity as an attraction in his Wild West Show. He took one look at her and left town in a hurry."

Dick frowned. "What else was we s'posed to get, Hank? The hoofpicks an'—a couple of rope halters?"

"Yeah." Hank took a long drink. "God, that's good.

Reckon they call her Calamity 'cause she sure as hell looks like one, huh, barkeep?"

The most famous woman on the entire frontier, Calamity Jane had a trim figure, hands of creamy whiteness and a wonderful wealth of long, glossy hair. She was of medium height and symmetrically built, and she dressed in a carefully tanned costume of buckskin, the vest being fringed with the fur of mink. She wore a jaunty Spanish sombrero and the boots on her dainty feet were of patent leather. Her face was slightly sunburned yet showed beauty, especially in her eyes that were black and piercing. And now, almost mortally wounded, Calamity Jane lay stretched out on Bessie Burt's bed.

"How come you to be so desperately wounded?" Bessie Burt asked the beautiful girl in tender tones.

"I fell under fire while trying to protect my husband, the notorious outlaw Deadwood Dick," gasped Calamity Jane. "You have a kind face. Tell me, is Deadwood Dick, my sweetheart, still alive?"

"So you are the wife of Deadwood Dick, the famous road agent!" ejaculated Bessie Burt. "There is nothing to fear for, Calamity. Deadwood Dick escaped from the lynch mob on his great white stallion."

Calamity Jane's lovely face relaxed and her lips parted in an angelic smile. "You can never know how happy you have made me. Now, if it be God's will, I can die in peace and contentment."

"You were wounded almost unto death," Bessie Burt smiled. "But I have staunched the terrible flow of blood. And I do believe that you will not perish."

"Listen, the trout are bitin' like nobody's business over at Sandy Bottom," Luke said, "and there ain't been no Indians seen around for a long time. C'mon! We'll ride my mules. Hank, you got a box of hooks and sinkers, ain't you?"

An hour later the three fishermen, Luke, Hank and Dick Clarke were well out of town on their way to Sandy Bottom. Passing the road that led to Deadwood, they saw a weatherbeaten old hulk of a stagecoach pulled off to the side of the road.

"Wonder how long they'll leave that coach sit there like that," Dick said. As they rode closer on their mules he saw several bullet gouges in the tough wooden frame of the coach. "I can see why they call it the bad-luck stagecoach," he added.

"You know the whole story there?" Luke asked. "That coach's been held up more'n any other one. Some say 200 times. Folks killed every time she went out. They worked 'er way back along the Overland, gettin' held up all over the place. Guess she was robbed about a dozen times around here before that last time, when the driver was shot and every other driver swore off drivin' it. She's been sittin' off the road there near on to a year now, I reckon. She's plain, pure bad luck."

"Heard old Buffalo Bill was thinkin' of buyin' it for his Wild West Show," Hank said.

"He already bought it," Dick told them. "Ma Hollis said he got it for somethin' like $75."

"That's so?" Luke kicked his mule. "We better get a move on to Sandy Bottom."

A sudden shot rang out and the masked man uttered a cry of pain and dropped his pistol as he clutched at his injured wrist.

"Thought you had the drop on me, did you, you sneaking, cowardly villain?" The handsome, athletic stagedriver bounded gracefully back into the seat of the stagecoach, brandishing the revolver that had appeared as if by magic in his hand. "Stand aside, all of you. The man you see before you is none other than Deadwood Dick himself!"

"You are Deadwood Dick, the fearless road agent?" cried the other masked bandits, who fell back before his bold gaze. "But how is it you are driving the stagecoach?"

"An errand of mercy!" cried Deadwood Dick. "This coach must be pulled into Deadwood by these faithful horses ere midnight! And any man who stands in my way shall die like a dog!" Thus saying, he cracked the whip over the horses' heads and sent them flying over the hill. Two of the masked bandits were foolhardy enough to pursue him, but Deadwood Dick's revolver spoke twice, and each bullet unerringly found its mark.

Hardly had he lost sight of the bandits than Dick glanced to his right and his keen eyes narrowed. A war party of at least 100 Sioux bore down toward him from the mountains. Lashing the whip over the racing steeds he cried, "Giddap! You noble beasts will have to be swifter than lightning to be on time!"

A fair-haired maiden stuck her head from the coach window and cried, "Can we outfly both time and those onrushing savages, or is all lost?"

"Never fear," said Deadwood Dick coolly. "I will defend you with my very life, and these brave steeds will race like the swiftest eagles in flight!"

Deadwood Dick kept on being a dashing Robin Hood-Sir Galahad right on up to the 1890s, and tens of thousands of readers around the country decided that he was every bit as real as the other characters mentioned in the paperback Westerns, such as Wild Bill Hickok, Calamity Jane, Preacher Smith, Poker Alice and Buffalo Bill.

As for Dick Clarke, he took a crack at ranching and tended bar for a while. But mainly he was a stablehand.

The next important event in the Deadwood Dick saga took place in 1927, when the only reported Indian massacre was when a drunken Sioux ran over a white man in a Model A Ford. That year a fellow by the name of Bert Bell came by the stable where Dick Clarke was employed, "Hi, Dick," he said.

Old Dick was about 70 by then, but he was still spry from years of healthful exercise with a pitchfork. "Howdy," he said.

Bert Bell lit a cigarette. "Say, Dick, how would you like to be Deadwood Dick?"

"Huh?"

"Your name's Dick. You been in Deadwood most of your life. How would you like to be Deadwood Dick?"

Bert explained that the local chamber of commerce was inaugurating Deadwood's "Days of '76" as an historical holiday and they needed somebody to be Deadwood Dick. "We'll get you a fancy suit of buckskins some place," Bert told Dick, "and we'll send you off to Washington to invite President Coolidge to come out and see us for the big celebration."

"Well, my job—"

"We'll get you a leave of absence. And we'll pay you for your time lost."

So Dick Clarke did it. They bought him a fancy frontiersman-type outfit, put a long-haired wig on him and flew him off to Washington as Deadwood Dick to chat with Cal Coolidge and invite him back to the Black

Hills, where the President would be able to have a rip-snorting time and try on a big, feathered Indian bonnet.

Dick got his picture taken maybe a million times in Washington, and the papers printed stories about Deadwood Dick Clarke being in the capital. Everybody got the idea that he was the real McCoy.

Bert Bell swore he had no idea this would happen. After all, he argued, when you see Santa Claus ringing a bell on a street corner around Christmas time, you don't necessarily figure him for the bona fide resident of the North Pole. But that's just what happened. By the time the "Days of '76" were over, the country was convinced that Deadwood Dick and Deadwood Dick Clarke were one and the same.

Also, when it came time for Clarke to turn over his buckskin uniform and go back to pitching hay, he got pretty indignant. By now, he, too, was convinced that he was Deadwood Dick. Matter of fact, he was more convinced than anybody. He started speaking of the other old-time plainsmen who had been his partners on the trail and began mourning the passing of the buffalo and all. It got so the mere mention of Hickok or Calamity Jane—or even General Custer—would bring a tear to his eye. And, though he was getting a bit on in years to do any riding or shooting, he loved to recall his uncanny feats of horsemanship and marksmanship. People paid him to be an attraction at shows and celebrations, and he began making more money than he'd ever made in his life.

A wily old gent, he had several narrow verbal escapes during his declining years. A tourist once asked him an embarrassing question about the rifle he carried as part of his costume. "Tell me, Mister Deadwood," he said. "How does that gun work?"

Deadwood Dick flushed a deep scarlet. "Humph!" he snorted. "Asking such a question of a man like me is a downright insult!"

In the early 40s, Dick Clarke at last cashed in his chips and made the final, long journey to the Happy Hunting Ground. They did not bury an ex-stablehand in "that narrow grave, just six-by-three." They laid to rest, with proper respect and ceremony, a renowned plainsman and Indian fighter. Somebody took the trouble to count heads at the funeral and duly reported that there were more people seeing Deadwood Dick off than there had been at Wild Bill Hickok's and Calamity Jane's funerals put together.

Deadwood Dick Clarke would have appreciated that. And Ed Wheeler, had he not been long dead, would have died laughing.

THE WOMAN WHO CONQUERED VIRGINIA CITY

*Adah Menken was a temptress from her flashing
eyes to her toes. When she arrived in the richest,
rowdiest town in the West, the men started pawing
the ground like bulls.*

In early March of 1864, a young reporter for the
Territorial Enterprise was properly enchanted by the vision of a gigantic nude woman on the slopes of Sun
Mountain above Virginia City. The naked female was the
focal point of a huge, 100-foot-long poster. The painting
portrayed her strapped to the back of a wild mustang,
and above the dramatic scene bold letters spelled out:
THE GREAT MAZEPPA! A growing crowd of miners gathered around the young reporter to stare with hypnotized
fascination at the gorgeous poster on the mountainside.
For a long time, no one spoke. This was an age when
speculation about well-turned ankles made for spicy conversation. The girl in the painting was well-turned from
feet to forehead, and no speculation was called for. It
was all there to see. Overwhelmed, the boys just looked.
Finally the reporter, a Missourian named Sam Clemens

who wrote under the name Mark Twain, found his voice long enough to say, "What the hell—!"

"By God!" A husky, bearded mining engineer slapped Twain powerfully on the back. "That there must be Adah Isaacs Menken! She's comin' to Virginia City!"

"The Menken!" a grizzled powder monkey yelled. "She'll put this here town on the map! Why, she's the greatest—"

Someone else in the crowd caught the name Menken and bellowed, "Yippppeee!" as he pulled his revolver and started blasting holes in the sky.

The Menken! Within an hour, the most fabulous boom-town of its time was filled with the magic name. Work around the site of the Comstock lode came to a halt. If you wanted a drink, which everyone did, you had to fight your way into a saloon. The Menken! Beauty, glamour, sex, charm—everything that was female and wonderful was wrapped up in that name. During the celebration, two men were shot on "C" Street and a drunken Chinaman was knifed in Maguire's Bar.

"It's my duty as a reporter," young Mark Twain decided in Moore's Pavilion, "to give that girl her come-uppance. After all, put her clothes back on, and what have you got?"

Had Twain not been well-liked, he would doubtless have been shot on the spot. The town's rugged characters blanched at the thought of putting Adah's clothes back on. Then they tried to explain that, dressed or otherwise, the Menken was purely magnificent. A few of them had seen her. All of them had heard of her.

"In that part she plays in *Mazeppa*," a scholarly faro dealer said, "she's really strapped to a wild stallion and rides up a man-made mountain on the stage. She's damn near been killed a dozen times."

Twain was still adamant. "She sounds like a glorified circus rider to me. And that's what I'll say in the *Enterprise*. When I finish with her, she'll just keep riding that mustang clear back to New York."

Adah Isaacs Menken and Virginia City came together at the peaks of their skyrocketing climbs to fame. The Washoe Mountains with their incredibly rich Comstock lode, were generally conceded to be composed almost entirely of silver. Since the rush in '59, when the gold miners found that the sticky black stuff they had been throwing away was silver, Virginia City had earned the reputation of being the toughest, wealthiest little metropolis in the world. At the outbreak of the Civil War, the Comstock was a primary objective for both the South and the North. General Terry tried to secure the Washoe Mountains for the Confederacy, but his few armed rebels couldn't hold out when the North built Fort Churchill practically on top of the Comstock and manned the fort with half the soldiers in California. To this day, there are those who stoutly maintain the Confederate States would have won the war, given the wealth from Virginia City. Certainly the flood of dollars rolling out of the mountains would have kept the Southern armies going a long time.

Despite hitting stupendous veins of silver, one of which was solid metal 6 feet wide, the miners had a hard life. Cave-ins were an everyday occurrence. Temperatures in the mines went as high as 160 degrees Fahrenheit—there was a stream of naturally boiling water in the Ophir Mine—and outside, in the wintertime, it was brutally cold. One man's feet had to be amputated, along with other parts, when he sat down in the snow to rest a few minutes. Also most of the water in Virginia City was poisonous. Hundreds of men got sick and many of them died before someone discovered there was gold, silver and arsenic in the water. Mark Twain was among the first to bring to public attention the fact that the town's H_2O could not be taken straight. You had to neutralize the water with a couple of generous slugs of whiskey.

The "Washoe Zephyr," a wind that blew out of the Washoe Mountains and reached hurricane strength, also plagued the residents. It blew cabins down regularly, and once it picked up a mule and hurled it off a ridge. The Zephyr snuck up behind Bill Harley one time and slammed into him so hard that it blew him right out of his boots. It blew the first Catholic Church down the slope and two miles across the desert, smashing it to kindling wood. When the Zephyr was acting up, the citizens stored valuables such as ammunition and medicinal whiskey underground. They even lugged two pool tables into a cave so they could play a few quiet games while the earth above trembled and shook under the blast of the wind.

Not a man in Virginia City would ever forget the

short, bloody Piute war. For several nights and days the town was surrounded by 10,000 Piute braves. When the sun went down, hundreds of Indian campfires could be seen stretching across the desert for miles. One hundred and five men went out to chase away the redskins. About half of them got back alive, some four days later. They had been ambushed at Pyramid Lake. Those miners who had been taken alive had been crushed under large rocks and burned alive in campfires by the Indians. The men of Virginia City garrisoned their streets and waited for the Piutes to come to town. They were armed with sawed-off shotguns, pistols, bowie knives and picks and shovels. "Them Pah-utes mebbe'll git me," a black-bearded miner grumbled, honing up the edge of his shovel. "But I'll dig m'way through three or four of 'em first."

Then one morning a steam whistle blasted happily from where lookouts were stationed on the ridge. "Soldiers!" A bullwhacker bellowed down. "Soldiers from California to drive off them heathen Pah-utes!" The only disappointed man in Virginia City was an engineer named Smith who had made a home-made cannon out of the trunk of a pine tree and mounted it over Devil's Gate so it would rake the canyon entrance to Sun Mountain. The Piutes were scattered into the desert and were never again a threat to the city.

Not long after, as the Civil War threatened to break out, Fort Churchill went up. And a strange thing began to happen to Virginia City. Since a large portion of its burly miners were millionaires, someone got the idea that the town needed elegance. After all, the poor grade ore from the Ophir—which would have been top grade ore in many silver mines—was used to pave the streets. What other town in the world literally had streets paved with silver? Buildings began to go up that were as plush and opulent as anything New York or Paris had to offer. Spiral staircases, marble floors, crystal chandeliers and magnificent mirrors were imported from San Francisco. One snobbish hotel insisted that no knife fights take place in its lobby—the blood might stain the new rugs.

Virginia City's *Territorial Enterprise* was the best newspaper west of the Mississippi. While visiting the town, the country's leading humorist, Artemus Ward, became great pals with Joe Goodman, the publisher, and his sidekick Mark Twain. At a dinner the paper gave in his honor, Ward proposed a toast. "Gentlemen. I give you the northern part of Canada."

"Northern Canada!" the assembled party agreed enthusiastically, drinking huge glasses of champagne.

Later Mark Twain frowned and said, "Say, Art. Why did you give us Northern Canada?"

"Because," Ward said simply, "I have no use for it myself."

Add to fantastic wealth and literary significance a glittering theater called Maguire's Opera House, and you have Virginia City in 1864; a perfect place for show folks to display their talent. And now The Menken, the greatest of the great, was coming.

Combine the outstanding characteristics of Marilyn Monroe, Babe Didrikson, Claire Booth Luce and Gypsy Rose Lee. Stir up and multiply by ten, and you have a reasonable image of this astonishing personality who set the world on its ear 100 years ago. The Menken was an actress, an athlete, a poetess, a sculptress and the world's first genuine strip teaser. The gorgeous creature was indisputably a ball of fire in the boudoir, which may have had something to do with her being an honorary Captain of the Dayton Light Guards. She spoke seven languages fluently. Most important, within her breathtaking framework there beat the heart of a wild, free soul that rebelled violently against everything normal and dull in the world.

Due principally to the fact that she loved to make up interesting stories, Adah's life is one vast confusion of details.

Picture a wide Texas prairie with maybe a thousand blood-crazed Comanches hurtling over a hill toward a lovely young girl. A tall, handsome man on a fine horse sees what's going on from a hilltop nearby. His name is Sam Houston. He dives his horse down the hill at breakneck speed to get to the poor, desperate girl first. He shoots at the Comanches five times, and seven Comanches are killed. Then he leans low on his pony, scoops the pretty girl into his arms and races away. "Never fear," says he. "I will protect you with my very life."

"Thank heaven," says she. "I was a bit worried there, for a moment."

They escape from the onrushing Indians in the nick of time, or you might even say, by a hair's breadth. Houston adopts the beautiful girl as his daughter, and she grows up to become the fabulous Menken. All of this, of course, never happened. But it was one of Adah's favorite lies. In time she even had an Indian chief raising his tomahawk to chop away her scalp just as Houston came barreling up.

The truth is, no one knows exactly when Adah was born or what her family name was. The place was just outside New Orleans, the time, about 1835. Some 21 years later, she married Alexander Isaacs Menken, whose name she retained when she became a world-wide celebrity.

In 1857, a theater manager named James Charles was reading a manuscript on the stage of his empty theater, when he heard a voice say, "Are you Mr. Charles?"

Looking up, he found himself staring into the biggest, softest pair of bedroom eyes he had ever seen. He stood up and mumbled, "Uhhh, yes."

Adah favored him with a smile that almost caved in his knees. "I want to become an actress, and I thought you might be able to help me."

"Do you have any professional experience?" he asked her.

"Oh, I'm afraid not."

"Doesn't matter. I was just curious," he apologized.

Adah starred in *The Lady of Lyons*, Charles' next production, in Shreveport, and within six months, she was taking the big city of New Orleans by storm. It is impossible to judge whether Adah could act or not. No one noticed. No one cared. Adah was Adah and that was all that mattered.

The Menken visited New York, where she met Frank Queen, editor of the *Clipper*, the *Variety* of its day. After one look at her, Queen was entranced.

"By the way, Mr. Queen," Adah said, fluttering her eyes, "I've a little poem I thought you might consider running in your paper."

"The *Clipper* never publishes poetry," Queen said. "But that's all right. We'll run your poem." And so it went.

No one man could hold down The Menken for long. Alexander, her first husband, was lost in the shuffle, and Adah met John C. Heenan, better known as "Benecia Boy," the more or less recognized heavyweight boxing champion of the world. She married him.

This started a big fuss, because Alexander Menken had never divorced Adah, though now he hastened to do so.

By the time the nation's newspapers got through playing up her bigamy, she was the most famous and scandalous woman of her time. As indignant editorials pointed out, good girls did not become actresses, and if they wrote poetry, they kept it modestly hidden in their diaries. What's more, they did not go around marrying at random, especially pugilists.

Leaving Adah to face these publicity bombshells by herself, Heenan sailed to England to fight the British champion Tom Sayers. And that was the end of him. Adah divorced him and Sayers whipped him.

Around the outbreak of the Civil War, The Menken got herself arrested in Baltimore for carrying a Confederate flag onstage. She married a political satirist named Newell, who wrote under the name Orpheus C. Kerr (a pun on "office seeker") but he didn't last long either.

In New York, in early 1861, a promoter named Smith asked Adah to play the lead in a play called *Mazeppa.* "It's always been pretty successful," he told her, "and I'd like to get you to play the lead in it. The play's built around Byron's *Mazeppa*. It's about a Tartar prince who gets tied to a wild horse and sent into the mountains to die."

"But it's a man's part," Adah said.

"That doesn't make any difference. Think of the furor it would cause to have a woman play the part of the prince—especially a woman like you." He laughed. "Of course you don't really get stripped and you don't really ride a wild stallion up a mountain."

The Menken eyed one of her diamond-encrusted hands thoughtfully. "What if I were stripped? What if I did ride the wild horse?" Smith was staggered by the suggestions.

On opening night New York went wild. The Menken, stripped down to thin, flesh-colored tights, was strapped to a mustang that went racing up a two-foot "mountain" ledge 30 feet high before disappearing into the wings. A beauty stripped of her clothes! A death-defying ride! And the whole play was based on Byron's poem, so it had to be called art! The Menken's performance rocked New York like an earthquake and sent tremors around the world.

Now, on the sixth of March in 1864, Mark Twain and Dan DeQuille, another *Enterprise* reporter whose real name was Bill Wright, stood together at the bar of the

Sazerac and discussed the forthcoming Menken appearance.

"They'll love her here in Virginia City," DeQuille grumbled. "Any ugly female tough enough to visit this town is automatically a raving beauty."

"I say she's nothing but a circus rider," Twain said. "I've been making up clever insults all week. For example, we could devote our critical review to the role played by the horse. We could say that even though it didn't have too many good lines, it ran away with the show."

"Or," DeQuille added, "when the horse turned around, we thought for a minute the theater manager had come out to make an announcement."

"One thing's sure," Twain muttered, "I'm not going to call The Menken an actress just because she has a beautiful body. That's all she is. A body."

The next night Virginia City's streets were alive with excitement. Maguire's Opera House was a blaze of lights and lanterns. Revolvers pounded the night air with increasing enthusiasm, and miners bellowed happily as the time for the big show drew closer.

Inside the theater, only the richest men in the area had seats. There was a crushing crowd standing at the rear. One miner made an abortive attempt to watch the show while hanging from a chandelier, but Maguire put a stop to that just before the chandelier and the ceiling were about to part company. Nat Redding, a gambling man, was wearing a jacket with diamond buttons worth $7,000 apiece. The boys in the front three rows were worth better than $200,000,000. Someone in the back of the lobby shot three holes in a picture of Edwin Booth and was thrown out before he could decide what to shoot at next. The *Enterprise* was represented by Twain, DeQuille and Goodman, its whole editorial staff.

At eight o'clock the boys quieted down, as the thick curtains rolled silently away to reveal the stage. At the sound of Adah's first words, the audience very nearly stopped breathing. Her low, husky voice was as thrilling as a soft kiss on the ear. Then, when she made her entrance from the wings, the enchantment was complete. If a man had dared sneeze, he would have been strung up.

In the second act the chips were down. The villain pronounced his decree: "Lead Mazeppa hence. Strip her of all her garb! Lead out the fiery, untamed steed!"

As one man, the audience strained forward in its seats. Would they actually do it? The horse was supposed to run up a simulated mountain at the rear of the stage, along a treacherous zigzag path. Suppose it slipped? The Menken could be killed. For that matter, would they really strip her?

For the boys in Virginia City, Adah allowed herself to be stripped bare to the waist. As the soldiers ripped away her clothes, a thousand hearts in the audience thumped wildly, then skipped several beats altogether. Before they had fully recovered, the beautiful girl was tied to the bay stallion and went thundering up the steep incline. As the stallion's hoofs disappeared 30 feet up above the stage, the curtains swung closed.

A mighty roar of approval shattered the stillness of the theater. Nat Redding clapped so hard he lost a $7,000 button, and he couldn't have cared less. Maybe "God never got to Virginia City," but The Menken was a satisfactory replacement. From that moment on, the boys worshipped her. They didn't even hold it against her that she had kept some of her clothes on.

When Twain and DeQuille got back to the *Enterprise* office to write their reviews, DeQuille said, "What are you going to find fault with?"

Twain loosened his sweat-soaked collar. "I'm going to find fault with the English language. It hasn't got the words to describe such a magnificent creature as The Menken!"

The *Enterprise* reviews were so superlative as far as Adah was concerned that the rest of the cast felt slighted. At the next night's performance, some of the other actors and actresses threw in an occasional ad lib poking fun at the paper's reporters. Finally, in the third act, Adah strode onto the stage furiously. "I demand that everyone in this company apologize to Mr. Twain and Mr. De-Quille!" she shouted angrily. "I won't step on this stage again until you've done so!" The Thespians eventually did apologize, and Adah gained two lifelong friendships.

Twain, DeQuille and a rich, handsome miner named Tom Peasley took Adah under their collective wing and showed her Virginia City. The Menken was almost as enchanted with the city as the city was with her.

On a tour of the mines, the ground beneath them shaking with underground blasts, Adah told Mark, "I love the names you give these mines. The Wake-Up Jake,

The Let Her Rip. The Gouge Eye. How did you ever think them all up?"

"Well," Twain replied modestly, "to be truthful, I didn't think them all up."

The Menken went down into the Ophir Mine and boiled an egg in the hot natural spring there. She set off charges of dynamite and laughed like a little girl to see tons of dirt and rock fly into the air. She bucked the tiger with the boys at a faro table and played a good man's hand of poker.

Tom Peasley may not have been as smart as Mark Twain, but he was better looking, and during her stay in Virginia City, Adah became his mistress. With instinctive good taste, the miners did not talk much about it. That was the way it was, and they were flattered that this almost mythological goddess had accepted one of their number so completely.

Menken Street suddenly appeared on maps of Virginia City. A new mine was christened "The Menken." Another group of admirers who were starting up a company called it "The Menken Shaft and Tunnel Company," and printed stock certificates with her picture on them. Adah was given 50 shares of the Menken Mine as a good luck gift. The shares were worth $5,000. Two weeks later they were worth $50,000.

One night after her show, Adah was making the rounds of the town with her friends. Twain, Peasley and a dozen others were with her as they approached a large crowd of men behind the Sazerac. "What's going on here?" Peasley demanded. "Make way so The Menken can watch!" The boys opened up to let the group through. In the center of the mob, a couple of the town roughs were boxing. A redheaded mining engineer was getting the best of another man, and in a moment it was all over.

As the engineer was catching his breath, someone called out, "The Menken can do everything else! I'll bet five to ten she can beat ol' Red with her fists!" The man was promptly hushed. Such a thought was improper, and the miner who hushed him bruised all four knuckles badly.

But Adah yelled right back, "Benecia Boy taught me a few things while I was married to him. I'll take Red on!" There was no holding her back. She took off her outer layers of skirts to allow for footwork and stepped into the ring of miners with Red. The engineer was horrified. Smiling nervously, he backed away before The Menken's attack. Adah was quick as a cat, and Red was suddenly knocked to one knee as a small, powerful fist walloped him on the point of the chin.

"By God, she staggered Red!" a laborer cried in astonishment. "No kiddin', she really clouted him!"

Red's temper flared up, and he put out a hand to defend himself. The next thing he knew, the wind was knocked out of his lungs by a hard shot to the solar plexus. Forgetting he was fighting a girl, he blinked and threw several roundhouses that fanned empty air. Out of nowhere, another small, strong fist sailed into his vision, and he stumbled back as it landed on his jaw. Red saw stars. He was vaguely aware of being hit twice more, and then he was on the cool earth, and someone was pouring some poisonous town water in his face. He had been out about three minutes.

Virginia City was up all night celebrating The Menken's victory. There were even those who wanted to pit her against Heenan himself. After that incredible exhibition, the lowly miners, working at four dollars a day, chipped in and bought Adah a bar of solid silver worth $2,000.

These gambling, drinking, carefree days were the happiest in The Menken's life. She swore she would live in Virginia City forever, and when she said it she meant it. One night, though, confiding in Mark Twain, Adah said, "I really thought I'd spend the rest of my life here, but now I'm not so sure. I have an idea I'll die in Paris."

During a performance a few days later, Adah's horse slipped on its upstage dash. Actually, The Menken was able to release herself instantly by letting go of the cords which bound her loosely. But she missed death by inches, when the falling horse grazed her, as its thousand pounds slammed shoulder down on the stage. The boys started breathing again when Adah leaped onto the back of the horse and went up a second time, evidently unhurt. Still they worried about her every time she did the stunt after that.

One morning about a month after The Menken's arrival in Virginia City, Tom Peasley went to her hotel to pick her up for a ride in the desert. Adah was gone. She had left on a stage in the middle of the night. No one ever did find out why she left so suddenly, without a word to any of her friends. Possibly, it was because she realized she was tubercular, and knew that sooner or later her strength would begin to fail her. Virginia City, as Adah knew it on its crest of vitality and fame, was not a place for failing strength.

Neither Virginia City nor Adah had long to go when they parted company. By the end of the year, it became evident that the bonanzas of silver were giving out. Mark Twain left for San Francisco. People stopped shooting each other so frequently. The heart of the lusty boomtown faded away. It soon became a more conservative place, where arguments were settled with conversation or court procedure instead of bowie knives and pistols.

As for Adah, she married once more, in New York, for no particular reason. She and her husband, James Barklay, hardly got to know each other before she was off to England and the Continent. She delighted English audiences with several plays, including *Mazeppa*. For a time she was the mistress of the poet Swinburne, an undersized sickly young man with one of the homeliest faces in London and a remarkable ability to take simple words and construct beautiful phrases out of them.

Paris was Adah's greatest triumph, though. Within a few nights after her opening in the French capital, she was the acknowledged theatrical ruler of France. She was called the "most fascinating combination of devil and angel that ever wore skirts." She received thousands of offers of marriage. Menken hats, Menken coats and Menken shoes were manufactured by the trainload; everything she wore or touched became "Menken," and everyone wanted one just like it. They even made Menken shaving mugs, with a picture of Adah on a bay stallion adorning the side. Napoleon the Third was rumored to be after her, but Alexander Dumas, *Père*, won her as his mistress while showing her the town—his town—of Paris.

Adah spoke a few words of encouragement to a young actress playing a small part in a theater a few blocks away from where she was appearing. The young actress had considered quitting the theater, but decided against it after the kind words from Adah. Her name was Sarah Bernhardt.

Twice within one month, during her third year abroad, Adah's horse slipped on that perilous mountain slope at the rear of the stage. The first time, her horse's neck was broken. Though she herself was unhurt, she couldn't continue that night. She sat with the horse's head in her lap and cried over the unfortunate animal. The second time a horse miscalculated and went off into space, several bones in The Menken's hand and wrist were broken and a thrashing hoof caught her below the throat. She joked about her injuries, spent as little time under a doctor's care as possible and went back to work. By early 1868, it was getting harder to make that ride. Tuberculosis was killing The Menken.

In Virginia City at that time, nothing was as it had been in the days when Adah and the boys had lived at the wild, happy peak of a silver-studded era. The old-timers kept up with the news of Adah through papers, magazines and talk. They were pleased when The Menken was quoted in Paris as saying that Virginia City was the most rugged, wonderful place in the world. They were puzzled when Swinburne called her "Adah, of the Seven Husbands." She had only been married four times. They had no way of knowing that The Menken had made the sad young man even sadder by dropping him and that Swinburne was poetically calling her a prostitute. They wouldn't have cared. The only one who would have cared was Tom Peasley, who loved Adah until the day a drunken gambler shot him in the chest. To those who were left, Adah was a goddess who had passed their way.

When Adah died on August 19, 1868, everyone who had known her lost something of their own lives that day. The Menken dead! And Virginia City nothing but a ghost of the old, rambunctious boomtown! How things changed! A town, a girl. Vital and vivid one minute, brimming over with life. The next minute, dying or dead.

The day they heard of her death, some of the oldtimers who were gathered in the now quiet Sazerac learned that Swinburne had written an epitaph about Adah that was judged to be one of the most beautiful lines in the English language. A bullwhacker who couldn't read too well, recited it slowly from a paper he held before him: "Lo, this is she that was the world's delight."

An old miner blinked his eyes, downed his whiskey and put the glass gently on the bar. "The world's delight." He nodded. "That was Adah."

THE FIRST STAGECOACH
ROBBERY

Tom Bell was making quite a name as a badman until he pulled the wildest caper the West had ever seen.

It was a few minutes before nine o'clock on the morning of August 11, 1856, when Bill Dobson entered the tiny office of the Langton Express Company in Camptonville, California. The bell over the door tinkled and the express clerk, a thin, nervous little man, hurried in from the back room. "Thank the Lord it's you who's going to ride with the Marysville shipment this morning, Bill," he said breathlessly. "It's the biggest one we've ever handled."

Dobson leaned his tall, slender frame partially across the counter and shifted his wide-brimmed hat back on his head so that his black, curly hair poked rebelliously out from under the brim. "What is it, Al?"

"Dust, of course," the little man whispered excitedly. "A box weighing around 340 pounds."

Bill whistled softly, almost silently, and pushed a forefinger thoughtfully against a tray of the scale set up on

84

the counter. "How the hell much does that come to in dollars?"

"One hundred thousand."

Dobson went to the side of the room and took his rifle from the messenger's gun rack. "Who's going to be riding whip on the run?"

"John Gear's scheduled to drive."

Bill said simply, "He's a good man." Then he left the office and walked slowly along the board sidewalk to a broad side street where stablehands were harnessing six fresh horses to the stagecoach.

John Gear came out of the stable and nodded to Dobson. "You ridin' shotgun?"

"Yep."

"From the way the boys in the express office are actin', you'd think we oughta have a troop of cavalry with us. They're as flighty as a bunch of hens with a fox in the coop."

"They say we'll be packing 100,000 iron men in the box."

The driver ran his fingers through his short beard. "Maybe a troop of cavalry wouldn't be a bad idea after all." He crossed to the waiting stage and began to inspect the horses that now stood in their harness, straightening the reins, feeling the belly bands for tightness, speaking to the horses in a low, soothing voice.

In a few minutes he drove the coach out onto the main street where the passengers for Marysville were gathered. Gear arranged their luggage in the rear boot, making mental notes of the people he would soon be responsible for. There were nine of them. Two were miners with hardset, unhappy faces whose claims had undoubtedly run dry and who were heading for better diggings. Two were Marysville merchants who had been to Camptonville on business. There was a woman named Mrs. Tilghman, the wife of a Marysville barber, who had spent a few days with friends. Finally there were four Chinese laborers who had somehow wangled the $12 fares for the trip. They got aboard silently, their braided queues hanging stiffly down their necks.

At the last moment Dobson emerged from the Langton Express office followed by two men who stumbled awkwardly under the weight of the heavy box they carried between them, toward the coach. Dobson and Gear helped them heave the solid box laced with iron reinforcements up into the stow box under the driver's seat. This done, they took their places and Gear was reaching for the reins when the express clerk Al hurried out to the street with a short, heavy man panting behind him. "Wait a minute, John," Al called. "This here's Mr. Rideout, the owner of that shipment. He's decided he wants to go along with it."

"Fine, git on board," Gear said, arranging the leather ribbons in his left hand.

"But riding in a coach makes me seasick," Mr. Rideout complained.

The driver glanced at him as one might look at a bug crawling on his boot. "Well, damn it, make up your mind."

"I'd like to follow along behind on my horse. It's tied in front of the express office, here."

"Suit yourself." Gear shook the reins in his left hand and reached for his whip with the other as Dobson settled back with his rifle over his legs. The long whip arched back over the stage, then gracefully coiled forward with whistling speed so that the tip snapped like a rawhide firecracker over the lead mare's ear. The coach lurched forward, its leather thorough braces creaking and squealing and its iron-rimmed wheels rumbling swiftly over the hard-packed dirt road.

As the swaying vehicle wheeled away from Camptonville that morning with the diminutive form of the dust buyer riding behind, no one suspected that this particular trip would become a never-forgotten incident in the story of stagecoaching; that on the 40-mile jaunt to Marysville they were about to take part unwillingly in the first stagecoach holdup in the history of the West, and that some of them would not step down from the coach.

John Gear and Bill Dobson were two of the finest drivers and guards in the state. Gear, a man in his middle 40s, was the sort of man who caused the phrase, "Knight of the Lash," to be coined. He knew every foot of road in the California gold fields, always knew the faults and strong points of every horse in his team, and knew stagecoaches so well that he could tell by the feel of his fanny against the seat if a rear wheel was coming loose. A lean, bronzed man who could spit tobacco straighter than most men could shoot, he was capable of a roaring battery of oaths that would make race horses out of tired plugs, and he could disintegrate a fly on the back of his lead horse with the tip of his whip. He could put a stage over a slippery, steep mountain road at full speed in the rain, the careening wheels flipping mud off the edge into eternity, while chatting congenially to his companion on the seat about the merits of homemade whiskey over the store-bought variety.

Dobson, a younger man with keen eyes and big, quiet hands, had the reputation of being both a dead shot and a man who never backed down from a fight.

Although they were both professionals, both realistic enough about their jobs always to expect the worst, they could not have been too seriously concerned about the danger of their being held up. In the first place, no bandit could know about the box of gold beneath them. In the second place, no one had ever stuck up a stagecoach. It simply wasn't done. It was considered far too risky even for the most daring bandit—what with a crack-shot guard sitting beside the gun-toting driver and most of the passengers, as a rule, also armed.

But on that particular day, there *was* a bandit who knew about the gold shipment and daring enough to attempt anything. He was a tall, blond man, a surgeon turned outlaw who had never yet been impressed by the fact that a thing hadn't been done before. He was known as Tom Bell and he had been doing unprecedented things all his life.

Several miles ahead of the stagecoach on the road to Marysville, Tom Bell and five of his men sat quietly in their saddles. He repeated instructions to each of them, explaining in detail the complete plan of the impending hold-up. Then he said, "The coach will be here at about 3:40, so we've got plenty of time before it arrives. Keep a watch on the road. I'm going to get some shut-eye."

Bill Gristy, one of his henchmen, chuckled knowingly. "You must need it. That red-headed wench looked to be a lively one."

Bell dismounted, lay quietly down under the shade of a tree with his hat over his eyes and calmly went to sleep. The other men whispered among themselves and cast anxious glances through the trees toward the road from Camptonville over which the stage would come that afternoon.

If Tom Bell dreamed as he rested under that tree, it was probably about the redhead Bill Gristy had mentioned. It would have had to be a much wilder dream for him to foresee what would take place in the soon-to-be-popular Western business he was initiating, the business of robbing stagecoaches. Before 30 days had passed, other crooks would be enthusiastically emulating his inspirational idea. Everyone would be going stage crazy and trying to get in on the criminal act. But Tom Bell, sleeping soundly as befitted a man of clear conscience and iron nerves, would be the pioneer, the father of the art of sticking up stagecoaches.

Contrary to popular opinion, California did not always have stagecoaches to rob. In the first year of the West Coast gold rush there wasn't a coach running farther west than Independence, Missouri.

When poor John Sutter failed so spectacularly with his lumber mill on the American River in '48 and '49, however, it soon became sparklingly apparent that golden California would not long be satisfied with the horses, wagons and few worn prairie schooners it currently boasted for transportation. In a state where you could get $50 for a used shovel and land sometimes brought $1,000 a square foot, it was obvious that the wealthy citizenry would be clamoring for the swift, relatively comfortable travel that only a Concord coach offered, and that they would be able to pay high prices for it.

The first Concord stagecoach reached San Francisco on June 24, 1850, and a beauty it was. Adorned with ornate gold scrolls and curlicues, and sporting fancy damask curtains at the windows, the gorgeous vehicle had doors that were covered with multi-colored landscapes while its strong ash body was flaming scarlet. Its tall wheel spokes were appropriately painted canary yellow to match the gold dust that every miner carried in his own leather pouch.

This elegant and graceful Concord coach, forerunner of countless of her sisters that were already on their way to the West, had more than beauty to recommend her, however. She was the toughest vehicle that ever thundered through a pass to the rhythm of pounding hooves, or clattered wildly over the stones in a dry creek bed with whooping Indians in fierce pursuit. Using the principal of the leather thorough brace, which caused Mark Twain to call her a "cradle on wheels," she rocked and swayed over the most rugged mountain roads. The shocks of deep holes or rocks banging against the wheels were absorbed by these long straps that passed under her body and were attached to C-shaped braces on the front and rear axles. The Abbott-Downing Company in Concord, New Hampshire, had been building these inimitable coaches since 1813, and while they liked to doll them up, they had wisely learned to make the bodies strong enough to stop Indian arrows and discourage lead slugs. The Concord weighed about 2,500 pounds and cost from $1,200 to $1,500. In the gold country they sometimes paid for themselves in a week of steady rolling, since they could accommodate nine passengers on the inside and, in a pinch, a dozen more adventurous souls on the swaying top.

By sea and by land the luxurious coaches came to California in ever-increasing numbers until by 1856 the staging business in the territory was in full swing. Although most of the lines were concentrated in the gold fields of northern California, other branches had penetrated far out of the state into Oregon and Nevada.

The strange fact was, though, that through the first few years no one tried to hold up a coach. With their blazing colors they could be seen from miles away on a clear day. They were often forced by lame horses, washed-out roads or other adverse acts of nature to slow to a walk or come to a halt, making easy, limping targets for bandits. Yet they chalked up uncounted thousands of miles over a period of more than five years in that rough and lawless era of the gold rush days with only two losses worth mentioning. Once a stubborn driver tried to take his coach across a deep, swift river swollen by spring rains. The coach made it all right, but the driver fell out of his seat and was drowned. Another time, an express box with $600 in it that had been sitting on the sidewalk waiting to be put into the stage that was due, mysteriously and unaccountably disappeared into thin air. By coincidence, a part-time stablehand next door disappeared into thin air that same day.

Otherwise, despite shipments often totalling several thousand dollars, stage companies were left strictly alone. Since the stages were well guarded and filled with passengers any number of whom might turn out to be first-rate gunslingers, the assorted banditry of the times, if they thought of stagecoaches at all, justifiably thought of them as being uncomfortably akin to rolling arsenals. It took someone of an unusually brave, audacious and even imaginative turn of mind to take the first step. Tom Bell was that man.

The one outstanding fact about Tom Bell was that he didn't scare easy. After that, his story becomes a little confusing. To begin with, Tom Bell was not Tom Bell. He was Doctor Thomas J. Hodges. He took the name of Bell when he first went into crime because there was an outlaw of some notoriety in California already using that monicker. For him to use the name too would confuse lawmen, and if there was anything Tom dearly loved it was to bewilder police officers. The joke was fairly effective, and for months sheriffs and marshals throughout several counties were wondering how Bell could be positively identified in the same afternoon at two robberies 200 miles apart. Then it became apparent that one Tom Bell was tall, blond and blue-eyed while the other was short, stocky, brown-eyed and bald as a cannonball. Later, the original Tom Bell was inconsiderate enough to die of a stretched neck and the prank could go no further for the doctor-turned-outlaw. The reason the respected man of medicine went into banditry in the first place will never be clearly known. Some say he was driven to it by unfortunate circumstances. Others claim he had a wide streak of hellishness in him that had to come out one way or the other.

Born in Rome, Tennessee, around 1830, Tom was well liked as a young man and did fine in the medical profession. When the Mexican War broke out, the young doctor joined the Tennessee Volunteers as a surgeon and served with distinction in the front lines. Around 1850, when he was as handy with a gun as with a scalpel, Tom arrived in California where he intended, as did thousands of others, to make a fortune. He first practiced medicine for a while, but found it suddenly dull. He tried his hand at mining and found it hard work. He next took to gambling and found it expensive. Finally, along with a hard case named Tex Wiley, young Tom took to banditry and found he had a natural talent for that occupation, a talent which would lead him into a short, but highly distinguished career. Tom and Tex started off by borrowing a string of good horses long enough to sell them at a nice profit. Pleased at the results of his first extra-legal sortie, Tom took the last name of Bell and became a full-time outlaw.

Sometimes alone, sometimes in the company of Tex or other hoot owl friends, Tom now began marauding through the gold fields, relieving lonely travelers of their burdensome gold dust, freeing saddle horses from the narrow confines of their owners' pastures and in many other ways generously giving lawmen over the state valid excuses to take long, healthy rides in the fresh air.

The peace officers, in an ungracious and lucky moment, caught Tom once and showed their complete lack of appreciation by putting him in the jail on Angel Island in San Francisco Bay for an indefinite stay. The minions of the law did not know that the man they held was a doctor, however. When the prisoner complained of being ill, they sent an innocent practitioner to see what was ailing him. Bell's symptoms, and the way he explained his aches and pains, soon terrified the prison doctor. There was no doubt in his mind that this prisoner had malaria. The frightened prison doctor couldn't get Bell off the island soon enough, and he had no trouble escaping once he was on the mainland.

Tom decided at this point that if he were going to be a highwayman, he might as well be a holy terror. He got together as rugged a bunch as California had ever seen, including men he'd met in jail and those he'd known on the trail. There were Monte Jack, Bill Gristy, Jim Smith, Ned Connor and English Bob. He developed powerful passions for four things—a good fight, a good wench, a game of cards and good whiskey. But his earlier training never left him, so he became a curious cross between a lusty outlaw and a well-mannered gentleman.

Not satisfied with an undisciplined mob of rowdies such as most outlaw gangs consisted of, Tom showed genuine ability as an executive and an organizer by the way he whipped his men into shape as an operating unit. His robberies, which became bigger and better all the time, were carried off with excellent planning and timing. Before long, Tom had established a regular initiation procedure for newcomers to his gang, which included schooling in the use of gun and knife. New members also had to give an oath of loyalty in all sincerity. As his band grew larger, Tom gradually set up a large network of hideouts in private homes, saloons and inns throughout the gold fields where passwords or secret signs would guarantee entrance and good treatment for anyone under his command.

Just to maintain good relations with his boys, and perhaps to assuage his love for a good scrap, Tom had a standing challenge that he could whip any member of his gang. Lots of his tough comrades took him up on his offer, especially since Tom allowed that he would use their choice of weapon, be it bare knuckles, knife or gun. The fact that no one died as a result of this playful entertainment was not due to genteel fighting standards, but rather to Tom's ability as a doctor.

A husky Mexican, new to Tom's band, once remarked that he was the best knife fighter north of the Rio Grande. Tom was pleasantly drunk, so he said quite gently, "You mean the second best, *amigo*. Isn't that so?"

"No," persisted the stubborn man, "I'm number one. The best."

Tom sighed deeply and called to Monte Jack, "Hey Monte. Lend me your bowie knife."

The two of them parried gingerly back and forth a few seconds. Then Tom caught the Mexican's blade on the guard of his own weapon in a beautifully timed thrust that would have done Jim Bowie's heart good, forced his opponent's arm up and back and caught the man's wrist from beneath with his free hand. Then, in what seemed to be one, swift motion, he slashed his blade down across the man's bicep, raised one knee and slammed the fellow's arm down across it. The man's muscles were cut to the bone near the shoulder and his arm broken at the elbow. That stopped the fight. Tom then patched the Mexican up neatly, all the while patiently explaining what mistakes the poor rascal had made. Between clenched teeth, his ex-opponent muttered that Tom was the best knife fighter north of the Rio Grande, and maybe even south of the Rio Grande, too.

It was on the tenth of August, 1856, that Tom received the information from one of his express company spies that led to his starting the business of stagecoach robbing. It is believed that he had been wanting to try a stagecoach stick-up for some time, and had been simply waiting for word of one big enough to make the risk worthwhile. Tom planned his attack with military precision. Having been told that the Camptonville-Marysville coach was carrying $100,000 in gold, he chose five of his best men to help him attack it.

"We'll strike in the area just past Dry Creek," he told them. "That's quite close to Marysville, and they'll be feeling perfectly safe when they get that far. There's plenty of thick woods around the road to get away in. Also, the trees will make it possible for us to be right on the stage before they know it. Three of us will take them from each side at exactly the same moment. Coming on them that way, we probably won't even have to fire a shot."

As it turned out, due to a freak happenstance that no one could have prepared for, shots were to be fired. Enough shots to drown out a Fourth of July celebration.

Mr. Rideout, the diminutive gold-dust buyer, was sick to death of the trip from Camptonville. Not only did riding on stagecoaches make him sick, but following them made him sick, too. He had discovered to his sorrow that the miserable vehicles kick up great billowing clouds of dust on a hot, dry day. He was choking to death. He hated stagecoaches.

To save himself from expiring altogether, it occurred to him that it might be a master stroke to ride on past the stage and precede it instead of following it as he had been doing for so many miles. He spurred along the side of the road, waved at Gear and Dobson as he passed the coach, and galloped ahead. Rideout had trouble pacing his tough little pony with the stage, however, and he had soon left it some distance behind.

At Dry Creek, only a few miles from Marysville, Rideout slowed his mount to a walk. The road angled to the right here, but there was an older trail known to Rideout that forked off to the left. The two routes ran nearly parallel for some time before coming back together again farther along. Since the unused path was lower in the valley, and cooler, Mr. Rideout decided to take it instead of the usually traveled stage road.

Up on the main road a few minutes later, Bill Gristy called to the sleeping Tom Bell. "Tom! The stage just came into sight!"

Rideout had gone off the trail before he had come within the view of Bell's men. Now they could see the coach rolling swiftly toward them.

"Juan, Bob, Hank!" Tom ordered. "Get across the road and cover your faces! Come out when you hear me tell the stage to halt."

The three men rode quickly across the road, still hidden from the men on the stagecoach. Within a few seconds, there was no one visible and no sound to be heard.

Mr. Rideout had been on the lower path several minutes when he happened to glance up toward the road and noticed a movement. Then he saw three men who were hidden from the road itself but clearly visible to him.

"Curious," he thought. Then the thing suddenly made horrible sense to him. The men were masked.

The bandits saw him as he whirled his horse to race back and warn the stage. There was a moment of hesitation while they wondered what to do, whether to let him try to warn the coach or whether to leave their posts and try to stop him. They decided on the latter course and crashed their horses recklessly through the thick underbrush down the side of the hill. They managed to head him off just as the first sound of the rumbling stagecoach came to their ears.

The little gold-dust buyer had plenty of grit in a pinch. He reached for his gun in the face of hopeless odds. One of the bandits fired a shot, a shot meant to make him leave his gun alone. Unfortunately, of course, the shot also warned everyone in the coach that there was trouble ahead.

Tom Bell and his two men plunged out upon a stage that bristled with cocked guns—and found they had no support from the other side of the road. The peaceful country air was suddenly split wide open with the thunder of blasting gunfire. The rifle in Bill Dobson's big, steady hands knocked Bell off his horse with its first shot. The team of horses pulling the stage came to a rearing, screaming halt as Monte Jack raced by them, filling the stage with lead. From where he lay, Bell now shot Bill Dobson through the arm. Bill dropped his rifle.

The stagecoach door on the far side banged open as soon as the stage was stopped and a white man and the four Chinese passengers erupted from it, sprinting away into the woods. They say the speed of the racing Chinamen caused their queues to stand straight out behind them. None of the five men was ever heard of again. Bell, only slightly wounded, swung back up on his horse. With the guard wounded and the passengers deserting, his was a clear-cut victory, even if the three men he had posted on the other side of the road had mysteriously disappeared. He was already wondering how to spend $100,000.

The situation was completely in control when he heard his missing men crashing back up through the brush on the far side of the road. Bill Gristy had dismounted and, holding his gun on the coach, now walked toward the forward boot to haul down the loot personally.

But young Bill Dobson was the sort of man who is never smart enough to know when he's licked. The nerves had come alive again in the hand of his wounded right arm, and he could work his fingers once more. His rifle was in easy reach. Hearing the sound of approaching horses and realizing the band was getting reinforcements, he knew that his move must be made now or not at all. He also knew that he would be a dead man if John Gear wasn't a brave man clear through.

His voice boomed, "Drive on, Gear!" He snatched his rifle up and a bullet whined near Bell's face. John Gear slapped the reins viciously, cracked his whip and bellowed like a madman at his team. The frightened horses plummeted ahead in swift unison, nearly lifting the coach off the ground as it lurched instantly into movement. Bill Gristy was knocked flat as the stage's large rear wheel slammed against him. Monte Jack was so stunned, he was momentarily paralyzed and sat stock-still in his saddle, staring with blank, astonished eyes at the escaping coach. Tom swung his mount about and sped after the stage, shouting for the three men who had just regained the road to join him.

A couple of passengers still in the coach, encouraged by the sudden and totally unexpected reprieve, filled the air with an enthusiastic rain of bullets.

Bill Dobson turned in his seat, ignoring the savage pain in his wounded arm, and aimed his rifle back over the bouncing roof of the stagecoach. His first unhurried shot caught one of Bell's men square in the center of the forehead, just below the rim of his hat.

The chances of retaking the $100,000 in the face of the withering fire with Marysville so close, were pretty slim. So Tom called a halt and the bandits brought their horses to dancing, snorting stops on the dusty road while the speeding coach made good its getaway.

"Where the hell were you imbeciles?" Tom snapped. Then, without waiting for a reply from the crestfallen men, he shook his head and suddenly grinned. "I would certainly be pleased to have that shotgun messenger riding with me."

Unfortunately, it was no grinning matter when the embattled stage lumbered to a halt in Marysville. Dobson was wounded in the arm. John Campbell, one of the Marysville merchants, had been shot in the head and was just barely alive. Another man had been shot through both legs. And Mrs. Tilghman, the only female passenger, had been killed instantly.

The peaceful town of Marysville immediately became one big lynching party. All they needed was someone to lynch. Dobson, Gear and Mr. Rideout, who had got away when his three captors had hurried back to help their comrades, gave lengthy descriptions of the men who had perpetrated the outrage, and there was no doubt in the minds of the local law enforcers that the masked bandits were part of Tom Bell's gang. Tom Bell was the man they were after. And Tom Bell's luck was running out.

The first posse included most of Marysville and it thundered out of town only a few minutes after the battered stage came to a halt there. Bell eluded them, but he must have sensed they were after him with a sinister purposefulness never before shown. Knowing that his gang was too big, that he couldn't possibly trust all of its scattered members even though they'd been thoroughly indoctrinated, he broke it up and went into hiding where only a few trusted lieutenants could find him.

Tom would have probably been able to hole up successfully until the excitement wore down, except that one of the lieutenants he had trusted was not worthy of that trust. Bill Gristy betrayed him.

Bill was riding south with a friend and they decided to spend the night in a little town called Knight's Ferry. Gristy knew that some of the lesser members of the gang had been picked up, and he'd heard that some of them had been shot to death, so he wasn't in a very happy frame of mind. In town, he was recognized as one of Tom Bell's top men, and when he and his friend sat down to dinner in a restaurant, they found themselves waited on by a sheriff and four deputies holding five fair-sized cannons in their hands. Bill acted tough and close-mouthed for a little while, but with threats on the one hand and promises to go easy with him if he talked on the other hand, he broke down. He told the lawmen everything he knew, including the hideout where Bell was staying.

A posse quickly gathered together and rode in a southwest direction toward the ranch Bill had described. The posse found the ranch deserted. The ashes were stone-cold in the fire, and there were no signs of life anywhere in the lonely valley where the cabin was located. They settled down to wait. The day turned to night, and then another day came.

A certain Judge Belt from Knight's Ferry was a member of the posse, and he was an incredibly stubborn man. The rest of the men wanted to go back home. There was no proof that Tom Bell had ever even been in this lonely cabin. Gristy had lied to them. But Judge Belt insisted on waiting. He had a feeling that Tom lived here, and that he would be along shortly. They waited four days before the judge finally admitted that they were wasting their time. That morning, the morning of October 4th, they saddled their horses and started back to Knight's Ferry.

They all started back, that is, except one man, a man named Price who wanted to ride in another direction. Price had been roped into the posse by chance. He didn't live in Knight's Ferry and had to take another route home.

Once again a solitary, unexpected rider was to play a part in what was left of Tom Bell's life, this time with disastrous results.

Beyond the open valley, Price left the others and cut through the woods. A naturally quiet person who knew the value of silence on the frontier, Price walked his horse at an easy pace in the soft ground. That is why he saw Tom Bell, and Tom Bell did not see him. Price didn't know it was Bell, but he got a glimpse through the trees of the back of a tall man sitting a large buckskin. The man was obviously watching the retreating posse from his vantage point, and had not been able to see Price leave the others. Price had heard somewhere that one of Bell's favorite horses was a big buckskin. That was all he needed. Soundlessly, he hurried along and joined the posse again farther along the trail.

With that sort of luck against him, Tom didn't have a chance. Later that morning, while he was talking with a friend a little distance from the ranch cabin, he suddenly sensed someone behind him and whirled, his hand on his gun. But it was too late. A few members of the posse had dismounted and managed to sneak through the woods to within a few feet of him. They were holding cocked rifles and pistols, and looked nervous enough to use them.

Although the judge was in the posse, they gave Tom no chance for a hearing, not even the pretense of a trial. There was a tall sycamore tree nearby and they threw a rope over its limbs. The judge figured other posses might conceivably be on their way and he simply didn't want to take the chance of sharing the glory of capturing and killing Bell with anyone else.

Tom asked for a chance to make a full confession, but even that wasn't granted. His final act on this earth was to drink a shot of whiskey. Sitting on his horse, with the noose already around his neck, he was handed a bottle and allowed one last, long drag. Then the judge slapped Tom's horse on the flank and the buckskin lunged forward, leaving the man who pulled the first stagecoach robbery dangling at the end of a rope, as he kicked away his few remaining moments of life. If Tom Bell's life and death proves anything at all it is simply this: Stagecoach robbing wasn't the easy or glamorous profession it is sometimes made out to be. It was the roughest, toughest and worst paid occupation the West had to offer. The only ones who could count on a square meal from the stages were the hard-working gents who ran them, and the stout-hearted horses who pulled them.

THE INDIAN SLAYER

Sam Brady liked corn liquor and girls, but killing Indians was his real love. He bagged his first scalp at ten and didn't quit until he had two hundred more.

Old man Brady could smell an Indian from two miles upwind. But this night, something went wrong. He was down in bed with a fever and his senses were not as alert as usual.

The two Brady boys, John and Samuel, were busy with their chores as darkness settled over the lonely cabin on the western Pennsylvania frontier. John, just turned 18, was tending the horses in the lean-to 50 feet from the cabin. Young Sam, a strapping ten-year-old, was farther off in the woods, fetching home an armload of firewood.

The Delaware warriors struck swiftly and without warning. From deep in the shadowy woods, young Sam saw five or six of them rush silently across the small clearing and into the open cabin door. At the same time another half-dozen savages sprung up from the ground around his brother.

"Look out!" Sam yelled. But his strangled cry was lost

in the fierce yammering and whooping that went up from the Delawares.

A big, nearly naked warrior, with white stripes painted on his chest and face and a narrow wedge of hair in the center of his otherwise clean-shaven head, struck John from behind with a tomahawk. He shrieked in savage elation as John crumpled, then took out a razor-sharp knife and started to scalp the dying boy.

The firewood fell from Sam's arms as he watched in helpless terror. Dark figures rushed from the cabin, and fingers of flame began to shoot up inside the door. The big Delaware who had killed John dragged the scalped body to the cabin and threw it into the spreading fire. Then, leading away the Brady horses, they were gone.

Sam ran to the cabin, but the intense heat drove him back from the door. He sat down on the ground and wept as the flames roared and crackled, mounting higher into the black sky.

Hours later, by the light of the quarter-moon, he went into the smoldering remains of the cabin and dragged out the charred body of his brother. But his father's body was not there. For the first time, Sam realized that the Delawares had taken him alive.

It would take too long to get help, the nearest neighbors were 11 miles away, the nearest settlement 17 miles. The boy pushed the grief and fear out of his mind and forced himself to think clearly. John always had his musket close by when he was outside the cabin. He usually left it in one corner of the lean-to while he took care of the horses. Sam ran to the lean-to and groped in the darkness. The musket was still there. Clutching the gun, which stood slightly taller than he did, Sam started in the direction the Indians had taken.

He came upon their camp about two hours later. But he was too late. The Delawares were sitting around a low-burning fire, where the remains of what had once been a human being was bound to a thick, charred stake.

Right then, something twisted in young Sam Brady's mind—something that was to make him different from other men. From that moment on, he lived for just one reason—to kill Indians.

The Delaware who had murdered John was standing alone by the fire. As the powerful savage stretched and yawned, Sam leveled his musket, balancing the heavy

100

barrel over a low branch of a tree. Aiming carefully, he pulled the trigger. As the gun roared, the big Delaware stiffened, then fell forward into the fire, dead.

Tossing the heavy musket aside, Sam rushed away in the dark, heading toward Cooper's Settlement, many miles away, on the Allegheny River.

By the time the Delawares realized what had happened, it was too late for them to trail their unseen enemy in the darkness. The next morning, they discovered a footprint in the sand near the small creek where they had made camp. One of them knelt down to examine it. "What kind of warrior is this?" he asked in the guttural Delaware tongue, spreading his thumb and forefinger over the small print. "He is no bigger than a child."

"Maybe he is a man of magic, and can melt away into nothing," another brave suggested, a trace of awe in his voice.

And that was the first of many legends that were to spring up around Samuel Brady—legendary frontiersman and Indian fighter.

After the death of his father and brother, Sam was shifted from one relative to another in western Pennsylvania and the Ohio country beyond. For a short time, he lived with an aunt in Philadelphia, learning how to read and write and behave in society.

The boy worked hard to earn his keep wherever he was living; he wanted to be a burden to no one. But he worked even harder to train himself as a killer. Saving his pennies, he got three dollars together and bought an all-steel tomahawk with an axe-edge on one side and a piercing spike on the other. By the time he was 14, he could use it with more deadly efficiency than most adult frontiersmen. In a land filled with men proud of their ability with knife, tomahawk and musket, Sam Brady stood out even as a youngster.

At 17, Sam was a tall, slim, deceptively good-natured red-head who dressed habitually in fringed buckskins. He made his living as a trapper, stalking through the woods with the casual grace and strength of a panther.

One morning he visited a small village on the Ohio River, known as Beaver, to sell some skins. A friend named Rahway hailed him. "Some nice pelts you got there, Sam. You hear about the Widow Smith?"

"No."

"Since her old man died last year, everybody's been

telling her she ought to come into Beaver to live so she'd have some protection from the redskins. But she wouldn't do it," Rahway shook his head sorrowfully and shot a squirt of tobacco into the dusty road.

"So what happened?" Sam eased the pack of beaver pelts off his shoulder.

"Some time early this mornin' a bunch of Mohawks raided her place out by Broad Creek. Made off with her and her six-year-old daughter."

"Took them alive?"

"Yup. But you know that don't count for much. Chances are their hair's decoratin' some longhouse right now. Pity. Bunch of men from Beaver went after them, but had to give up. Trail ran out."

"Think I'll take a look myself." Sam handed his pelts to Rahway. "Turn these in for me at the trading post."

"Sam, you oughtn't go by yourself!" Rahway called after him.

But Brady was already on his way to the Smith cabin on Board Creek, moving at a long-striding, easy run that he could keep up all day and all night.

The Mohawks hadn't burned the cabin, but the inside of it was a jumbled mass of broken furniture and scattered household goods. There had been three braves, Sam decided, though the white men from Beaver had almost obliterated most of the signs. The Mohawks were heading toward the Ohio, and Sam started after them. Watching the trail keenly, he saw that at first the warriors had been carrying the Smith woman and the child. But half a mile along, they had put the woman down and forced her to walk.

Near the Ohio, there was a wide stretch of rocky ground, and Sam could see where the party from Beaver had been fooled. One of the Mohawks had gone back into the woods at a slight angle, leaving enough trail for the white men to follow. Then, doubling back on the rocks, he had rejoined the others on the river bank, where they probably had a canoe waiting.

Sam examined the rocks along the water's edge and found an almost invisible chip of wet birchbark where a canoe had been beached. They must have paddled upstream, he reasoned, for Beaver lay in the other direction, and he set off up the river at his tireless jogging pace.

After a two-hour run, Sam's sharp eyes spotted a thick,

unnatural-looking pile of brush on the far side of the river. Holding his musket and powder-horn in one hand, he swam to the other side. It was the canoe. Evidently the Mohawks had picked up their horses here. He began to run at full speed.

The sun was moving low into the west when Sam caught sight of the Mohawks and their prisoners. The braves were riding their horses easily, certain that they had lost their pursuers. They were headed northeast through a broad valley, evidently toward their village.

Sam ducked out of sight behind the hills forming the right shoulder of the valley and ran some distance ahead of the raiding party. Then he came down into the valley at a point where the trees were heavy enough for him to hide. He stood behind a thick oak which the Indians had to pass; his musket was cocked and ready.

As the Mohawks approached, they were laughing and joking in low voices. One brave held the little girl in front of him as he rode. Her mother, hands tied, was riding with another brave. The little girl began to cry when the group was almost abreast of Sam, and the savage cuffed her viciously. Then he tangled his fingers in her long, blonde hair and made a joke about what a fine scalp it would make. He brought up the rear as they went single-file past the oak.

Sam slid the tomahawk from his buckskin belt, balanced it lightly in his right hand, and let fly. The weapon whirled silently, swiftly through the air and buried itself in the back of the Mohawk's head. The brave tumbled off his horse to the ground.

The warrior holding the woman spun around and saw his dead companion. His immediate reaction was to whip out the knife in his loincloth to kill his prisoner. As he raised the knife, Sam's musket bellowed and the Indian fell lifeless to the ground.

The last warrior galloped straight at Sam, his tomahawk raised over his head. As the horse thundered down on him, Sam gripped his rifle like a club, sidestepped, and slammed the butt across the Mohawk's forehead. The swinging tomahawk slashed Sam's right arm, but the Indian was knocked off his horse. Sam flung himself on the stunned Mohawk and clamped steel fingers around his throat. Soon the Indian's body went limp.

"Oh my God, my God, my God!" the Smith woman cried. She was on the verge of exhaustion and hysteria.

However, when Sam cut the thongs around her wrists, she calmed down a little. Gathering the weeping child in her arms and hugging her close, she turned to Sam. "God bless you. You saved our lives." Then she noticed his wound. "You're hurt . . . your arm. Let me bandage it for you."

As she fussed over him, Brady took note for the first time that she was a handsome woman, slender and young with long, soft, auburn hair. She tore a long strip of cloth off the hem of her petticoat and bound it tightly around the wound on his arm.

"It's not deep," Sam said, shyly.

"Still needs fixin'," she said in a firm voice that brooked no argument.

After she had finished, Sam caught the three Indian ponies and they started back home, with Brady carrying the little girl in his arms. They reached the Smith cabin after riding all night.

While the woman, whose name was Elizabeth, got some sleep, Sam put the cabin back into shape. That took most of the day. Then, while he took a nap, she cooked supper for them, waking him when it was done.

Elizabeth smiled at him over the table when they had finished eating. "You seem so young and so innocent, now. Yet back there, you were so—so savage."

Sam was young and innocent. Blushing, he shrugged his shoulders and mumbled noncommittally, "Ummmm."

Elizabeth was silent for a moment, glancing at her daughter who was sound asleep in the far corner of the room. Then she said, softly, "You will stay with me tonight, won't you?"

"Probably be a good thing," Sam agreed. "Also you ought to make plans to move into Beaver. It's not safe this far out."

"Yes. I'm going to do that."

"Good." Sam stood up uncomfortably. "Well, I'll go out and sleep in the open."

"No!" Elizabeth stood up beside him, and there was a look in her eyes and an edge to her voice that made Sam's throat go dry and tight. "I won't hear of it. You'll sleep in here."

Sam did, and from that point on he slightly reoriented his life. It was still dedicated to the pursuit of Indians, but he decided there was room in it for the pursuit of attractive women, also.

Word of the widow's rescue and Sam's killing three Mohawk warriors spread along the frontier, and he was invited to join a newly organized outfit called The Pennsylvania Rangers. There were never many more than 100 Rangers in this small, tough crew. But each man was a rugged, experienced and fearless fighter. The Rangers operated as trouble shooters, wherever the Indian threat was greatest. Sam figured that was as good a way as any to collect scalps.

A message, delivered to the captain of the Rangers one day in 1774, said that an unknown number of Cayugas had massacred two families about 40 miles north. Sam was part of a 15-man force assigned to hunt down the marauders.

The next morning they arrived at the scene of the massacre. Both houses, about a stone's throw from each other, were burned. There had been seven victims— men, women and children. One of the women had been tied to a stake and burned in her front yard.

"Them Cayugas usually ain't this bad," one of the veteran Rangers muttered. "They must really be stirred up."

Studying the ground, Sam said, "There were a lot of them. I'd say maybe a hundred."

The sergeant in charge of the buckskin-clad fighting men shook his head. He was an older man, and he thought a youngster like Sam ought to be seen and not heard. "Naw. You're readin' the same tracks over again. Warn't more than twenty or so."

"I still say you ought to go careful."

"I'm runnin' this bunch, and we'll do like I say. You ain't scared, are you, young feller?"

"No, I'm not scared," Sam said.

"Let's go, then!"

The next day they caught up with the Cayugas As Sam had predicted, there were at least 100 warriors— an unusually huge war party—waiting in ambush for the Rangers in a wooded valley. A chilling war whoop rang out, and the air was filled with whistling arrows. Six Rangers went down in the first volley of shafts, then the survivors were overwhelmed by a solid wall of screaming, onrushing Cayugas.

Sam got off one shot that knocked down a howling brave. Then he slung his musket over one shoulder and met the full force of the Indian charge with his knife in one hand and his tomahawk in the other.

He split one skull with his tomahawk and drove the knife deep into the belly of another redskin.

Chopping and slicing, he bulled his way through the Cayugas surrounding him. For a brief time the sergeant had been fighting at his side, but now he was alone. Slashing his keen blade across the throat of one last brave, Sam broke into the open and ducked quickly into the forest. Loading his musket as he ran swiftly through the trees, he wheeled about to see what had happened to his friends.

Not one of the Rangers had survived, except Sam. The fighting was over. Several of the Indians were coming after him now, and a feathered shaft thumped into a tree at his side. One Cayuga was a short distance ahead of the others. Sam shot him, turned and continued to run.

One Ranger against a howling mob of braves. Most men would have been panicked. But as he ducked and weaved to avoid arrows, Sam was thinking fast. He recalled that his party had passed a canyon off to the left about an hour before the attack. He headed for it as fast as he could run.

Glancing back from time to time, he saw that about 30 of the Cayugas were still bounding after him like deer. The Cayugas were famous as fast runners. If he slipped just once, he wouldn't have a second chance to get away from them.

At last he reached the canyon. It was about 50 feet deep, with absolutely perpendicular sides, and it was about 20 feet wide at the top. Gaining every bit of speed that he could, he raced to the edge, gave a mighty thrust with his right foot and went sailing into the air in a desperate leap. The wind rushed past his face, and he caught a glimpse of the rocky canyon bottom far below. Then he hit the far rim and went down on all fours. Scrambling to his feet, he ran into a clump of trees a few yards away.

The first Cayuga to burst into view was a husky, fleet-footed buck. He considered making the leap, but at the last second, he realized it was too much, and veered away. Brady finished loading his musket and shot him, turned and ran on.

A quarter-mile away, he stopped on the crest of a hill and turned to look back. The Indians were gathered at the edge of the canyon, but none of them had dared try the jump.

Later, some curious Rangers took the trouble to measure the width of the canyon. Brady had broad jumped better than 22 feet.

By the time he was 19, Sam was the most famous Ranger in the frontier country. This was 1775, the year that General Daniel Brodhead, who was in charge of all military forces in Pennsylvania, asked Brady to visit him in Philadelphia.

"You're damned young to be a sergeant," the general said, drumming his fingers on his desk as he studied Sam.

"Yes sir." There was nothing else Sam could say.

"Humph!" Brodhead grumbled. "And you're the youngest captain I've ever seen."

"Beg pardon, sir?"

"I said, *captain*. I've read reports on you. I've talked to men who have fought beside you. And now that I've seen you, Brady, I'm putting you in charge of the Pennsylvania Rangers. Your rank is captain."

"Well, I'll be damned—sir."

"Quite possibly you will, Captain. I understand you're as handy with a pretty wench as you are with a gun and a knife."

"Those reports are a little exaggerated, sir," Sam grinned.

"I trust my sources implicitly." Brodhead smiled, then became serious. "What do you think of the trouble between England and the colonies?"

"I'd hate to fight the English," Sam said thoughtfully, "if it comes to that. But the way England's been behaving toward us—" He hesitated and then went on in a rush of words, "I'd rather be a dead man than live without being free."

Brodhead nodded slowly. "Good. As for the fighting, it may come more quickly than you think."

Captain Brady rarely hit a bottle, but when he did, the bottle knew it had been hit. That night in Philadelphia, he celebrated his unexpected promotion by polishing off three bottles and becoming gloriously drunk.

The next morning, when he was on his way back to western Pennsylvania to take command of the Rangers, a girl in one of Philadelphia's more popular sporting houses took a sip of coffee and said, "Last night was one of the worst nights I've had in years."

Across the breakfast table, another girl shrugged and said, "I had a quiet night, except for one fellow. He just about did me in."

"Same with me," a third girl agreed. "I was only with one man, but it was enough for me. His name was Captain Sam Brady."

The second girl's mouth dropped open in surprise. "Brady! Why that's the fellow who was with me!"

And the first girl shook her head, and said, in a small voice, "Me, too."

When the war came in '76, it didn't really change things much for Brady. He had been fighting Indians all along, only now they were called mercenaries, paid by the British to do all the damage they could to the rebelling colonies.

Once, while chasing some Senecas, Sam was separated from the others in his command and surrounded by 15 braves. He fought his way out, killing two of them, the rest hot on his heels. The outraged Senecas were having trouble trailing Sam, for he always ran lightly and left few signs of his passage. But suddenly his trail became extremely easy to follow. There were clear footprints—something Sam never left—that led up to a thick grove of trees. At the rim of the grove, his prints turned off into an open field. Exactly half-way out in the wide, flat field, the footprints stopped. Brady, seemingly, at that point had disappeared into the air.

"How can this be?" the Seneca chief demanded.

"Brady has great magic," a brave said. "He cannot be harmed by weapons. He must have changed himself into a bird."

"Let us go back to our lodge," another whispered, the sound of fear in his voice. "The gods watch over Brady."

The chief wasn't sure how the gods stood. But to get Brady's scalp would mean prestige and glory beyond his wildest dreams, and he didn't want to give up easily.

"He has disappeared. But maybe he will reappear again. I will wait and see. If any man is brave enough, he can wait with me."

Two warriors remained with the chief, and the others headed back toward their village to the north. The three remaining Indians sat on a log not far from the grove of trees.

As soon as the main force of Indians was out of earshot, a thunderous *boom* came from the forest and all three Indians went sprawling off the log. Brady rushed out of the grove and found the chief dead. The other two, who were wounded, he killed with his tomahawk.

Brady had fooled the Senacas with a simple ruse. He had walked half way out into the soft dirt of the field. Then, stepping backwards in the prints he had already made, he had retraced his way to the grove.

While the three Senecas sat, waiting for him to "materialize" again, he had overloaded his musket so that it would fire an unusually powerful blast. "Surprised me more than it did them," he told a friend. "I figured to kill one and maybe wing another. But getting all three of them was a stroke of pure luck."

Brady found out later that one of the Senecas, who had fallen behind the others on the way back to the lodge, had heard the loud single shot. He reached the scene after Brady was gone and found the three dead Indians —all with bullet wounds. Now the legends really began to bloom. Not only could the fabulous Brady disappear in the middle of a field, but he could shoot three men with one shot! Obviously the gods were on his side.

Brady and his men did a great deal to keep the redskins off the neck of General Washington's army. Sam was always at the right place at the right time. After the war was over, General Brodhead said, "Captain Brady has done more than any man I know to help in the victorious conclusion of this struggle. Here is a man who during these trying years killed at least a hundred savages with his own hands, and stopped God knows how many more from harassing our armies from the rear."

There was a big fuss about giving Sam a medal for his services, but while he did get to Philadelphia, he didn't manage to make it to the dinner given for him. He wound up drinking and enjoying Philadelphia's fancy women instead.

In the 1780s, while Sam was still a young man, the Indian troubles in the Pennsylvania-Ohio country began to subside. And maybe he became a little careless. In any event he was riding through an Ohio forest on a scouting trip with two Rangers when they found themselves trapped by an Iroquois war party. The word had gone out among the Indians to take Sam alive, but his two comrades were filled with arrows. Brady was able to kill only two warriors before he was dragged from the saddle by a small

109

army of braves. It was the only time in his long career of Indian fighting that he was captured. They tied him from his wrists to his elbows with thick rawhide.

"Men say bullet, arrow not kill you," the war chief said. "Maybe fire kill you." He ordered his men to knot a stout rope around Sam's neck, and they led him back to their village. There, he was guarded by four warriors who kept him surrounded and never took their eyes off him.

When evening came, a great fire was prepared, and the chief came to taunt the prisoner. "You will be burned at stake." He grinned tightly. "You got magic for that?" He glanced at the flames shooting up from a pile of blazing logs, off to one side. "We wait for fire to die. Coals burn slower. Hurt more."

The braves erected a freshly cut stake in the center of the village. When the flames died out, Sam would be tied to the stake and the glowing coals would be heaped around him.

About a quarter of an hour later, the chief nodded significantly to Sam's guards. Two burly braves cut the thongs that bound the white man's legs and hands. They prodded him with their knives. Feigning fear and weakness, Sam leaned on his captors for support as they led him to the stake. He sagged against the thick pole and put his hands behind him docilely.

As the other Indians busied themselves around the mound of glowing coals, Sam was left unguarded except for the chief and one guard who was preparing to tie his hands.

"White man afraid to die?" the chief grunted.

"Hell no!" Sam roared suddenly. Breaking away from the stake, he smashed the chief in the face with a savage roundhouse punch and sent him crashing back onto the hot coals. As the guard came up behind him, Sam whirled, kneed him in the groin and broke his wrist over his knee. Taking the brave's knife, he sprang away into the darkness. Another warrior blocked his path—Sam stabbed him and rushed on. As he reached the edge of the clearing, an Iroquois fitted an arrow to his bow. Without breaking step, Sam hurled the knife at him. A fountain of blood spurted into the air as the blade smashed into the Indian's throat. Then Sam was running like the wind through the trees.

That night, instead of slowly roasting over a fire, Captain Brady made his way back to a nearby settlement where there was a particularly attractive, dark-haired young lady he knew.

But, in the years that followed, the Indian threat almost ended, in the country that Sam loved so well. He finally became so discouraged at not having enough to do that he got married and settled down to three or four peaceful years.

Sam Brady died at the age of 41. There are those who say he died of a physical disease, possibly leukemia. But those who knew him best claimed that, after killing upward of 200 Indians, Captain Sam Brady died of plain ordinary boredom.

REVENGE TIMES TWENTY

Only two of the twenty men who murdered Murrieta's wife escaped his terrible vengeance. And they killed themselves before he got to them.

"I'll show you what I'll do to that killer Murrieta if I ever lay eyes on him," the tough, half-drunk miner growled. Striding across the crowded, noisy saloon, he placed an ace of clubs against the wall. A path was quickly cleared to the bar as he swaggered back to his cronies there, loosening the revolver in his belt as he walked.

"Say that ace is Murrieta," he snarled. "Watch!"

Whirling around to face the card, he grabbed the gun in his belt. But before its barrel had cleared, a handsome young Mexican at a nearby monte table stood up, his right arm describing a swift arc. A scalpel-sharp knife flashed through the air and thudded into the center of the card, burying itself to the hilt.

In the stunned silence, the Mexican smiled at the awe-struck miner who stood frozen, his gun still not completely drawn. "And that," he said pleasantly, "is what Murrieta would do to you. He dislikes wasting bullets on mining camp tramps."

The miner, his face gray and tight, dropped his hand from his gun. No one in the room moved.

"Come, gentlemen," the young man laughed. "All evening you've been talking about what you would do to poor Murrieta if you had a chance. You have your chance. Won't someone accept this cordial invitation to kill me?"

His hands were far from the pearl butts of the twin .44s in black leather, silver-engraved holsters at his side. Still no one moved.

"Ah," the Mexican sighed. "This is very sad. I had hoped to do a favor for one of you. There is a $5,000 reward for me," he reminded them. "Plus the $10,000 I carry myself and offer as a prize to the man who can take me. Will not one of you brave men who would like $15,000 for such a simple bit of work have the common courtesy to shoot me?"

He glanced around the room. It was so quiet he could hear the tense breathing of the monte dealer at the table before him. "Very well." He shrugged his shoulders in resignation, walked to the far wall and withdrew his knife. Stepping to the door, he left the saloon quietly, mounted the coal-black mare waiting in the shadows, and rode away at a casual canter.

Inside the saloon, as soon as the hoofbeats had faded away, a small riot began as eager men drew their guns and stampeded the door for a shot at Murrieta's back. Every armed man in town mounted and thundered into the night after him, but it was as though Murrieta and his black mare had ridden into the dark sky. They had disappeared completely.

Part legend, part ghost, part insane killer and part charming gentleman, Joaquin Murrieta was the most feared, hated and loved man in all California during the early 1850s.

At the height of his incredible career, it was said that Murrieta could assemble an army of 2,000 men within two days. Countless Mexicans, resentful of the fact that California was in American hands, hoped that one day he would decide to regain the state for them, and were certain that if he tried he would succeed even if he had to crush the entire United States Army in doing so. Yet these same worshipful Mexicans, along with every other

113

citizen, trembled at the mention of his name and cringed at the very thought of traveling at night. Joaquin was, after all, a demon, and who can say what a demon will do?

If a traveler had ever done the slightest favor for Murrieta, or if the bandit for some reason felt pity for him, he would not only be allowed to proceed at will, but would probably be given money or food if he needed it. If the victim had crossed Joaquin or did not appeal to his sympathetic nature, that man might be found later spread-eagled on the ground, his eyes gouged out and his tongue and ears cut off. It was not a worthwhile risk to take.

As for defending oneself against Murrieta, that was simply impossible. His superhuman acts and inhuman cruelty led many to believe that he was Satan himself come to wander the face of the earth, and that he could only be killed if he were shot in the heart with a silver bullet.

The truth is that Joaquin Murrieta was quite human. The motive that led him to become the most famous killer and bandit of his time was a very basic human drive—revenge.

His story began when a man named John Sutter found gold in his California mill stream. The fabulous rush of '49 brought tens of thousands of adventurers from all over the world to California. Among the swarming immigrants, Americans, Europeans, Chinese and Mexicans who poured into the new, raw land, was a man named Jesus Murrieta. Accompanying him were his younger brother, Joaquin, and the boy's bride, Carmen. Carmen's parents were well-to-do Spanish aristocrats. Joaquin, a remarkably handsome, slender youth, had been too proud to stay with Carmen's family or to take advantage of their money. He had preferred coming to the "Golden State" to make his own fortune through the honest, hard work of mining.

Setting up camp at Murphy's Diggings, the two brothers staked out a modest claim and began working it. They were mildly lucky, more so than the Yankees to either side of them, and their jealous neighbors soon became openly hostile.

One morning a band of them gathered around the two men. Caleb Smith, a grim, heavily muscled miner, threatened Jesus with a small pick and growled, "Who told you greasers you had any right to pan around here?"

114

"We have staked a claim properly," Jesus answered firmly. "Under the treaty of Guadalupe Hildago, Mexicans have the same rights in California as Americans."

"By God," Caleb snarled, "if there's one thing worse'n a greaser, it's a edicated greaser! Cut out the fancy gab and listen here. This's good U.S. property all around here, and no greasers ain't allowed in Murphy's Diggins!"

"Damn right!" another muttered as the crowd moved forward menacingly.

Joaquin said nothing, but moved to stand quietly beside his brother. He held an old but efficient-appearing long rifle gingerly in his hands.

Bill Lang, at whom the gun happened to be pointing, blanched and said, "Well, boys, we warned 'em. Now let's give 'em a chance to clear out without no trouble."

When the surly group had left, Jesus turned and said to his brother, "These people are not so bad. They are angry because their luck is poor. We must forgive them."

For the next few weeks there was no trouble, but Joaquin sensed the growing animosity of the Anglo-Saxon element in Murphy's Diggins. The Murrietas continued to be moderately lucky. They panned several hundred dollars' worth of gold and Joaquin bought a small cabin which Carmen promptly made comfortable.

Then one day Jesus bought two horses from an American on his way to Stockton. A few days later Jesus loaned one mount to a friend while Joaquin saddled an old mare he had had for several months. The three rode to town. At the first saloon they passed on the outskirts of Murphy's, a mob of shouting miners burst out into the street to stop them.

"I swear them's the very two horses!" Bill Lang bellowed. "Stole off me night 'afore last!"

"I bought these horses," Jesus said. "I've a bill of sale home to prove it."

"Anybody can write up a phony bill a' sale," Caleb Smith roared, snatching the reins. "Oney way we can protect us Yankees' rights is to hang these two dirty greasers that stole them horses!"

"Get a rope!" someone yelled. "No use wasting any time!"

"Let's string 'em up from the saloon rafters!"

"Here, I got a rope!"

Jesus and his friend were dragged from their horses. Joaquin leaped from his mount fighting wildly to free his

115

brother. A revolver barrel crashed against his head from behind knocking him to the ground where he was kicked and beaten furiously. He lost consciousness for a short time. He opened his eyes just in time to stare in horror as the ropes were being pulled and the two kicking men were lifted into the air. Jesus' body gradually stopped thrashing. His body quivered as though on that warm morning he were suddenly cold. Then there was no movement.

When Joaquin stumbled into his cabin he was crying. "Quick, Carmen," he muttered. "Get me my gun. They have murdered Jesus. I will kill them all."

With tender persuasion, Carmen made him lie down. He told her what had happened as she cleaned the blood from his hair and put cold cloths on his bruises.

"Please," Carmen whispered, "don't torment yourself with thoughts of Jesus. One terrible mistake will not erase another. Jesus would not want you to kill on his account."

"But then what should I do?" Joaquin asked, his jaw set tight.

"Let us leave the gold camps and get away from this greed and hatred," she said softly. "Let us go to Mexico and build our own ranch as we have always wanted."

Joaquin finally agreed that Carmen was right. They decided to stay a week or two to settle their affairs, sell the cabin and try to take a little more money from the claim to help them get started with a ranch.

A week later, while they were eating dinner late at night, the cabin door crashed open. Caleb Smith and Bill Lang, with a crowd of drunken miners behind them, barged into the room.

"What happened to your brother didn't teach you a damn thing, did it?" Caleb demanded.

Joaquin dived for a knife but they were on him before he could reach it. A rifle butt cracked down on his skull. Screaming, Carmen rushed toward him but a husky man grabbed her and laughed as she fought him.

"Someone look for the dust this greaser took off California property," Caleb commanded.

They tied Joaquin with his arms above his head. Then someone produced a rawhide whip. Joaquin said nothing as Caleb ripped the shirt from his back.

"About ten apiece ought to do it," Lang said.

"Still figger a greaser has rights around here?" Caleb

116

grunted as he lashed out with the whip. Joaquin's eyes blazed with pain and fury as the rough leather sliced the skin from his back. Caleb took ten strokes, then another miner stepped up, and another.

"I've found his gold," a man cried jubilantly. He began dividing it with the others, as the whipping continued.

As his back slowly changed to a pulp of torn skin, Joaquin only ground his teeth tighter together. No cry came from him. Carmen's screams had broken down into low, heart-broken sobs. When, after an eternity of agony, they cut him down more dead than alive, Joaquin slumped to the floor, his eyes dull, half-conscious coals of burning hate.

"Well, men," Caleb drawled. "Now that we've a finished with business, how 'bout a little pleasure! I ain't seen a better looking wench than this here in all Californy, even if she is a greaser!"

Stepping to Carmen, he caught her dress near the neck and ripped down with all his strength.

Joaquin, crumpled on the floor, unable to control even the muscles of his fingers, stared with glazed, maddened eyes as every man in the crowd made obscene, drunken jokes while one after another they raped Carmen. She was still struggling weakly when Hammond, one of the last men to take his turn, lost his temper at her resistance and hit her repeatedly with his clenched fist.

In the morning an elderly Mexican woman, a friend of Carmen's, discovered them. After two days Joaquin could move around with great effort; his back was beginning to heal. Carmen was brave. She fought against the weakness within her. But on the third day she called feebly to Joaquin. She smiled at him and groped for his hand, and then she died.

In the instant that Carmen died, the demon came to life in Joaquin. For a long time, as he stood beside her, he was too shocked with grief to know it was there. Then it came raging into the front of his mind and his grip tightened on the delicate, lifeless fingers in his hand. Kneeling beside Carmen, he buried his face in his hands and made a fierce and bitter vow.

Three weeks later, in early 1850, Caleb Smith finished a card game with friends. After laughing about how "that greaser sure high-tailed it," he started riding toward his cabin half a mile away. On the lonely trail a riata flicked over his head with the deadly speed of a striking snake. The next moment Caleb was lying on his back looking up by the light of the moon at a tall, grim figure. His hand fumbled for his gun but the swift pressure of a knife blade against his throat stopped him. Now he saw Joaquin's face clearly, but it was no longer the face of a 21-year-old youth, it was the face of a devil.

"Don't kill me," he gasped. "Hammond and Lang started it." Then, in sniveling desperation, "I'll give you my gold!"

"I will take your gold, and that which you took from me," Joaquin hissed. "After you die."

In the rock-steady hand, the knife bore down slightly, breaking the skin. "For God's sake," Caleb pleaded. His high-pitched shriek became an insane gurgle as the knife finished its unhurried downward path. They found him there when the sun came up. Carefully carved on his forehead was the single, large letter "M."

Two nights later Hammond heard the soft whisper of a riata as it brushed past his ears. The rope snapped taut and he was dragged from his horse. Whirling on the ground, he grabbed for his gun, but Joaquin lunged out of the night and nearly cut off his arm. Grasping his wounded arm, Hammond began sobbing hysterically. "Put the knife away," he begged. "If you're going to kill me, use a gun."

The blade shone wickedly in the dim light. "Don't. I can't stand a knife—being cut," he whimpered.

They found Hammond's body later on with numerous knife wounds in it, no one of which would have killed him. The letter "M" was gouged into his forehead.

Of the 20 men upon whom Joaquin had sworn vengeance, 18 were left. Seven of them moved en masse to Marysville in an attempt to escape. Murrieta followed them there and through one full week he killed a man a night. Five of them died slowly by the knife. Two, who had carried their guns with them almost constantly, were shot between the eyes.

The name Murrieta spread over the entire state; it became synonymous with death. Joaquin used the money he took from his victims freely. He bought a splendid pair of revolvers, a late model rifle and knives of the finest steel. In fulfilling his sworn vengeance, he would live or die by his weapons and his ability to use them. During the day he holed up in the mountains. At night he prowled the towns and valleys on a blooded black

118

mare, watching and waiting. Thieves, bandits and cut-throats began seraching for him through the wilds of Calaveras and El Dorado Counties, where he usually could be found. They were awed by his magic name and reputation and wanted nothing except to be associated with him. Soon a tight-knit band of killers had gathered around him. His original plan to kill the 20 men was now enlarged in scope. With ruthless cynicism he murdered people as the normal man might casually step on ants. But those left on his personal list were marked for special attention.

Strangely, there were still within him, and powerfully so, such qualities as loyalty, generosity and sympathy. Four horsemen surrounded an old man named Whitten one night as he was driving a buckboard to Murphy's Diggings. The leader's keen eyes recognized him before any of the others could shoot.

"Hold!" Joaquin shouted. "Señor Whitten," he continued, "how are things with you?"

Whitten answered frankly, "Not too well. A fire burned a lot of stock in my store and now it looks like I'm gonna be killed."

"A fire? How much did you lose?" the man on the black mare inquired with grave concern.

"About five hundred dollars."

There was a faint thump on the seat of the buckboard beside Whitten and the man on the mare rode away with the others after him. When Whitten arrived in town he found a pouch of gold dust worth nearly a thousand dollars on the seat. At first, he couldn't figure out the reason for the windfall. Then he recalled that he had once given a pretty girl a few spare yards of material for a dress. Her name was Carmen Murrieta.

A valuable but sinister addition to Joaquin's rapidly growing band was Three Finger Jack Garcia. Three Finger had caught a rifle slug in his right hand, hence the name. His favorite boast was that blood had the same effect on him that whiskey has on most men. "The sight and smell of it makes me wild drunk," he told Joaquin. "And the more I see, the more I want."

In due time he had an opportunity to demonstrate how this ghastly craving affected him. Murrieta's gang succeeded in capturing four miners outside the camp known as Hell's Delight. When the prize captives were brought before Joaquin, his eyes became narrow glints of fire.

119

"Jack," he commanded, "come here and meet four of the men who had the pleasure of lashing me and murdering my wife."

Garcia, a broad grin spreading over his face, removed his sombrero and bowed deeply toward the four miners who stood petrified with terror.

"Since you are more expert than I," Joaquin continued, "I'm curious to see what unusual entertainment you can devise for them."

Garcia nodded and placed the tip of a long-bladed knife in the low-burning fire. The screams of his victims pierced the clear blue sky throughout the entire day, and, as a final gesture, Three Finger quartered each man by tying his limbs to four nervous, half-wild ponies and stampeding them. When the dust had settled and Three Finger had finished with his fun, parts of bodies were scattered all over the valley.

In the next few months, Murrieta brought his own shattering brand of vengeance to 18 of the 20 men who had inspired his infamous career. The other two escaped him in the only possible way; they committed suicide before he could get to them.

By now Murrieta was the most wanted man in California, his band had swelled to nearly 100 men, and unheard-of rewards were being offered for his capture.

The sheriff of Stockton, in a desperate attempt to enlist traitors in Murrieta's camp on his side, nailed a poster to a prominent tree on the main street. It read: "Reward for the capture of JOAQUIN MURRIETA. $5,000 DOLLARS. Dead or alive."

As the sheriff walked back to his office, a good-looking young Mexican, one of the crowd which had watched in curiosity, rode his black mare up closer to the tree for a better look. He pursed his lips thoughtfully, then, taking a pencil from his pocket, casually added another line before trotting on down the street.

A moment later a wild chorus of yelling voices brought the sheriff back on the run. Pushing his way through the mob around the tree, he read the new line: *And I will pay $10,000. Joaquin Murrieta.*

Within seconds a rapidly formed posse pounded down the street in angry pursuit of Joaquin. As usual, he had completely disappeared.

As Murrieta's fame became international, sober army men all over the world who did not believe him supernatural paid him the even higher compliment of believing him a military genius. Within 24 hours, he would strike at half-a-dozen points all the way from Tulare Lake to Sierra City and back again, some 600 miles. While posses and cavalry scurried to the north, Murrieta would strike in the south. When the cursing lawmen or soldiers galloped back south, Murrieta would flash down out of the hills once more to the north. His system was to divide his men into self-operating companies. With a chosen man —Claudio, Jose Ochovo, Manuel Sevalio or Florencio Cruz, each a hardened, experienced fighter—acting as lieutenant of each separate group, Joaquin would set up a master plan whereby they would have every enemy in the territory running in the wrong direction while a single troop of bandits galloped down on an unprotected area to rob stages, loot small settlements or hold up runners of gold shipments.

Many military experts favorably compared Murrieta with the young Napoleon. The few times armed forces accidentally got near Joaquin, the outcome was tragically similar. Like Bonaparte, Murrieta directed his men into quick, tight maneuvers that invariably left the pursuers outflanked and confused and put them in the unfortunate position of being blasted to pieces by his fighting men.

Murrieta had an unorthodox but highly effective network of signals operating among the hundreds of Mexican families in California who were sympathetic toward him. If a washwoman hung up two sheets with a red piece of clothing between them, it meant danger. Or if at night windows were lighted in a certain fashion, they carried a message that could be read as far as the light could be seen.

Estimates were made that at its peak Murrieta's band numbered well over 200. Joaquin and his bandits have been likened to Robin Hood and his Merry Men. But while Murrieta was capable of great generosity and kindness, the similarity ended there, for his men were hardly lovable scallawags. One evening Three Finger Jack Garcia and a few men captured eight Chinese miners. Tieing them together by their long queues, they herded the shrilling innocents into camp. There, Jack walked down the line of Orientals, slitting each one's throat as he went.

Three Finger had an insatiable appetite for slaying Chinamen, and, according to conservative figures, he murdered 200 of them during his bloody years. Luis

Vulvia, another gang member, was perhaps a worse psychopath. It has been said that his bestial crimes would have nauseated Jack the Ripper.

Periodically such companionship palled on Joaquin and he rode out of the hills several times a month to enjoy himself in towns near his hideouts. His youth and fine manners convinced people that he was probably the son of a wealthy rancher. Murrieta was understandably the main topic of conversation, and the young Latin would listen with interest as others talked about the bandit king's latest exploits. Often, when angered by braggarts who were forever going to kill him, he would tell them who he was, then stalk out in disgust as they became speechless with fear.

One night in late 1852 a member of the band who had made secret arrangements to betray his leader asked Joaquin if he might accompany him into town. Murrieta agreed, and the trap seemed complete as they settled down to a card game in a busy saloon. When the sheriff and a small army arrived, the traitor sprang away from the line of fire and pointed at Joaquin.

"That's him!" he shouted. "That's Murrieta!"

Murrieta instantly overturned the heavy card table, scattering cards, chips and men across the room. His guns appeared magically in his hands and the first .44 slug nearly tore off the top of the Judas' head. Joaquin now faced half a hundred armed and resolute men waiting for the panic-stricken card players to scramble out of the way so they could kill him. His next bullets, fired swiftly from the hip, blasted out every light in the saloon. In the pandemonium that followed, screams and curses mingled with the echoing roars of wildly firing revolvers. "Don't let him get away!" the sheriff bellowed, blasting at a suspicious shadow that moved near him.

"I got him!" two men yelled at once.

When the smoke had cleared and quiet was restored to the room, the bartender struck a match to a new lamp. Besides the treacherous bandit they grimly counted six dead men. Murrieta was gone.

Joaquin returned to camp weak with laughter. He had holstered his guns after shooting out the lights, and had walked calmly out the back door.

The California Legislature, aghast at the fact that the 24-year-old desperado and his men had killed a thousand men and stolen an immeasurable fortune from luckless citizens, authorized a company of Rangers to devote their full time tracking down the outlaw. Captain Harry Love, a veteran of the Mexican War under General Zachary Taylor, was put in charge of the expedition.

On the morning of July 22, 1853, the Rangers rode into Arroya Cantova near Tulare Lake and came upon a small group of men just waking up.

No one was more surprised than Love when the only man in his company who knew Murrieta by sight, a Texan named Byrnes, pointed at one of the men in the camp and shouted in great excitement, "That's Murrieta!"

The dark-eyed bandit leader immediately reached for a gun and the battle was on. Three Finger Jack Garcia grabbed a revolver and ran. Murrieta sprang to the back of a pinto and tried to escape. A bullet hit him in the back and another struck the pinto. As Murrieta turned to fire, the animal fell, pinning him. Before he could squeeze out from under his horse, two more slugs tore into him. The other Mexicans in the camp were shot down as they jumped to their feet.

Three Finger was caught in some bushes where a volley of bullets ended his grisly career.

In order to prove he had killed Murrieta, Love ordered Joaquin's head cut off. Three Finger's hand was removed at the wrist as further substantiation. After all rewards had been paid, the head was sold to a theatrical entrepreneur who exhibited it to thousands of people eager to pay a dollar for a glimpse of all that remained of the famous and mysterious Murrieta.

According to records of the California Legislature and history books, the saga of Joaquin Murrieta ends there. Almost everyone was happy to know that at last he was dead and his outlaw band broken up.

But there are some curious points to consider. Love was indeed fortunate to enter Murrieta's camp so easily when Murrieta *always* posted lookouts. Murrietta was known to be a handsome, slender man, yet the displayed head had a large nose, thick lips and a bull-like neck. Murrieta had a scar behind his right ear from a blow received when his brother was hanged. The head had no mark. Love's victim had dashed for a pinto. Murrieta's coal-black mare was not in the camp.

There are those who are convinced that Murrieta was not killed by Ranger bullets. They believe that he had tired of an outlaw's ilfe and left his command to Three

Finger Jack Garcia. They say the brilliant young bandit, as always, was one step ahead of the law, and that he finally felt, after the deaths of those he had sworn to kill and more than 1,000 others, that his revenge was complete.

They like to think that Joaquin Murrieta quietly rode south to Mexico, to build the ranch he and Carmen had dreamed of.

THE INCREDIBLE PRISONER
OF YUMA

*Rather than break his word, the quiet "Professor"
passed up one chance to escape. Then, singlehanded,
he started—and stopped—the West's wildest jailbreak.*

From where they stood, the distant prison looked
like a giant stone box lying in the sand. Above it, tiny
specks that were six-foot buzzards swam tiredly in the
pulsing heat that covered the desert.

Halley, the guard, shifted his Winchester to lay it
crosswise before him in the saddle. "That's it," he told
the blond, heavy-shouldered young man walking in
front of the sweating horse. "Ain't much on the inside,
maybe, but it's sure better than being outside."

"Why?" the blond man asked.

"Well, Rogers, outside in three directions, you got a lot
of fire-hot desert where a man can't live long. And in
Yuma town, behind us, prisoners are shot on sight."

"You mean it would be hard to escape?"

"Impossible. Even worse than the desert or gettin'
shot in town is the 'Paches. They love to find a prisoner.
Coupla' weeks past they got hold of one of our boys and

125

spread-eagled him face up. They pinned back his eyelids with cactus needles. When we found him he was blind and crazy. He died in a coupla' days."

Rogers squinted through the blazing sunlight at the circling vultures above the prison. Guessing his thoughts, Halley said, "Birds'll go for a man, too, once he's too weak to move. They've et a few."

"Cheerful place," Rogers said.

"Let's move along." Halley touched a spur to his mount. "You seem a likely lad," he continued, a friendly note in his voice. "Keep out of trouble. The boys wouldn't want to have to shoot you or drag your carcass off the desert."

On that searing hot day in the 1880s when John Rogers was escorted to the Territorial Prison at Yuma, it was generally agreed that Yuma Prison was a killer. A bleak, impregnable fortress of solid granite, it was referred to grimly as the American Devil's Island. Scorching temperatures, the deadly Arizona desert, savage Apaches and the prisoners themselves—the most vicious outlaws and murderers who ever ranged the frontier—combined to make it a sweltering hell where the death of an inmate was about as important as the death of one of the bug-eyed lizards that sunned themselves around the jail—or perhaps even less so, since the lizards were valued as fly-catchers.

Nobody suspected, though, that John Rogers would turn out to be the most incredibly stubborn man ever entered on the jail's records, or that his epic escape plot would become a legend in the history of the West.

When the monstrous iron gates clanged shut behind them, Halley took Rogers straight to Warden Smith's office. Smith's secretary, who was used to hardened gunfighters, cattle rustlers, rapists and knife killers, threw a piece of paper across his desk and mumbled belligerently, "Fill this out with any pert'nent data about yourself."

When Rogers had finished writing and handed the paper back, the secretary glanced at it and snapped, "What are you, loco?"

"No," Rogers said, his jaw tightening.

The secretary passed the paper to the warden, who grumbled, "What's all this damned nonsense? Graduate of Oxford—B.A., LL.B. and all this other stuff. And here!" Smith glared at Rogers. "A professional violinist!

126

Are you sure you haven't got us mixed up with the Hotel Astor?"

Rogers said in a low voice, "Quite sure."

"Put him in the 800 block," Smith told Halley. "And watch out for him. He's a troublemaker."

Striding through the dark, fetid corridors, Halley said, "Them things you put down. They true?"

"Yes."

"You ought've explained to the warden. He's O. K. if he thinks you're square with him. Far as he's concerned, you're just another con doing time for robbery."

Rogers didn't answer.

It was soon obvious that Rogers had written the plain truth about himself. He seemed to know nearly everything about everything and he spoke several languages fluently. Some of the inmates began referring admiringly to the erudite young newcomer as "Professor." One night a guard borrowed Eli Benton's ancient, battered violin and passed it through the cell bars to Rogers. Benton had sworn nothing but squeaks, grunts and groans would ever come out of the thing. But Rogers felt the catgut strings gingerly, worked with the screws and rubbed a small dab of candle wax into the bowstring. A few minutes later, soft, lovely music was penetrating the darkest corners of Yuma Prison like silver shafts of dancing moonlight. It was strange to hear in that murderous hellhole.

Through his learning, about which he was almost painfully modest, Rogers quickly became the final authority on any and all arguments among the prisoners. Because of his musical ability and his unassuming, easygoing personality, he also became increasingly popular. This was bitterly resented by Nate Buckner, self-pronounced boss of the inmates. Nate was a dark, wiry man who was reputed to be a cousin of John Wesley Hardin and was on speaking terms with every gunslinger in the Southwest. He had gathered half-a-dozen tough lieutenants about him and set up an iron-fisted hierarchy in the jail. For every cigar, shot of whiskey or homemade knife that changed hands, Nate got a kickback. Seeing in Rogers a threat to his power, he decided to slap the blond violin-player down. In the prison yard one afternoon he got his chance. He was sitting in the shade of a wall with five cronies when Rogers walked by. The two mounted guards

127

with .45s at their hips and Winchesters stuck in their saddle holsters had ridden to the far side of the yard.

"Hey, Blondie," Nate called out. "Where's your violin?"

Rogers glanced at him. He didn't answer.

"While we're at it," Nate continued, "I've been meanin'
to tell ya', stop makin' that goddamned sissy racket. No
more fiddlin', see?"

Rogers looked at him contemptuously. "Go to hell,"
he said.

"Lewt," Nate snapped at a gigantic, muscle-heavy
man sprawled near him. "You gonna let that sissy fiddler
talk to us that way?"

"Tell Nate here you didn't mean what you said," Lewt
drawled.

"I mean it."

"Damn you," Lewt complained, shifting his huge body
slowly erect. "Now I'll have to make you 'pologize."

Rogers turned slightly to face him, his blue eyes glinting
dangerously. "Try it," he said.

With his friends following, Lewt plunged angrily at
Rogers. He saw Rogers' shoulder move, but the whipping
fist was faster than the eye could follow. He was vaguely
aware of having run into what seemed to be the wrong
end of a kicking horse. Then he was out. The others
jumped Rogers from all sides and he became a furious,
human tornado, twisting, surging, plowing among them
and slashing out brutally with fists like solid rocks.

When the guards broke it up, Rogers was still standing,
blood running from a cut on his mouth. The others hadn't
got off so easily.

"Great God in Heaven," the prison doctor muttered,
summing it up officially. "I don't mind a dead man 'cause
he's no trouble. But I got a busted jaw, three broken ribs
and a concussion on my hands. This can't go on!"

Warden Smith found Rogers in his cell. "What have
you been trying to do?" he snarled. "Cripple everybody
in the place?"

"No," Rogers said mildly.

"Did you start the fight?"

"With six against me?" Rogers raised an eyebrow.

"Answer me," the warden growled. "Did you start it?"

"You know Nate Buckner. Your question is too absurd
to answer."

"All right, Rogers." Smith turned and walked away.

In a few minutes, two guards came for Rogers. They led him deep into the bowels of the prison. At the lowest level he was put into a deep hole dug out of the dirt. This was solitary, the snakepit, as the men called it, where an incorrigible received two slices of bread and a half glass of water a day until he either begged for release or died.

"Anything you want us to tell the warden?" a burly jailer demanded.

"Tell him he's wrong."

"You tell him."

They fastened the stone covering over the top of the hole and Rogers was left in a soundless, timeless dungeon.

Four weeks was the longest time anyone ever had been left in the snakepit up to the time Rogers was put in it. Each day the warden asked the guards whether or not the prisoner was ready to admit he was wrong and tell him who had started the fight. Each day the guards shook their heads glumly.

After three weeks Smith growled, "He can't last much longer."

"No, sir," a guard agreed. "He's startin' to crack up already. This mornin' he told Mike that Schopenhauer was wrong, that if he'd done some time in the snakepit his whole attitude would've changed. But we ain't got no Schopenhauer around here, sir."

Smith glowered at him and the guard retreated, still puzzled.

After a full month, the warden visited the pit personally. "Look here, Rogers," he called down to the thin, bearded man lying on his back and blinking at the feeble light of the candle Smith held, "if you want to stay here and die, it's all right with me. On the other hand, why don't you use your head and admit your error?"

"The question," Rogers gasped for breath, "the question is ridiculous and you know it."

"Don't be a fool!"

"This has become—a matter of principle."

Warden Smith went away cursing.

When eight weeks had passed, the warden's morning question to the guards had changed. Now it was, "Is he still alive?" Each day they reassured him that it didn't look as though anything could kill Rogers. But Smith was beginning to wonder. Somehow, as it always does, word had spread around that a superman was being slowly murdered by the warden of Yuma Prison over a trifling matter. If Rogers did die now, Smith would be called on for an explanation. Furthermore, the warden had allowed another disquieting thought to enter his mind. Rogers had obviously been telling the truth about his background. What if his family or personal friends turned out to be influential people back East? What if he died and they found out about it? Smith's reason for letting him die would sound pretty silly in court.

During the 11th week, Rogers was still alive and adamant, but Smith couldn't stand it any longer. Storming down to the pit, he unlocked the chain that held the stone in place. Opening up the pit, he raised his candle and said bitterly, "Rogers! Are you still alive?"

Through lips cracked like dried-out old leather, Rogers finally said, "Yes."

"Do you want to tell me you were wrong?"

Painfully, but without hesitation, the answer came, "No."

Calling the guards, Smith ordered, "Get that idiot out of there. We've got other prisoners, too. He can't monopolize the pit forever!"

Two men carried Rogers to his cell. A week later he was playing the violin again. After another few days he banged two heads together. One of the heads belonged to a prisoner. The other was the property of a guard who was laid up for nine days.

"I see," Warden Smith told him grimly, "that you've got back some energy."

"That's right."

"Why did you hurt those two men?"

"They were both arguing. They were keeping the boys in Block 800 awake."

"It's not your place to stop arguments," Smith said acidly. "We'll use your energy to better advantage."

As punishment, the warden put Rogers on the rockpile with a sledgehammer, hoping the furnace-like heat and grueling labor would tame or kill the impossible prisoner. For several weeks Rogers thrived on the murderous rockpile, growing stronger and healthier every day while others collapsed all around him. When a worker fell, he was thrown back into his cell. There he sometimes recuperated but more often died, his life literally pounded out of him by the blasting sun and harrowing work.

One morning an inmate's arms became paralyzed. He didn't pass out, but he couldn't lift the hammer. A stocky guard rode over and bellowed, "Git to work, damn you!"

"Stop that nonsense," Rogers said. "The man is sick."

The guard's face purpled with rage. He grabbed a rawhide whip from his saddle horn and snarled, "This'll make 'im work!" As the whip curved back, Rogers sprang forward, dragged the big jailer from his saddle like a sack of potatoes, and shook his sledgehammer in the man's suddenly gray face. "You hit him and I'll knock your mediocre brains out!" he threatened.

Rogers could have killed the guard and the others knew it, so they didn't shoot him. They sent him to Smith for disciplining. Smith muttered to himself and decided Rogers was hopeless. As a matter of duty he had him lashed severely. Rogers took the long, cruel beating in stubborn silence, shook the pain out of his wide shoulders, and stalked in angry dignity to his cell.

For the first and only time in his career, Smith had to admit to himself that a prisoner was too much for him. In a remarkable turnabout, he tried to plot some way for Rogers to escape. When the Ladies' Club of Yuma, five miles away, was about to have a party, the warden offered to lend the women "a superb violinist" for the evening. The club accepted gladly.

The afternoon that Rogers was to go into Yuma, Smith visited him in his cell and said, "You can't go to a ladies' club in prison clothes. We'll fix you up with a suit."

"I was about to suggest that," Rogers agreed.

When he was dressed and ready to go, Smith said, "One other thing. I can't spare a man to guard you tonight. You'll have to go into Yuma alone."

"Oh?"

"Naturally, I'll have to have your word that you'll come back all right."

Rogers hesitated, then said, "You have it."

Smith saw him to the gate and watched happily as his nemesis trudged off in the direction of Yuma. That night the warden ordered a special dinner and invited three of his officers to join him. They reported later that he smiled and joked as he never had before, and a pleasant time was had by all.

The next morning he nodded cheerfully to his secretary before sitting down at his desk.

"Good morning," the secretary said. "Rogers reported in at about 1 o'clock."

Smith's mouth opened and shut soundlessly. Then he said, "He did? Good. Good."

"The guard on 800 block has the suit of clothes."

"All right! Stop bothering me," the warden grumbled, turning to the papers on his desk.

Rogers had been a great success at the party and he had walked all the way back to Yuma in the middle of the night. Smith had made the mistake of making him promise to return. He had returned.

For the next few weeks Rogers was amazingly docile. He injured no one, jailer or prisoner, and was in reasonable control of his now famous temper. The truth was he was too busy with important thoughts to bother with day-to-day trivialities. He had made up his mind to escape, and when he put his scholarly mind to work on the problem, he wasn't satisfied with any halfway measures. His plan was not simply to get away himself, but to arrange a mass break in which every last prisoner in Yuma would win his freedom.

Desperate convicts, usually lifers, had tried regularly to break out of Yuma. With sharpened spoons and filed-down, iron bed legs, they had often labored for years to scratch their way through the thick granite walls, carrying the tiny bit of dust collected each day into the yard in their pockets and letting it blow away across the sand. They had never succeeded. Others, who had tried dashes over the desert, had been found, as Halley had warned Rogers, tortured by Apaches or dead from thirst and exhaustion.

While returning from the party at Yuma, Rogers had noticed that there was a train leaving for Phoenix every night at 11:30. He wanted to time the break so that the prisoners could board the train, take it over and, using it as transportation, scatter themselves over the entire Southwest.

As for getting out of the prison, he decided the attack should be made shortly after dark and should be aimed at the main gate, where it would be least expected. There were six guards along the walls armed with Winchesters. Directly above the gate there was a mounted Gatling gun with two men always on duty ready to operate it.

Rogers worked the complete plan out in his mind. When he had allowed for every contingency and perfected each detail, he began his indoctrination of the other men.

Nate Buckner and his gang had healed from their wounds by now, but still bore hard feelings toward Rogers. When he approached them in the prison yard, they frowned sullenly.

"Sorry about that misunderstanding," Rogers said.

"Where'd you learn to fight?" Lewt asked with grudging admiration.

Rogers ignored the question. "How would you boys like to get out of here for good, say next week?"

This was the sort of talk they liked. In a few minutes, Rogers was their acknowledged leader and even Nate was quietly taking instructions. When he had made himself clear on the method of escape, Rogers stared at the eager faces around him. "That's all except for one thing," he said. "Under no circumstances will any of you hurt the guards."

"After what you done to us, you're worried about hurtin' people all of a sudden? How come?" Lewt demanded.

"You fellows asked for it," Rogers told him. "Most of these guards are all right. I don't want them killed or hurt. Either that's understood or the break is off."

They reluctantly agreed to handle the guards gently.

When Rogers moved further along the wall to spread the word, Nate muttered, "We'll go 'long with his idea, 'cause it's a good one. But once we get goin' don't let nobody stand in the way."

Rogers chose a night when Warden Smith was not at Yuma. That evening the prisoners were especially quiet and well behaved. The guards who had never faced a mass escape before, didn't recognize the ominous silence by the peaceful atmosphere and they relaxed visibly, joking among themselves. As night shadows blacked out the yards below, the guards on the walls waited impatiently to be relieved for dinner.

When the replacement guards could be heard marching up the stone steps to the top of the wall, there was suddenly a wild yell, "Prisoner loose! Outside the walls!"

Instantly the wall guards turned to search the darkness for a glimpse of the escaped man. At the same time the footsteps of the approaching guards increased, quite naturally, to a fast run.

There was no escaped convict, and the "guards" were

prisoners Rogers had stationed in the prison kitchen, knowing they would not be missed until night roll call. Now they clattered along the walls, overwhelming the unsuspecting jailers who didn't realize the trick until it was too late.

Within 30 seconds, the prison was a shrieking bedlam. Rogers had placed men in key positions throughout the entire jail, and they sprang into swift action. The great majority of men, who were still in their cells, bellowed to be let loose. Rogers was the first man to be released. Racing down the hall, he plunged into the main yard and yelled, "Throw the keys!" to his men on the wall who had taken them from the chief guard. A moment later he opened the great iron gate. Inside, men were running from cell to cell, rapidly unlocking each door.

Rogers ran to the top of the wall and nearly tripped over the guard Halley lying at the top of the steps. Kneeling down, he felt blood pouring out of a knife wound in Halley's back. "Who hurt this man?" he asked the two convicts who were holding rifles on the other guards grouped before them.

"Nate did," one answered. "You didn't expect anyone to take that stuff about not hurtin' guards serious, did you?"

Rogers jerked a handkerchief from his pocket and started to stop the flow of blood, his mind hurtling swiftly through some unpleasant thoughts. Yuma was a hell hole, but was that fact alone enough to justify letting these men out? What about the people, innocent, hardworking people, who were bound to suffer at the hands of these men? They had tasted freedom only a few minutes and already one man was hurt badly. Rogers' jaw tightened into a hard line.

The bleeding stopped now. Rogers glanced into the yard below. On the far side he could see Nate and Lewt leading horses from the prison stables.

Noticing Rogers' angry face and sensing trouble, one of the jailbirds turned his Winchester toward him. "Don't get any big ideas. It's too late."

Rogers said flatly, "The break's off."

"You're crazy!" the man behind the rifle sneered.

Lunging with the speed and force of a mountain lion, Rogers whipped one arm up and knocked the gun from the man's hands while his coiled fist buried itself in his stomach. The man said, "Ohh!" and crumpled. Before the other convict could turn, Rogers kicked his legs out from under him, dumping him into the yard 30 feet below. "Get on the Gatling gun," Rogers told the guards. "Shoot anyone who tries to come up the stairs. We can stop them in the yard."

Leaving the guards, Rogers sped along the wall. Above the gate he saw Nate and Lewt galloping toward the exit. Yelling at the top of his voice he jumped down to the yard directly in front of the gate. The horses, terrified by the shouting figure which had plummeted into their path, reared high, shrilling their fright. Lewt was thrown, dropping a rifle he held, and Rogers bounced to his feet, dragging the squirming Nate from his saddle before he could draw the Colt he had strapped to his waist. Rogers flattened the gunman with a crushing right to the face and kicked Lewt in the head as he started to get up. Then, as the first wildly screaming prisoners surged into the yard toward the gate, he turned to close it. He got the key in the lock, but before he could turn it, a dozen madly clawing, scrambling prisoners were on him, tearing him away. As he fell, Rogers saw the rifle Lewt had dropped on the ground before him. Grabbing the Winchester by its barrel, he fought his way into a standing position throwing men from him like a rearing giant. A convict was fumbling with the gate, trying to unlock it. Churning through the massed men, Rogers grabbed him by the neck and threw him to the ground. Then, standing with his back to the gate, he lashed out wildly using the rifle stock as a club. His raging attack drove the frantic men back for an instant, and he whirled, turned the key in the lock, and threw the key far away into the dark prison yard.

"Kill 'im," someone shrieked as the main body of prisoners flooded through the yards and surged toward Rogers. "He locked the gate!"

A hundred crazed prisoners charged at Rogers. He braced himself, then hurtled among them, blasting a path through their roaring lines with the now bloody gun stock.

Suddenly there was a coughing thunder as the Gatling gun above was cranked into action. The first warning shots whined over the prisoners' heads. At the same time a staccato burst of rifle fire came from the off-duty guards who were now organized in the main building and ready to cut loose from behind the prisoners.

The convicts knew the next shower of bullets would

cut them down mercilessly. They backed away from Rogers. In seconds they were transformed from madmen to sullenly milling prisoners. Within an hour they were all back in their cells.

Five weeks from the day of the break, Warden Smith called Rogers to his office and said, "There are those who think you should be hung for starting the riot, and those who think you should be given a lifetime pension for stopping the escape. On my recommendation the state has decided to give you a full pardon. I'll be glad to be rid of you."

"The feeling is mutual."

The next day Rogers walked out of Yuma Prison and the huge iron gates crashed together behind him, shutting the well-dressed, free man outside.

Halley, his knife wound cured, was on duty on the wall. "What I first told you, don't go no more," he called down. "In your case now, it's better being out of Yuma Prison than in it."

"I think I prefer it," Rogers smiled.

"Don't come back."

John Rogers never did. He disappeared completely, leaving behind only the legend, the legend of a scholarly gentleman and two-fisted wildman who singlehandedly started and stopped the damndest mass jailbreak in the history of the Southwest. Yuma Prison itself has long since ceased to exist. But the story of John Rogers goes on forever.

SAM COLT WAS
A CURIOUS MAN

*Military experts called him a crackpot, but Sam
never lost faith in the amazing revolving gun that
tamed the Wild West, revolutionized warfare and
altered the course of world history.*

One evening, a young seaman off the brig *Corlo*
wandered beyond Maidan Park toward the native section
of Calcutta. He was of medium height, his shoulders were
unusually wide and his eyes unusually alive and sharp.
Otherwise there was nothing to distinguish him from a
thousand other seafaring men in the city. But the three
hooded men following in the growing shadows behind
him, needed no excuse for murder. It was their religion.
Members of the dreaded *phansigars,* they had taken an
oath to kill all the foreigners they could to please their
God, *Kali.*

They closed the distance quickly as the young American started up a dark, winding alley in the direction of
the port, to the left of the sprawling native quarter. The
sound of a light, quick footstep behind him warned him
an instant before a thin cord whipped down across his
face toward his throat. The *phansigar* had been profes-
sionally trained in the art of assassination. He was an

expert. But before the cord could tighten, the sailor lunged swiftly backwards, cracking the Hindu in the jaw with his head and hitting him in the stomach with his right elbow. One *phansigar* was out of the game.

Whirling as the first thug fell, the sailor found his way blocked by the remaining two *phansigars*. They advanced, expecting him to run. He charged instead. One went down under a fist that struck like a battering ram. The other discarded his garroting cord and leaped forward with a curved knife. The sailor ducked the swinging blade and rushed down the alley. He tripped in the dark, rolled once and was on his feet again instantly.

He was pretty fast on his feet. His pursuers fell behind, and, eventually, he made it back to his ship. Panting hard, he stopped for a moment under the lamp burning above the gangplank. Before going aboard, he reached into his jacket pocket and pulled out a strange-looking gun. Inspecting it carefully, he sighed with relief. It had not been damaged in the fall.

This particular gun would have meant nothing to the *phansigars,* if he had pulled it on them in the alley. In fact, it would have meant nothing to anyone in the year 1831. It was the first revolver in the history of the world, and it was made of wood.

Samuel Colt, age 16, put the wooden model back in his pocket and started up the gangplank. As he reached the top, a friend called out to him. "You look the town over, boy? What'd you think of it?"

"Well," Sam answered slowly, "I thought it was very interesting."

Sam Colt found almost everything about life interesting. A curious man, he had a relentlessly inquiring mind and boundless energy to back it up.

At the age of four, he was given a miniature brass cannon. It was the kind of toy a normal child stands behind and yells, "Boom, boom!" Not Sam; no phony "booms" for him. He borrowed some gunpowder from his father's hunting horn, tamped it into the cannon and touched it off with a long, lighted stick. The resultant blast blew the toy to smithereens and knocked Sam flat. He was overjoyed at the success of his project.

Another time when he was seven years old, Sam came into possession of an ancient horse pistol that was not in working order. He promptly swiped some household goods from the Colt residence and traded them to a gunsmith in return for repairing the pistol.

An afternoon or two later, there was a vast roar from a nearby valley. Members of the family and servants rushed out of the house in a body to find out what had happened. When they reached the valley, they saw Sam walking slowly toward them.

"Noise?" the lad replied sweetly to their excited questions. "I didn't hear anything out of the ordinary." The truth was, he had overloaded his pistol, and it almost blew up when he fired it. With his first shot, young Sam had also blown a small sapling nearly in half. Then, realizing that adults frowned upon this sort of activity in seven-year-olds, he had hidden the horse pistol carefully.

The Colts were one of the wealthiest and most respected families in Hartford, Connecticut, during Sam's early childhood. When he was 11 years old, his mother died, and shortly after that Christopher Colt, his father, met with business reverses. Colt sent his three older sons to work for friends and relatives, in return for board and keep.

Sam was indentured to a farmer for one year. During this year in the country he learned two things: one, he hated farming; two, the men outside of the safe, comfortable cities were desperate for a repeating firearm. The best they had come up with so far was a double-barreled rifle or pistol. As soon as you went beyond that, it seemed, you needed a team of oxen to drag the weapon around. For that matter, even a twin-barreled rifle was heavy and inconvenient, and for practical purposes, two pistols had many advantages over one bulky, double-barreled affair. It looked as if firearms had gone just about as far as they ever would go.

Sam was intrigued. He would get out that old horse pistol of his and stare at it after the chores were done at night, trying to visualize how you could get more barrels onto a gun without increasing its weight.

When his year of farming was up, Sam's father put him to work in a textile factory he had started in Ware, Massachusetts. Nothing could have pleased Sam more. Here all sorts of tools and chemicals were available to him for the first time. Sam was an assistant to the factory chemist, and after hours he was, as ever, a menace. He tried rigging four barrels onto a single breech. The contraption weighed about 50 pounds, and one night, all four barrels

139

accidentally discharged at once and nearly broke the boy's arm. Then he had the idea of putting several loadings into one barrel and touching them off one at a time, starting with the front load. This didn't work either. A 12-year-old inventor's life is a hard one.

Discouraged and bruised, Sam turned his attention to a newfangled and nearly unknown gadget, the galvanic battery. Almost immediately, the youngster discovered something no one had ever known before—gunpowder could be exploded with electricity. He also discovered that an insulated wire could carry electricity under water. Not realizing that his son had hit on a principle that would someday revolutionize naval warfare, old Chris Colt told Sam to quit fooling with explosives, please, before he blew the plant up, and to pay more attention to the textile business.

At the age of 15, Sam printed up a leaflet and distributed it around the town of Ware: "Sam'l Colt will blow a raft sky-high on Ware Pond, July 4, 1829."

Even a nervous father couldn't stand in the way of his son putting on a purely patriotic exhibition.

On the morning of the Fourth of July, Sam made a few last minute adjustments to a battery he had hidden in some bushes by the pond. Later, a large crowd gathered to witness a raft being blown sky-high. It was a lovely day, and the citizens were dressed in their holiday best, as they clustered around the edge of the pond.

As Sam knelt to touch off that first naval mine, he didn't notice what a strong current had swung the raft beyond where he had anchored the explosive. There was a sudden, awful roar as the dynamite thundered underwater, and hundreds of gallons of mud and water arched high into the sky, inundating the festive crowd in a wet, mucky avalanche.

Sam was not tarred and feathered, although there were some people so mad at him they would have enjoyed doing it. Something almost as bad happened. His father, who was a few dollars ahead of the game now, sent him to school at Amherst. His stay there was relatively successful until a mysterious explosion set the school on fire.

It was at this point that Sam was sent to sea. As an apprentice seaman, he could not take the wheel, but whenever possible, he would stand near the helm, watching the majestic ship plunge into the waves. One warm night in the Indian Ocean, he watched idly as the helmsman heeled the ship gently to the starboard. As the wheel turned, he noticed that each of its wooden spokes fell into a clutch so that it could be locked at any given position. There were rivets fastening each spoke at the outer edge of the wheel. Suddenly Sam found himself imagining that the rivets were revolving chambers, held perfectly in line by a clutch. Then he visualized a stationary barrel to receive cartridges that were loaded in the revolving chambers. And so the revolver was born.

Sam set to work with a knife, carving his concept of a "revolving gun" out of a block of wood. Many parts had to be discarded or laboriously remodeled, but gradually the model took form.

By the time the *Corlo* reached Calcutta, the wooden gun was complete. Sam just had time to look the town over, do battle with the three murderous *phansigars* and get back to his ship before sailing time. The English and the *phansigars* were doing their best to wipe each other out at the time, and Captain Spawlding didn't want to lose any of his crew to those deadly nooses.

As soon as the brig docked in Boston, Sam hurried home to his father. Christopher Colt was pleased with the boy's model gun and promised to have two of them made by the best gunsmiths available. Sam promised to return to Ware and help the factory chemists until the work had been completed.

Unfortunately, Chris Colt had no imagination and could not sustain his original enthusiasm. After talking to some good gunsmiths, who assured him that the revolver was nothing more than an amusing trinket which could never work and which, incidentally, would cost several hundred dollars to duplicate in metal, Chris was soured on the whole idea. But to satisfy Sam, he had a couple of cheap guns made up by a third-rate mechanic. Sam took one look at the finished products and knew they would never work. One of the revolvers simply refused to revolve. The other blew up in Sam's hand when he fired it. Physically, he was not hurt; emotionally, he was deeply wounded. Obviously, his father had no faith in him.

Sam told the old chemist with whom he worked, "Half of growing up seems to be the knack of keeping faith in yourself."

The next day he was gone.

Sam's only ambition now was to raise enough money to make fine models of his gun. Inspiration came to him in the form of "laughing gas." He had become familiar with nitrous oxide at Ware, and had witnessed the weird effects it produced in people who inhaled it. He got a supply of the gas and started giving demonstrations on the street corners of various towns. Within a few weeks he had collected enough by passing his hat to rent a theater. He advertised:

COME ONE—COME ALL!
AMUSEMENT—ENTERTAINMENT—THRILLS GALORE!
COLT AND HIS LAUGHING GAS!
MASONIC TEMPLE—JULY 29TH

He almost went broke at this point. Religious fanatics throughout the country were in the middle of a campaign against laughter, thrills, entertainment, or any form of frivolity. His first theater engagement fell flat.

Next time his pitch went something like this:

Doctor Coult, (late of New York, London and Calcutta) respectfully informs the Ladies and Gentlemen of Lowell and vicinity that he will lecture and administer Nitrous Oxide or Exhilarating Gas, November 29th at Town Hall. The peculiar effect of this singular compound upon the animal system was first noticed by the celebrated English Chemist, Sir Humphry Davy. He observed that when inhaled into the lungs it produced the most astonishing effects upon the Nervous System. Some individuals were disposed to Laugh, Sing and Dance, others to Recitation and Declamation and the greater number had an irresistible urge to muscular exertion such as wrestling, boxing and other innumerable fantastic feats....

Doctor C. has exhibited the extraordinary powers of this Gas in many cities in America, to Ladies and Gentlemen of the first respectability. He has administered it to more than 20,000 individuals, and has taken it himself no less than 1,000 times . . .

No proper churchman could cry out against education, so "Dr. Coult's Scientific Lectures" became all the rage.

There were drawbacks to playing straight man to a jug of nitrous oxide. In Boston a giggly lady who had inhaled one too many slugs of the gas started taking off her clothes. With the amount of clothes she was wearing, the project was an ambitious one. She was down to her last petticoat, when Sam managed to push her into the wings where a stout stagehand held onto her.

Rushing back onstage, Sam could see that the more pious members of the audience were shocked and offended by the woman's breach of etiquette. He tried to placate them. "Unfortunate woman. On rare occasions nitrous oxide has the terrible effect of making one feel that he or she is burning up. The subject attempts to remove as much warm clothing as possible in order to cool off. Some of the greatest scientific minds of the century are at present experimenting with this odd phenomenon. Indeed, it is believed that with proper control it may one day be possible to ward off colds by breathing a certain amount of this miraculous gas. Now, who would like to be next to submit, in order that we may learn still more about the marvelous qualities of this compound?"

No more ladies volunteered that night, but the clergy was reconciled to Sam's purely academic pursuits.

Another time, a giant blacksmith became violently homicidal under the influence of the gas.

"You!" he bellowed, lunging at Sam. "I'm going to kill you right now!"

Sam raced backstage with the big man right behind him. When they were behind the curtain, Sam turned and caught the giant squarely with a solid, hammering right to the jaw. The would-be killer slumped to the floor.

"Tie him up," Sam told the stage manager. Walking on stage again, he explained to the audience, "The last subject, understandably, is so embarrassed by his little outburst that he's ashamed to come back on the stage." He glanced toward the wings, where they were tightening cords around the blacksmith's thick arms. "He's actually blushing and wants to apologize to all concerned for his brief, irrational behavior."

The youthful "Doctor Coult" had several months of clear theatrical sailing through New England and half a dozen Southern states. When he had saved enough money, he headed for Washington and filed his invention with the U.S. patent office. A few days later, in Baltimore, he hired a top gunsmith to make two working models of his gun. Once the work was under way to his satisfaction, he moved farther west to bring the benefits of laughing gas to Memphis, Natchez, New Orleans and St. Louis.

Several months later he returned to Baltimore to see how his revolvers were coming along. John Pearson, the gunsmith, had completed one of the two guns. He took it out of his safe and handed it, wrapped in soft leather, to Sam. Colt unwrapped it slowly. The metal gleamed dully in the light coming through the shop window. Pearson had done a splendid job.

Sam held the gun in his hand, tested it for balance, then broke out the cylinder. As he examined the firearm, trying not to show his pride and pleasure, he said casually, "What do you think of it, John?"

The master gunsmith, looking at the gun that was to revolutionize warfare and alter the course of world events, said, "It's all right, for what it is."

Sam glanced up at him. "What do you mean?"

Pearson shrugged. "I mean, it's interesting and I guess it'll work all right. It's a real interesting novelty."

Sam Colt held in his hand the weapon generations of men had yearned for. Yet, he was going to find that most men, like Pearson, were so blind, so totally lacking in good sense and imagination, that they would not recognize the fabulous value of his revolver even when it was demonstrated to them.

Sam arranged to have Pearson make up several additional samples of the gun, in various calibers, and also to make up a rifle operating on the same principle. Such a large order was going to cost upwards of $3,000, and Sam was low on cash. He traveled to Canada, where "Doctor Coult" had never been heard of yet, to try his luck there.

It was a bust. For some reasons, Canadians simply were not intrigued with nitrous oxide. Sam advertised diligently, and tried both the "amusement" and the "scientific lecture" approach with equal lack of success. Soon Pearson was howling for money to continue his work in Baltimore.

With the "Doctor Coult" act laying eggs clear across Canada, Sam's alert mind turned to other possibilities. There was almost 100 per cent difference in the price of broadcloth in Canada and the United States. Since it was selling for half the price north of the border, the United States had declared an extremely large duty on it.

On a cold January morning Sam drove a light carriage across the border between the Dominion of Canada and the United States. Slapping their gloved hands together, the guards grumbled as they examined the vehicle.

"Man could freeze to death on a day like this," Sam said sympathetically. "They ought to build a good-sized customs house so you fellows could search carriages inside of it, out of this wind."

"You're right," a sergeant grunted. "They don't give a damn what happens to us. Go ahead on through."

Sam entered the country with several hundred yards of broadcloth concealed under a false floor he had rigged up within the carriage. With the profits he cleared on his first smuggling venture, he went back north and bought twice as much broadcloth.

Next time over the border it wasn't such a cold day. A careful guard noticed the bottom of the carriage, and the contraband was seized.

Sam was not jailed, but he was broke again. Pearson's work in Baltimore promptly ceased. At this low ebb in his career, Sam got a letter from a friend in Richmond, Virginia, claiming that Colt's Laughing Gas act could clean up in that amusement-minded town.

In Virginia, Sam began to rake in the green stuff hand over fist. In his correspondence with Pearson, he arranged for the gunsmith to hire a couple of helpers to push the work forward at a faster pace.

Then, to his delight, he learned that the Virginia Militia was preparing to buy a large order of pistols and muskets. He hurried to the commanding officer to demonstrate his pistol, with which he had become a dead shot, and to explain that he also had revolving rifles under construction. Pearson could increase his small shop's output tremendously on a go ahead from the militia; he could move to larger quarters and hire additional workers.

When the commanding officer of the militia refused to see him Sam was stunned. As he stood at the receptionist's desk, wondering what his next step should be, the officer walked out of his office and passed Sam.

"Sir," the young man said earnestly, "I have a multiple-shot firearm that will make Virginia's militia the best armed fighting force in the world."

"Nonsense!" was the brusk answer. "I know a little about you. A comic scientific entertainer. Hundreds of men like you have hundreds of schemes to defraud responsible citizens."

Sam followed the officer outside to where a hack was waiting. "But, sir, if you'll only examine the gun."

"I haven't time to waste."

Sam took the revolver from his pocket and sighted on a fence post that stood in a field across the street, about 100 feet away. He emptied the revolver into the post in less than four seconds, each shot pounding true into the wood. Through the rolling roar of gunfire, the post quivered under the impact of the lead.

The officer was too stupid to be impressed. "If you ever repeat that performance, I'll have you arrested," he snapped.

The hack lurched down the street, and Sam was left standing alone, bewildered and hopelessly defeated by arrogant idiocy.

He returned to his room and lay on his bed, staring at the ceiling. One thing was plain. He would have to give up the theater as a means of supporting himself. No one took an entertainer seriously. Gradually, his self-confidence began to return to him. He would devote his full time to promoting his revolvers. That was the only way.

Quitting show business forever, Sam next managed to borrow $1,000 from members of his family, on the terms that he pay back the loan with interest and surrender 50 per cent interest in the company he proposed to found.

Now, at 21 years of age, Sam took out patents in England, France and Prussia. Returning to America, he established a factory in Paterson, New Jersey. The Patent Arms Manufacturing Company was doomed to failure from the very first. A cousin of Sam's, Dudley Selden, was made business manager of the concern, and Cousin Dudley kept a tight hold on the company purse strings. Sam wanted to change the costly, laborious system of arms-making as it had existed for centuries—one gunsmith making one complete gun and then going on to the next. He wanted to install a production line in the factory, whereby each gunsmith would work on one or two specific operations in the manufacturing of many guns. He wanted his revolvers to be made with interchangeable parts. But such ideas were beyond Dudley's poor comprehension. He refused to let Sam squander company

146

funds on "foolhardy experiments." "We'll turn out our guns the good, old-fashioned way," he said righteously.

"Let's at least advertise," Sam pleaded. "Tell the public something about our product. We should buy space in newspapers, put on shooting exhibitions and give braces of our guns to important people."

Dudley was shocked. It was beneath the dignity of a corporation to advertise, he said. And as for demonstrations and giving away guns, was Samuel crazy? They were in business to work, to sell guns—not to give them away!

Under constant financial pressure, Sam journeyed to Washington to interest the government in his guns. After a great deal of double talk and red tape, the government agreed to hold an official test of his revolver. Just when this official test would take place, they could not say.

At his hotel one night, Sam struck up a chance acquaintance with Lieutenant James Hillman of the South Carolina Militia. Hillman was wildly enthusiastic about the guns. He not only bought a pair on the spot for his personal use, but insisted that Sam demonstrate them before the Militia Board.

The Board was unanimously impressed with Colt's weapons and was prepared to order 300 "turning guns" and 200 "revolving rifles." All they asked was a guaranteed delivery date. Another arms-maker, named Eli Whitney, was prepared to deliver good quality muskets and single-shot pistols at a moment's notice.

Sam sent word to his factory to speed up production and to let him know immediately the earliest delivery date that could be set. Cousin Dudley blandly wrote back that the factory couldn't possibly speed up production until the militia order was signed and paid for.

By the time they had finished bickering, the disgusted militia had purchased their needed firearms from Whitney's company.

Not long after this, the United States government finally got around to testing the Colt revolvers. An august body of seven high-ranking officers examined the revolvers at length and tried them out on the West Point firing range. To the everlasting glory of the Army, these profound thinkers decided that the Colt revolver, "from its complicated character, its liability to accident and other faults, is entirely unsuitable to the general purposes of military service."

A colonel in the group later voiced his private opinion.

"It's a clever gadget, but for real fighting it would never stack up to the good old musket with buck and ball and a full powder horn!"

The Navy tested the gun independently and came to the same conclusion: "Useless as a weapon. It will never work." If possible, the Navy went one step beyond the Army in lunacy. Sam had recently perfected a waterproof cartridge, the first in existence, which the naval authorities considered an "interesting novelty."

Two groups of fighting men, however, did realize the utility of the revolver. Both of them were groups who spent a great deal of time battling for their lives instead of battling for lunch tables in Washington's crowded restaurants as did the deskbound military dilettantes.

Colonel William Harney's command in Florida was being wiped out by the shrewd, hard-hitting Seminoles. The colonel managed to swing a deal to buy four dozen of Sam's revolving rifles. He and his men considered them a godsend.

The Texas Rangers, a new law-enforcement agency in the Southwest, was fighting Mexicans, Apaches, Comanches and assorted outlaws in an attempt to defend the Republic of Texas. Sam Walker, a Ranger captain, was sent to purchase all the Colt revolvers he could get his hands on.

The two Sams got together in New York. Colt, knowing Walker had traveled all the way from Houston to see him, expected some small word of praise for his invention.

Walker, a tall, skinny, taciturn man opened the conversation with, "If you're gonna invent a gun, why in hell don't you invent a goddam good gun?"

Taken aback, Colt quickly rallied to the defense of his brain-child. "It's the best goddam gun you ever saw!"

"Now looka-here," Walker continued, "the biggest bore you've made so far is a .34 caliber. Why goddam it, that hardly stings more than a Texas horse fly! What you got to do is build a man-sized sidearm like, say, a .44 caliber. And you need a good trigger guard. What do you want a man to do? Blow his own head off by accident? Then you got to get a handle to fit the size and shape of a man's fist. Taper it off more at the top. And another inch or two of barrel wouldn't hurt either, for accurate distance shootin'."

The two men developed a great regard for one another,

and out of their discussion was born the famous Walker Colt, a .44-caliber six-shooter considered by many to be superior even to the later, fabulous Peacemaker.

Walker was purchasing agent for a poverty-stricken band of fighters. He could only afford to have 70 of the Walker Colts made for the Rangers. Sam, by practically threatening to murder Cousin Dudley, succeeded in getting the company to forego its own profits and give the Texan 100 guns.

Despite Walker's harsh criticism of Sam's .34-caliber guns, he admitted, before leaving New York with his small arsenal, that they were selling for as much as $300 on the frontier; the Eastern selling price was $28.

Sam's favor to Captain Walker was the straw that broke Cousin Dudley's back. From that point on, he refused to forward any money at all to Sam for travel, promotion of the revolver, or anything else. He was signing the company's death warrant and the board of directors, composed of staid businessmen, backed him up. Within a year, the company folded up.

Sam was slowed down, but far from stopped. In the face of a current increase of international tension, he began to promote a plan based on the same principle by which he had attempted to blow the raft sky-high many years before. His idea was to fill the nation's ports with submarine mines which would blast approaching enemy ships to kingdom come.

In the meantime, he met an inventor, Samuel Morse, who had thought of another use for electricity. Morse's idea was to communicate over a wire by spelling out letters with electrical impulses. Colt's reaction was: "Wonderful! Brilliant! What an ass I am not to have thought of it!"

In 1841, as he was preparing to present his case for submarine mines to the government, Sam received word that his brother John had been arrested for a particularly brutal murder in New York.

Tried, convicted and sentenced to hang for the crime, John was found dead on his cell cot shortly before the day set for his execution. Apparently, he had stabbed himself, rather than take that awful drop from the scaffold.

When the tragedy was over, Sam went back to promoting his submarine mine. Remembering his theater days, he decided to appeal to public opinion through drama. Consequently, he set off numerous underwater explosions off Coney Island, and newspapers all over the country ran exciting accounts of Colt's incredible waterspouts.

"The beauty of the submarine mine," Sam told everyone, "is that it allows our coasts to be defended without risking the life of a single American boy." This point was so telling that Congress was obliged to consider Colt's invention.

Sam's strongest opposition came from the United States Navy—any Navy man knew the only maritime defense was a bigger navy than the enemy's; Colt's silly submarine mine couldn't possibly do any damage to a stout man-of-war. The officer who laughed the loudest at Sam was a thick-necked gent named Matthew Calbraith Perry. Commodore Perry said he would like to see a harmless waterspout stop a thick-hulled gunboat. Happily, Colt accepted the unintentional challenge.

Appropriately, the test was scheduled for the Fourth of July, 1842. An old, strongly built gunboat, the *Boxer*, was towed into position off Castle Gardens, where viewers on both the New Jersey and New York shores could watch. Sam was permitted to drop his mine into the water a few feet from the old vessel. It floated about ten feet under the surface. Reeling out wire, Sam's small boat then proceeded to a warship a mile and a half away.

A hush fell over the scene as the time for the test drew nearer. Five seconds, four seconds, three seconds, two seconds—

A mighty roar sent thousands of gallons of water churning high into the air. The *Boxer* was completely hidden from sight for a brief time by a curtain of falling water. When it cleared, the *Boxer* was gone. All that remained of the gunboat were a few chunks of debris floating here and there.

Everybody was dumbfounded and awestruck except Commodore Perry. His sanity might be questioned, but never his courage. "I'll bet you couldn't sink me with one of those things if I was sailing down the Potomac River," he said. He fully intended to try it, too, but Sam wouldn't let him take the risk.

Perry had brought up an interesting point, though. Could Colt's mine blow up a ship under sail? Although he refused to blow up a ship with the commodore and a crew aboard, Sam agreed to another demonstration in the Potomac. Well before the weather-beaten schooner used in the test arrived near the mine, her crew and officers abandoned her. The schooner moved on majestically until she was abreast of the submerged mine. Then Sam touched off the explosive. There was a horrendous blast and the schooner was turned into chunks of driftwood. For some time Sam commuted between New York and Washington sinking bigger and tougher ships to demonstrate the potency of his submarine mine. The tests ended with the total destruction of a 500-ton man-of-war on the Potomac, a spectacle which Congress adjourned to witness. Since their navy was rapidly becoming smaller the nautical brass finally had to concede that Sam Colt had something there, all right. But that was about as far as they went. The government officials paid Sam for his time and expense and said that they would keep him in mind and if they ever needed any submarine mines they would call on him.

About this time, Samuel Morse suggested that Colt join him in his expanding telegraph business. Sam contributed his underwater, insulated cable so that they were able to lay telegraph wires across the bottom of bays and rivers, instead of building expensive lines over or around waterways. Sam, personally, laid the first cables connecting Manhattan Island with Brooklyn and New Jersey. It was a profitable undertaking, and he was making more money than most men ever see in their lifetime. Still, he had not yet begun to hit his stride.

The Lone Star State was up to its ears in trouble. The Mexican government had been irritated no end when Texas was admitted to the Union, and the provisional president of Mexico, Santa Anna, decided he was going to take Texas away from the Yankees. General Zachary Taylor rushed down to discourage Santa Anna, there was an exchange of unpleasantries, and the Mexican War was on.

Old Rough and Ready soon discovered that one man armed with a brace of Colt revolvers was equal to a patrol of men with conventional arms. A Lieutenant Thornton was surrounded by a platoon of Mexican soldiers. He had two six-shooters, and in no time at all, it seemed as if the Mexican platoon was surrounded by Lieutenant Thornton. He nearly wiped out the opposing force singlehandedly, then rode calmly back to the Texas lines. In dozens of other cases, wherever there were a few Colts, the tide of the battle was rapidly turned, regardless of the superior number of Mexicans.

Taylor sent Captain Sam Walker east at top speed to contact Colt. Walker found his old friend in New York, at the Carlton House.

"I want 1,000 pistols in a hurry," Walker said. "Name your own price this time."

"I haven't got a gun shop," Sam told him. "It went out of business quite a while ago. Matter of fact, I haven't even got a model to copy."

When the Ranger had explained the desperate situation, the two of them spent hours combing New York for a Colt without success. Returning to the hotel in the middle of the night, they sat down at Colt's desk, and Sam drew specifications for his revolver from memory. The next morning they went to Whitneyville, Connecticut, and contracted with Eli Whitney to have the parts for 1,000 guns made up.

A few weeks later, Walker headed back for Texas with his revolvers, stipulating that he wanted 1,000 more as soon as possible.

At last, with the money he had saved from working with Morse, Sam was in a position to go into the arms business on his own. He set up a factory in Hartford, in a small, three-story building on Pearl Street.

As soon as he got into production, Sam gave braces of beautifully engraved and decorated guns to Captain Coffee Jack Hayes and Brigham Young. Through presenting these elaborate gifts to men of action whose opinions were respected, Sam received a lot of good advance publicity. Soon orders for his weapons began to filter in from France, England, Russia and China.

After the Mexican War, one of his best customers was the Government of Mexico. South of the border, they had learned the value of Colt's guns the hard way. Every Mexican wanted to be armed with a sixgun. He received endless orders from the Western frontier, too. Business was so heavy that Sam had to keep an English warship waiting a week while he finished an order of guns for Her Majesty's officers in South Africa.

In order to keep up with swiftly multiplying orders, Sam had to operate at maximum efficiency. At last he realized his ambition of a smoothly functioning assembly line. He was, from all evidence, the first man in the world to institute mass production methods. He personally trained each of the growing army of men working for him, and as soon as he was satisfied that the factory could operate without him, he took off on a business tour of Europe.

In Turkey, Sam easily arranged an audience with the sultan. Colt's name had spread around the world like wildfire. The sultan presented him with a richly jeweled snuffbox, and Sam gave the Turkish ruler a fine set of guns.

"They are exquisite," the sultan said through his interpreter.

Sam nodded proudly. "Yes, the Russians thought so. They liked them so much, they ordered 10,000 of them."

When the interpreter translated this message the sultan frowned thoughtfully. "Well, come to think of it, I guess I could use about 10,000 of them in Turkey, too, just to be on the safe side."

Sam didn't think it necessary to explain that he had sold the Russians that huge order of guns after mentioning that the Turks were buying revolvers by the boatload.

Back in America, Sam learned that practically everyone who had ever made anything from a cap pistol to a squirt gun was suing him. From Eli Whitney down to the humblest gunsmith, they were all claiming that Sam Colt had infringed upon their patent rights. With fame and fortune, he found, there also comes a great deal of annoyance. He was to be in court for one suit or another, continually, until the end of his life.

One canny lawyer, attempting to prove Sam's patents invalid, claimed that a revolving firearm had existed as far back as the 15th Century. Sam and his lawyers asked for time to prepare their defense. At the next session, three of Sam's workmen staggered into court carrying an ugly, cumbersome machine that weighed in the neighborhood of 200 pounds. This, Sam's lawyer explained, was an exact replica of the ancient "revolving gun" that the opposition had been discussing so eloquently before. "Would the learned counsel like to continue his discussion of the similarity between the weapons?" he asked tartly.

The suit was dropped.

Sam built a new factory on the outskirts of Hartford that was the epitome of modern design and efficiency.

His treatment of his employees was a century ahead of its time. He insisted on the unheard practice of giving them a full hour for lunch, and even built a large social hall and equipped it with games, books and other recreational facilities. He also built excellent houses for his workers near the factory. As for the factory itself, it was kept spotlessly clean, and the vasy armory was spotted with wash basins with hot and cold runing water, soap and towels. Sam did one more revolutionary thing that was regarded as completely ridiculous by other employers—he guaranteed his workers old-age pensions.

Deciding to branch out, just in case peace on earth came to pass in his lifetime and guns went out of vogue, Sam got into the willow furniture business. When he learned that the best willow craftsmen in the world lived in Potsdam, Germany, Sam informed his German agent that he would like to hire all the workers in the town. The agent wrote back and said it was impossible. These people had been living in Potsdam for close to 15 centuries, and they didn't want to move. Besides, the workers wouldn't leave their families just for higher pay in America.

Sam said that was understandable, and instead of moving the workers, or even the workers and their families, he proposed moving the whole town to America, brick by brick and person by person. In the end, Sam only had to duplicate the town of Potsdam near the arms company and bring the residents' household possessions to Hartford. So the buildings remained in German territory, but everything else—men, women and children, beds, tables, chairs and kitchen dishes—was moved across the Atlantic. Sam never did make any money on furniture, but the Potsdamers, it developed, were fine musicians, so Sam let them make up an official company band. It was judged to be one of the best in Connecticut.

The English were the most stubborn and unreasonable people on the face of the earth as far as Sam was concerned. He spent half a dozen fortunes trying to open a factory in England. Apparently, they resented an American making guns for them and hamstrung him in every way they could, despite the fact that the Crimean War was just around the corner and their soldiers were poorly armed. But after the Charge of the Light Brigade, they realized that good guns were a matter of life and death and begged Sam to sell them his Colts.

154

Sam was neutral. He sold England arms, then he went to Czar Nicholas' court and offered to sell the Russians arms, too.

The czar was in the market for 100,000 muskets, but he didn't have the facilities to train his soldiers in the use of such a modern weapon. He insisted that Sam let one of his military experts accompany him to America to examine the guns and to receive instructions in their use. This presented a problem, with the powerful British Navy controlling the sea, but it didn't phase Sam. He took the inspector along as his valet. They stopped off briefly in London to see how Sam's factory was going, then sailed peacefully to America.

Within the next few years, Sam married a Hartford girl named Elizabeth Jarvis and built her a tremendous mansion overlooking his arms plant. A boy was born to them.

Sam saw the Civil War coming long before most men. While other Northerners made laughing remarks about sending a few schoolboys down South to quell the rebels, Sam was certain there would be a stupid, fierce, bloody war that would go on for years. He set out to arm the North as quickly as he could, certain that the Union would need all the help it could get.

Some say the Civil War killed Sam Colt, that he couldn't stand seeing the country he loved tearing itself to pieces. Whatever the cause, his health declined rapidly in 1861. He died at his home on the tenth of January, 1862, at the age of 47.

Shortly before his death, Sam was attacked from the pulpit by a preacher, who claimed that his "infernal machines" were vicious, mass killers. "Men do not need such instruments of violence!" he insisted.

One night the preacher was beaten and robbed.

Sam sent him a Colt with the following brief message: "Please accept my sympathy and a copy of my latest work on moral reform."

THE SAGA OF
THE PONY EXPRESS

Nothing ever stopped a Pony Express rider—not Indians, outlaws or nature. In a tough spot, he saved the mail first, his horse second and his own skin last.

The lone rider crouching low over the pommel of his saddle rode hell-for-leather down the sandy slope, his powerful gray mare stretching her nose straight out and straining every ounce of her 1,200 pounds of muscle to achieve more speed. They hit the flats below the slope, and the mare, responding to the expert pressure of the rider's legs, flew across the sagebrush-spotted desert, her streaming mane whipping the air. Her thundering hoofs were a blur of pounding speed.

On the crest of a long, low ridge a mile before him, the rider saw an Indian lope into view on a painted mustang. Within a few seconds, more than 20 other Indians appeared at the rim of the crest, strung out in a wide line that blocked his passage. "Pah-Utes, Betsy," he whispered in the ear of the big, clean-limbed mare beneath him. "Cain't go around 'em, so we'll plow right through the middle of 'em."

He could have whirled his mare around and retreated

safely, since the gray could outrun any Indian pony ridden by any Paiute in the country. But such a thought never occurred to him. He touched the loaded, spare cylinder in the left pocket of his jacket, just to make sure it was where he could get it in a hurry. Then he pulled his Colt from its holster and barreled toward the waiting war party. Cocking quickly and firing slowly, he knocked two of the Paiutes off their horses, as the gray mare hurtled through the line of Indians. The warriors, armed with rifles and bows and arrows, tried to block his way, but the rider and horse roared right through them and on across the flats. As he turned to fire back at the Indians, his Colt's hammer fell on a spent shell, and he took out the fresh cylinder and reloaded. The Paiutes chased him for about a mile, whooping and shrieking while they cut loose with arrows and bullets. He sent three more of them sprawling onto the hard-baked floor of the desert, before his mare pulled away from the slower Indian horses.

Forty minutes later, the rider pulled to a stop near the Dry Creek Express station. The station attendants came running out at the sound of the mare's hoofs. The rider patted the unusual saddlebags he carried and said, "Mail." Then he let go of the reins, leaned far out of the saddle and fell to the ground, dead.

"Jesus God!" one of the attendants muttered. "Old Joe must have a dozen arrows stickin' in 'em!"

A young man hurried up, leading a fresh, prancing, gray mare with a deep, powerful chest. He glanced briefly at the dead man, took the bloodied saddlebags off the exhausted mare, and less than a minute later, was racing on into the West. The first attendant watched the rider galloping swiftly out of sight. Turning to his partner, he shook his head. "Nothin' on God's green earth stops these fellas."

The other man knelt beside the dead rider. "You oughtta know by now the Pony Express ain't just a mail carryin' company." He added softly, "It's closer to a religion!"

The Pony Express was in existence for only 19 months, from early 1860 to late 1861. It was made up of less than 100 riders, and less than 500 horses. The horsemen carried mail by quick relays over the 2,000-mile stretch between St. Joseph, Missouri, and Sacramento, California.

But the Pony Express was greater than the sum of all its parts. It operated on sheer audacity, courage and stubbornness. It struck such a chord in the heart of the nation that it will be remembered forever. More important, it was the Pony Express that first united America into a single nation. In the 1850s, from a practical standpoint, the Missouri River was closer to Europe than to California. America was two, widely separated countries—one in the East, the other in the vague, faraway, almost mythical West. When the government in Washington made Utah a Territory, the news went from New York by boat to Panama. There it was carried over the isthmus to another boat. The second boat took the news to San Francisco. From Frisco it was taken to Salt Lake. It was nearly three months after the event that the Mormons heard about it.

Two of the first men who tried to fill the desperate need for a fast news service were Major George Chorpenning and his partner, Captain Absalom Woodward. After risking his neck a thousand times, Chorpenning wound up broke. He sued the Post Office Department, which had annulled his contract when the going got too rough, but he never collected. Woodward risked his neck once too often. He and five other men were carrying mail between San Francisco and Salt Lake. Woodward's body was found months later filled with arrows; no trace was ever found of the others.

A man named John Butterfield got a stage route going between St. Louis and San Francisco in '58. It swung as far south as El Paso, Texas, and was hundreds of miles longer than a direct route through the Rockies. The Post Office paid him $600,000 a year to carry mail, but it still took close to a month to get information from one half of the country to the other, if the Butterfield stages were running on time. America was still two nations, separated by a gigantic wedge of blistering desert and high walls of rugged mountains.

In early 1860, a tough young stage driver named Sawed-Off Cumbo was hoisting a drink in a San Francisco bar, when a tall, equally rough-and-ready-looking gent moved up beside him. "Hear you can ride," he said.

"Ride?" Sawed-Off said. "Why hell, I won't even bother with a horse it takes less'n six men to saddle." He tossed down his drink. "Who wants to know can I ride?"

"Me. Bolivar Roberts."

158

"I've heard the name. Heard you can tell a mule from a mustang, yourself. What you want with me?"

"I'm hirin' for an outfit in Kansas. Name of Central Overland and Pike's Peak Express Company. Some call it the Horse Express. Figure to take the mail straight through from St. Joe to Frisco in good time."

"What'ya call good time?"

"New York to Frisco, coast to coast, in ten days."

"Ten days?" Sawed-Off's jaw dropped with amazement, and it took real will power to force the sagging jaw back into place. "Say no more, mister," he said at last. "Ten days is absolutely impossible. And any outfit crazy enough to try it, is an outfit I'd be pleased to work for."

All through the West, agents recruited men to ride for the Horse Express, soon to be established by Russell, Majors and Waddell, a giant freighting concern with headquarters in Leavenworth. They were looking for the top riders and toughest men to be found in a land filled with fine horsemen and fearless fighting men. They gathered together the most colorful, capable crew ever assembled on the frontier. Besides Sawed-Off Cumbo, there were Broncho Charlie Miller, Tough Littleton, Bill Cates, Whip Randall, Cyclone Thompson and more than 70 others like them. Muleskinners, wranglers, miners, sailors and bullwhackers, they had four things in common: they were lean; they were confident almost to a point of cockiness; they were honest; and they could ride anything that had room between the ears and the tail for a saddle.

At the same time, the finest horseflesh available was bought up by the Overland. Those days, a fine horse went for $50. The Horse Express was paying between $150 and $200 for its animals. Way stations—sometimes a cabin, sometimes a cave in the side of a mountain—were thrown together along the route, with main stopovers at places like Fort Kearney, Julesburg, Fort Laramie, South Pass, Fort Bridger, Camp Floyd and Carson City.

The whole country was tense with excitement as April 3, 1860, came closer. This was the day the Horse Express, which the people instinctively renamed the Pony Express, was to pick up the mail at St. Joe and try the incredible task of getting it to Frisco within eight days. Gamblers were offering odds of 100 to one that the mail wouldn't even get through, let alone in eight days, for the high passes were still frozen in deep drifts of snow and ice.

If one man can be given credit for the success of the Pony Express, that man was William H. Russell. When Bill Russell first spoke of his Express idea to his partners, Majors said, "Every outfit that ever tried the direct route has gone bust, Bill. Only way to do it is to have the Post Office back you up. And the Post Office won't do that unless you're already running the mail successfully. They might not even do it then, they're such all-fired idiots in the Postal Department."

"How much would it cost us to start?" Waddell asked nervously.

"Well," Russell said lightly, "I figure we could make a start with $100,000."

Waddell, who was the cautious, mousy type, took his money out of the company as soon as possible. Russell and Majors had the courage to stake their huge financial empire on the success or failure of the Pony Express. "I'm a businessman," Majors told Russell a few days before the historic third of April. "And this is absurd from an economic point of view. We've sunk nearly a quarter of a million dollars into the Pony before the first letter's been carried. We've put in nearly 200 stations across a country two-thirds dominated by Utes, Paiutes, Comanche and Sioux. If we don't get government help fast, our whole freight business could go down the drain." He rubbed his shaggy mustache absently. "But you know, Bill. If this works, it'll bring the country together. And even if we take a loss, there's a lot of satisfaction in doing a thing like that."

Russell nodded. "Hear the latest that the Postmaster General had to say? Old Joe Holt says our Pony Express is, 'Completely out of the question.' "

"There's some hope, then," Majors chuckled. "He's never been right about anything yet. Well," he shrugged, "everything from carrier pigeons to camels have tried to bust across that monstrous country between here and the Pacific. Pretty quick we'll see what the best riders and best horses in the country can do."

Bill Richardson paced angrily back and forth in front of the St. Joseph railroad station. It was April third. Bill had drawn lots with the other Pony Express Riders and had won the honor of racing the first lap with the mail.

The Leavenworth *Times* had run a three-inch-high head-line that screamed: "CLEAR THE WAY AND LET THE PONY EXPRESS GO THROUGH!" Other papers had been equally enthusiastic in every part of the country. There was a huge crowd milling around the station, and a brass band was booming out a blaring version of *Camptown Races*. Richardson's fine-limbed, blooded mare was pawing the ground impatiently. On her back was the small, tough saddle designed especially for the Pony Express. Over the saddle, with slits cut to hook around the cantle and pommel, was a thin, square blanket of leather with four padlocked pockets, two on each side. This was the *mochila*, the Pony Express saddlebags for carrying the mail. Bill was dressed lightly; short-heeled boots, blue whipcord pants and a red flannel shirt topped off with a gray Stetson and a buckskin jacket. There wasn't an ounce of unnecessary weight in the compact Landis saddle, or in Bill's pockets. He had even swapped a heavy, gold watch for one that weighed a few ounces less. He was sweating with eagerness to go.

Ironically, the train bringing mail into St. Joseph was late. It would have been laughable that the iron horse couldn't get the mail to the flesh-and-blood horse on time, except that it was too serious for laughter. The train was due at four o'clock. It got there at six. A railroad executive had a speech all ready, but Bill grabbed the packet of mail, rushed to his horse and was halfway out of town before the railroad man had said, "Ladies and gentlemen."

Less than an hour later, Bill came in sight of the first way station, more than 20 miles from his starting point. As he approached the shack, he took a small horn from the side of his saddle and blew it to alert the station attendant, so that no time would be wasted. But the rolling hoofbeats of the horse were signal enough. When Bill pulled up in front of the station, the attendant was waiting with a fresh, saddled horse. "Where the hell you been?" he demanded. "You're two hours late!"

Before he had finished the sentence, Bill had swung the *mochila* onto the fresh horse and was starting away. "Explain later," he yelled back. "*Adios!*"

Bill rode 80 miles at a full gallop, wearing out half a dozen magnificent horses. He was only an hour late when he passed the mail to Bob Rising, his relief.

161

"What happened?" Bob asked as he took the *mochila* and fastened it over his own saddle.

"Train late. Luck," Bill panted. That was all the time there was for explanation. Bob's spirited mare reared once, then plunged on toward the West.

On the San Francisco end of the Express, the sendoff, in true California style, was gay and festive. There were speeches, several bands playing at once, parades, fireworks and guns blasting the air. Hank Hamilton, the rider who had won the honor of starting off with the eastbound mail, allowed a pretty *senorita* to put a string of bells around his mare's neck. The first part of his race would be a simple boatride to Sacramento.

At Sacramento Hank was the first man off the boat, and he was nearly out of sight before the boat captain thought to blow the boat's steam whistle to cheer him on his way. He arrived at Placerville, where his relief, Warren Upson, was waiting, half an hour ahead of time. Warren had the toughest part of the 2,000-mile stretch, not counting Indians. He had to go up and over the wicked Johnson Pass, where snow drifts were piled as high as 30 feet.

A Placerville miner standing near the young man offered some advice. "Looky here, Warren. Nobody can git up over the Pass. Friend o' mine tried 'er in snowshoes and didn't make it. You better wait a while less'n you git yourself killed or froze."

Warren couldn't argue with him—the man was right. Wordlessly he took the *mochila* from Hank, whirled his pony and plunged up the trail toward the wicked, snow-covered peaks.

The horse Warren was riding was not a blooded animal like those most used on the Pony Express. Those long-legged, deep-chested animals were fine for open country. But for the snowed-in mountain country, there was nothing to match the small, tough mustang, whose heart Warren could feel beating against his legs. This wiry mount could kick and plunge and fight his way through snows where the racier beasts would kill themselves.

A blizzard roared down off the peaks as they reached the foothills, and the going was almost impossible, but Warren never thought of turning back. The mustang plowed on toward the summit lost above them in the blinding storm. Trails and landmarks were blotted out as they neared the Pass. Warren finally got off and led his pony, for fear he might accidentally ride off a precipice.

They came to a ravine with steep slopes on both sides of it, and Warren felt a tug on the reins as he started through. The mustang balked. Puzzled, he turned to see if the animal was lamed. It didn't seem to be favoring any leg, but it was trembling slightly and refused to move forward.

A sudden, low whispering noise made Warren whirl back toward the ravine. The volume increased to a throaty rumbling, and finally into a thunderous roar, as thousands of tons of snow and ice boomed down off the left side of the mountain and buried the ravine in a huge, white sea. When the deafening noise and churning mists of snow had settled, the pass was blocked, and would remain blocked for months. Where the snow had come down off the mountain, there was a solid sheet of ice. The only place to go was over the top of the mountain. "To hell with the Pass, anyhow," Warren muttered to his horse. "We'll take the scenic route."

And somehow, through that bewildering blinding maze of tortuous ice and snow, they got over the mountain. When at last they were moving downhill again, Warren realized that he was about as lost as one man can get without the help of two others. He got on the mustang and gave it its head, and the wise, sure-footed little horse took him through the blizzard and down out of the mountains. At the first swing station, the courageous mustang was able to rest, but Upson had just started. After four changes of horses, he arrived half-dead at Carson City, 85 miles away from Placerville.

"I'm late," he muttered to his relief rider.

"Late?" the man laughed, slapping him lightly on the shoulder. "Hell, man the Donner party wasn't in no worse fix up there than you was!" He jumped into the saddle without touching the stirrups and hooked his toes in, as his mount sped on to the East.

Within a few days, somewhere out in that vast expanse of wilderness, the mails from East and West crossed, as two unknown horsemen hurtled past each other with a whoop and a brief wave of the hand. Under impossible conditions, the immense expanse of land between St. Joseph and San Francisco, still referred to vaguely on most maps as "The Great American Desert," was bridged in ten days. The best time ever made before was more than cut in half. Europe was suddenly much farther

163

away from the East Coast than California. America was, for the first time, one nation in fact as well as theory.

Newspapers and citizens, from one end of the country to the other, went wild. Loved ones at the far edge of America were no longer in another world; they were only ten short days away. The Pony Express riders were the heroes of the hour. At least everybody thought so except the Post Office Department. For reasons best known to themselves, the postal authorities refused to recognize the Pony Express. Butterfield's Stage continued to collect $50,000 a month from Uncle Sam for its mail services. The Pony, which moved like lightning, and made the Butterfield news obsolete by the time the stages got there, was getting exactly nothing. In the first days of its existence the Pony Express was going broke.

Bill Russell and Alexander Majors had a short, bitter talk one night after supper. "What in the devil is the matter with that fool Holt?" Russell said, biting off the tip of a cigar with a disgusted grind of his teeth. "It costs us $16 an ounce to deliver mail. And our charge is $5 an ounce. We're losing 11 iron men on every ounce. And we're better than twice as fast as anyone else."

"We're not only losing money," Majors grunted, "we're losing riders. It'd be easier to face a firing squad than to face the routes some of them have been riding. The Paiutes killed three of them between Salt Lake and Placerville in the last couple of days. Some of the boys are quitting."

Russell watched the smoke of his cigar curling up over the table. "As long as my money lasts, I'm staying with the Pony. I believe in it."

Majors nodded. "I know how you feel, Bill. You can count me in to my last dollar."

The riders on the Pony Express had a creed: "When in trouble, save the mail first, your horse second and your own skin last." When the scorching desert or mountain blizzards were not testing this creed, the Indians were. The redskins had never seen such swift horses as those on the Pony. They decided that those odd-looking leather saddlebags contained a sure-fire, powerful medicine, and they were determined to get *mochilas* to toss over their own horses, so that they would run as fast as the wind.

Where most men on the frontier had their choice of a hundred different routes to avoid Indians, the Pony

164

riders could only go from one swing station to the next. It was the easiest thing in the world for a few ambitious bucks to sit around and wait for the Pony boy to ride right up to them. Although countless attacks were made on the riders, only one *mochila* was ever lost. One rider, one horse and one *mochila* left a swing station in Nevada and disappeared as though a giant, invisible hand had snatched them out of the desert.

In May, nearly 10,000 Paiutes went on the warpath, and Nevada and parts of Utah became a huge battlefield. Hundreds of settlers were killed and tortured, and their homes were burned to the ground. But the Pony riders kept taking the mail through.

Reining up before the Cold Spring Station one afternoon, Pony Bob Haslam found it leveled by fire. He took the time to check and see if either of the attendants were alive. He found them in the charred remains of the station. They had been tied up and left to burn to death in the fire. The livestock had been driven away. As he mounted again, Pony Bob saw smoke signals rising thinly into the clear blue sky before him. From the tracks around the ruined station, he knew it must be a large warparty. He took a long breath and slowly exhaled. "Let's move on with the mail, horse," he said, urging the mare into a quick lope toward the next station.

At the next stop, Sand Creek, the attendant came out with a fresh horse. "Pah-Utes got Jim yesti'day," the man said. "He went out to hunt for deer. He never came back."

"I ain't gonna take that horse Sam," Pony Bob said. "You swing onto 'er yourself and ride along with me. Redskins got the boys back to Cold Springs. They'll be along here pretty quick now, I'd reckon."

"Well, okay, if you say so," the attendant agreed reluctantly; he hated to leave the station he was responsible for. "You know Injuns better'n me."

"Yep. Get a move on."

They rode about an hour. The sun had settled behind the hills to the west, as they topped a high ridge and glanced back at the shadowed prairie. At this distance, the station looked like a tiny, square dot in the immense barren space behind them. As they watched, a swarm of miniature figures raced toward the building, and a moment later, they could see flames leap into the air.

"Glad you made me leave," Sam whispered.

After a few more minutes of riding, the two men circled a large boulder and ran into a camp of 30 or 40 Paiute warriors. "Follow me—fast!" Pony Bob ordered. "Yeeoowhh!" he shrieked, charging straight into the amazed warriors. A few of them were on horseback, but most of them were seated in a circle. They scrambled to get out of the way of the screaming demon bearing down on them. One brave raised a rifle and Pony Bob shot him through the chest. The mare smashed into two running Paiutes and knocked them sprawling into the hard sand. And they were through the warparty, riding at a furious clip that soon left the Indians far behind them.

Pony Bob and the men like him would not let ten or 10,000 Paiutes stop the Express. But Alexander Majors and Bill Russell were tired of having their men murdered. They called a halt to the Pony Express and demanded that the government do something to protect the riders. The government did nothing, until 110 civilian volunteers went out to fight the Paiutes and were nearly massacred in June. Then it belatedly sent a troop of Army regulars against the Indians. The savages were scattered, and the Pony Express, after a delay of about four weeks, went back into action.

From this time until the end of the Pony Express, there was never another break in the schedule. As a schoolteacher in Nebraska said: "I could look out my window and see the Pony rider coming, and when he sped by the schoolhouse, I knew it was exactly nine o'clock. I could set my clock by it."

Nature, savages and outlaws still plagued the Express riders, however.

A man who dealt severely with the outlaws was William F. Cody, better known in later life as Buffalo Bill. According to Bill, one time he knew there were outlaws on the path ahead, so he put a spare *mochila* on top of the real one. Sure enough, two armed thugs held him up at a bend in the pass. Young Bill threw the spare *mochila* square into the face of the nearest badman, shot the other and rode quickly away.

Another man, who worked for the Express, was William Butler Hickok. Wild Bill, then known as Duck Bill because of his unusually shaped nose, had a job as station attendant. He got in a fight with a fellow named McCanles. According to Bill's story, McCanles and a group of nine husky, armed confederates jumped him for no

166

reason one day, and he wound up slaying the whole gang with his gun and a knife.

You wrap up all the godlike myths of Buffalo Bill and Wild Bill Hickok, and toss in a dash of Cossack, and it is not a bad picture of most Pony Express riders. Pony Bob Haslam, when two other riders were laid up, once rode at a full gallop through 400 miles of rough country. "You get any rest at all?" a friend asked him later. Bob grinned. "Some. Mostly in the saddle. The horses knew the way as good as I did. But they didn't allow for my height. Three times they ran under low branches while I was dozin'. I am the only fella I know who's got 30 to 40 mighty short ribs in his chest." Jack Keeley once spent nearly 40 hours in the saddle without a rest. He wore out 32 horses before he lay down. Jack slept 20 hours and got up ready to ride again. Sawed-Off Cumbo got so tired once, he put three slugs into an oak tree. It was bitterly cold, and the branches were crackling like shots under the pressure of frozen sap. Sawed-Off figured somebody behind the oak was shooting at him, so he blazed back at the hidden enemy.

Toward the end of 1860 the Pony was entrusted with carrying perhaps the most vital news reports that have ever gone from one seaboard to the other. Lincoln was elected President on November 7, 1860. At least four horses were ridden to death, as the Pony Riders raced across the wilderness with this crucial message. Soon after this, in California, tens of thousands of Southern sympathizers organized an armed rebellion against the Union. Fifty thousand guns from Springfield, Massachusetts, were somehow delivered into their hands, and it was their plan to make Sonora and California an independent republic, then throw their strength behind the Confederate states. The Pony Express hurtled across the continent with the news, and brought back instructions from Washington for the defense of California. The way was now cleared for the tensely awaited inauguration address. To a great extent, war or peace depended on what this tall, shambling newcomer to the American scene would say in his speech. Fierce storms lashed the frontier after Lincoln's address, but the Pony—even though two horses were lost in quicksand, one in a flooded river and two others in mountain blizzards—got the President's words to the Pacific in record time. And it

167

was the Pony which thundered into the West with news of the firing on Fort Sumter.

Despite the gallant achievements of the Pony, it still did not receive any government help—even though the government relied completely on the Pony now. Butterfield's southern stage route was controlled by the South, but to the end, it was lavishly supported by Congress and the Post Office. Butterfield was getting as high as $60 and $70 for carrying a letter, most of which funds came out of the U.S. Treasury. Finally, the stage route was ordered to move north, and it joined up with Wells-Fargo. During this same period, the Pony was getting $3 for each letter it carried, although the expense of carrying a letter had risen to about $18. Russell and Majors, operating at a tremendous deficit, had sunk their fortunes into the Pony. Russell, a broken man, finally called it quits, and Majors kept the Pony going briefly by himself.

Things got so bad a rider galloped into his home station and said, "Payday! Got my money?" The riders were paid from $50 to $100 a month.

The super at the station said, "Yep. Just one thing. If you git paid, the horses ain't goin' to eat."

"Yeah?" the rider said. "Things are that bad? Well, hell, the horses gotta get their grain."

Majors soon sold out to Wells-Fargo. As if purposely waiting for such a move, Congress immediately voted to give Wells-Fargo $1,000,000 a year to help the outfit carry the mail. They had never given the original Pony Express one cent through the long, turbulent, hellish months that it had brought, and held, the nation together.

Wells-Fargo kept the new Pony going for a while, but the one thing that could whip good men on good horses was now coming into its own—the telegraph wire. The tall, skinny poles had been edging farther and farther westward. Congress offered $400,000 to the company that would string wires across the frontier. In October of '61 the job was done, and the Pony Express was dead.

Bill Cates was the last rider to make that final, lonesome ride. He hit the last swing station between Placerville and Sacramento. Then a mile from the station, his horse stuck its foreleg into a gopher hole and fell without warning. The horse was all right, but Bill's leg was broken by the weight of the horse landing on it. A stagecoach pulled up a few minutes later, and the driver saw Bill trying to crawl to his horse which was grazing a few feet away from him.

"C'mon," the driver yelled, jumping down from the high seat. "Lemme give you a hand. We'll take you and the mail into Sacramento."

"Like hell you will!" Bill exclaimed. "Pony Express don't need no help. I'll make it!" He tried to stand up but could not.

A passenger got down from the coach and walked over to Bill. "Howdy, Bill. Reckon I could ride relief for ya'?"

Cates looked up and swore. "Sawed-Off Cumbo! Hell yes! Just so's it's a Pony man who takes 'er in. That's what matters."

Sawed-Off leaped into the saddle, swung the mare around and sped away toward Sacramento. Bill Cates watched as the rider disappeared around a distant bend in the road, and the dust from the flying hooves settled slowly. "Damned broke leg," he muttered through clenched teeth. He grunted with pain as the driver helped him stand. "But that mail'll get there the way it ought. Carried by a good man on a good pony."

DEVIL OF A MAN

The wildest hell-raiser of them all, Jack Slade lived most of his life with a gun in his hand and died with a rope around his neck.

A lone horseman rode into the little town of Julesburg, Colorado, one memorable November day, causing all kinds of commotion. At sight of the straight, tall figure in the saddle, people along the busy main street whispered frantically to one another and broke into quick walks or running steps that took them off the main thoroughfare onto sidestreets. Doors slammed as businessmen ducked into their offices. Windows thumped down and curtains were gingerly parted so that peering eyes could get a better look at the stranger who rode his big pinto so well.

As the horseman passed the barbershop, the barber, a new man in town, laid down his razor and said, "Who's that feller? What's all the fuss about?"

"That's Slade, the new Overland Super, come to take his job today," the man in the chair answered. "And," he continued nervously, "since Jules Beni ain't gonna like giving up his job, someone's likely to get kilt in the next ten minutes."

170

Joseph Alfred Slade, the man on the pinto, was destined to become a legend in the West. Roaring drunk, Slade could clip off a man's jacket button with a revolver at 20 paces. Half drunk, he liked to gallop his snorting stallion into a barroom and blast the tops off a row of whiskey bottles. A powerful man, he was once shot six times with a .45 Colt—and walked away. A drinking man, he was the wildest hell-raiser of his time.

Slade's first definitely sober yell was voiced in 1829 in Carlyle, Illinois. After a quiet childhood and a few years in school, he joined Company A of the First Regiment of Illinois Foot Volunteers at the outbreak of the Mexican War. His Army sidekicks renamed him "Jack" and taught him what a few shots of firewater can do to gladden a man's heart. Both the name and the taste for liquor stayed with him the rest of his life.

Back in Carlyle after the war, Jack got into a friendly argument with the local Goliath, a giant of a man who didn't like to lose arguments. One thing led to another and they finally stepped outside to settle the dispute to everyone's satisfaction. In the terrific scrap, Slade's opponent quickly got down to the roughest form of street fighting which, added to his great size, made it look temporarily like a one-sided battle. Never one to come out second best, Jack promptly grabbed a heavy boulder and walloped his adversary over his bull-like head with it as hard as he could, with the result that his enemy stopped living.

A short while later, Jack arrived at the far bank of the Mississippi, safe from Illinois law, and headed for high adventure in the West.

Slade's first few years in this new, raw country are obscure, but in the middle 1850s he went to work with the Overland Line. His solid reputation as a fighter was established one day while riding between two Overland stations with a friend. Three Sioux warriors swooped down on them to collect a couple of easy scalps and Jack's reception was short and to the point.

His partner on the trip said: "Slade was the fastest man I ever hope to see. The Indians charged us, and before I had time to think what to do, he pulled his gun and fired what sounded like one, close-echoing shot. It was really three separate shots. Every redskin was dead before he hit the ground."

This was a neat bit of work that brought Jack's name

to every man on the Overland, but the whispers that followed were sinister. Jack cut off the ears of the three savages and strung them around their ponies' necks. Then he slapped the horses away to carry the souvenirs back to the tribe. It is significant that Indians caused Jack little trouble after that. When they heard he was around, they made it a point not to be.

Big Ben Holladay, owner of the Overland Line, and Ben Ficklin, his right-hand man, finally decided that Slade was the man to take over the agency at Julesburg, the meanest, toughest town on the entire Overland Line. Located near the South Platte River one mile east of Fort Sedgwick, starting point of the Bozeman Trail, Julesburg was the major stopover along 300 miles of Overland Trail which formed the Sweetwater Division. In taking command of the station at Julesburg, Jack automatically became superintendent of all stations of the Sweetwater run, a job that would have made any man but a Jack Slade start looking for other work.

Not only were there knifings and shootings at every drop of an ace of spades along the rugged 300 miles, but the man whose job Slade was taking was the most hated and feared man in that part of the country. His name was Jules Beni, and Julesburg was named after him. A grizzled, slovenly gorilla of a man, Beni was getting a kickback on every dishonest dollar made in his territory. He liked his job.

So it's no wonder Beni's eyes narrowed viciously as he watched a square-shouldered man swing down off his pinto outside the Overland office, on November 3, 1859. In a moment Jack Slade entered the office and handed his credentials to Beni, without saying a word. Jules glanced at the papers and then into Slade's eyes.

"Ben Ficklin never did like me," he rumbled deep in his throat, "but he's got no call sending a new man around who won't last out the week."

"I'll last," Slade said softly.

Jules sat down behind the heavy oak desk in the center of the office. "I'll tell you this, Slade. If someone else don't kill you, I'll damned well do it myself."

Jack leaned forward, resting his hands at the edge of the desk. "It's been tried. I'm giving you two hours to get out of town and when you're out, I want you to stay out."

Beni snarled and his hand disappeared suddenly as he

172

grabbed at a gun in the desk drawer before him. Jack couldn't see the revolver but he figured it was there. Surging forward, he whipped the big desk off its short legs and slammed it into Jules as though it were a box of matches. Jules, his chair and the desk crashed into the corner of the room in a splintered, undignified heap. Swearing furiously, Jules struggled from under the desk looking for his lost weapon.

"If you find that gun, you're a dead man." Jack had pulled his own revolver and it was leveled at Jules.

"Get your stuff. Get out."

Jules glared at Slade several full seconds before his own gaze dropped. By looking deep into someone else's eyes, a man can sense who is master, and Jules suddenly realized that he was not. In a few minutes he was gone. The erstwhile strongest man on the Overland Trail had been dethroned, and in his place was a man who would not be considered simply strong, but who would be thought well nigh immortal through the length and breadth of the Overland. In the few minutes these two men spent together, there began one of the most vicious personal feuds in the West's history; one in which both parties would be supposedly killed, before their final terrible meeting.

Jack Slade rode over every foot of the Sweetwater Division, learning the land perfectly. He gave the Julesburg station a thorough overhauling and settled down to inspire a fear of law and order in the hearts of the renegades and killers who lived in his domain.

One day, as the first snowfall of winter was threatening in a gray morning sky, a westbound stagecoach rumbled over the frozen dirt road into Julesburg. The driver hurried into the Overland office and told Slade that four men had robbed the stage two miles out of town. Jack got some men together and they saddled up quickly. Then, their horses' hooves thundering over the solid, cold earth, they raced down the main street and out along the line. Blissfully unaware of the new Overland man, the thieves were taking no pains to cover their trail. Within two hours Slade and his men caught them. Taking the part of judge, jury and executioner, he hung all four of of them to a high gate post and hurried back to town in time to beat the threatening storm.

Before a month passed, he hung two more men who

had been stealing horses. A half-dozen hangings began to dishearten even the roughest men in his jurisdiction. There was talk of murdering Slade in every saloon on the Sweetwater, but no one quite felt that he was just the right man to do it. Jules himself was living in a cabin 30 miles west of his old headquarters, and while he drank prodigiously and talked fearlessly of revenge, his visits to Julesburg were rare and he avoided Slade.

Not satisfied with eliminating the out-and-out lawlessness in his kingdom, Slade now began to work on the more or less legal racketeers. Some hay for Overland stock was accidentally burned, so he bought several bales from a local farmer. After it had been delivered, he found that it was half willow branches and weeds. He promptly collared the unfortunate farmer and chained him to a heavy log near where the half-and-half hay was stacked. Then he set fire to the poor quality merchandise and threatened to throw both farmer and log into the blazing mass. The miserable seller of hay was hysterically apologetic and promised in tears to raise his standard of business to a higher level. Slade said he had a good mind to chuck him in the fire anyway, just for the hell of it. When he finally unchained the farmer, the terrified man couldn't get out of Julesburg fast enough. Business ethics in the district showed a marked improvement after that.

During those peacemaking months of '59 and '60, Slade changed the way of life of every person along his Overland empire. He also changed his personal way of life by marrying a girl named Virginia Dale who could outride any man on the Sweetwater and outshoot most of them, and who was so good looking that a few years later Virginia City was to be named after her. As a settlement, Virginia City was originally named Varina City after the wife of Jefferson Davis. But within a short time it became Virginia City, as it is today, in honor of Jack Slade's wife.

As a married man, Jack led a tranquil life for about three months, but a calm existence dulled his senses. It very nearly caused his death.

In the late spring of 1860, he spent an evening at a Line station about 25 miles west of Julesburg with Jim Boner and Phil James, the attendants. In the morning he rode on toward the next station to make a routine checkup. An hour later Boner noticed that Jack had left his revolvers hanging near his bunk.

"Phil," Jim yelled to his partner, "Slade has gone off without his guns and I'll just bet that Jules shoots him if he gets a chance."

The two men leaped onto their horses and galloped off to catch up with Jack.

They were too late.

Slade arrived at his destination and dismounted. He sat on a wagon tongue and talked for a few minutes with a boy who was a helper at the station, then stood up and started toward the building.

Jules was standing in the door.

Slade's jaw tightened as he realized he was unarmed, but he said nothing. Jules pulled his revolver and started shooting. He emptied the Colt .45 without missing once, and still Slade stood erect, defying all known laws regarding the impact of .45-caliber slugs. Then, stiffly and awkwardly, Slade started walking toward Jules. Cursing with mixed amazement and fear, Jules rushed to where his horse was tied at the side of the building and drew a double-barreled shotgun from the saddle. Whirling, he let loose with both barrels at almost point-blank range, and buckshot tore into Slade in a hundred places. Only then did Slade buckle and slump to the ground. Jules sprang to his horse and spurred out of the station at a dead run.

Moments later, Boner and James arrived to find the station attendants looking down at the riddled body of their friend.

"Damnation," James uttered.

"Never saw a man so dead in my life," said an awed station attendant.

And then the dead man moved and whispered an angry curse. Slade was alive.

The closest doctor was at Fort Laramie, 167 miles away. Slade's friends rode the entire distance without stopping, halting only for seconds to change mounts. They made the same time on the way back. When the haggard doctor saw the stricken man, he declared the case hopeless, saying he had never seen a living man with so much lead in him. But Slade's fantastic strength nourished a spark of life that gradually grew and cheated the Grim Reaper out of what he must have thought was a sure thing.

The health and strength of Jules was proved in a rather remarkable manner at the same time. While Slade

175

was recovering from his wounds, several of his enraged comrades hunted Jules down and captured him. They strung him up and rode away leaving him for dead.

Jules's spine was not broken, however, and within a few minutes he was cut down by two fellow thugs who had watched the hanging from a distance. That night, aside from a stiff neck, Jules was in excellent shape for a dead man. Having developed a distaste for being hung, though, he moved to Rocky Ridge where there was less chance of the process being repeated.

By the time Slade recuperated, Rocky Ridge had become a worse hellhole than Sweetwater had been. Big Ben Holladay decided to put Slade in charge of both divisions, and he told him, "Jack, I want you to get Jules and let everybody know you got him."

Slade was pleased to be in action once more. Like the devil he was, he strode in where both angels and fools feared to tread and began jamming law and order down the throats of the more reluctant citizens of Rocky Ridge.

One Sunday morning while riding alone, Slade was ambushed by eight men who silently took him to a remote cabin where they intended to murder him at their leisure. Jack asked if he could say good-bye to his wife and one of the men left camp in the direction of Jack's home.

After a few hours he returned with Virginia Dale riding haughtily beside him.

Wordlessly the beautiful girl brushed past the men into the cabin where Jack was being held. Half a minute later Mr. and Mrs. Slade stood in the doorway of the cabin, Jack holding two cocked revolvers and Virginia leveling a third six-shooter in a most businesslike manner.

"Because you boys let me see my wife, I won't kill you," Jack told them. "Now lower your gun belts very carefully."

The two Slades galloped away leaving eight thoroughly disgruntled, disarmed men locked inside the cabin.

The unsuccessful attempt to murder him irritated Jack. He held Jules completely responsible for it, although he never knew whether the Frenchman had originated the scheme to capture him. The fact that he would carry several ounces of his enemy's lead to the grave with him added to the irritation, and Ben Holladay's words about getting Jules helped the mania along. Jack's revenge, when it came, may have been the result of long and careful thought. It may have been inspired by a hard morning of harder liquor. Whatever the cause, his vengeance proclaimed him a fiend incarnate throughout the West, and this reputation went to the grave with him as sure as the lead from Jules' guns.

Two of Slade's friends were riding through the hills in the early morning when they found Jules sleeping in a shack and took him prisoner. They forced their surprised captive to dress and started the long trip back to Julesburg.

It was noon when they presented him to Jack in a saloon where the Overland superintendent had been drinking most of the morning.

Jack's blue eyes darkened and he said, "I've been waiting to meet you for a long time, Jules."

Jules growled an obscenity, but he was afraid. He had every right to be.

"Let's tie him up out here." Jack led the way through the bar. Thirty feet behind the building they tied Jules to a snubbing post.

Going into the bar with his friends, Jack bought a round of drinks. Then he went to the back door of the saloon and pulled a gun from his holster. The first time the revolver roared, one of Jules' fingers was blown off. Slade holstered the gun and went back to the bar for a few more shots of whiskey. After several minutes he went back to the rear exit and shot again, this time tearing a chunk of flesh out of Jules' arm. Jules fell to his knees and whimpered deep in his throat like a great, sick bear who breathes heavily and knows he is dying. The bartender, his face pale, started to drink long, nervous gulps of his own liquor. The two men who had brought Jules in joined Slade in one more drink, then made uncomfortable excuses and left the saloon as Jack walked back and shot Jules' kneecap away.

It was a long afternoon.

News of this terrible thing Slade was doing traveled swiftly up and down the Overland. Those within hearing range trembled whenever a pistol shot came to their ears. Women bit their lower lip and prayed as they worked in their homes. Men listened grimly and were silent. Slade was the law. Besides, everybody knew he had received

177

enough punishment at the hands of Jules to have killed half a dozen lesser men.

A man cannot tell another man what to do with a cowardly killer who has attacked him unarmed and shot six balls of a .45 and two barrels of buckshot into him. And yet what Slade was doing now was not human. Nor was it animal. It was the work of the devil.

It was late afternoon when Slade fired a final shot into Jules' limp and mutilated body. After drinking nearly two quarts of whiskey he still knicked the battered corpse neatly from the saloon door. He paid for his drinks at the bar and then walked slowly out of the back door. Over the body of Jules, he leaned down steadily. The barman, watching him, stared with new horror as Slade pulled a knife and carefully sliced off the two ears of his dead foe. Straightening, Jack replaced the knife, thrust the two ears in his pocket and walked away. The barman, who could usually pour a rock-steady drink after seeing a man shot, closed his saloon for the next two days.

For the next few months, anyone with a dishonest thought in his head, thought also of the manner in which Jules had been taken out of circulation and went elsewhere to try his illegal schemes.

Bored, Slade began making a science out of getting as drunk as possible, riding his mount into saloons and shooting hell out of any targets that took his fancy. Everyone in his domain would vouch for the fact that he often shot buttons off men's coats while heavily in his cups. This fine accomplishment was slandered by some people who insisted he would occasionally do it the easy way, facing the buttons head on, which would lead to the untimely demise of the owner of the button.

In the summer of 1861, Joe Plante, the owner of a general store outside Independence Rock, wrote Slade a letter. Two "bastards" named Charley Bacon and Harry Smith had murdered a neighbor of Plante's, Doctor Bartholomew. They had done some work for the doctor, then shot him in an argument over wages. They'd then forced the doctor's widow and children out of the house and had settled down to wait and see if the "great Jack Slade" would do anything about it.

Jack sent back a typically pithy message. "Get two ropes ready."

Slade, Plante and two friends found Bacon and Smith

playing cards and drinking in their recently acquired house along with a ratty looking crony known only by the name of Pete.

Bacon made a dive for his gun that was on a couch at his side. Slade shot him through the shoulder to discourage that course of action.

"What'll we do with this one?" Plante asked, gesturing toward Pete.

"Since he likes their company so much, he can keep it," Slade said. "We'll hang them all together. But first," he commanded, "I want you three to give me all your money."

After they'd emptied their pockets, the two thoroughly frightened killers and their quivering sidekick tried gamely to make a show of bravery. They asked Jack's permission for one last drink. Receiving it, they raised their glasses with trembling hands and Bacon toasted, "May we all meet in hell."

Twenty minutes later they alone knew whether the toast had been fulfilled.

An hour later, word was racing from mouth to mouth that Jack had murdered an innocent man as well as robbing his victims. Since Slade didn't say much about it to anyone and also because it held less excitement value, no one even bothered to tell what Slade did right after the killing. It's a fact, though, that he hunted up the Bartholomew widow, offered his sympathies and asked, "How are you fixed for money?"

"Well," she said hesitantly, "I'm sure I'll be all right."

"This may help a little for a starter." Jack put $523 on the table.

"I couldn't," Mrs. Bartholomew muttered huskily.

"Some fellows thought it might help your kids."

"Well, perhaps, since they thought of it that way."

The widow wanted to go back east to Omaha, so Jack sold her ranch for her at a little more than it was worth. At the same time, Virginia sewed outfits of clothes for the children and gave Mrs. Bartholomew some of her best dresses. Slade himself bought the tickets for the family to go to Omaha.

When he and Virginia saw the Bartholomews off on the stake, the widow tried to thank them but could not. Her voice choked up and words would not come. She kissed Virginia, then leaned forward suddenly and kissed Slade on the cheek.

179

With the close of the Bartholomew incident, both of Slade's divisions again became too peaceful and the only way he could enjoy himself was by causing his own excitement. There just weren't enough bars in the 500 miles of Rocky Ridge and Sweetwater to keep him happy with his drinking and smashing, so he started making long trips to Denver and points west. To further brighten his life he sometimes dressed in fancy clothes. On one visit to Denver he bought a beaded buckskin suit at the astronomical price of $750. This not only brought more color into his existence, but gave rise also to good-natured insults from friends who knew him well enough to dare joking with him. The insults in turn, gave rise to stimulating brawls in which Jack had great fun decimating saloons. He developed an uncontrollable passion for riding wildly into bars and testing his marksmanship on bull's-eyes such as shot glasses and bottle tops. Though he had started this habit some time before and continued it all his life, he never found a horse who would share his enthusiasm. Every one of them reared, bucked, plunged and kicked frantically, all of which added to the general amusement. Slade also reveled in finding huge, gaudy mirrors and windows, for he obtained much joy from pulverizing them with tables and chairs.

When all the smashing was done though, and he sobered up, he would revisit the scenes of destruction and pay without question for all damage done. Many barmen along the Overland counted on Jack for most of their profit. If he and his friends came to a saloon, that saloon owner knew he could count on a brisk trade of whiskey through the night and then be able to get twice the price of broken mirrors, windows and assorted furniture the next day.

With all Jack's glorious carnage, however, it was a mediocre store in Fort Halleck with only small windows that caused him to part with the Overland Line.

Gorgeously plastered one afternoon, he rode a half-tamed buckskin into a store to purchase some tobacco. The buck reared and caused Jack to slam his head against the ceiling. Three soldiers and the storekeeper thought this was funny, and laughed.

Jack laughed, too, and shouted, "I'm glad we've all got a sense of humor!" Then he spurred the pony right through the flimsily constructed counter, picked up the storeman by the scruff of the neck and heaved him out

180

the door. Dismounting, he tossed one of the charging soldiers through the window nearest him. It was a fiasco, because the man got stuck in the frame and Jack had to throw the other two soldiers out the door. While his pony smashed out a section of wall with his hooves, Slade warhooped with joy and showed his contempt for the merchandise in the shop by flinging it into the street. Then he went elsewhere for his tobacco.

The store happened to belong to a sutler. When Jack returned the next morning to pay for the fun, he found an Army Captain kicking through the wreckage and cursing furiously. As soon as the officer realized it was Jack Slade who had committed the outrage to United States Army goods, he calmed down, but coldly refused payment and stalked away.

At that time, the Army was the biggest customer of the Overland Line. When, through official channels, the company received a request to change the superintendent of the Rocky Ridge and Sweetwater Divisions, it was tantamount to a command. Big Ben Holladay fought the "request" as long as he could. He tried to explain that Slade was the best peacemaker on the Overland Trail, which was to the advantage of the military. The Army brass remained adamant. In 1862 Slade and the Overland Line parted company.

After that Jack turned to independent freighting and almost immediately distinguished himself by doing the impossible. In the late fall of '62 a merchant named J. B. Hardy had a large, valuable cargo stranded at the mouth of Milk River. A Missouri steamboat had set out too late in the summer to get the goods to Fort Benton. The skipper had unloaded the stuff at the Milk River to be transported by land, but he had overlooked the rather important fact that there was no land route between the river and the cargo's destination, Varina City. If the merchandise were left it would spoil. And Hardy could find no freighter who would try to get it out with winter coming. Slade was intrigued by the impossible situation. He hired a gang of good drivers and they plunged recklessly to the Milk through a wilderness never traveled by wagon before, snatched the cargo out of the freezing clutch of Old Man Winter and fought their way through unbroken, virgin territory to Varina.

Jack liked Varina City so the next summer he moved to a ranch two miles outside the town.

Virginia, an intelligent, willful woman, started a subtle campaign to stop Jack's heavy drinking. She encouraged his home interests and despite Slade's hellion reputation they became known as one of the handsomest, most charming couples in all Montana. Virginia was especially popular among the people of Varina and Jack had the pleasure of hearing various citizens begin changing the appellation of that town from Varina to Virginia City.

Jack occasionally left his wife to go out and have a few drinks with the boys, but in general his drinking for a time was moderate and his behavior reasonable.

This gently enforced sobriety and sedateness looked good on the exterior, but internally the devil in Jack was growing each day, grumbling and straining to be let loose.

On the first of March, 1864, the demon in him came shrieking out, driving him on to one last, long drunk to end all of his drunks. As he loped away from home, Virginia did nothing to stop him. She'd seen it coming. She knew better than to try changing a man like Slade in too short a time, and she could not know what the coming nine days were to bring.

Slade arrived in town and was soon surrounded by several boisterous friends who had been looking forward to a wild time for nearly two months. During the last weeks Virginia City had been deadly calm due to the sudden realization of the terrifying power of the Vigilantes. On January 14th, this grim band had hung the notorious Henry Plummer and his gang en masse. It was enough to make even thoroughly law abiding gentlemen think twice before spitting on the board sidewalks.

Jack Slade entering this quiet, icy tense atmosphere with alcoholic intentions, was rather like shooting a wild stallion into the midst of an elderly ladies' tea social. By midnight he and his friends were ranging hilariously from bar to bar, the lesser drunks whooping it up and raising general hell while Jack, the happy, human bull dozer, wrought havoc, smashing and shattering bars, windows and mirrors to his heart's content. He bought constant drinks for the house, giving Jules Beni's ears as token payment and then putting them back in his pocket. News of his turbulent activities spread quickly throughout Virginia City and to Nevada City, a mining town one mile away, where Captain Williams, executive officer of the Vigilantes, listened with an expressionless face and said, "A man's got a right to get drunk once in a while."

The next day Slade was back at it again. Companions joined him and left him in shifts for no one could keep up with his pace. Stories of his feats traveled swiftly from mouth to mouth during the next few days as he continued his wonderful marathon of drinking and wrecking. Each man who repeated tales of Jack's bacchanalian prowess added to the telling of it until people had serious doubts as to whether the man was a mortal. He never slept, said the yarns, but went from day to day and night to night becoming more wide-awake and jubilant as he went along.

Many Virginia City stores were closed by prudent owners who waited impatiently for Jack to bring his rampage to a halt. Discreet townsmen kept their houses dark at night. Slade had killed no one so far, but the whole town fearfully retreated into itself as day after day, the one-man siege continued.

On March 8th, after eight days of drunken orgy, the Vigilantes began to lose patience. Captain Williams told his irate followers to give Slade one more day. They agreed with their executive officer's suggestion.

That night Jack and several carousers decided on a bit of culture and entered the Virginia City Theatre where a dramatics group with more thespian zeal than common sense was daring to put on a play. Slade, as might be guessed, was soon bored with the heavy dialogue and attempted to brighten it up with lusty, gleeful ad-libbing. The actors refused to enter into the gay spirit of the occasion, especially when Jack shot out the footlights and the play was postponed in the second act. Later that night Slade's jolly crew wandered back and forth between the few bars that were not now boarded up, singing and shooting.

In the early morning of the next day, Jack saw the milkman making his rounds and bought a gallon of milk to quench his thirst. Sitting alongside the driver in the front seat of the wagon, he raised the unfamiliar liquid to his lips. Just then an optimistic member of his gang blasted three shots from his revolver at the morning star. The horse pulling the wagaon jerked nervously forward, making Jack spill some of the milk over his shirt. This struck Slade as an opportunity for great merriment. Roaring with laughter, he held the gallon container over the milkman's head and slowly emptied its contents over the frightened man.

At noon Sheriff Fox of Virginia City at last approached Slade timidly with a warrant for his arrest for disturbing the peace, made out by Judge Alexander Davis. Slade was angry and indignant. He ripped the warrant into slivers of paper and threw them to the ground. Fox was told in eloquent terms that he would be shot if he ever attempted such an unfriendly bit of skulduggery again. Later, Slade saw Judge Davis and threatened him, too. Jack had a derringer against the judge's forehead for several seconds to lend authority to his threats while he talked. Both sheriff and judge were brave but intelligent men. They agreed to let the matter drop.

In the late afternoon, though, a high man in the Vigilantes, Alex Topance, hunted Slade down to warn him that the Vigilance Committee had had enough. "Slade," he said sincerely, "get your horse and get out of town or there will be hell to pay."

Jack knew that Topance was not a joking man. He said, "I'll leave after a while. But first I'm going to have a few more drinks."

Thus began a sinister comedy of errors. Topance thought Jack was ignoring his warning. He went to Nevada City and told Captain Williams that Slade was still going strong. The executive officer started collecting a small army of men to march on Virginia City and take Slade by force.

But Jack had meant what he told Topance. After a few drinks he walked out onto the darkening street and headed for a store owned by the president of the Vigilantes, Pfoutz. There, as he had done countless times along the Overland, he apologized for whatever trouble he had caused and offered to pay for all damages.

While Slade was talking to Pfoutz, Captain Williams, backed by more than 200 miners, cowmen and merchants, came into Virginia City and asked where he could find the "devil."

Gathering in numbers, the Vigilante mob moved on to Pfoutz's store and crowded around it.

Surrounded by men holding cocked revolvers and rifles, Williams opened the door of the store and said, "Slade, I want you. Come on out."

184

Genuinely puzzled, since he had been in the act of making retribution for his behavior, Slade asked, "What do you want with me?"

"Come along and ask no questions," Williams commanded.

Pfoutz, although president of the Vigilantes, did nothing to interfere with the action of the executive officer. Someone produced a rope and a few feet was cut off the end of it to tie Slade. Then they marched him along to a spot where the remaining length of hemp could accomplish its grim purpose.

As the mob rumbled mightily along the street, a friend of Slade's rushed breathlessly to Jack's home to tell Virginia what was happening.

Virginia had a horse that was known throughout Montana for its speed. Within seconds she swung to her saddle and galloped furiously toward town in a fearless, headlong race in absolute darkness over steep, rocky terrain where any misstep could mean her own death. Soon she could see flickering lights in the tiny, faraway buildings. Her long black hair whipping in the wind, the magnificent woman hurtled swiftly through the night.

While Slade tried vainly to reason with Williams, an experienced Vigilante expertly looped a hangman's noose into the end of the rope.

Scores of people in the crowd cried out to stop the hanging, but the small group of Vigilante leaders under Williams went ahead anyway. One man whom Slade had befriended threw off his coat and shouted, "You'll murder this man over my dead body!"

Several rifles swung ominously toward him, hammers clicking, and he dropped to his knees sobbing.

Williams knew that Virginia Dale would have been informed of Slade's danger by now and that she could stop the hanging if it were not done before she arrived.

"Men, do your duty," he said gruffly.

"Oh, my dear wife!" cried Slade as the noose was drawn tight about his throat. He died with no fear in his heart, a prayer for Virginia on his lips and Jules Beni's ears in his pocket.

When Virginia's mount thundered into town, she knew she was too late. The mob had melted away into little knots of people along the street. There were many sympathetic, ashamed faces in front of the Virginia Hotel.

She jumped from the saddle and ran into the lobby where she found Jack's body lying on a couch.

"We just brought 'im in," a young friend of Slade's told her. "Didn't want you to see—"

Virginia, tears blinding her, whirled angrily on the friends gathered silently about her husband. "If you couldn't stop it why didn't you shoot him?" she demanded fiercely. "I would have shot him! No such death should have come to such a man."

Then she kneeled near Jack and put her head on his chest. In the morning two women who were close companions of Virginia's went to try to console her. She had knelt beside her husband through the entire, long night, without moving.

Virginia hated the town bearing her name so violently that she refused to bury Jack there. She ordered him a coffin lined with tin and filled it with alcohol to preserve Jack's body. In the spring, when the snow-filled passes became negotiable, she transported the coffin 400 miles to Salt Lake City. There, on July 20, 1864, the devil of a man was finally buried, after having reposed almost five months in the highly potent liquid he loved so much in life.

THE THREE LIVES
OF BAT MASTERSON

Bat was the kind of a man who could do most anything he set his mind to—gunning down buffalo or outlaws, gambling, fighting or writing a column for a newspaper.

It was summer in Dodge City, Kansas, biggest boom town and railroad junction in the Far West. Into the shouting, teeming crowds swarming along Front Street, one June morning in 1872, rode young Bill Masterson, an ancient muzzle-loading long-gun crossed on the saddle before him. A handsome six-footer with a high forehead and large alert eyes, he attracted more attention than most strangers in town. Josiah Wright Mooar, an old-time buffalo hunter, was particularly impressed with the way he sat his horse and held his gun. Mooar, who was trying to fill out a buffalo-hunting crew, walked over to the kid as he swung down from the saddle. "Son, you lookin' for a job?"

"What kind of a job?"

"Buffalo crew. Skinnin' or stackin'. Top pay. You can make maybe $100 a month."

"I'm your man. My name's Bill Masterson."

"I'm Joe Mooar."

They shook hands on the deal and two days later moved out of Dodge with fresh supplies and a full crew.

Bill soon learned the buffalo-hunting business. He worked a short while as a stacker, spreading the hides taken from the day's kill out flat over an acre or two of prairie. The hides weighed about 300 pounds apiece, and they had to be dried a full day, on each side, under the blazing sun. When the sun had done its work, the hides weighed about one third of their original weight and were almost as hard and stiff as cast iron. They were then ready to be stacked into carts and hauled back to the railroad station at Dodge for shipment to the East.

Masterson quickly moved from stacking to skinning, and eventually, when someone in camp discovered he was a dead shot, to the top of the trade, which was hunting.

Most men consider themselves lucky if they can make a go of one career. Bat Masterson took on three and was successful in all of them; he was a buffalo hunter, a gunman and gambler, and finally, an editor on a famous New York newspaper. He was unbelievably fast and accurate with a gun, he was intelligent, and he was courageous. He was one of those rare people who can do most anything they set their minds to, and do it well.

His full name was William Barclay Masterson. The nickname "Bat" came along later when he served as a deputy under Wyatt Earp in Dodge City. As a boy, he helped work the family farm in Iroquois County, Illinois, along with his father and his brothers Ed, Jim and Tom. Then at 16, he decided that farming was not for him. He wanted excitement. Always appreciative of a good editorial phrase, he followed Horace Greeley's dictum: "Go West, young man . . ."

With his Sharps "Big 50," Masterson soon made a name for himself as top hunter in Joe Mooar's crew. "There was absolutely no danger," he later wrote of his buffalo-hunting experiences. "It was on a par with shooting cows in a pasture, except on occasion, when an injured bull would charge a hunter. You did have to know something about buffalo, though, to do the job right. A good hunter shot to hit the buffalo's brain. Hit properly in the head, the animal would fall within a few feet of where he was shot. If you hit him in the heart, he could run four or five hundred feet before going down, and that might set the rest of the herd running, too."

Joe Mooar liked a rough, tough crew under him. It was his one sure way of protecting himself from the bully-boys who made a profession of stealing hides from the honest hunters. Indeed, many of Mooar's men were convicts themselves. These assorted murderers and thieves were, for the most part, belligerently loyal to Joe. But once, a fellow named Jason Cook tried to sell Joe and his friends out. Jason wandered out of camp one night, just before the crew was about to head back to Dodge with the buffalo hides. Most of the boys, exhausted from a grinding week's work, were sleeping soundly, but Bill Masterson, a light sleeper, woke up as Jason was moving out of the light of the campfire. He became suspicious and pulled on his boots and followed the man.

Half a mile out of camp, Jason joined a gang of waiting confederates who had carts all ready to pick up the valuable skins. Ten minutes later, as they were starting their highjacking operation, Bill Masterson's clear voice came firmly through the night. "We've got you surrounded. First man that moves, dies."

It's likely he would have kept them surrounded, too, all by himself, except that Jason panicked and made a break through the silver moonlight playing down on the scene. When he ran, the others scattered too. Masterson fired his Big 50 just once. A few minutes later Mooar and the others joined him. The only trace of the crooks was a stream of Jason's blood trailing off to the east. They all got away, but Mooar was satisfied; his hides were safe.

"Any man who can surround a whole gang with a single-shot rifle is a good man to have next to you in a gun fight," he said.

The truth of that statement was demonstrated when Masterson and eight other people held off some 300 Arapahoe and Cheyenne Indians for 21 days at the Battle of Adobe Walls.

Adobe Walls was a trading depot consisting of several small buildings and corrals. Joe and his brother, John Mooar, left Masterson and the rest of the crew there while they went back to Dodge for supplies.

Among those staying at Adobe Walls were: Jim Hanrahan, the owner of Hanrahan's Saloon; Tom O'Keefe, a blacksmith; Bill Olds and his wife, who ran the small restaurant there; and completing the list, Bill Masterson, Billy Tyler and a few more buffalo hunters.

The big Indian war party that swooped down upon the buffalo range was as well organized as it was swift. Two camps of hunters were wiped out before they could fire a defending shot.

Adobe Walls was sleeping peacefully at two o'clock in the morning, unaware of the onrushing redskin juggernaut. Then something happened that has not been explained to this day. There was a loud, cracking noise from the ridgepole supporting the roof in Hanrahan's Saloon, the largest and most solid building in Adobe Walls. Instantly, the men sleeping there woke up. Masterson lit a lamp and they examined the ridgepole, a thick beam, about two feet in diameter. To their surprise, they found it was as solid as ever. They could think of no reason why it should have snapped.

The men scratched their heads, and Hanrahan poured a drink around as they started talking it over. It was getting on toward morning, anyway, and there was no real point in their going back to bed.

Whatever the noise was, it saved their lives. They were wide awake half an hour later, when the Indians silently surrounded the camp and prepared to take it by surprise. Masterson's keen ears picked up the sound of unshod horses moving over rock, and he went outside to investigate. He saw the savages advancing over the crest of a nearby hill and ran back into Hanrahan's to give the alarm. "Get your guns," he said. "Trouble coming."

When the Indians swarmed into Adobe Walls, they found they had grabbed a mountain lion by the tail. Masterson assembled everyone in the saloon, and under his leadership the handful of men made a formidable fighting force.

The whites had every available gun loaded and ready for action; the trading post had practically unlimited guns and ammunition. Each man would fire one gun, drop it and pick up another, repeating the maneuver about ten times.

The warriors screamed past Hanrahan's, pouring arrows and lead slugs into the building. With Masterson's Big 50 setting the beat, a mighty chorus of firearms answered them. Thinking that there were at least 100 men

190

inside the building the redskins retired to think the whole thing over.

Masterson knew that a war party as large as this one must have attracted considerable attention on its way to Adobe Walls. "All we have to do," he told the others, "is sit tight until help comes. It's bound to get here sooner or later."

"Maybe not," Billy Tyler grumbled. "Maybe nobody knows the spot we're in."

At daylight the Indians made another rush upon the small, determined saloon-fortress. Hanrahan was a miserable marksman, so he made himself useful by serving up drinks to the others as they blasted gaping holes in the enemy lines.

Masterson kept the consumption of alcohol down to a point where the men could feel a glow, but their eyes and trigger fingers were as steady as ever. Probably no warriors were ever jollier at the height of a battle. In attack after attack, 300 crazed savages charged, only to be repulsed each time. Everybody was feeling pretty good, except Tyler. The liquor wasn't helping him.

As evening came, he complained, "I'm not goin' to stay here and get myself killed! I'm gonna make a break for it!"

"Calm down," Masterson said. "Joe Mooar will be coming back this way soon, even if no one else does. And Joe'll head back for Dodge to get help."

"Joe may walk right into 'em! He may be dead already!"

"You don't know Joe," Masterson grinned.

Tyler couldn't let well enough alone. A few minutes later when no one was watching him, he pulled down a barricade and leaped through a window. He'd gone about 50 feet when a slug from an Indian rifle went through his neck and dropped him. A couple of braves crept up through the evening shadows to collect his scalp. At the same time, Bill Masterson charged through the saloon door.

Masterson and the Indians reached Tyler at the same time. In the saloon, they were afraid to shoot for fear of hitting Bill, but as it turned out, he didn't need their help anyway. Shooting his Big 50 from the hip, at a dead run, he cut one Cheyenne nearly in half. As the other warrior started to raise his gun, Masterson was on him, swinging the Big 50's cannon-sized barrel. It collided with the red-

191

skin's head, and he went down as though his legs had been blown out from under him. Masterson tossed Tyler over his shoulder and ran for Hanrahan's as half a dozen Cheyennes on horseback thundered over the hill to run him down. He plunged through the door to safety as his friends picked off three of his pursuers. But after all this trouble, poor little Billy Tyler was dead. He was the only one who was killed in the siege.

It was three weeks before government troops arrived to rescue the men trapped at Adobe Walls. At the rate the fighting was going, if the U.S. Army had delayed much longer, the Indians would have been completely wiped out.

From the troops who frightened the war party back into the hills, Masterson learned that the marauding Indians had been responsible for several raw atrocities in the neighborhood. Five women had been taken captive by a band of braves after their men had been killed. They had all been assaulted, and two of them had been roasted over a slow fire. One of the women had all of her hair pulled out, handful by handful.

While the rest of his friends went back to Dodge, Masterson joined General Nelson A. Miles as an Army scout under Lieutenant Baldwin.

During the period that he served as a scout, he picked up an interest in books from the officers with whom he associated. He read everything they could supply him with: drilling manuals, the Bible, the biographies of Julius Caesar and the plays by William Shakespeare. His schooling on the farm back in Illinois had been limited, but now he found a new teacher in every book he came across. Lieutenant Baldwin recognized that his unusual young scout had an alert and intelligent mind, and encouraged his appreciation of reading and writing. It was his help and encouragement that shaped Bill's future career.

Masterson served with distinction at the Battle of Red River. From then on, the Indian threat in the territory became less and less through the years.

About this time, Masterson met a young man he'd known briefly as a buffalo hunter; a slim fellow with sandy-blond hair, piercing eyes and a firm, quiet voice. His name was Wyatt Earp. They liked each other right away. Earp was just making his mark in the territory as a lawman. He'd been sheriffing at Newton with considerable success, and he told Masterson that a job as deputy was waiting for him any time he wanted to quit scouting.

Later that year, Masterson moved on to Sweetwater, Texas, still serving as a civilian scout. Here he met the one girl he truly loved, and through his whole career in the West, he never loved another.

Bill was having a drink with some Army friends in the Blue Ox Dance Hall in Sweetwater, when he saw a pretty blonde across the room. He looked at her and she looked at him, and things looked pretty good to both of them. She didn't have the familiar come-hither commercial gleam in her eyes.

They got to talking. Her name was Alice and she was a dance-hall girl; no more no less. She didn't frequent the rooms on the second floor at the drop of a dollar. She dressed prettily, came to the hall and danced with the boys, drank with them sometimes, and then went home alone. Within a few days Bill and Alice were in love.

If everything had gone right, Masterson might have disappeared from the history books. He might have married, settled down and lived quietly ever after. But fate was as fickle and cruel those days as it is now, and things didn't go right. A cavalry sergeant named King had his heart set on Alice.

One night Bill and his sweetheart were dancing together when King plunged into the room, a sixgun in each hand.

Alice, looking over Bill's shoulder, saw King come in. "Look out, Bill!" she screamed and whirled so that her body was shielding Masterson.

King cut loose with both .45s as Alice spun into the line of fire. Masterson shoved her aside and whipped his revolver out of its holster. His first slug killed King. Instantly, he dropped to his knees beside Alice. She was dead. King had got off one well-aimed shot.

"Say, Masterson," someone whispered after a moment. "You better look to yourself or you'll bleed to death."

The bullet that had killed Alice had been deflected and hit him high up in the thigh. It was only a flesh wound, but it was bleeding badly.

It had all happened so fast, Bill couldn't quite believe it for a while. When full realization of the tragedy struck him, he stood and limped out the door.

A few days later, Masterson rode into Dodge City and looked up his brother Jim who had moved there a few months earlier. His leg wound was healing, but it still caused him to limp, and he had to walk with a cane.

"What are you going to do now?" Jim asked.

"I don't know. Haven't thought much about it."

"Wyatt Earp just took over as marshal," Jim said. "He's offered me a deputy badge. I know damned well he'd give you a job."

Bill shook his head. "Not with a game leg."

As soon as Jim told Wyatt that Bill was in town, Wyatt hurried over to see him. "Even crippled I'd rather have you for a deputy than anyone else I know," Earp growled. He hauled a badge out of his pocket. "Pin this on. You're enforcing the law in Dodge City with me as of now."

Before the day was out, two cowboys saw Bill Masterson limping down Front Street, his new badge pinned onto his shirt.

"Dodge must be hard up for policemen," the first one remarked loudly. "Now they're hiring 'em with one leg."

"You know why that is," the other said. "If they had two legs they could run away and hide."

"That ain't it at all," the first laughed. "Truth is, if they're half dead in the first place the city don't lose so much when they're killed." He drew his gun and fired at the ground near Bill.

"Are you two gentlemen finished?" Masterson asked quietly. "Because if you are, I'm running you in for disturbing the peace."

The two cowboys had just started to roar with laughter when Bill flattened them with his cane.

A third puncher rushed out of the adjacent saloon to revenge his fallen pals by shooting the new deputy sheriff "between the eyes." His six-gun had not cleared leather when Bill Mastersons' cane creased the side of his head.

"Holy jumpin' hell!" an old bull-whacker mumbled. "Did you see the way he wuz battin' them around?"

"Yeah," his drinking partner agreed in a properly subdued voice. "He's better with that bat than most men are with a revolver!"

Thus did Bill Masterson become "Bat" Masterson. By the time his leg had healed and he'd thrown away his cane, the honorary title had caught on and he was never known as anything else for the rest of his life. Roughly three dozen craniums were thoroughly dented by Bat's cane in his debut as a peace officer. Indeed, there are those who claim Dodge City heaved a sigh of relief when he tossed away his bat and moved through the streets of Dodge with only his Colts at his hips.

Dodge City passed the most peaceful and law-abiding summer in its short, hectic life that year of '76. Wyatt and Bat knew that it was impossible to stop all the rough stuff. Dodge was the terminal of the cattle drives, where the Texas cowhands were paid off after being on the range for as long as six months at a stretch; it was the headquarters of the buffalo hunters; it was the nearest town the soldiers from Fort Dodge could come for excitement and high times. There were bound to be ruckuses. So they set a deadline at the railroad. South of the deadline where the red-light district and the tough dives were located, a man could raise hell pretty much as he pleased. North of the deadline no man could carry a weapon, and even disturbing the peace with a loud warwhoop might mean a night in jail. It was a sensible arrangement, but the wild element in Dodge resented it. The Texans, in particular, felt they needed more elbow room to carry on, come payday. But since none of them wanted to tackle Bat or Wyatt personally, a few well-to-do ranchers kicked in to import Clay Allison for the job.

The morning Clay rode into town, he already had some 18 or 20 killings behind him. Wyatt got the news of his arrival just before breakfast. He and Bat discussed it in the hotel restaurant over their coffee.

"You need some backing," Bat said.

"No. I'll have to see Allison alone," Wyatt disagreed as he lit a cigar.

"I don't mean that. I mean he's going to have friends backing his play. I'll just even things up."

Bat crossed Front Street a few minutes later and wandered up toward Second Avenue.

Wyatt came onto the street straightening his big black hat. He was about half way to the Second Avenue intersection when Clay Allison stepped out of a doorway and approached him. Within five seconds, the street was cleared of traffic.

"You Wyatt Earp?" the hired gunman demanded.

"I'm Wyatt Earp."

At this point Allison seemed to have very little left to say. He glanced nervously up and down the street, trying to keep his eyes on Wyatt at the same time. Finally he muttered something about Earp's having killed a soldier who was a friend of his. Although this was not true, Wyatt said simply, "What business is it of yours if I did?"

Allison, at last, backed down completely, aware that from his point of view the whole affair was a miserable fiasco. He got on his horse and rode slowly toward the outskirts of town. He turned once and rode back toward Earp. Then he brought his pony to a sliding halt in front of Wright and Beverly's store. "You dirty bastards were supposed to back me up!" he yelled. He wheeled his horse and galloped out of Dodge.

A group of Texans gathered behind the window of Wright & Beverly's hung their heads sheepishly. Across the street, leaning casually against a wall was Bat Masterson.

After an interlude of several relatively peaceful months, Bat, his brother Jim and Wyatt decided that being peace officers in Dodge was becoming a bit of a bore. Wyatt went to Texas and Bat and Jim stayed on in Dodge as gamblers. In the meantime, Bat's older brother Ed had moved west and wanted to try his hand at wearing a badge. By June of '77, Bat was a highly successful gambler and had maneuvered his brother Ed into the post of assistant marshal. The marshal, a giant of a man named Larry Deger, was all muscle and no brain, and Dodge had deteriorated into as tough a town as it had ever been.

One morning, a little fellow named Bobby Gilmore was standing in front of Fred Zimmerman's General Store and telling a few friends how he wished the good old days of peace and quiet would come back. Marshal Deger overheard Bobby's remarks and told him to shut up.

"I will not," Bobby said. "I'm an American. I can say what I want."

Bat wandered up as Deger grabbed Gilmore by the neck and threw him into the dusty street. The marshal kicked the little man when he tried to get to his feet and vowed that he was going to put him in jail after he had roughed him up.

196

"You aren't going to rough him up or put him in jail," Bat said. "Leave him alone."

"Who's gonna make me?" Deger bellowed. He was drawing back his right foot for another kick at the prostrate Gilmore when Bat kicked his left leg out from under him. The big man was up again instantly, roaring with rage. Bat knocked him down twice before a bunch of Deger's friends piled onto him. Seven men had to fight every inch of the way to get Bat to jail, but they finally succeeded.

Bat was fined $25 and costs. When the City Council next convened, however, it remitted Bat's fine and apologized to him publicly for the miscarriage of justice.

In any case, Bat decided it was time to start wearing a badge again. He promptly ran for sheriff of Ford County and won handily. Since Dodge was the county seat of Ford County, Bat spent most of his time there. Deger, who had more prudence than valor, spent the rest of his term in office as marshal of Dodge City muttering quietly into his shot glass at his favorite bar.

It is to Bat's credit that he almost always made arrests without having to resort to gunplay. But the time was coming when he would have to use his guns in the most famous—and infamous—gun battle in Dodge City's history.

Ed Masterson's first shooting scrape as assistant marshal of Dodge City led indirectly to the later and deadlier gunplay. His first call to pull a gun came one night when Texas Dick Moore and Bob Shaw got into an argument at the Lone Star. Bob yelled loud and clear that Texas Dick had cheated him of $40.

"Talk like that'll get you a slug in the guts," Dick warned.

"I'll say it again," Bob shouted. "You cheated me out of forty dollars!"

Ed entered the Lone Star just as Bob Shaw had pulled his hogleg and was about to bombard poor Texas Dick.

"Put up that gun!" Ed commanded sharply.

"Keep out of this!" Bob snarled.

Shaw then began blasting at Dick, who was heading toward an exit.

At this point, Ed clouted Bob behind the ear with the barrel of his Colt, as was fitting and proper. But he clouted Bob too tenderly. Instead of flooring the badman, it merely irritated him. He turned and shot Ed in the chest. Ed dropped, flipping his gun from right to left hand as he fell, and shot Bob through the arm and leg. Wounded as he was, Ed held out until help came. They found him covering Shaw and several of the gunman's friends. As soon as his fellow officers arrived to take over, Ed passed out cold from shock and loss of blood.

When he came to, Bat was leaning over him. "You'll be all right, Ed," he said softly. "And you did a fine job. But damn it, when the time comes to buffalo a man, buffalo him! Sometimes you have to be as mean as a wolf in this job. Otherwise you'll get yourself killed."

In a few months Ed was up and around once more, as good as ever. But unfortunately he didn't take his brother's advice.

On April 9, 1878, a little after nine o'clock at night, Ed and his assistant deputy, Nathaniel Haywood, heard several pistol shots from south of the deadline. They hurried across the tracks and found a rugged gang of Texans in the Lady Gay Dance Hall who were bent upon having a wild old time of it.

One of the punchers, Jack Wagner, had made a good start at drinking Dodge dry. He was still sober enough though to be plenty dangerous, and he was packing a gun. Ed asked Wagner for the revolver, and the cowpoke grumbled a little but handed it over. Ed then located the ramrod of the outfit, Al Walker, and gave him the gun, suggesting that Walker check it with the bartender as required by law south of the deadline. Walker said he would, and Ed and Nat left the Lady Gay.

Within two minutes, the lawmen made a quick turn of the block and were passing the Lady Gay once again on their way back to the north side of the deadline.

Wagner and Walker were leaving the dance hall at that moment, and Ed saw that Wagner was still wearing his gun.

Ed stepped over to the puncher and said, "I'll take that gun."

"Like hell you will!" Wagner growled. "I'd just like to see you try to take it!"

The other cowmen in the Texas outfit started out the door at the sound of Wagner's angry voice. Nat said that one of them poked a gun in his face and pulled the trigger, but the gun misfired. At this point, Nat took off up the street for help, leaving Ed to face the cattlemen singlehandedly.

In the meantime, Bat heard a few scattered shots and walked across the tracks to investigate. There were more shots, shouts and the sound of a scuffle. He broke into a run. He was in time to see Ed, ringed by armed Texans, stagger back under the impact of a heavy-caliber gun, fired so close to him that his clothes caught fire.

Seeing Bat, the Texans cut loose on him. Bat's guns bucked furiously in his fists, roaring and coughing fire. His first volley cut Wagner, literally, to pieces. Then he turned his fire on Walker who ran a short distance and collapsed. The other Texans were now in full retreat, dodging into narrow alleys, diving through windows, crawling under porches and doing anything to get out of Bat's withering, deadly fire.

Suddenly there was nothing more to shoot at. There was a moment of intense silence, then a roar of voices as people flooded out onto the street from every direction.

"Hey Bat!" someone called. "Ed's over here. In Hoover's Saloon!"

Bat went into Hoover's and found his brother stretched out on a table. Ed looked up and tried to speak, but he couldn't get the words out. He gave Bat a good-natured grin. Then he died.

This was the second time someone Bat loved had been the victim of vicious, stupid gunfire. And each time he had been powerless to save them. The fact that he had avenged both murders was small consolation. Bat walked aimlessly through the lonely streets of Dodge the rest of that black night, talking to no one and thinking his own dark thoughts.

Charlie Tinkam, a friend of Bat's, said later: "From talking to Bat after the death of his brother Ed, I got the idea he'd decided all killing was senseless and useless, and that he was going to do his best to do right by his badge without ever shooting to kill again. He ordered two new .45s from Colt's Manufacturing Company that same week. He wanted them 'easy on the trigger,' and he wanted them nickel-plated with gutta-percha handles. He wanted the front sights a little higher and wider than usual, with barrels about the length of the ejector rods. Same time he sent for them, he ordered the complete works of Shakespeare and a volume on 18th Century English poets. I know he was looking forward to getting those books a whole lot more than he was looking forward to getting the guns."

The killing of a lawman—despite the immediate and drastic revenge it received—encouraged the cowboys, drifters and assorted badmen of Dodge to regain some of their confidence. As sheriff of Ford County, Bat couldn't spend all of his time at the county seat, and while he was away, the town went wild. Horsemen galloped through the streets, blasting away recklessly at the stars or the sun, depending on the time of day. Tinhorn gamblers cropped up at all the gambling halls. Two young cowboys devised an interesting contest one night. Trying to imitate William Tell, they shot each other's hat off two or three times, until one got to laughing too hard and accidentally blew his friend's head off.

The City Council finally brought Wyatt Earp back from Texas to serve as city marshal again. Masterson and Earp were together in Dodge City when Dora Hand was murdered.

The shooting of Dora Hand was as tragic and sensational a case as Kansas had ever seen. Dora Hand was the most beautiful girl in Dodge City. While she was, admittedly, a successful prostitute in Dodge's busy red-light district, she had many qualities that set her above and apart from her professional sisters. She had played the role of frontier Florence Nightingale on numerous occasions, nursing the hurt or sick with tender devotion. She was kind and generous to a fault in everything she did. Any man who insulted Dora in Dodge City, most likely would have been raised on a rope in short order.

Her killing was a fearful blunder.

A Texan named Kennedy had fallen out with Mayor Kelley. Kelley had taken exception to something Kennedy said and punched him in the nose. Kennedy, a habitual troublemaker, rode out of town nursing his nose and a grudge.

That very day Mayor Kelley left for Fort Dodge and turned his home over to Dora Hand and one of her girl friends for the night.

Not knowing this, Kennedy came back to town in the middle of the night. Walking his horse quietly, he crept up to Kelley's home and emptied his pistol through the thin outside bedroom wall. Dora was hit by one of the slugs and killed instantly. Without realizing his mistake, Kennedy raced out of Dodge at full speed.

Earp, Masterson and a young deputy named Bill Tilghman headed for Wagon Bed Springs on the hunch that the killer would try to escape into the desolate Indian territory. They rode all night and all the next day. Finally, certain that they had bypassed him, they laid an ambush in a small valley through which their quarry would have to pass, if their idea was correct.

A short time later, Kennedy came riding along the trail. He did not see them until he was within shooting range. Then Bat rode out and called, "You're under arrest, Kennedy!"

The Texan spun his horse around and galloped back in the direction he had come from. Bat took careful aim with one of his new Colts and pulled the trigger. Kennedy was knocked sprawling from his horse, his arm shattered.

On the way back to Dodge, the prisoner asked if he had succeeded in killing Kelley. When Wyatt Earp told him what had happened, Kennedy cursed Bat furiously for not killing him. "Dora Hand once grub-staked me when I was down and out," he cried. "I deserve to die!"

Bat killed no one else during the remainder of his term in office. He shot a lengthy list of unscrupulous characters, from crooked poker dealers to horsethieves, but he always drilled them neatly in an arm, a leg or a shoulder.

On one memorable occasion, the celebrated comedian Eddie Foy was almost certain that Bat Masterson was going to kill him. Eddie was playing Dodge for the first time. The day after his debut a group of quiet but determined men called for him at his hotel. The handsome, smartly dressed young man who was the leader of the crowd introduced himself as Bat Masterson. The comedian was a bit surprised; he expected Bat to be at least eight foot tall, with a killer's vicious, narrowed eyes and half a dozen huge revolvers dangling from his hips.

Foy was even more surprised when Bat said in a cultured, well-modulated voice, "We're terribly sorry to disturb you, Mr. Foy. But as you are aware, most of the town saw your opening act at Ham Bell's Varieties last night. Consequently, the citizens of Dodge City have formed a committee to carry out the town's decision in regard to you."

"Decision?" Foy looked puzzled.

Bat nodded slowly. "After seeing you on stage, the people of Dodge have decided the only thing to do is hang you."

Several men standing behind Bat who, Foy observed,

looked like alarmingly desperate types, surged forward and led the unhappy comedian into the street.

At first Foy tried bravado. But the unsmiling man went quietly about the business of leading him to a large tree and bringing up a horse for him to sit on. As they tied his hands behind his back, with Masterson supervising all the details carefully, a large crowd began to gather.

For the first time, it occurred to Foy that they actually might be going to hang him. His heart pounded nervously as someone threw a rope over the branch above him and pulled it until the noose hung level with Eddie's head.

Masterson at last broke the long silence. "Mr. Foy," he asked, "before we go ahead, is there any last word you'd like to say?"

Foy gulped down his panic and wet his lips. "Yes," he said.

"What is it?"

"Could I buy all you boys a drink?"

The crowd roared with laughter and approval at Foy's last words. Slapping him on the back, they untied him and helped him from the horse. Everyone retired to the Long Branch, where the hanging was conceded to be one of the most successful of the year.

By the time 1880 rolled around, Bat was losing interest in his position as sheriff of Ford County. The adventurous, glorious days of Dodge City were declining. Buffalo hunting, along with the buffalo, had died out. The Texas cowboys, who had once stormed the town, were dwindling in number as farming pushed farther west and other cattle markets came into existence. Also, there was more money in professional gambling.

Early in '80, when Wyatt Earp moved on to Tombstone to take the job of federal deputy marshal there, Bat resigned too. About that time Jim Masterson, against Bat's advice, went into partnership with Al Peacock in a gambling house and dance hall. Peacock was a sharp, hard-faced dealer who had an unsavory background and who moved in tough circles. Jim, the perennial little brother, took Bat's advice as a personal offense and promptly threw in with Peacock.

Bat was ripe for a deal that Dave Rickabaugh offered him. "I own the Oriental, the finest place in Tombstone," Dave told him. "Certain parties are trying to take it over. I want men with a gunslinging reputation to work for

202

me to discourage 'em. If you take me up, I'll make it worth your while."

After due consideration, Masterson moved to the Oriental in Tombstone, along with Luke Short who also had a name as a good man in a fight.

There was plenty of action in Tombstone. Luke got into a gunfight with a mean gunman named Charlie Storms shortly after their arrival and put several holes in poor Charlie before Bat broke it up.

A few weeks later, two ungracious visitors visited the Oriental when Bat was on duty alone. They amused themselves by tossing yellow chips into the air and trying to shoot them in midflight.

"I'll have to ask you gentlemen not to carry on like that," Bat said politely. "Rules of the house."

One made the mistake of swiveling his gun in Bat's direction and found his arm dangling helplessly at his side in no time at all. Bat shot the other in the shoulder as he tried to finish what his friend had started.

"Now you two boys just move along and don't be so rough next time you're in the Oriental," Bat admonished them. The truth of the matter is, they avoided the Oriental altogether from that time on.

Bat served as a deputy to Wyatt once or twice and was just getting to enjoy Tombstone when he got a letter from a friend in Dodge City. The letter said that his brother Jim was in trouble up to his eyebrows. It seemed that Al Peacock and Jim had a falling out. Peacock and the tough bartender who worked for the two partners were out to kill Jim.

Bat took the first stage out of Tombstone to Deming. At Deming he caught the train to Dodge. One thought was uppermost in his mind. He had lost his girl in the fight at Sweetwater and one brother in Dodge. It wasn't going to happen again if he could help it.

The train pulled into Dodge at noon on April 16th; it was half an hour late. The engine slowly chugged to a halt and Bat hopped off the passenger car, his bag in one hand. As he looked up and down the platform, he saw Peacock and Updegraff, the bartender, standing near the station. They turned away as Bat approached them and started to walk rapidly toward Front Street.

"Wait a minute, you two," Bat called. "I want to talk to you!"

They bolted and took cover behind the nearby caboose,

pulling their guns as they ran. Both opened fire from their protected position, and Bat dropped quickly behind the railroad grading. Shooting wildly, the two men raked the street behind Bat with lead. Shells plowed into Hoover's Liquor Store, the Long Branch Saloon and Mc-Carty's Drugstore.

Bat finally had a clean shot at Updegraff. From the way the two men had reacted when they saw him, he thought they might have already killed Jim. So when he pulled the trigger, he wasn't interested in simply winging Updegraff. He shot to kill. With Updegraff out of the fight, Peacock threw down his gun.

As soon as the shooting was over, Bat allowed himself to be arrested and taken to jail. He was only held briefly. To his relief, he learned upon his release that Jim was still alive.

Updegraff lived a few days then died. Most of the citizens of Dodge were relieved that it was he, rather than Masterson, who had died. But there was a new reform element in town, led by the new mayor, a pious crook named Webster. Out of petty spite, Webster insisted that Bat be fined $8.00 for "unlawfully and feloniously discharging a pistol upon the streets of said city."

A crusading newspaper, the Walnut City *Blade*, who was spearheading Webster's drive for a town completely under the mayor's thumb, editorialized: "It costs $8.00 to shoot a man through the lung in Dodge City. Such was Bat Masterson's fine." It didn't go into the proper etiquette one should observe when two other men start using you for target practice.

Dodge City had changed. It was no longer honestly dishonest. Its one time healthy, hell-for-leather deviltry had given way to stealthy, sneaky corruption. Disgusted with Dodge, both Bat and Jim left town a few months after the Updegraff shooting. Bat moved on to Trinidad, Colorado, where he leased a gambling concession.

One morning he got a telegram from his old friend Luke Short. Luke was in trouble. He had moved back to Dodge from Tombstone and taken over the Long Branch. Always a good businessman, Luke hired a cute girl to play the piano and sing for his customers. Consequently, the Alamo, next door to the Long Branch, began to lose business. Luke returned to his place one evening to find the doors locked by order of the sheriff. His silver-voiced songstress, being automatically out of a job, had instantly accepted an offer to sing for the owner of the Alamo.

Bat was not particularly surprised at these events, since the owner of the Alamo was none other than the honorable Mayor Webster. To add to Luke's woes, the mayor had run him out of town.

Bat sent word to Wyatt Earp, who promptly gathered some of their old friends together: Charlie Bassett, Frank McLane, Neal Brown and Billy Potillion—all champion gunslingers.

Bat, Wyatt and Luke's other friends arrived in Dodge, set up a semi-legal "peace commission," consisting of themselves, and took the town over. A chastened Mayor Webster changed his high-handed views overnight, and Luke Short's raw deal was miraculously turned into a square deal for all concerned.

With that score settled, Bat Masterson next tried his luck in Deadwood, Leadville, Ogallala, Tombstone and Cimarron, looking for excitement and adventure.

When the Santa Fe and the Rio Grande railroads were having a small war over a track right-of-way, a Santa Fe agent came looking for Bat.

"This is the story," he said nervously. "Man named Palmer has a whole army aboard a train. They've killed a couple of men at Cucharas, and they're heading to Pueblo to take over the Santa Fe's railroad property. We've already started making a fort out of the old Pueblo roundhouse, but we need someone to take over when it comes to actual fighting."

Bat accepted the assignment.

When General Palmer and his army arrived at Pueblo, they found the doors of the roundhouse barred with heavy timbers. Inside, with a smaller army and a couple of Gatling guns, was Bat Masterson.

There was a tense moment as Palmer weighed the possibilities of storming the fortress. Usually a determined man, he couldn't quite bring himself to give the order to attack. He had heard too many stories about Bat Masterson. Palmer's treasurer, realizing that both armies were composed of mercenaries, suggested talking to the men in the fortress under a flag of truce. He figured they could buy off the opposing army by offering them more money than the Sante Fe was paying them.

Bat wanted to remain loyal to the Santa Fe, but his

men didn't see it that way. They couldn't see any sense in fighting, if they could get more money by surrendering. At last Bat was outvoted, and the fight was averted.

On another occasion, an eccentric millionaire named Soule wanted to move the county seat of Gray County, Kansas, from Cimarron to Ingalls. He hired Bat and another veteran gunfighter, Jim Marshall, to take a gang of fighters to Cimarron. They were to raid the county courthouse, swipe all official county papers and the county seal and take them to Ingalls. Soule was convinced that if he could get all official county documents to Ingalls, he could succeed in making Ingalls the new county seat.

This sounded like good fun to Bat. He and Marshall got to Cimarron with a platoon of hired scrappers. Leaving their men outside, the two of them rushed into the courthouse and began gathering up the documents.

In the meantime, word had spread through Cimarron of what was going on. A mob of irate citizens marched on the courthouse, many of them armed. In the face of howling criticism and whining bullets, the mercenaries outside fled, leaving Bat and Jim inside to face the music.

It is a tribute to the gunslingers' marksmanship that they managed to hold the enraged mob at bay for several hours without killing off half the population of Cimarron. With all the flying lead, an innocent bystander two blocks away was the only fatality. It is highly unlikely that either Bat or Jim shot the fellow, but when they surrendered after several hours of siege, they were tried for murder.

Their defense was unique. They claimed they couldn't have murdered the man because they didn't even know him. And if one of their bullets had accidentally hit the poor fellow, it was only because they were deliberately firing over the heads of the mob—and, incidentally, firing to protect their own lives.

Eventually, they were released, with a warning that if they ever showed up in Cimarron again they would be immediately hanged.

Bat's love of good books, reading and writing shaped his final destiny. Following the turn of the century, he realized that the West as he had known it was dead. He moved to New York and managed to get a job as a writer with the *Morning Telegraph*. He wrote well and

206

his byline soon became common. Bat developed a tremendous interest in sports, especially boxing. He felt that a man, if he is a man, is bound to have fight in him, and that he should have some way of getting that fight out of him. Boxing was the most civilized way of accomplishing this, Bat thought.

In time, Bat became a well-known and respected sports writer. Later, he became an editor with the *Telegraph*.

On October 25th, 1921, Bat died of a heart attack at his desk. He was 67 years old.

The boom of six-guns is far removed from the clatter of typewriters, yet, somehow, they both seemed right for Bat. His sophisticated editor and writer friends probably would have agreed that the simple prayer Bat's Western friends said over him was just about right.

"Lord. Take care of this man."

THE MAN WHO
MARRIED ANNIE OAKLEY

Frank Butler could shoot rings around any man in the country. But he fell in love with "Little Miss Sure Shot" and sacrificed his own career to make her world famous.

On Thanksgiving morning of 1875, a crowd began to gather in a field on the outskirts of Cincinnati. The people were in an excited, festive frame of mind. Word had been passed that a shooting match was to be held, and at this time, when every backwoods hamlet in the country could muster a legion of crack shots, shooting was more than an idle pastime or sport. It was practically a way of life. And since the local champion was about to take on a flashy professional who specialized in blasting tiny glass balls out of the air, this match promised some very fancy shooting.

A man called to a friend, "Hey, Ed! You still think that Butler fella can beat little Phoebe?"

"Sure, I do. I'd bet my shirt, but I got myself ten dollars here. . ."

The bet was covered, and throughout the crowd others

put up their money or argued over the outcome of the contest.

At 9 o'clock, a Cincinnati hotel manager named Frost arrived in a buckboard with two young girls and drove slowly through the gathering to a point near the center of the field. Frost had set up the match. Butler, a trick shot who was making a road tour with a theatrical group, was staying at Frost's hotel. The manager had offered Butler a sporting wager of $100 a side to shoot against the hunter who supplied his hotel with wild fowl. He hadn't bothered to mention that the hunter was a 15-year-old girl.

In a few minutes, another rig pulled into the field. The driver was a tall, strongly built young man with clear, steady eyes and a handsome face. He smiled and waved as people greeted him from all sides. Reining up beside the buckboard, he jumped down and said, "Morning, Frost. The other fellow here yet?"

"Like to introduce Phoebe Mozee and her sister Louise," said Frost. "Phoebe's the girl who's going to shoot against you."

Frank Butler looked down in wonder at the slender, poorly dressed girl who stood nervously beside the hotel manager. He took off his wide-brimmed hat. "I'm very happy to know you, Miss Mozee."

The girl blushed and managed to stammer, "Pleased to meet you."

Frost said amusedly, "Phoebe's a little on edge. She's never shot in a real match before."

Smiling in a friendly fashion at the girl, Butler said, "I know just how you feel. I've never shot against a girl before."

While Frost and some of his friends carried crates containing 50 live birds to the target line, Butler talked to Phoebe Mozee in a low, gentle voice. By the time the match was ready to begin, the crowd had grown larger and the slim girl was obviously suffering from acute stagefright. As the two of them stepped out toward the designated firing line, Butler ginned and said, "Don't worry about the folks watching us. Just pretend you're giving me a few pointers in shooting. That way, it'll be kind of fun."

She gave him a quick, appreciative look and relaxed visibly.

"Pull!" she called.

The first bird flew up and she brought her shotgun smoothly to her shoulder, blasting it from the air.

"Dead!" came the announcement from the traps.

"Say," Butler said with genuine delight, "you're good." He shifted his gun and yelled, "Pull!" A moment later, the second reply came, "Dead!"

They fired 25 shots each at that historic meeting. Little Phoebe Mozee, her confidence built up and paying no attention to the audience, killed every bird instantly and came through with a perfect score. Butler, perhaps over-confident—or, although he would never admit it, perhaps being gallant in a manner typical to him—only winged the last bird that sped into the air. Phoebe Mozee was the winner by one point.

The nervous little girl Frank Butler encouraged into winning that shooting match was, of course, the future Annie Oakley.

Everyone knows about Annie. They know how the back-country youngster, who was born in a log cabin, took her first shot when she was nine years old, blowing the head neatly off a running quail and busting her nose under the recoil of the ancient muzzle-loader. They know that she was world-famous in her twenties as the in-credible Little Miss Sure Shot, adopted daughter of Sitting Bull and adored sweetheart of millions, who could use a polished bowie knife for a mirror and, shooting a six-gun over her shoulder, split a playing card at 50 feet. They know she was the darling of European royalty who once shot the ashes off the Kaiser's cigarette. The Mag-nificent Girl of the Plains with her Magic Rifle was a legend even in her own time.

No one knows about the man she married. Yet if it had not been for Frank Butler, there never would have been an Annie Oakley. He was the one-in-a-million man who could have taken Phoebe Anne Oakley Mozee, a timid backwoods girl of Darke County, Ohio, and made her into the most admired, sought-after and famous woman of her generation.

Born in Ireland in 1850, Frank E. Butler was a cheer-ful, happy-go-lucky kid despite a childhood that would have embittered most youngsters. There was never any money in the family and Frank had to work almost as soon as he was able to walk and talk. When he was eight, his parents left him in the care of a narrow-faced, vicious aunt. He never saw them again.

After a few years with the spinster, Frank ran away. He hiked to the sea coast and hung around the waterfront trying to get a berth on a ship. The likable kid soon made many friends, including the captain of a clipper ship bound for America. The skipper took him aboard as a galley boy and Frank peeled potatoes all the way to New York City.

Now 14 and big for his age, Frank claimed he was 18 and worked at a variety of jobs. He sold papers, delivered milk, was a deckhand on a fishing vessel and even served as apprentice to a glass blower. One thing he learned as an apprentice was that he couldn't stand working indoors. If he couldn't spend most of the day out in the sun and fresh air, he was miserable. Frank also discovered that he loved guns and dogs, and paradoxically, poetry. He saved for months to buy a handworn copy of Shakespeare. His first gun was a Spencer with a split stock held together by wire that he bought from a cavalryman in the Union Army. A friend gave him a flop-eared mongrel, and the happiest days of Frank's youth were spent hunting and reading in the woods outside the city. He was a natural marksman, and it didn't take him long to find that spare change could be picked up by competing with gents who were more adept at shooting off their mouths than their guns.

In 1870, the owner of a stock company heard of this good-looking kid who could throw a pebble into the air and shatter it with his rifle. Since good shooting was always a heavy drawing card in the gun-conscious towns along the road, he asked Frank if he'd like to squeeze a trigger for regular pay.

Butler took as naturally to the theater as he'd taken to guns. He had a flair for showmanship. One of the first routines he worked out was a take-off on William Tell. By this time, he had acquired a large white poodle named George. He trained George to sit up and balance an apple on his head. Then Frank would walk to the far side of the stage, whirl around and shoot his rifle from the hip. The apple would be broken of course, and the kicker of the act was that George nonchalantly picked out the largest chunk left, carried it to the front of the stage and lay down to chew on it in a bored manner. This brought down the house.

Frank came to be as good with a revolver as he was with a rifle, and he'd make a split-second draw to demolish the apple. He also added a human assistant named Billy Graham, and they toured under the billing of "Butler and Graham."

Between 1870 and 1875, Frank was considered by many to be the top marksman in the nation. Wherever he went, there was a standing challenge to meet anyone and everyone in any kind of a shooting match they wanted. He never lost, although he was put up against the finest amateurs and professionals in every section of the country to shoot at everything from frightened turkeys peeping over logs to lighted candles swinging in the dark. He'd laugh and tell a few jokes while he was shooting. And everyone would go away liking him, even though he'd just shot circles around the local contender.

On one of the rare occasions that he lost his temper, a hulking Southerner he'd just won a match against said, "Well, you damn Yankee, I'll bet you three dollars, I can shoot the ear off that poodle of yours."

Frank grabbed the gun as the large man was lifting it to his shoulder, broke it over a tree stump and flattened the offender with one ferocious punch.

With all this rugged young man's charm, and the fact that women were falling all over him, he wanted nothing to do with the fairer sex. His mother had deserted him. His aunt had mistreated and bullied him. He felt that women were a great mistake in an otherwise well-ordered world. His dog felt the same way about it and on general principle would bare his teeth in a threatening snarl if any female approached within five feet.

"Butler and Graham" were on the road with *Uncle Tom's Cabin* on that Thanksgiving morning in Cincinnati when little Phoebe Mozee outshot Frank by one point. On that fateful day, the Irish lad not only lost the shooting match, but he lost his usual distrust of women as well.

As the crowd began to break up, he made his way to Frost's buckboard where Phoebe and her sister were waiting for the hotel manager. "I'd be pleased, Miss Mozee," he said, "to take you to dinner by way of congratulating you for the fine shooting."

The young girl was flattered and flustered to a degree where she found it difficult to talk. Simply visiting the big

212

town and being the center of attention for a short while was a great adventure to her, and now this—it was almost too much.

She finally said, "Well, I've promised my sister that I'd—"

"Perhaps she'd like to join us."

Her sister Louise said uncertainly, "My husband might—"

"Bring him, too," Frank laughed.

His laughter put them at ease and they agreed to meet him later on, with Louise's husband, Joe.

That was a splendid day for the future Annie Oakley. She had dinner in a restaurant for the first time in her life, and with Frank sitting beside her, everything she did seemed just right. He gave them tickets to the show, another "first" for the Mozee girl, and after Frank shot the apple off George's head, the dog completely ignored both his hatred of women and the maxim that the show must go on. He calmly trotted down to the first row of seats where he put his woolly head on the thrilled girl's lap and refused to budge.

The next day the show was on the road again and Phoebe Mozee went sadly back to her cabin in the hills, probably resigned to spending the rest of her life with the memories of those fabulous 24 hours in town.

But a few days later, instead of riding his mule straight down the trail below the cabin, the postman came up to the clearing before her house and yelled five wonderful words, "Phoebe! You've got a letter!"

In the letter, Frank explained that he wasn't a man for writing much, but that George had been after him to send a note saying hello. And that stubborn dog was so insistent that Frank finally had to give in and write it, because George's penmanship wasn't too good. Phoebe wrote back to George and said she'd enjoyed meeting him.

It wasn't long before the correspondence between her and the poodle got pretty hot and heavy. At Christmas, George sent her a five-pound box of chocolates and mentioned in his letter that Frank had swung a deal whereby the show would be coming back through Ohio in a little while. Phoebe, not to be outdone, made herself a brand-new dress for when George would be passing through.

The show got there in late spring. Frank told Phoebe

that he was ruining his wrist writing all those letters for George, and the only thing he could see to do was for her to marry George's owner so that she and the dog wouldn't have to go on sending letters forever.

Phoebe cried about this suggestion for a little while and then agreed it was a good idea.

They were married that year, 1876, on June 22.

Frank started calling Phoebe by her second name, Annie, and she went along with him while the "Butler and Graham" act continued as before. Frank also began to fill in Annie's neglected education, both by teaching her himself and putting her in good schools whenever they were in one place long enough.

A few weeks after they were married, Billy Graham got sick and couldn't go on the stage.

"Guess you'll have to take his place," Frank told Annie. "And I want you to exchange shots with me. You toss the glass balls in the air like you've seen Billy do, and I'll bust them. Then I'll throw some of them up and you break them."

Annie was mute at the idea of trick-shooting on the stage. She just nodded.

"Close your eyes when you throw the balls or you might get hurt by the exploding glass," Frank said. Then, while she tried vainly to get Billy's buckskin outfit to fit her slender figure, he hurried to the theater to change the bills.

Some people watching sharpshooters have a tendency to think of them as being infallible. Frank knew the opposite to be true. He knew that if Annie's nerves didn't hold out, or if she made a slip, he stood to have his head blown off. But he had every confidence in his wife.

Annie couldn't make Billy's costume do, so she wore street clothes on the stage that night. Frank went through his part of the act. Then it was Annie's turn. The crowd watched her intently as she picked up a rifle from the table in center stage and backed to a wing. Near the other wing, Frank took the first ball gingerly in the palm of his hand, then tossed it lightly above his head.

Annie swung the gun to her shoulder quickly, caught the shining sphere in the sights, jerked the trigger—and missed. There was the roar of the rifle followed by the very distinct and separate pop of the ball as it broke on the stage floor. The audience suddenly became painfully silent. Someone in the balcony snickered. Frank caught

Annie's anguished eyes and held them with his own. He grinned at her, gave her a second to collect herself, then threw another ball. Reassured, Annie shattered it and the audience howled with approval. The team of "Butler and Oakley" was on its way. A natural-born showman, Frank picked Annie's two middle names for billing and from then on she was known as Annie Oakley.

Frank taught Annie all there was to know about show business. He taught her that good shooting by itself could be deadly boring. You could blow a pin in half at 30 paces and it wouldn't be half as effective as hitting a milk bottle which would explode into a thousand pieces. He taught her the importance of the element of danger. If people think there's a chance of a performer being injured, they'll flock to the show from miles around. Therefore, Frank worked out the bowie knife trick and another shot in which one of them would swing a ball around his head for the other to hit. Other famous targets were the dime held between thumb and forefinger, the ashes of the cigarette held between Frank's lips and the flame of a match held in the hand.

From stock touring with their own act, they went with the Sells Brothers Circus in 1880. Here they ran into the crooked circus followers, the cappers, grafters, shell artists and con men who drifted with the big top and were ever ready to clip anyone, with a variety of deals ranging from complex swindles to a simple, stout blow over the head in a dark alley. This was the first time Annie had seen life in the raw. Since she'd been brought up by Quaker parents, Frank knew she'd need protecting. He banged a few heads together and word got around that the Oakley girl was not to be tampered with in any way, shape or form.

One good thing came out of the Sells Brothers run. Frank devised a spectacular horseback routine in which they would riddle targets while charging before the audience on galloping horses. Their act became quite famous and while they were in New Orleans, they were approached by Bill Cody and Nate Salisbury, partners in "Buffalo Bill's Original Wild West Show."

They made a deal to go with the "Bill Show" as it was called, and then Frank did a typical and amazing thing. He scratched himself out of the act. Putting aside all thoughts of himself, deliberately ignoring the fact that he was throwing over his own fine reputation as a sharp-

215

shooter and entertainer deluxe, and forsaking the normal desire of any performer to bask in the admiration and applause of admirers, he bowed quietly out. He believed Annie could go farther at this time without him. He managed the act, and he still assisted Annie, but the posters no longer read "Butler and Oakley." They were now, "Annie Oakley."

Because of Frank's clear-thinking decision, Annie Oakley was no longer part of a very good performance. She was now an awe-inspiring combination of rugged plainsman and feminine charm, unique in the theatrical world. Thundering across the arena of the Wild West Show on a gorgeous Palomino and blasting impossible targets right and left through a halo of powder-blue smoke, she rode and shot her way into the heart of the nation.

Within a few short months, that aristocratic old faker of the plains, Buffalo Bill, was cringing at the mention of her name. He knew that the vast majority of people who flocked to see his show were doing so to see Annie Oakley. Salisbury convinced him that money was more important than wounded dignity, so Bill kept Annie with him. At Frank's suggestion, the great chief Sitting Bull joined the show. Then, with Frank and the show's press agent, Major John W. Burke, egging him along, Sitting Bull proclaimed Annie as his adopted daughter. He called her *"Machin Chilla Wytonys Cecelia,"* which meant, "My Daughter, Little Sure Shot."

Since the memory of Custer's Massacre at Sitting Bull's hands was still vivid to Americans, this "adoption" meant hundreds of thousands of dollars' worth of free publicity. Sitting Bull admired Frank and Annie immensely and went along with the stunt willingly.

While Annie was skyrocketing to fame, one of Frank's favorite pastimes was discrediting crooks who used trickery in an attempt to imitate her. A woman trapeze artist worked a six-gun into her act. She would hang by her heels on the trapeze, and each time she swung to the far end of the arc would fire the revolver, hitting a bull's-eye set up at the end of the tent. There would be the bark of the gun, followed by the metallic whang as the bullet struck home. This was a fair-to-middling trick, except that Frank proved the woman was shooting blank cartridges and a crony was standing behind the tent hitting the gong with a hammer each time she fired.

Another entertainer rigged up a piano with an elaborate system of levers topped by small white disks. The theory was that he shot and hit the disks so accurately and rapidly that the levers in turn caused the piano to play. On a hunch, Frank bribed a stagehand to empty most of the shells from the fellow's rifles. When the "trick shot" ran out of ammunition in the middle of the next performance, the piano played merrily along under its own power, operated by an automatic roller.

Other frauds shot out candles placed against boards. Any gun expert knows that all you have to do is hit the board and the vibration will extinguish the candle flame. By running a pin through a cigar or cigarette, you only have to touch the pin with your teeth when someone fires in your general direction and the ashes will fall as though shot. Frank loved to expose such practices because he and Annie had always depended on honestly fine shooting as the base of success. He hated to see phonies cash in who couldn't hit the tent they were standing in two times out of three.

The "Bill Show" played to packed houses at Madison Square Garden in New York, and then sailed overseas to conquer Europe.

Here, as Frank wanted it, Annie was always in the limelight while he stood just beyond in the dark, always ready to help and guide her, to let her absorb his strength and tremendous self-confidence.

Edward, Prince of Wales, was among the first to admire Annie's unique abilities. He and his entourage watched the lengthy spectacle with mild interest. They sat through The Landing Of The Pilgrims, Pocahontas Saving John Smith, The Prairie Fire, The Stagecoach Holdup, Custer's Massacre, The Pony Express and half a dozen other assorted scenes portraying frontier Americana. But when Annie galloped into the arena with her blazing guns, they were spellbound.

A short time later, Buffalo Bill came running toward Frank waving a piece of paper in his trembling hand. "The Prince of Wales wants Annie to shoot a match with The Grand Duke of Russia!" he stuttered. "If she accepts, she'll have to lose! It'd be a disgrace to beat a member of royalty."

"Now calm down, Bill," Frank said. "Naturally, she'll accept. And naturally, she'll win."

The Duke was a real sharpshooter, but he simply

wasn't on Annie's level. He hit 35 out of 50 difficult targets. Annie hit 47.

After this, Queen Victoria asked Annie to give a command performance. Like everyone else, Her Majesty was thrilled with the Oakley brand of shooting and at the end of the exhibition, she gave the Ohio girl a pair of opera glasses fashioned of gold and mother-of-pearl.

Buffalo Bill could stand it no longer. He'd been playing second fiddle to Annie too long, and now when the Crowned Heads of Europe ignored him in favor of her, he called it quits. The Wild West Show returned to America while Frank took Annie on to capture the Continent.

The Butlers were an immediate success in Europe, but the strain of countless shows was beginning to tell on Annie. One cold night, she tried to build a fire in their Paris apartment and Frank found her crying bitterly before the fireplace with smoke curling out into the room.

"The chimney's clogged," she wailed.

"Now don't you worry," Frank said. He unbuttoned a rifle bag and strode to the fireplace with the gun. There was a rapid tempo of thundering rifle blasts and when he stepped back, the fire was burning briskly. He'd cleared the flue in an unorthodox but highly efficient manner.

Then he took his tearful little girl in his arms and told her they were going to cancel all engagements and go home for a long vacation.

They stayed in Ohio for a few months and when Annie was completely rested, they went on to various stage shows. Later, Buffalo Bill found business falling off, put his ego momentarily aside and asked them to come back with the Wild West Show for another European tour.

In Germany, Kaiser Wilhelm II was fascinated by Annie's uncanny shooting skill and asked her to clip the ashes off his cigarette. Buffalo Bill nearly had a nervous breakdown, but Frank told Annie to go ahead. People all over the world got an ecstatic thrill when they read that a lead slug fired by Annie Oakley had sped three inches from Wilhelm's head.

They returned to the United States and stayed with the Wild West Show until 1901. In that year, the show was speeding south on a special train when it crashed head on into an express.

Frank was two cars behind Annie. He fought and shouldered his way through the wreckage to where she lay unconscious and bleeding to death. Somehow, he

218

stopped her bleeding and got her out of the twisted mass of steel.

She was partially paralyzed. Frank stayed at her side constantly through the following months that slowly turned into years. Then one day, she had improved so much that he gave her a gun and bet a dollar she could outshoot him. She wasn't shooting too well, but he managed to lose the dollar.

Frank was concerned about Annie's health and wanted to settle down, but she felt this would be admitting defeat. Annie's happiness was the most important thing to Frank, so he agreed to let her go back to show business. They went on the road, played to Army camps during the first World War and gave shooting lessons in their spare time. Then, in 1921, they were in a serious automobile crash.

This second accident marked the end of their professional lives. Annie was never in good health from that time on, and she died on November 3, 1926. The man who loved her, who had purposely given up his own career in order to further hers, who had in her own words "raised her from nothing," simply refused to eat after she died.

He joined her in death 19 days later.

They are buried side by side in a little country cemetery in Ohio, and people who knew them like to think that a poem Frank once wrote has finally come true:

> Some fine day I'll settle down
> And stop this roving life;
> With a cottage in the country
> I will claim my little wife.
> Then we'll be happy and contented,
> No quarrels shall arise,
> And I'll never leave my little girl
> With the raindrops in her eyes.

APACHE REVENGE

*When the white men slaughtered his family and
wiped out his village, the young Apache brave went
on a wild rampage of revenge that made him the
most feared warrior of the Old West.*

A company of Mexican cavalry passed the Indians
far to the left just at high noon. Goyathlay, scouting the
left flank, heard the distant, shrill whinny of a horse. He
lifted his right arm, and the long column of Bedonkohe
warriors in the valley disappeared silently among the
trees and rocks.

Sprinting almost to the top of the hill, Goyathlay
dropped and crawled to the summit. The sun-baked
earth was warm on his broad chest. His watchful, dark
eyes studied the broken plain below. From a deep arroyo
half way across the plain, the lead horse appeared, shaking its head. The rider was a squat, powerful Mexican
with gold at his shoulders. Soon the entire column was in
sight, a great, black snake winding lazily over the broken
plain toward Arizpe. One frightened pack horse, carrying two large sacks, plunged and fought the reins as a
mounted soldier tried to lead him.

Goyathlay watched until the cavalry was gone. The

Bedonkohe were at peace with Mexico, but the warriors walked with a soft foot nevertheless. He turned to the empty valley below and raised his muscular left arm. Mangus Colorado, the chief, rode toward Goyathlay.

"One company of Mexican horse soldiers. Moving to Arizpe," Goyathlay told him.

The chief stared thoughtfully at the tall young warrior. "Were their horses weary?"

"No. They were excited."

Mangus Colorado twisted his pony in a standing turn and rode back to the head of his braves. The party continued on toward their camp, which was half a day's march to the north, in the Kaskiyeh Valley. Goyathlay's thoughts went ahead to his wife, Alope, who was waiting for him in camp. Coming to trade in Arizpe had been a great adventure for her. She had never been to Mexico before and, since there was peace, she had begged Goyathlay to take her with him. He had finally brought along Alope, their three children and his mother.

The women, children and a few older men had been left in camp while the braves went to Arizpe to trade. Goyathlay had given two mountain lion skins and seven bearskins for five arm-lengths of fine red cloth and three strands of colored beads. Alope's eyes would sparkle when she saw the cloth. Then he would show her the beads, and she would cry out in a little voice at their beauty. They would give the children some of the beads to play with.

The sun had settled low in the sky and the Bedonkohe were nearing their camp when Goyathlay saw one of their advance scouts hurrying back to Mangus Colorado, who rode at the head of the column. The chief spoke briefly to the scout, then called the warriors to him. Goyathlay waited impatiently at his point of lookout. Soon Toklonnen trotted away from the assembly and up the side of the hill to join him.

"What has happened?" Goyathlay demanded.

"No one knows," Toklonnen said. "The scout says there is no smoke from the camp."

"I will ride ahead and see what has happened," Goyathlay said.

"No," Toklonnen told him. "Mangus Colorado says we must wait until dark. There may be enemies near."

Goyathlay, for the first time in his life, knew real fear.

Not the exciting fear that comes from tracking a mountain lion and hearing him cough nearby, or from riding a wild horse for the first time. This was the cold, still fear that hurts the chest.

When the moon was standing on the rim of a mesa to their right, Goyathlay heard what sounded like the muffled cry of a hoot owl from the valley. The Bedonkohe began moving cautiously ahead. Near the camp, Goyathlay heard a faint sound behind a large rock. Drawing his knife, he crept toward the noise and came upon Nadastin, the wife of Chokole, clutching her son to her breast. She was sobbing silently. The boy was dead; the clotted blood around the wound in his side looked like caked, black mud in the moonlight.

"Mexicans?" Goyathlay whispered.

"Yes," she whimpered.

"Are they still near?"

"I don't think so."

"Alope?"

"I don't know. There are many dead."

"Stay here. I will tell Chokole you are still with us."

Hurrying into the camp, Goyathlay saw that the tepees were all down, their contents strewn wildly about. Scattered among the shadows on the ground were bodies in grotesque, unreal positions. For one horrible moment a vivid picture of how it must have been flashed through Goyathlay's mind. The Mexican cavalry galloping down on the peaceful camp; the screams; the shrilling horses; slashing, wet-red sabers, the merciless, leveled lances; running children trampled in the swirling dust beneath the cruel hooves.

Then the picture passed. Racing to the remains of his tent, Goyathlay searched frantically through the moon-drenched wreckage. There was nothing. But Alope was a swift runner. Perhaps she had escaped into the woods or hills.

Then, close to a long line of scrub oak behind the camp, Goyathlay came upon Alope's body. Even in the dim light he recognized the moccasins and bracelet he had given her. Her head had been severed just below the chin. She lay all in a heap with their two younger sons. The oldest boy lay slightly beyond them facing back toward Alope.

Goyathlay sat on the ground and put his hand to his eyes to erase the picture.

After a long time, Chokole's voice came to him, "Goyathlay."

He opened his eyes and looked at the warrior. "What?"

"It is not good for you to stay here."

"My mother?"

"She is not with us. She was in the tent of Tiamo when they struck."

"Oh."

"You must not stay here," Chokole repeated.

"Nadastin is still with us," Goyathlay said.

"I have seen her," Chokole mumbled. "Do not stay here." Then he was gone.

Goyathlay looked again at the body of Alope. If she had been alone, she would have made it to the scrub oaks. But she had tried to save the two boys.

Standing up, he walked to the oaks. Running his fingers over the blanket of fallen leaves, he found they had been pushed down evenly by moccasined feet, not crushed by soldiers' boots. His oldest son had been hiding here; Alope must have commanded him to run ahead. He had seen her fall and rushed back to help her. Kneeling, he put his hand on the back of the dead boy. He could be proud.

Goyathlay stood and walked very slowly, like an old man, through the camp. Parts of low-voiced conversation drifted to him.

"The Mexicans still pay for the scalp of a Bedonkohe."

"And they say they are at peace with us."

"In gold they will give one hundred dollars for the scalp of a brave, fifty for a woman and twenty-five for a child."

"There are sixty who are no longer with us."

"Goyathlay lost five."

"They are great warriors against women and children."

In the camp, the women had begun to wail for the dead.

Goyathlay walked wordlessly by the clustered groups toward a stream near the camp. Staring into the quietly running water, he thought of the gods of his people—the Giver of Life and the Child of Water; and last of all, he thought of the Killer of Enemies. Perhaps Killer of Enemies was the strongest god, for the other gods were helpless without him. One could not have life or families, trade in peace or hunt deer, with enemies surrounding him. Killer of Enemies was the only true god.

Goyathlay thought of his past life. He remembered the games he had played as a child; throwing marbles to the line, piling rocks to build a fortress against the white men, sneaking up soundlessly on grazing deer and buffalo. As he had grown older, the games had improved. Once, when he had a made a fine throw with a warclub, bringing a rabbit down in mid-air, Mangus Colorado had told him, "You will grow up to be a fine warrior if you ever stop yawning."

At 12 years he had received the name "Goyathlay," meaning The One Who Yawns. He couldn't help yawning. He loved to sleep. It was especially hard to stay awake when his mother had visitors and he had to sit in the wickiup and be polite. He always tried to hide the yawns, but his mother was sharp-eyed.

At 16, Goyathlay found he never got in trouble for yawning when Alope visited with her mother. Her bright eyes and mischievous smile made it impossible for him to feel tired.

The next year was a great one for Goyathlay. He was admitted to the Council of Warriors; the boy was now a man. His first action was to visit Noposo and ask for his daughter Alope.

Noposo eyed him shrewdly. Rolling oak leaves tightly around a long, thin core of tobacco, he lit the crude cigar and passed it to Goyathlay. "What can you give me for her?" he asked.

"I have three good ponies. Young and strong."

The old man took a long puff and blew smoke thoughtfully into the air. Then he said, "Alope words hard. She is a good girl. Many men are interested in her. It would make her happy if a warrior offered six ponies for her."

Goyathlay choked on the cigar smoke. "Six ponies?"

"Yes," Noposo said. "Other braves will come to talk with me. You better think it over."

That evening Goyathlay spoke to Alope. "Your father is a big thief," he told her.

"Why?"

"He is asking six ponies for you."

"How do you know?"

"I spoke to him."

"You did?" She smiled. Then the smile stopped. "And you don't think I'm worth that many ponies?"

"The three that I offered him are very good animals."

Alope stamped a knee-high moccasin hard on the ground. "There are others beside the one who yawns!"

"You just don't know the value of a good horse," Goyathlay explained.

Alope turned and strode away.

Goyathlay rode north the next day. When he returned, after ten days' absence, he had three horses with him.

Goyathlay tied the required six mounts in front of Noposo's wickiup. The old man smiled and called Alope out. Then he went back into the wickiup and, following tribal law, told his wife that she was now Goyathlay's mother-in-law and could never look at Goyathlay or speak to him again.

That night there was dancing and everyone drank too much *tiswin*. Alope's eyes reflected the stars and Goyathlay was happier than he had ever been.

Over the years, Alope had borne him three healthy sons. She had pounded corn to make him bread, had patiently scraped, chewed and worked the animal pelts into buckskin. She had always been there when he needed her, in their 12 summers together. And now—the thought struck him like a knife—he had not been there when she needed *him*.

For a moment he considered plunging his knife into his chest and joining his family in the Underworld. Then he remembered his chosen god, Killer of Enemies. He had to live to follow that god.

In the morning Chokole found Goyathlay by the driver. "Those who are no longer with us have been put to rest," he said. "We are returning north."

Goyathlay found the horses and unpacked his beads and cloth. He piled them with Alope's other possessions on the tattered remains of the tepee. From his quiver, he took his fire drill and a pinch of shredded juniper bark which he placed on a flat piece of sotol stalk on the ground. Twisting the thin, round drill between his palms, he soon sparked the tinder. He cupped it in his hands and blew until it burst into flame. Then he put the fired tinder under the red cloth. When the pile was burning fiercely, he joined the others as they started north. The Bedonkohe believed anything that was burned went underground with the dead. Alope, his mother and children would have the tent, the cloth and the beads.

Goyathlay spoke to Mangus Colorado. "We will return south for revenge?"

"Yes. First we must get more warriors, and we must put the women and children out of reach of the Mexicans."

At their permanent camp in the north, Goyathlay said to his chief, "My father's father was Maco, chief of the Nedni. They will listen to my voice."

"Go, then, and ask them for warriors."

Goyathlay talked to Chief Whoa and his Nedni braves a few days later. "You are my brothers and friends," he said. "If you come to war with the Bedonkohe, you will lose many men. But it will be to protect your women and children, for the Mexicans may attack you next."

"We cannot kill all the Mexicans," Whoa said.

"We can make them fear us," Goyathlay told him. "Or we can wait until they overrun our land and kill all of us. If you are afraid, say so and I will go to the Chokonen. They are warriors, not old women."

The Nedni braves muttered angrily. "I am for fighting!" one cried.

"And I," shouted another. "What will the Mexicans do if we let them kill our people without revenge?"

Goyathlay left the Nedni with a promise of the tribe's entire strength, 100 warriors.

Instead of heading south, back to his own village, he rode west to the land of the Chokonen. After six days, guards waved him by and he topped a hill where he could see the home of the Chokonen in the valley below. There were many small fires in the village. As he entered the circle of wickiups he saw they were making ready for war. Men were holding their arrows over glowing coals, to fire-harden the tips. Others pounded animal blood and cactus quills between smooth rocks; the mixture would be allowed to stand in the sun and ferment to make poison for the arrows. Still others came into the village carrying straight branches from mulberry trees to be used in making bows and lances.

Goyathlay found the Chokonen chief, Cochise, making a new saddle. He was stretching wet rawhide over a cottonwood frame. When he saw Goyathlay he said, "We have heard of the massacre at Kaskiyeh. Our hearts are heavy for our brothers."

"I have come to speak for warriors."

"You need not speak. My braves will go into Mexico with you."

Back at his own village, Goyathlay reported to Mangus Colorado, "Whoa will have one hundred warriors. Cochise, one hundred and twenty."

"You have done well. We will have more than three hundred braves. Now we must prepare for war."

To Goyathlay it seemed the preparations for war were long and tedious. He dreamed often of Alope and his family.

Finally, Whoa and Cochise rode in with their warriors to join the Bedonkohe. Buckskin was placed over pots to form drums. The number four was holy, so the drummers beat out a steady tempo that went: *thump tum tum tum, thump tum tum tum, thump tum tum tum*. Other villages relayed the message, and soon drums were echoing throughout the hills.

That afternoon the chiefs decided on a safe valley into which they would send the women and children to be guarded by older men and a few picked braves.

At nightfall the drums began booming out with greater frenzy, and a holy fire was built by the witch doctors for a war dance. A powerful *shaman* stepped into the light of the fire with a rifle and began the weapon ceremony. With his finger he made four crosses on his body and called upon the four thunders—black thunder, yellow thunder, blue thunder and white thunder. Grasping the rifle with both hands he chanted: "The stock is the earth, the barrel is the moon, the moving pieces are the whirlwind . . ." He repeated the ceremony with a bow and arrow, thus insuring the accuracy and deadliness of the Indian weapons, and at the same time guaranteeing misfires and inaccuracy to enemy weapons.

When the actual war dance began, the thunder of the drums increased. The chiefs called the warriors by name: "Chokole! What will you do when we meet the Mexicans?"

Each brave sprang into the circle of fire and demonstrated how he would fight. He shot imaginary arrows, trampled the enemy underfoot and drew his knife and slashed savagely at the invisible foe. The other braves voiced approval of his actions as he leaped about the fire by grunting, "Wuh! Wuh!" in time to the drums.

When Goyathlay's name was called, he simply walked in a circle around the fire once, holding up his right hand to indicate that he would be there. A Nedni brave yelled with derision. "He lost five," a Bedonkohe warrior reminded him, and the Nedni was silent.

After the war dance, Goyathlay walked through the sleeping village and to the top of the hill. For a long time he stood there still and silent, thinking of Alope, his children and his mother. Soon he would begin his vengeance. He said a wordless prayer to the Killer of Enemies.

When the sun rose, the women and children began their trek to safety, escorted by those who were to guard them. The warriors bound for Mexico put on sacred buckskin headbands to protect them in battle. They wore only loincloths, moccasins and a rawhide thong tied about their stomachs; the thong could be pulled tight if they became hungry and there was no food. A few of the wealthy men had flintlocks or a treasured percussion rifle, but most of the 300 carried bows, arrows and knives, as well as a spear or war club. Their hair was twisted together in a scalplock at the back, to form a convenient handle for anyone brave enough and strong enough to lift their scalps. The *shamans* and those who wanted to frighten their enemies painted themselves black with charcoal, and red and yellow with ocher.

Then, on a sunny morning in 1859, the combined Bedonkohe, Nedni and Chokonen tribes moved south, some on horseback and others pacing tirelessly beside them, toward the city of Arizpe to avenge the Kaskiyeh Massacre.

They arrived at the outskirts of Arizpe on the day when the time-*shaman* moved the 14th bead beyond the knot in his necklace. In two weeks they had met no one. From the hills outside the city they saw the gates swing wide and eight soldiers gallop forth under a white flag to meet them in truce.

The Indians waited patiently in a long line in the foothills while the eight-man party drew near. At 50 yards the leader of the Mexicans raised his arms and called, *"Paz!"* Bow strings sang as a cloud of arrows whined toward the white men. Leisurely, the Indians retrieved their arrows and made a human mound of the eight soldiers. On top of the mound they stuck the white flag of truce.

A company of infantry with a two-wagon supply train charged angrily out from the city to face the war party.

228

The Indians melted into the hills like rain drops falling into a river.

The captain of the infantry company was under the impression that the enemy was retreating and he was pursuing. As he whipped his crop down on his stallion's flank, an arrow thudded into his chest. There was a panicky retreat as whoops and shrieks filled the air and murderous arrows poured into the Mexicans from all directions.

Goyathlay was at the end of the Mexican force near the supply train. He sent an arrow into the driver of the lead wagon, then another into the soldier beside him who was groping for the reins.

"Toklonnen, Chokole!" he shouted. "Take the second wagon!" He sprinted for the driverless vehicle and leaped into the seat as two or three braves ran for the other. Rifle balls snarled past him as he bellowed at the horses and slapped the reins on their backs. A soldier lunged at him from under the canvas-top of the wagon. Goyathlay's war club cracked his skull. The horses leaped forward, swinging around and away from the noise. Once out of firing range, Goyathlay turned and saw the other wagon bouncing behind him with Chokole in the driver's seat.

The firing stopped soon after, and the rest of the infantrymen retreated to the flats surrounding Arizpe in front of the city gates. When the chiefs saw the captured wagons they were pleased. Both were loaded with food, guns and ammunition.

Whoa took a rifle from its box and said, "This is good. The men who know rifles must teach the others to load and shoot."

Mangus Colorado glanced at the sun and said, "The day is short. No more soldiers will come out before morning. We can start now. Use as few bullets as possible."

The glow of pink in the east signaled the beginning of the next day. Before the sun was free of the horizon, the gates of Arizpe swung open once more and the entire military might of the city—two companies of infantry and two companies of cavalry—came forth to crush the Indians. The man at the head of the cavalry was the squat, powerful man Goyathlay had seen long before, leading his men away from the Kaskiyeh Massacre. He and two other scouts hurried back into the hills to report.

"Four companies. Two on horse, two on foot," Goyathlay told the chiefs. "One of the mounted companies is

229

the one that made the attack on the women and children at Kaskiyeh."

Cochise nodded. "It is in my mind," he said, "to let Goyathlay command the warriors in this battle. Few have lost as he has."

Mangus Colorado stared with stern eyes at his young brave. "He has earned the honor by taking the supply wagons yesterday."

Whoa said, "His father's father was Maco, chief of the Nednis before me. Good blood flows in his veins. It shall be as you wish."

Goyathlay, standing where he had given his report, could not find his voice for a moment.

"I told you once," Mangus Colorado said, "that you would be a good warrior if you would stop yawning long enough. Are you going to stand silent?"

Goyathlay's voice came suddenly, and rather than betray his nervousness, he spoke sharply. "If I am to command this battle, none of you chiefs may fight," he declared. "It is better if there is only one leader." The chiefs nodded. "I want no warrior to use a rifle who did not have one before yesterday. We must use the weapons we know. The horses are to be taken to the rear. This battle will be fought on foot, and it will be fought with clubs, knives and spears."

A few minutes later Goyathlay led his swarm of fighting men to a rounded, thickly wooded mountain near which the Mexicans would pass. To 30 select riflemen and 30 expert bowmen he said, "Hide yourselves in the woods near the top of the mountain. Don't shoot when the scouts pass. Begin shooting only when the Mexican leader rides past the tall rock at the far side of the pass."

At the foot of the mountain, the plain was heavy with trees. Two hundred yards from its base was a stream which cut six feet straight into the ground, leaving a bank which was a natural breastwork. Goyathlay hid the bulk of his warriors out of sight behind the stream's bank. "Don't muddy the water," he cautioned. "The Mexicans may look at it downstream."

Fifteen minutes after Goyathlay had given his final orders, the Mexicans' Indian scouts appeared, hurrying before the column. They would stop and twist their heads from side to side, their eyes traveling nervously over the terrain, their noses quivering in search of any unusual odor. Then they were gone.

After five minutes there was the familiar tinkling of steel on steel. This time Goyathlay was near enough to hear the creaking of leather as the soldiers shifted their weight in the saddles. First came the two companies of cavalry, the squat man riding in the lead. Behind them were the foot soldiers, their rifles held at high port instead of balanced across the shoulder. On and on they came. Goyathlay had never seen so many soldiers at one time. He estimated that there were 800 of them. It would be a bloody fight.

The leader was almost to the tall rock. The enemy's whole flank was exposed to the marksmen on the hill. One of the Indian riflemen moved to take careful aim and started a loose pebble rolling. A tense, keen-eyed Mexican cavalryman shouted a warning and whirled his horse in the direction of the sound. Instantly the thunder of battle crashed through the air. Rifles roared from the hill, arrows flashed in the sun, wounded horses screamed and plunged, men cursed and shouted. Realizing his predicament, the Mexican commander screamed the retreat: *"Vayamos para el rio!"*

The Mexicans backed slowly through the trees toward the river, returning steadily the fire from the hill. Every Indian at the river was watching Goyathlay. Gripping a war club and a knife in his hands, he vaulted from the high bank. Seconds later they were all up and charging the bewildered Mexicans.

Goyathlay had a fleeting thought of Alope and his children lying dead in the moonlight as he leaped at the nearest Mexican. Then, as the man sagged to the ground with his head clubbed into a bleeding mass, Goyathlay burst into the middle of the fight, his club and knife dealing out death.

The trained cavalry horses could stand gunfire or cannon, but the surging army of Indians was too much for them. The Indians fought the animals as well as their riders, and in the stampeding confusion the cavalrymen lost control over their terrified mounts. At such close quarters their lances and rifles were worthless. They struggled to draw their only usable weapons, sabers. The infantrymen were no better off. Their clumsy rifles were not made for hand-to-hand combat, and if they withdrew to reload, the marksmen on the hill picked them off.

As the fierce battle raged, the squat Mexican captain tried to set up a hasty defense in a small clearing. Goyathlay hacked a bloody path through the blue-coated enemy toward him. The captain saw him coming and rode down on him, swinging viciously with his sword. Goyathlay ducked and tried to parry the blow with his war club. The club was knocked from his hand, but the sharp blade missed him. Goyathlay grabbed the officer by the waist and dragged him from his mount. As the squirming man fought to slash at him again, Goyathlay ripped the captain's throat with his knife. Blood spurted from the dying man's neck and spilled onto his uniform.

Whirling, Goyathlay plunged savagely into the nearest mass of soldiers, fighting now with only his knife. But the knife was enough. The Mexicans had seen the powerful warrior driving through their lines, crushing skulls and chests with his war club, slashing so fast with his knife that the eye could not follow. They had seen their captain, the most feared fighter among them, go down like a child before his onslaught. Now they bawled in sheer terror, *"Madre mia! Beware the Unholy One!"*

They retreated before him like leaves before a howling wind.

Goyathlay was invincible. His warriors, inspired by their leader's incredible strength and courage, fought as they had never fought before. By ones, twos and half dozens, the Mexicans deserted and fled wild-eyed down the valley toward Arizpe, never realizing—or caring— that they outnumbered the Indians nearly three to one.

After two and a half hours of battle, the fighting thinned out rapidly. The field was littered with bodies, and the sharpshooters on the hill had run out of ammunition. Goyathlay and four warriors charged the final group of Mexicans, and when the dust had cleared, only Goyathlay and Toklonnen stood. Goyathlay's knife had finally snapped off in the body of a soldier.

Two cavalrymen who had been sent from Arizpe to try to find out what had happened, galloped onto the scene. Goyathlay dodged as the soldiers raised their rifles and fired, but Toklonnen was hit. As the two mounted men spurred toward Goyathlay to finish the job, he snatched a spear from a fallen brave's hand. Leaping to one side as the soldiers sped past with lances lowered, he drove it into the nearest rider, breaking the spear and hurling him to the ground. The man groped feebly for his sword, then died.

The second cavalryman swung in a tight turn and

thundered back. Goyathlay grabbed the saber from the first Mexican's lifeless grip and straightened to meet the charge. He knocked the sharp lance aside with the unfamiliar weapon and plunged the saber into the cavalryman as the horse brushed swiftly by him.

Goyathlay was the last warrior standing on the field. When the Indians who had been watching the battle from the hills arrived on the scene, their first task was caring for the wounded. This done, they unanimously proclaimed Goyathlay war chief over the Nedni, Bedonkohe and Chokonen tribes, the three groups that made up the Chiricahua branch of the Apache race.

Their choice was a good one. In the years to come, Goyathlay outfought and outfoxed 5,000 American soldiers and uncountable numbers of Mexican troops. With only 18 men, he terrorized the countryside on both sides of the Mexican border. He was the last great leader of Indian resistance in the United States.

The Mexicans who straggled back into Arizpe that afternoon were muttering and crying under their breath about *Jerome*—the "unholy one."

As soldiers are inclined to do, they had changed a sacred word into a curse. *Jerome* really meant "holy one."

Goyathlay was known from that time on as Jerome. He liked the name because it meant that he was evil to the Mexicans—and that is what Goyathlay intended to be. He would always be true to his god, the Killer of Enemies. The name Jerome is pronounced differently in Spanish than it is in English. The Mexicans say it, "Geronimo."

THE SAGA OF SAM BASS

Sam and his outlaw "army" almost put the Texas railroads out of business and had the best lawmen in the nation tearing out their hair—until a traitor did him in.

Sam Bass was born in Indiana—that was his native home. And at the age of seventeen, young Sam began to roam. He first came out to Texas, a cowboy for to be.

A kinder-hearted feller, you scarcely ever see.

Daniel and Elizabeth Bass raised a big family on their farm outside Mitchell, Indiana. Their fourth son, Samuel, was born on the 21st day of July in 1851. As a boy, Sam was a hard worker, quiet and industrious. His proud parents often boasted that he was the solid, dependable sort of lad who would grow up, marry one of the gingham-clad girls around Mitchell, and settle down on his own farm to be a respected citizen, raise up a family and live a long, peaceful life.

They had no way of knowing that their youngster would never have time to marry or settle down, that he was to lead a short, violent life that would be hammered to a close by the pounding bullets of Texas Ranger Colts. As for Sam's being a respected citizen, this surmise was not quite true, either. Sam was to become Texas' most beloved bandit, adored and venerated by half the people in his adopted state—but the other half would angrily insist hanging was too good for him. He was to become an almost mythical figure in the Southwest, a sort of legendary six-gun Robin Hood surrounded by lean-hipped Merry Men who thundered down out of the hills to rob the rich and give to the poor, and who blithely drove a legion of confused law officers almost to insanity—until a traitor entered his camp.

When he was ten, Sam's mother died. Then, while the boy was just getting over this great blow, his older brothers went off to fight the Civil War and news quickly came back that two of them had been killed. Sam's father never recovered from these shocks, and a little later, his health gone, the old man departed from this world, too.

Now an orphan, a tall, skinny youth who talked in a shy whisper and whose face reflected the thought that life was a pretty grim prospect, Sam was sent to a nearby farm to live with his mother's well-to-do brother, Dave Sheeks. They say that Uncle David welcomed the distraught boy with open arms—in one outstretched arm was a shovel, and in the other a pitchfork. Sheeks worked the boy day and night, seven days a week. In return, he generously saw to it that Sam had something to eat every now and then, and enough clothes to just barely cover his lanky frame.

During the years that Sam was literally in bondage to his uncle, his schooling was completely ignored. He never did master the complexities of reading and writing. Later in life, when he made his heavy, laborious signature, he often rested after printing the "B" so that the name sometimes had an unhappy way of looking like Sam B. Ass, a point over which even his closest friends never failed to chuckle.

The only cheerful moments that brightened the otherwise gloomy years Sam spent with his uncle were the times when he would hear exciting (and highly exaggerated) stories of the Reno Gang, a tough bunch of badmen marauding through the territory. They staged one holdup only a few miles from Sheeks' farm and by the time the news reached Sam, their loot was being estimated at $100,000.

That, Sam felt, must be the life. No worries, no cares. Just wander around having fun—and when you run short of cash, simply pull out your gun and take some.

When he was 17, young Sam told his tyrannical uncle he wanted some sort of an allowance or wages in return for his hard labor. Sheeks had never in his life parted willingly with a penny, and he wasn't about to change his ways, so the two reached an impasse. Around his 18th birthday, Sam saw clearly that he had to choose between being a serf for Uncle Dave indefinitely or striking out on his own. He didn't have the problem of what to pack; he simply walked off the farm and worked his way to St. Louis, from there moving on to Rosedale.

In Rosedale, Sam got a job in a lumbermill and decided life might turn out to be fun after all. He spent about a year there, and people just naturally liked the quiet, easy-going young man. It was at this time that Sam bought his first brace of revolvers and taught himself how to use them with notable expertness, although he thought too much of people to shoot them up in the then accepted manner, and made up his mind never to do so if it could be avoided.

One of his many friends, a man named Mays, told Sam he was taking his family to Texas, and young Bass decided to go along with them. They made their way in a prairie schooner to the town of Denton in the Lone Star State, and Sam went to work at a variety of jobs. He rode as a cow-puncher, then became a stablehand at the Lacey House, a hotel in Denton. Colonel William Eagan, a prominent Denton citizen who owned considerable real estate in the town and was also the sheriff, took a liking to Sam. He hired him as general handyman and later took to swearing him in as special deputy whenever Sam's particular talents were needed. These talents consisted of the rare ability to make friends right away with anyone. They say young Sam Bass could slap a coiled rattlesnake on the shoulder and invite it for a drink and the rattler would insist on buying. Sam had the knack of making a happy-go-lucky pal out of anyone, and he caused many potential gun battles in the streets of Denton to wind up as good-natured discussions in the nearest bar.

Sam was doing fine. But then, just after his 24th birthday, he did something that made him some easy money and eventually plunged him into a life of lawlessness. Sam bought a horse, and that was the beginning of the end.

> He made a deal in race stock, one called the Denton
> Mare,
> He matched her in scrub races and took her to the
> fair.
> Sam always coined the money, and spent it just as
> free,
> He always drank good whiskey, wherever he might
> be.

The horse's name was Jenny, and while she had no thoroughbred pretentions, the Denton Mare did have a wide streak of jackrabbit in her. Sam had always thought a salary of $25 a month was real riches, but when his friends talked him into running Jenny in a local scrub race and he wound up holding $100 in his slightly trembling hand, he suddenly had an entirely new idea of money. "Holy smoke!" he muttered. "This is a season's wages!"

When Sam drank, everyone drank, and that night everyone got roaring drunk, with Sam leading off at the bar.

Sheriff Eagen tried to talk him out of the horse-racing business, but Sam wouldn't listen to him. He had worked hard all his life and he had been poor all his life. He could plainly see that hard work and poverty are too often stablemates. Sam quit Eagan and made a small vow never to do another day's work as long as he lived. And whatever his critics may say, it must be admitted that Sam fulfilled that vow with the utmost tenacity.

He made a science of horse racing. He hired a tiny Negro jockey named Dick Eidson who weighed only a little more than the bridle Jenny wore. To cut down weight even farther, Dick used no saddle. On days when the diminutive rider had a hangover, they would spread a little sorghum on Jenny's back to keep the jock glued on when the mare whizzed down the track. Sam found that Jenny could do even better if she started from a two-foot bank built up behind her hind heels. At the races, in plain sight of the crowd, he and Dick would patiently dig up the track and pack a starting bank for the Denton Mare. If there were any complaints, Sam would begrudgingly offer his opponents a two-length handicap, knowing perfectly well that Jenny would hoot out from the bank like a low-flying rocket. Even with a three- and four-length handicap, Jenny rarely lost a quarter-mile race.

The money was rolling in at a rate almost equal to Jenny's uncanny pace. Sam paid Dick as much as $300 a race and treated his sorrel mare like a four-legged princess. At the same time he started going around with some high-living characters of the kind you always encounter around race tracks. He met Henry Underwood, a connoisseur of United States and Mexican jails, and he met a part-time badman Joel Collins. His association with such men caused folks to begin to pay some attention to the evil rumors a few hard losers were spreading. They said Sam doped horses. They said he paid stablemen to twist thin strands of baling wire around other horses' legs, wire that would tighten into the flesh as they ran and cripple them. Such talk wasn't true. Sam loved horses too much to mistreat them. But he did work a little confidence game with Joel Collins.

Joel would come into a town acting like a stranger to Sam, and sneer openly at Jenny. He would say he had seen the Denton Mare run and that she was nothing but an overrated plow horse who couldn't outdistance a flat-footed turtle with a sprained ankle. "As a matter of plain fact, stranger," Joel would say, "they got a horse in this town that can run circles around your nag. I got $200 that says Speedwell, the local champ, can win in a walk!"

"Why, my Jenny can beat that broken-down mule running backwards!" Sam would snort contemptuously.

The outraged citizenry, spurred on by patriotism and by Joel's confidence, would then zealously lay it on the line in support of the local horse and the team would move on to the next town, considerably richer. They took in most of Texas with this simple dodge, then moved up into Oklahoma. A few miles from Fort Sill, Sam found some Cherokee Indians who had justifiable pride in their swift mounts. He put Jenny up against the fastest pony the tribe could produce, betting cold cash against several of the redskins' horses. Jenny won, but the race was close and the Cherokees refused to pay up. Since there were about 30 of them, outnumbering Sam and his friends ten to one, Bass just shrugged his shoulders and left the camp. But that night he came back and took the Cherokee

238

horses he had won—plus a few extra for interest—and started back for Texas.

The Cherokees had long boasted that no white man could ever get into their camp undetected. When they discovered their loss, they were furious. They sent a rider to report the incident to the nearest sheriff, who immediately collected a posse and headed Sam off near the border.

The sheriff drew up a hundred yards from where Sam faced him on Jenny and called out, "Stop in the name of the law! I'm taking them ponies back to their rightful owners!"

"They're with their rightful owners!" Sam yelled back. He put a hand on each of his revolvers and added, "Before you take them, we'll wade knee deep in blood!"

Such was Sam's manner when angered that the sheriff thought his words over quietly and then rode back to tell the Cherokees their horses couldn't be found.

Jenny went lame after they got back to Texas and Sam regretfully put her out to pasture on a friend's farm. He was drinking down his sorrow over the loss of the Denton Mare when Joel Collins had an idea how Sam might invest the money he hadn't yet thrown away. He suggested that they buy some longhorns and drive them up north where prices were high. Sam forthwith bought a herd.

> Sam left the Collins ranch in the merry month of
>   May,
> With a herd of Texas cattle that grew some on the
>   way.
> Sold out in Custer City and then got on a spree,
> A jollier set of cowboys, you seldom ever see.

Sam made Joel his ramrod and they left Joel's ranch for Dodge City with a few forgetful cowboys they had picked up in various saloons around town. These *vaqueros* were so forgetful that they couldn't quite remember what Sam's trail brand was, and they were forever accidentally picking up stray cattle along the way. By the time they got to Dodge City the herd had doubled in size and the authorities in that town raised an embarrassing technical point of ownership. Naturally Sam couldn't remember where all the extra steers had come from, and he couldn't rightly recall where he had put the nonexistent bills of sale, so they drove the herd on into Nebraska where the authorities at that time were much less inclined to ask questions. The poor memories of everyone involved resulted in Sam's netting $8,000 after the boys had been paid off and all expenses met.

He and Joel next wandered down into Ogallala where the town was frantic with talk of the gold strike in Deadwood. It didn't take them long to catch the fever. They traveled to the Black Hills and joined the wild colony hastily assembling there.

Winter hit within a few weeks. The thermometer plummeted to 30 below zero and stayed there.

Sam promptly dropped most of his $8,000 in a worthless mining claim. He and Joel tried everything from professional gambling to running a bordello in the sprawling red-light district, but they went steadily down in funds. Even Sam's good nature was strained when spring came and they found themselves stone broke. Things were so black it looked as though Sam might have to break his vow and go to work again.

When knee-deep mud had replaced the snow along Deadwood's main drag, Sam told Joel, "Hell, I guess the only thing to do is rob a stagecoach." They found three other men low on their luck—Jim Berry, Frank Towle and Bill Reddy, who liked Sam's simple, straightforward idea. The five rookie robbers were so poor they had to steal the horses - they needed for the job, but on March 25th, 1877, they galloped their stolen steeds to a gulch three miles outside of Deadwood, tied red bandannas around their faces and waited patiently for the coach. When the stage lumbered into the draw beneath them, Sam called out, "Haul on those reins! This is a holdup!"

Johnny Slaughter, the driver, did exactly that. He stopped and held up his hands. Johnny was a fine, cooperative driver to stick up. But Bill Reddy aimed his scattergun at the tranquil man in the driver's seat and blasted poor Johnny nearly in two. The horses panicked at the thundering echoes of the shotgun volley and took off in a dead run for town, a strong box holding $15,000 bouncing safely in the boot.

Sam threatened to kill Reddy for the senseless murder. Reddy was so impressed with the way Sam expressed himself on this topic that he galloped away and was never heard of again.

240

Disgusted beyond words, the others rode into Deadwood to join in the general outcry over Johnny's untimely demise and to curse the blackhearted villains who had tried to rob the stage. Sam was so well liked that the law in Deadwood never did tie him up with the evil doing. Half a dozen stages were held up for minor sums during the following weeks. After each one, Sam was richer. But the local peace officers put his wealth down to luck at blackjack.

The trouble with robbing stages was, there wasn't any real money in it. You could count on a brass watch or two from the passengers and maybe $100 or so from the strongbox, but that was all. With so many coaches being held up, the shippers became wary; big shipments of gold were sent through when they were least expected, and even then the dust was cleverly hidden. One stage that Sam held up for its gold contained exactly nothing. The driver had only $30 on him, and since he told Sam he was getting married, Sam didn't take his money.

"Joel," Sam confessed later on, "I'm getting tired of risking my neck for flapjack money and a few brass watches."

Joel agreed that their plight was a sad one, and they were lamenting the deplorable state of the stagecoach-robbing business when a California renegade by the name of Jack Davis approached them. "Sam," Jack said, "if you're looking for gold, the place to find it is on the Union Pacific trains."

This was a pleasing thought. No one particularly liked trains anyway. They were thought of generally as the tentacles of a corporate octopus back East which was greedily grabbing up all the West. Also, rumor had it that a young fellow named Jesse James was doing well by sticking up trains. Sam liked the idea and made plans accordingly.

> On their way back to Texas they robbed the U.P. train,
> And then split up in couples and started out again.
> Joel Collins and his partner were overtaken soon.
> With all their stolen money, they had to meet their doom.

On the night of September 19, Sam rode at the head of five men toward the tiny station at Big Springs, Nebraska, where the eastbound Union Pacific was scheduled to make a water stop. Along with Joel and Jack Davis, he had recruited Jim Berry, Bill Heffridge and Tom Nixon. At a little before 10 o'clock, they halted their horses outside the ring of light cast from the stationhouse and put bandannas around their faces. Their horses snorted nervously as the 10 o'clock train rumbled out of the darkness and screeched to a stop. Sam rode up to the express car while his companions appeared out of the night to cover the conductor, engineer, brakeman and station attendant. Holding a .45 on the pertrified express-car messenger, Sam hoisted himself out of the saddle and into the car.

"Friend," he said softly, "how would you like to open that safe?"

The attendant stuttered that he didn't know how, and Sam believed him. Exploring the interior of the car, Sam found a heavy pouch near the safe. Opening it, he saw that it was filled with $20 gold pieces. "This is my meat," he told the messenger. "We won't have to bother with the safe." He called for Joel to come and pick up the pouch, then vaulted into the saddle and joined the others as they headed for the hills.

When they were some distance out of Big Springs, Sam ordered a halt. They spent nearly two hours counting the gold pieces. There were 3,000 of them. "Sixty thousand dollars!" Joel whistled. "That's what I call a good night's work!"

"Thing to do now," Sam told them, "is divide the money and split up. Posses all over Nebraska will be looking for six men. I'm going back down to Denton, and one of you can come along. Two of you go east, and two west. Chances are better that way."

Joel and Bill Heffridge decided to head west, while Nixon and Berry went east. Jack Davis elected to go south with Sam.

By sunup Sam and Jack were 20 miles along the trail. When the sun's beams flashed across the prairie at them, Sam took one of the $20 gold pieces out of his saddle bags and looked at it. It shone brightly in the sun. It was a newly minted coin with the year 1877 printed on it. The coins were brand-new.

"Almost too pretty to spend," Sam laughed.

In Kansas City the two riders heard that lawmen were fanning out all over the state searching for the desperate gang of train robbers. It wasn't rightly known who they were, but it was expected that they would be spending 1877 gold pieces right and left. Sam and Jack didn't spend any money. They traded their two good horses for an old plow horse and a beaten-down rig to escape suspicion. On their way south from Kansas City they were joined and escorted by a troop of soldiers who had been detailed to help in the manhunt. They were on the road together for several days, and Sam often remarked of that time, "I felt right safe with them soldiers to look out for me."

At Fort Worth, Jack Davis took a train for New Orleans. "I'm going down to South America and get me a ranch," he told Sam. "Why don't you come along? The States'll be too hot for you."

"'Oh, I reckon not," Sam said. "I kind of like Denton. It's sort of like a hometown to me. You be careful on that train," he cautioned. "No telling where them desperadoes will pop up next."

After Jack's train had pulled out, Sam visited a nearby saloon for a bit of refreshment. In the bar he listened with interest while others discussed the robbery. After half an hour a man rushed in with the latest report. An hombre named Joe Collins and his sidekick, Bill Heffridge, had been halted as a routine matter by a sheriff who had two deputies and a squad of ten soldiers with him. The two suspects had made a break and gone for their guns. They had been cut to pieces by murderous, point-blank fire from the soldiers' rifles.

Feeling slightly sick, Sam left the bar. He bought a fast horse and outfitted it the next day. Before he left Fort Worth, he got his second shock. Jim Berry had been cornered in Missouri by a posse and was now lying near death. Within three weeks, half of the gang had been shot up.

Sam made it back to Texas, all right side up with
   care,
Rode into the town of Denton, with all his friends
   to share.
Sam's life was short in Texas, four robberies did he
   do,
He robbed all the passengers, mail and express cars
   too.

Following little-known trails, Sam rode on toward Denton. He stopped at Cove Hollow, a lonely spot thickly overrun with trees and underbrush 30 miles outside of Denton, and set up a camp. Living there in the Hollow, he gradually began to regain his confidence. Sometimes he even rode into Denton at night to see some of his old buddies and cut up a few touches in the saloons. He ran into Hank Underwood again, and along with a likable gunslinger named Frank Jackson, they spent considerable time drinking and rousting about. Sam decided that no one outside of his close friends knew he was a holdup man after all, and with Bass picking up the bills, the trio outfitted themselves with new clothes, new horses and new guns and whooped out for San Antonio to go on a spree. In San Antonio they went on a wild round of wine, women and song—but Sam was throwing around too many of those shiny gold pieces. He often paid $20 for a meal, a cigar or a shoeshine, telling the astonished recipient to keep the change.

But then one night a venturesome blonde whom Sam had availed himself of from time to time came to where he was living. "There's some cops in town looking for you," she told Sam. "One of them's a Pinkerton man, and he's got two deputies from Denton with him."

"They interested in anything in particular?" Sam asked.

"I hear they're curious about a trail of 1877 gold pieces you've left all the way from Denton."

Sam thanked the girl, hunted up Underwood and Jackson, and headed out of San Antonio. He could have made it across the border into Mexico, but he told Jackson, "God damn it, Texas is where all my friends are. No one's going to drive me out of the state."

They rode back to their camp in Cove Hollow and, against Sam's advice, Underwood went on into Denton. "They'll claim you had a part in the Big Springs holdup, Hank," Sam told him.

Underwood had been in Denton exactly 15 minutes when Sheriff Eagan and three deputies jailed him. They suspected that he was the "Tom Nixon" who had been in on the U.P. robbery. Hank was so enraged at this "terrible miscarriage of justice" that he was speechless. A special deputy had him halfway to Nebraska for trial before the shock wore off and he started cussing at the top of his voice.

Sam and Frank hurried into Denton as soon as they heard of Hank's arrest. But the news had traveled too slowly, and poor Hank was already over the state line. They ran smack into Deputy Sheriff Tom Gerrin, who yelled for help and started blazing away at them with his revolver. Sam emptied his gun into the air. Gerrin, sure that he was about to have his head blown off, was so nervous he couldn't have hit the ground beneath him twice in a row.

Riding back to Cove Hollow, Sam realized that once a man is on the Hoot Owl trail, there is no turning back. He had been pretty idle lately, half thinking that no one would associate him with the U.P. holdup, hoping that it would blow over in time. But obviously he was now in the outlaw game for keeps. Sam and Frank moved to Hickory Creek, a little closer to Denton, where no one would be likely to think to look for them, then held up the stage at Weatherford just to keep in practice. Frank was jubilant over the $500 they got from the stage, but Sam told him it was nothing. "We'll round up a couple of boys and take on a train the next time," he promised.

Frank then uttered a classic understatement of the West. He shook his head thoughtfully and said, "It looks to me as if train robbin' might be gettin' kind of dangerous."

"I reckon," Sam admitted, "that there is some truth in what you say."

They put the deal up to an old friend of Sam's, Jim Murphy, who had a farm not far out of Denton. Jim liked the idea of robbing trains but didn't have the guts to go along. He used his father as an excuse, saying that the old man couldn't be left alone. Then they talked to Seab Barnes and Tom Spottswood about train robbing, and both Seab and Tom thought it offered a fine future.

Within the next two months, Sam completely revolutionized the railroad industry in Texas. He held up four trains in 48 days, a record that stands unbroken in all the gaudy history of the West. Lawmen from all over the nation swarmed into Texas until it was said that two out of every three people on the streets of Denton and Dallas were private detectives or official police—and the third man was one of Sam's gang. Newspapers all over the country outdid each other in front page spreads devoted to accounts of Sam and his "outlaw army." Estimates as to the number of the gang ran from 50 to 150.

245

On the night of February 22, 1878, Sam led his three men to Allen station on the outskirts of Dallas. When the Houston and Texas Central train chugged into the station, Sam entered the express car while the others held guns on the surprised railroad employees. They cleared out with $1,300 amid the usual hail of angry shots and made it back to Hickory Creek. Tom Spottswood wandered off and soon got himself arrested in town. Seab took sick. Sam's "army" of 150 men was now cut to one man. He and Frank helped Seab over his illness and then, on March 18, rode over to Hutchins to rob the Houston and Texas Central all over again. This time they only got $500, and the railroad men decided to put up a real fight as the boys galloped away. The air was filled with bullets and the express messenger chased them down the road on foot, yelling and shaking his fist. He might even have caught them except that the brakeman on his own train brought him down with a rifle ball in the leg.

The boys made it back to Hickory Creek and found Hank Underwood waiting for them there with another jailbird named Arkansas Johnson. Hank had broken out of jail and brought Arkansas along with him. They went through a few bottles of whiskey by way of celebrating the reunion, then got down to planning future operations.

On April 4, they tackled the Texas and Pacific Railroad at Eagle Ford, practically in the downtown area of Dallas. Only six nights later they popped up in Mesquite in time to catch the 11 o'clock train at the station. Frank Jackson lined up the station agent, engineer and brakeman on the platform while the other boys placed themselves at strategic points. Sam started for the mail car. Suddenly the conductor appeared on the platform with a small caliber pocket pistol and started shooting. The gun sounded like a little, yapping dog, and the conductor wasn't hitting within ten feet of where he was aiming, so the boys just laughed at him. Angered, the conductor ducked back into the train and came out a moment later with a heavy pair of .45 Colts. When he started blowing the station down in an irresponsible way with these small cannons, Sam regretfully shot him through the shoulder. Just to keep him from killing anyone. Several passengers added to the confusion by shooting from the train windows, and two armed guards on the train proved to be trigger-happy, too.

In the deafening roar of gunfire, Sam found that the

246

messenger had locked the mail-car door from the inside. He had to threaten to burn the car down before the stubborn little man would open it. Sam found only a miserable $150 in the car, and on top of that the messenger timidly inquired if he could have a receipt for the money so his boss would know that he hadn't stolen it himself. Any bandit but Sam Bass, listening to the good-sized war going on outside and finding a negligible $150 in loot, would have shot the messenger. But good-natured Sam patiently scrawled his signature at the bottom of a receipt and handed it over.

By the time Sam and his boys ran for their horses and rode into the night, the station was so pockmarked with bullet holes it looked as though the whole Civil War had been fought right there. Fortunately, no one had been killed. A few minutes after the shooting was over, a man named Gross came into the light of the station, pushing a reluctant figure before him. "Lookit here!" he bellowed. "I caught Sam Bass hisself, singlehanded!"

Gross had succeeded in capturing the train's fireman.

Sam had four companions, each a bold and daring lad,
Underwood and Jackson, Tom Spottswood and Seab,
Four of the boldest cowboys the rangers ever knew,
They whupped the Texas Rangers and ran the boys in blue.

The four holdups very nearly ruined railroading in Texas. People knew that Sam wasn't robbing passengers, but they didn't know when he might start, and they were cashing in tickets and refusing to ride trains all over the state. Express company officers were frantic as the harried officials tore their hair and tried to think of hiding places for valuables being shipped.

Figuring that Sam wouldn't let the banks off forever, citizens all over the state began drawing out their deposits.

Newspaper writers began to flock to Denton County, only to find all available hotel space taken up by police. U.S. Marshal Stilwell H. Russel was at the Windsor Hotel with 19 men. William Pinkerton, Allen Pinkerton's son, had taken over the LeGrand Hotel with a battalion of assistant investigators. Hordes of detectives hired by the railroads and express companies flocked through the territory. Federal investigators and local lawmen added to the chaos, while private sleuths, eager to catch Sam and collect the rewards that were growing every day, helped to make Sam's pursuit a comedy of errors. A bewhiskered gentleman in the streets of Denton dropped his beard. Blushing furiously, he tried to replace the false whiskers as he hurried around a corner. Two special deputies proudly brought in "Sam Bass," only to discover that their victim was another special deputy.

Topping the crest of the flood of lawmen, Major John Jones and Captain June Peak of the Texas Rangers arrived with 30 handpicked men to try their luck at catching Bass. Major Jones knew Sam couldn't be far away. He also knew Sam was even coming into Denton upon occasion but was so well thought of among the townspeople that no one would inform on him. Indeed, because he was so generous with the proceeds of his train robberies, they thought of him as a kind of Robin Hood.

Jones devised a simple plan. He began arresting everyone who had ever been known to be on particularly good terms with Sam, and trying to pump them for information. This meant arresting a goodly portion of Denton County, but Jones was a determined man. He quizzed Spottswood unsuccessfully, arrested Albert Pipes, Henry Herndon and Jim Murphy, all of whom were intimates of Sam, and all of whom were suspected of belonging to his gang. Within a few days he had made dozens of arrests and had even picked up Jim Murphy's old dad, for it was known that he had spoken to Sam on numerous occasions.

In the meantime, Captain Peak was scouring the area with his contingent of Rangers. They ran into other posses more than anything else, but they did have occasional brushes with Sam. Once the two groups spotted each other from clear across Cove Hollow, a distance of nearly 2,500 feet. One of the Rangers took a shot at the bandits and the slug tore a hole in Sam's rifle stock. The shot was pure luck, of course, but it made Sam so mad the others had to talk him out of going back to battle the Rangers at odds of about eight to one.

They even had the Army searching for Sam, and it got so the boys couldn't get a good night's sleep at the Hickory Creek camp. No one ever actually looked there, since it was so close to Denton, but troops of horses going by at all hours made too much noise for relaxation.

248

Sam moved out to Salt Creek to avoid the crowds. On the way there, they met two posses. In each case Sam passed his gang off as a team of express company agents, and solemnly agreed with the other posses that Sam Bass was a very elusive cuss.

At Salt Creek they found things a little quieter. They stayed there calmly while peace officers roamed in droves about the county, shooting at each other. Then, by sheer accident, the Rangers stumbled on the Salt Creek hideout.

Sam had another companion called Arkansas for
  short,
He was shot by a Texas Ranger by the name of
  Thomas Floyd.
Tom is a big six-shooter, and he acts mighty shy,
But I can tell you his racket, he's a deadbeat on the
  sly.

Sam only had a few seconds' notice. The Rangers were coming noisily through the underbrush on horseback, unaware that they were wandering right into Sam's camp. He warned his boys in a whisper and they hurried away, leading the nearest horses. When the Rangers found the camp, there was no one in sight, but they did succeed in getting Sam's provisions and half of his horses.

The next day the Rangers dropped off their captured horses in Denton and took out for the hills to continue their search. As they disappeared out of town in one direction, three riders came into town from the other direction. Sam had brought along Frank Jackson and Seab Barnes to reclaim their "stolen" horses. By high noon they had the stablehand tied up and they led their mounts at a leisurely trot down the main street of Denton under the noses of countless lawmen who were telling each other where and how to catch Sam Bass.

An hour later, Sheriff Eagan, Sam's ex-employer, found that Sam had reclaimed his horses. Eagan led a posse of 50 men out of Denton after the gang. A few miles from town the sheriff found a six-man party of Rangers who had run into Sam. Sam had wounded one of them and put all six afoot so they couldn't follow him. Eagan put a professional tracker to work and they kept on the trail until late at night. They finally heard the Bass gang moving up ahead of them and opened fire. There was a violent gun battle that lasted most of the night. In the morning it was discovered that two men had been wounded in the fray. It was also discovered that the "Bass gang" was a posse who thought Eagan's bunch was the Bass gang.

Where Sam had disappeared to, no one knew. Reports coming in from all over Texas indicated that every 24 hours Sam was in at least 200 places over an area of several thousand square miles. The most plausible tale was that of a Denton man who claimed he saw Sam sitting on his horse near Hickory Creek. In the distance a posse was kicking up dust as they hell-for-leathered it toward Palo Pinto where, according to the latest reports, Sam was in hiding. The Denton man added further that Sam was grinning a very quiet grin, like a fox watching a pack of yelping hounds who had gone off the trail.

Captain June Peak was in for a second break, though. On May 12, he and several men bumped into Sam's camp again. This time they drew blood. Hank Underwood was shot in the arm, an outlaw named Carter who had just teamed up with the gang was shot through the leg, and Arkansas Johnson was shot in the neck, a wound that turned out to be fatal. Even with his boys shot up somewhat, Sam managed to hold the Rangers off until nightfall when he got the survivors away. Underwood and Carter decided while nursing their wounds that this wild life was beginning to be a strain on them, and they left the gang to head for Mexico. Although newspapers across the country were still filled with stories about Sam's whopping big army of desperadoes, the number of badmen under his command was now exactly two. He had faithful Frank Jackson and Seab Barnes still with him. He didn't know it, but he was about to get a new recruit.

Jim Murphy was arrested and then released on bail.
He jumped his bond at Tyler and took the train for Terrell.
But Major Jones had posted Jim, and that was all a stall,
'Twas only a plan to capture Sam before the coming fall.

250

Major Jones had been busy all this time. He had talked to every person who knew Sam Bass and arrested everyone who could even vaguely be charged with aiding and abetting the fugitive. Jones was a shrewd psychologist and he figured the weakest friend Sam had was Jim Murphy. He told him that he sure hated to hold him and his dad in jail, but there wasn't much else he could do. It was especially a pity since at the rate things were going Sam never would be caught and the Murphys would likely rot away in prison before the law would have time to bring them to trial. When the idea of betraying Sam first came to him, he thought the plan was his own, but Jones had planted the thought very carefully.

"Maybe I could help you catch Sam," Jim told the major. "He trusts me. He told me I could join his gang anytime I wanted."

With Jones filling in, Jim evolved this plan of action: If he and his dad would be released from jail by the major, he would undertake to join Bass. Posing as the pal he had always been taken for, he would ride with them, find out when and where they were going to be at any given spot, and sneak that information to Jones so that the Rangers could be there waiting for them.

The major believed the plan worth trying—especially since it was his own. He let Jim go and Murphy went back to his farm outside Denton. He spent nearly three weeks trying to contact Sam. Then one morning, Sam, Frank and Seab all rode up to the front of the Murphy cabin.

"Does what you said about my joining up with you still go?" Jim asked Sam.

"Sure does. Always room for one more friend," Sam told him.

Jim said he had to do a few things around the farm and they all agreed to meet at Hickory Creek that evening. As soon as they were out of sight, Jim rode toward Denton where he met Sheriff Everheart of Grayson County. He told Everheart where the boys would be that night and the sheriff promised to be there with as many deputies as he could gather. Jim rode away feeling that the business of playing traitor wasn't as hard as it was cracked up to be.

There was just one thing wrong. Everheart never did show up. Either he thought Jim was drunk, or he simply didn't want to be the one to arrest Sam Bass. In any case Jim was now one of the band and he didn't like it. It seemed to him they spotted a new and bigger posse every ten minutes. As he remarked later on, "It was plumb risky for a fella to go ridin' around with them fellers." In Jim's defense it must be said that he was not the callous Judas he has often been painted. Perhaps he honestly felt the only way to get his father out of jail was by double-crossing Sam. Perhaps he was too much of a coward to defy the dreaded Texas Rangers. But, like everyone else who knew the outlaw, he loved Sam, and his conscience would, within a few months after his betrayal, drive him to committing suicide by taking poison.

> Sam met his fate at Round Rock, July the twenty-first,
> They pierced poor Sam with rifle balls and emptied out his purse.
> Poor Sam he is a corpse and six foot under clay,
> And Jackson's in the bushes, tryin' to get away.

Sam decided the thing to do now was rob a bank. Since most of the trains were carrying more guards than passengers, and the banks had been left alone up to now, they offered the most likely target. The band left Denton and started south. At Rockwall, Sam spent a chunk of his rapidly diminishing money buying Jim Murphy some new guns and equipment. He had always had a soft spot for the kid and had often helped him and his father out with money in the past.

They then wandered down through Terrell, Kaufman, Ennis, Waco and Belton. On the way, they posed as lawmen looking for the Bass gang, and the worse they were treated the happier Sam was. One old rancher refused to sell or give them anything to eat. "I've heard a heap about that Sam Bass," he said. "And I think a heap of him. I hope you never do catch him."

"Well," Sam told him, passing the old man a $20 gold piece with 1877 stamped on it. "I think the chances are pretty good he never *will* be caught."

The oldster looked the coin over carefully, grinned at Sam and said, "You Rangers are welcome here as long as you want to stay. And I don't want no money, so keep this."

At one point they purchased a dozen eggs from a woman. A posse appeared just as they rode out of sight.

The woman was still holding the $20 coin in her hand when the sheriff asked her if she had seen any men who might possibly be from the Bass gang. She said no one had passed her house in days.

Jim Murphy went into Belton on a pretext and managed to get a letter off to Major Jones. He told Jones that the gang was headed into Round Rock where they planned to stick up the bank. Jones got the letter and every Ranger in that section of the country headed for the little town.

On the way down to Round Rock, the outlaws stopped off at a bar in a tiny village along the way. Toward the end of the evening, Sam threw a $20 gold piece on the bar. "Let her gush," he philosophized. "It all goes in a lifetime." It was his last 1877 coin.

On the morning of July 19, they arrived at the outskirts of Round Rock. Frank Jackson went into town to look the place over. He came back and said. "I don't care for the looks of that town. There's a feller I saw down there who looks like a Ranger to me."

That afternoon Sam and Seab moseyed down into the town to check on Frank's findings. Round Rock looked peaceful and calm to them, and they found nothing suspicious about the loiterers they saw along the main street.

The next morning the boys rode slowly into the quiet town. There was only a few people on the sidewalks. They didn't pull up in front of the bank, but reined in their horses a few feet down the street in front of Kopperel's tobacco store. They walked casually into the store and bought some tobacco. They wanted to size things up before moving on to the bank.

Jim Murphy whispered to Sam that he was going outside to keep an eye on things. Once out on the street, he hurried away from his friends and the bank, certain that his letter had got to Jones all right and that the quiet town was going to explode at any minute.

In the tobacco store, Sam was just turning from the counter when Sheriff Grimes of Round Rock and a deputy came in. Grimes looked Seab Barnes over critically and made a slighting remark about Seab's having "too many guns." This was not the sort of thing to tell Seab Barnes when he was about to rob a bank. Seab was touchy under the best circumstances, but at this particular moment he was downright argumentative. He took one of his "too many guns" from its holster and nearly blew the sheriff's head off with it. Frank Jackson shot the deputy through the lungs as a wild slug from the deputy's pistol hit Sam in the hand. The three of them ran out onto the street to find that almost deserted thoroughfare suddenly filled to overflowing with Texas Rangers.

Seab was killed instantly by a slug through his head. Sam turned to help him and saw that he was dead. Sam's hesitation gave a Ranger the chance to shoot him square in the chest. Sam went down on both knees, then struggled to his feet. Frank Jackson, moving calmly and deliberately, got off his horse in the middle of the murderous fusillade, went over to ·Sam and helped him up onto his horse. With bullets pounding and whining all around them, they galloped back out of town, Frank helping to support Sam in the saddle.

Sitting on some wooden steps, his head buried in his arms, Jim Murphy cried as the two men galloped past him.

> Jim sold out Sam and Barnes and left their friends to mourn,
> Oh what a scorching Jim will get when Gabriel blows his horn.
> Perhaps Jim's got to heaven, there's none of us to say,
> But if I'm right in my surmise, he's gone the other way.

The following morning, the Rangers found Sam lying under a tree. Frank had done everything possible for him and had left a horse nearby in case Sam came around enough to ride. Then, at Sam's insistence, he had cleared out before the law came. Sam was still alive, and they took him back into Round Rock.

Major Jones tried all day to get him to tell who had ridden with him, but Sam would say nothing about them. He talked freely about the boys who were dead, but as for telling Jones anything that might help him catch those still living, he said simply, "It's against my profession."

When Jones brought up Jim Murphy's name, Sam said nothing, but his lips set themselves into a faint, sad grin. The long afternoon was settling into evening when Sam finally said, "The world is bobbin' around," and died. It was July 21, 1878, Sam's 27th birthday.

An outlaw he was, but folks realized he had made it a

point never to kill anyone, and he had given generously of himself and his money to all those around him. Texans proudly claimed the Indiana boy as their own, and any gun Sam had ever shot, any horse he had ever ridden, any glass he had ever taken a drink from, became a priceless treasure to its owner. In the years to come thousands of "authentic" Sam Bass revolvers, gun belts, rifles, hats, boots and spurs turned up all over the state. As the legend grew it became clear that there wasn't one house Sam hadn't visited, there wasn't one fireplace he hadn't warmed his feet before, and there wasn't one old-timer in the state who hadn't sheltered Sam Bass while the Rangers were chasing him.

The people of Texas put a stone over Sam Bass' grave. On it they engraved a question about their beloved outlaw that no man could answer. *"A brave man reposes in in death here. Why was he not true?"*

THE STORY OF
THE BRANDING IRON

*The custom never set well with their women but the
old-time ranchers wanted every possession they
owned to bear their personal mark. Although it had
its origin in ancient Egypt over 4,500 years ago,
branding reached a peak in the Old West when cattlemen needed indelible symbols to identify their far-
flung herds.*

The night before Jessie Harper was to be married,
he built a low-burning fire in the parlor of his Wyoming
ranch house and stuck his branding iron in among the
coals. Then he rode the short distance to his fiancee's
home and asked her to come over to his place to receive
a "special surprise" he had planned for her.

She agreed to the request, and, since courting in the
1880s was a refined process, they sat in front of the fire
for an hour before she finally broke down and demanded
to know what the surprise was.

Jessie, a sentimental fellow, told her to close her eyes
and bet her that she'd never forget that night.

She closed them and chatted merrily as Jessie got off

the sofa. "Now hurry up, Jess, I'm just dying to know. Don't you be a tease, Jess."

Suddenly, there was a spitting sound like ten mean cats in a hissing contest and Jessie's gal let out a yell that was heard from Yellowstone to Cheyenne.

Jessie, in his inimitable way, had paid the girl the supreme compliment when he stamped his brand on her.

He'd known it would hurt a little, but he also figured she would see the romantic side of it and recognize the fact that it proved beyond question, his eternal love and enduring affection.

But you can never tell about women.

The girl didn't marry Jess the next day, or any day thereafter, but preferred going through life explaining to other men how come she had a "Rocking K" brand on her right forearm.

Furthermore, she told Jess in a most ladylike manner that if she ever saw him again, she'd shoot him.

Branding, like Jessie Harper, has often been misunderstood. It did not begin in the West as many people believe. On the contrary, its origin cannot be satisfactorily traced due to the practice being so ancient. It's at least 4,500 years old.

In the tomb of an Egyptian King who ruled around 2,500 B.C., there is a very clear representation of three cowboys in loincloths. Two of them are holding a hogtied steer from kicking while the third old-time puncher is about to stamp-brand it on the rump. In a fire a few feet away, there are two more irons being heated up in preparation for branding the remainder of the herd.

Branded livestock was first introduced into America via the 16 warhorses brought here 436 years ago by Hernando Cortez on his search for gold.

In 1518, when those 16 ponies snorted through beach water and came splashing up onto the sand to be the first horses ever seen in the new world, each of them bore one of these three marks:

A modern cowpoke might call them the "Circle A," the "Crazy X" and the "Holy Cross," and he would be

257

able to name off half a dozen brands similar to each one within his own county.

The basic symbols with which men mark their animals have never changed. Take the "Frying Pan," "Hammer," "Spur" and "Hatchet" brands, reading from left to right:

Every one of these marks, plus thousands of others, can be traced back as deep as archaeologists can dig. From the beginning of time, every man who has worried about losing an object or been proud of a possession, has wanted to put his sign on it.

For 43 of the 45 known centuries of fire branding, it's been fairly commonplace to sear marks into the flesh of human beings. The ancient pharaohs thought as little of having their brands burned into the hides of their slaves as into the hides of their cattle.

The letter "F" was marked with a fiery hot piece of iron on Romans who were thieves or criminals—or in other words "Fugitives." Early Puritans in New England often felt morally obligated to fry the letter "A" in the foreheads of convicted adulterers with a searing iron. As late as 1832, "TF," for Traux Forces, was branded on French galley slaves. But the burning resentment people have always held against being so painfully identified has at last paid off, and today the branding of one's neighbor, wife or slave, regardless of the reason, has become pretty much a thing of the past.

While branding admittedly did not begin in the West, it is there, however, that the practice reached its peak of artistic and enthusiastic use.

A Western cattleman's brand had to mean something. It might be made up from his initials or his name. It might refer to his guns, cooking utensils, riding equipment, clothing or girl friend, his favorite whiskey, a good fight he'd been in or a sentimental memory. He might make a brand from the stars, the moon, the sun or lightning.

Will Rogers had a brand which he claimed reminded him of a fireplace he'd spent many happy hours loafing in front of. He called it the "Dog Iron" and it looked like this:

Will always said no rustler ever tried to run off with any of his cattle. After one look at Will's scrawny herd, he'd usually ride over to the Rogers' ranch and offer to loan Will the price of a bale of hay.

A Colorado cowboy had just married and was starting up a small ranch. He wanted to use the brand "OU2" in honor of his wife from whom he had borrowed two dollars to get married on. His little woman, though, devised a design that she preferred.

"But what the blazes will I call it?" he demanded. "It looks like nothing I ever seen."

"I don't care what you call it," she told him. "But I like that design. You think up a name for it."

All the way to the county clerk's office, the young rancher pondered the problem, taking the penciled outline from his pocket from time to time and complaining to his horse that there was just nothing you could call such an outlandish figure.

They say he stopped at a saloon, had three glasses of whiskey and bemoaned the fact that he had a loco wife before inspiration struck him like the flying hoof of a half-broke range pony. Forthwith, he strode to the clerk's office and registered his brand, under the name of "Crazy Woman."

Literally, hundreds of thousands of brands have been used throughout the history of America, but the average cowboy refused to be confused by them. He had a mind as devoid of fat as his lean, tough body. With a few simple facts to go on, he made the jargon of branding an easy one to understand. Here's about all he needed:

Running Brand: A straight iron rod with a curve at the end of it. With this type of branding iron, a puncher would actually draw the mark like a picture, and each brand would be slightly different.

Stamp Brand: A rod with the design of a brand fashioned at the end of it. With this, a cowman simply stamped the iron onto the rump of his animal and in one motion the entire mark was etched. Each brand would be identical to the other.

Trail Brand: An additional brand burned into cattle when various ranchers sold livestock to a single, large trail herd, usually being driven to market.

In reading brands, these words are helpful:

Lazy: Any number or letter on its side or back.

Rocking: A design joined to a half circle beneath it.

Flying: When a figure seems to have wings, it is usually called flying.

Connected: Any two figures joined together or making common use of a line.

Bar: Any straight, horizontal line by itself.

Thus the five brands below are "Lazy W," the "Rocking M," the "Flying Cross," the "J-F Connected" and the "Barbecue."

Mexicans, not satisfied with fighting an occasional war against "gringos," tried to make the lives of early cattlemen miserable by designing brands that meant absolutely nothing and then selling or trading their steers across the border. Their designs were beautiful, often masterpieces of balance and artful grace. But what would you call these marks?

Hard put as the ranchers might be for a name upon first sighting these pretty, meaningless designs, they would soon come up with names that make the marks look made to order. From the left, they call these four: the

"Spiked Circle," the "Flying Half-Circle," "Buzzard On A Rail" and the "Clover Cross."

Three really hard ones the Mexicans were suspected of having sent up purposely to make the Southwestern cattlemen turn to robbing railroads for a living, were these:

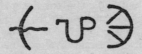

But the cowboys, hardened to this nonsense by now, took one long look, collectively bombarded a spittoon with shots of tobacco juice, and said, 'Why you boys have drawn a 'Snake in the Moon,' 'Seven Up' and a 'Broken Wheel.'" Which is what the brands have been called from that time on.

As the early years of the West rolled by, though 47 States of the Union will hate to admit it, Texas began pulling ahead in the world of branding ingenuity. L. Hammar told a short, pointed story on economics one year in the Lone Star State by branding his few steers with "No Money."

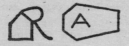

A man named Houser came up with one of the appropriate brands shown below, while a grim humorist with the handle A. Coffin devised the other.

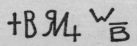

Other standouts in the country of the Alamo were Crosby, R. N. Fourr, and W. Barbee who registered as shown below:

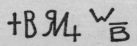

One Texas cattleman who had no brand at all owned an island situated a half mile out in the Gulf of Mexico. Since he was by himself, he thought quite rightly that there was no sense in taking the time and trouble to figure out a brand and burn it onto his livestock. The only problem was, that every now and then, during an exceptionally low tide, some of his more adventuresome cows would wade out and swim for the mainland. Many of them got tired and returned to the island, but a few of them made it to the other side. Sometimes, honest Texans would spot the errant livestock and send them back to the owner of the island. Sometimes, dishonest out-of-staters would find them and put their own brand on them. That's how they came to recognize and call wandering, homeless cattle the way they do. The owner of those unbranded cows and steers was a gentleman named Mr. Maverick.

Probably the most famous brand in the history of the West was born on the night that a happy-go-lucky cowpoke rode into town with a little money in his pocket and a big desire to play some poker. The cowboy, S. B. Burnett, warmed himself with a drink or two and then sat in on a mild game of draw. The game didn't stay mild long, for Burnett suddenly found himself in the luckiest winning streak of his card-playing days. No matter what he drew to, from an inside straight to a two-card try for a flush, he hit it. In that spectacular night of gambling, even wise men and their gold were soon parted.

By 3 o'clock in the morning, Burnett had won more money than he'd ever seen in his life and there was only one gent who could still afford to play with him, a wealthy cattleman who owned a good-sized ranch in the county. The rancher switched from draw to stud and back again in an effort to break Burnett's luck. It did no good. By 4 o'clock, he had lost a whopping pile of money to the unbeatable puncher as well as signing over a stack of IOU's.

"Tell you what I'll do," he said finally. "I'll bet you my ranch against all the money in front of you. One hand of draw to see who wins."

"Mister, you got a bet," Burnett smiled. "I've always wanted to own a ranch."

The cards were shuffled and dealt in tense, electric silence as even the bartenders left their posts to watch.

The rancher called for two cards and Burnett asked for three.

With a pleased expression, the rancher put three aces on the table face up. Burnett squinted wryly at his own hand and slowly spread the five cards to see what he'd drawn.

He laid four sixes down on the table.

By sunup, Burnett was on his new ranch, forging a new brand, the "6666" which he called the Four Sixes. The iron consisted of only one six which was stamped four times in a row.

S. B. Burnett made a piker of a man who broke the bank at Monte Carlo, for his luck never did run out from that day forward. Not only did his ranch prosper cattlewise, but a few years later an ocean of oil was discovered a couple of feet down under his land.

As a millionaire, Burnett joined the ranks of hundreds of cattlemen who have shown a fanatic loyalty to their brands by putting them on everything in sight. He put the "Four Sixes" on his oil derricks, trucks, linen, shirts, private planes, belt buckles, ties, bedspreads and even on his swimming pool.

The "Four Sixes" is a lucky brand in a further sense. There is no doubt as to how and why it originated. Many famous brands haven't a definite birthplace, in which case every State claims the marks as their own and offers as proof stories that have grown up around them. Arizona is usually credited with being the first to have the following brand. In any case, there can be little doubt that the accompanying yarn is more fact than fiction.

Not far from Phoenix, the story goes, two young brothers bought a small ranch with three or four dozen head of cattle. After the deed was drawn up, they decided to celebrate their purchase and spend the night carousing. They reached their new property in the wee hours, so drunk that it was all they could do to flop into bed.

Came morning, one brother forced his eyes open and finally made it outside to the well where he splashed water on his face and gradually came back to life. When he tried to wake up his father's other son, though, he met with no success. After being kicked and pummeled five minutes, the sleepy one rolled over and muttered, "Whatta ya' want?"

"Gotta get up. Lots of work to do around here."

"Go to hell," his brother mumbled.

"C'mon!" the awake one snapped. "We got to do some branding."

"You figure out a brand. You do it. I'm tired." With this, the less energetic lad passed out for good. When he came to late in the afternoon, he found that his brother had a poetic, and at the same time, vengeful soul. Their newly acquired cattle were branded—

$$U\backsim$$

His trained cowboy eye immediately recognized this as a biting remark on his attitude toward getting up that morning. This is how it reads. "U Lazy S."

The most classic branding insult though, was made by a woman rancher, according to old-timers. They say a pretty, hard-working gal married a good-looking but no-account fellow who was completely useless as a man and as a husband. Unlike other spouses, he didn't even have the glamorous faults of drinking and gambling, but just hung around the house sitting in the rocking chair, moping on the grass in the front yard or often just not bothering to get out of bed at all. The lady put up with her husband's lethargic behavior good-naturedly for some time, hoping that he would snap out of it. After a year though, he had even less get-up-and-go than ever, and she realized that he would go through life as a drowsy-eyed bum. Taking the initiative, she saddled a horse for him, filled a bag with his belongings and kicked him off the ranch. Then, as a back-handed honor, she made up a brand in memory of her constantly sluggish spouse:

$$2\backsim P$$

As long as it is remembered that the center letter must read "Lazy 2," it isn't much work deciphering the disgusted lady's brand.

In the earlier days of the West, cowmen didn't worry about rustlers because they marked their cattle at as many as six spots, sometimes using a different brand at each place. With signs on the right and left rump, right and left shoulder, and a couple of earmarks to boot, their livestock stood no chance of being rebranded by an industrious but dishonest neighbor. The hitch came when prices on cowhide became so high that a man couldn't afford to ruin the skin with too much burning. Cattle owners started to save the hides by branding just once on the left rump or slightly under the left rear leg near the belly.

Here's where rustling came into its own, for watch what can happen to the "Pick," "J-B Connected" and "Hat" brands:

$$\perp \mathcal{B} \frown$$

Since these marks are simple, a few adroitly added lines will instantly change them to the "Broken Wheel," "O-B Connected" and "Hashknife" brands:

$$\Lambda T\Lambda \quad \mathcal{CB} \quad \underline{\mathcal{I}}$$

There were two ways of knowing if a brand had been made over. One was the chance that the rustler would slip with his running brand and two lines would appear where only one should be. The second was by killing the suspect head of cattle and skinning it. From the underside of the skin, a twice-branded hide would show a darker line where the original imprint was made.

Finding a rustler and proving his guilt always took a lot of time and trouble, and even then over-lenient judges were likely to let them off with light sentences. So the cowmen took two steps to discourage rustling. First, they lynched or shot cattle thieves from time to time without the judicial blessing of a judge and jury. Second, they made their brands tough to disguise.

One rancher dreamed up a brand that must have given many a headache to many a rustler. It was composed of the letters X I T and it looked like the symbol below.

$$XIT$$

But no matter how smart a man gets, sooner or later, there always seems to be someone a little smarter. After many years of driving cattle thieves to drink, the X I T brand was mastered by an artistic crook who missed his calling when he didn't go in for painting phony Rembrandts. This imaginative thug boasted to cattle buyers that no one would ever be able to work over his brand and all the time he was selling cows legally belonging to the XIT ranch. He called his mark the "Star Cross," and this is the way it was made:

The Star Cross goes over the XIT in such a manner that the middle letter of XIT becomes the vertical line of the cross.

The all-time champion of clever branding, however, was not a rustler, but a man who was on the side of law and order. Once again, every State lays claim to being the spot where the drama originally unfolded, but Utah seems to have the jump on the others. About 100 years ago, a man named Ichabod Chapman is said to have developed a fine ranch in the northern corner of Utah. Since he trusted the other ranchers in the territory, he didn't bother with a complicated brand, but simply used his initials, "I C," as a mark.

Through the years, Ichabod labored long and hard to build up a good herd of cattle, and he at last succeeded so well that his fat, sleek cows and steers became the envy of everyone in that section of the country. Then, one day, while riding several miles from his ranch, Ichabod saw a few head of cattle grazing in a gully and went to see if they might be "I C" steers that had wandered away from his spread.

His honest mind was appalled when he dismounted and found everyone of the steers was branded with a mark which read, "I C U." The cattle evidently didn't belong to him, but they certainly looked familiar. Riding back home, the honest cattleman was in a sad quandary. He didn't want to accuse any of his neighbors of being a thief, nor did he want to lose his livestock.

Next morning, bright and early, Ichabod was happy and cheerful. Whistling between his teeth, he rounded up his cattle, and when he had finished with them, they all bore the perfect answer to the "I C U" mark. Their new brand was: "I C U 2."

The branding iron was the white-hot pen with which the cowboy wrote his own unique history in his own unique way. Humor, satire, pride, greed and dishonesty, along with all other human elements, have been charred indelibly into America's past by brands. And often they have told a story more clearly than words.

When a rancher named Hart lost his two sons in a stampede, he went to the barn and, his face set tightly, took down his branding iron. The change he made in that iron told what he felt more honestly and sincerely than any words. His brand had been a simple heart. When he finished working with it, this is how it looked:

His deep sorrow would last forever.

THE FABULOUS ORIENTAL

Hangout of Wyatt Earp, Bat Masterson, Doc Holliday and the rest of that high-rolling gang, Tombstone's legendary house of pleasure was the wickedest spot this side of hell.

The elegantly dressed gentleman who came through the ornate swinging doors paused, then glanced back into the street as several shots roared through the early morning air. When the shooting stopped, he crossed the thick carpeting to the gleaming, 40-foot mahogany bar with the huge, wall-length mirror behind it surrounded with dainty, carved-crystal decorations.

"Good morning, Frank," he said to the trim barman.

"Morning, Doc."

"I'll have a Silver Fizz, Frank."

The barman selected a large, sparkling glass and began to make the cocktail with expert hands. "Who won?" he asked casually.

"John McCallister."

"Thought so," Frank grunted. "One Arm Kelly never could shoot. Glad I booted them out. Hate to start off the morning with a killing in the bar."

The town was Tombstone in the year 1880. The barman was Buckskin Frank Leslie, who could have, had he been so crass, put 12 notches on his revolver butt. The gentleman ordering the Silver Fizz was Doc Holliday, gambler and gunman deluxe, who reportedly originated the handkerchief duel in which each opponent grabbed a corner of a handkerchief with one hand and went for his gun with the other. The place was the Oriental Saloon And Gambling House, the toughest, wealthiest emporium ever to have a piano concert in one room interrupted by the blasts of a fatal shooting in the next. It was given that exotic name because folks believed anything smacking of the Orient was luxurious and out of the ordinary. It lived up to its name with a vengeance, incorporating a paradoxical combination of superb taste and superb shooting, fine living and brutal murder. And like the flea-bitten prospector who once wandered through its swinging doors, lost $25,000 at faro in 25 minutes, and then wandered wordlessly back out of the door to disappear forever, the Oriental had an inscrutable, incredible personality of its own.

Tombstone, Arizona, was the shootingest, fightingest, drinkingest mining town that ever thundered through the pages of frontier history. It was called the meanest town in the world, and no one who had seen it ever took exception to the title. And the very heart of Tombstone was the large, square-fronted building in the middle of town called the Oriental Saloon And Gambling House. It was to the Oriental that the miners, outlaws, professional gamblers and gunmen, ladies of leisure and cowmen flocked 24 hours a day for a friendly drink, a friendly game or some friendly conversation.

Just how friendly an evening at the Oriental could be is indicated by the fact that an estimated 200 men held their last drink, poker hand or conversation in and around the Oriental's sacred precincts before being carried off to a six-by-three resting place in Tombstone's Boot Hill, their carcasses filled with various and sundry bullet and buckshot holes.

The Oriental was born, lived and died along with Tombstone itself, and their histories are as much a part of each other as Scotch and soda, poker and chips, bullets and guns.

When a stubborn prospector named Ed Schieffelin wandered alone into Apache land in search of gold, folks told him all he would find was his tombstone. He found neither. What he did find was the richest veins of silver this side of a prospector's dreams. The silver assayed at $15,000 a ton. As get-rich-quick experts flooded to the strike, he remembered what people had said and laughingly called the growing camp "Tombstone." A shrewd merchant named Vizina hauled in two rumbling wagons loaded with kegs of whiskey and got as close to the mine as he could. At the spot where his tired animals refused to pull the heavy load anymore, he set up shop. That was the beginning of the Oriental, and Tombstone grew up around it. At first men slept, worked and drank on the open ground. Then it became a tent town, and the biggest tent was the Oriental. Later on the canvas was junked in favor of pine planks dragged from the nearby hills, and the saloon became the biggest frame building in Tombstone, at the corner of Allen and Fifth Streets.

It had, of course, plenty of competition. The Lucky Cuss, Contention, Tough Nut and Grand Central mines supplied so much silver that 15,000 people crowded into the swiftly growing town. Rival establishments like the Alhambra, Crystal Palace and Bird Cage did thundering businesses every hour of the week. But the Oriental was *the* place in Tombstone, and until you had pushed in the swinging doors that led to its superb bar and gambling rooms, you couldn't rightly say you had been to Tombstone.

Through those doors passed the most colorful and deadly men of the West. They say Billy the Kid and Wild Bill Hickok were regular customers there, but that's unlikely. The watery-eyed Kid and the talkative Hickok were argumentative cusses, and those inclined to arguing had no chance to become regular customers at the Oriental. They didn't live long enough.

One such argumentative lad was Jack Peters. At a poker game he called George Beeson a cheat and went for his gun. Beeson was in an awkward psotion to draw, so he whipped out his bowie knife with his left hand and nearly decapitated Jack. Two days later, Beeson was shot in an argument with Hank Forrest. That was, in the Oriental's bizarre fashion, the way life went on—or just plain went.

Hal Bradshaw and Mike McIntyre were business partners. One day Bradshaw went out and bought a loud sport shirt with black, red and yellow stripes. All the way up Allen-Street, men laughed at him. Finally he could take it no longer. "I'll kill the next fool who laughs at this shirt!" he bellowed.

As the belligerent fellow started into the Oriental, his partner, McIntyre, was coming out. McIntyre went into hysterics. Bradshaw repeated his statement. McIntyre couldn't let well enough alone. He bellowed with laughter once more. Bradshaw walloped McIntyre a husky belt on the jaw. That got them both laughing. Then McIntyre shot Bradshaw right through his happy top row of front teeth.

It was a good joke and everybody thought Bradshaw was, in a way, lucky to have departed from this sad world in a peal of laughter. So everybody went into the Oriental and had a drink to commemorate the occasion.

Although the prudent Oriental patron carried eight to twelve pounds of weapons around his waist, what really set the place apart was that in many respects it was vastly more civilized than the fanciest joints in New York and Paris. In the few hectic years that Tombstone flourished, $50 million worth of silver was gouged out of the holes in the surrounding hills. That would be roughly comparable to $500 million today. And practically everyone who shared in that silver bonanza spent some of it in the Oriental Saloon And Gambling House. You could go in, slap the bar and order Tangleleg, Forty Rod, Taos Lightning or Tarantula juice. But you would be regarded as a bit of a hillbilly. The Oriental barman could, with perfect precision, concoct the finest cocktails, flips, mashes and sangarees. If a dullard behind the gleaming bar spilled a Blue-Blazer, poured a Pousse Cafe clumsily, or botched a Kentucky Mint Julep, he would be shipped back to New York promptly, quite possibly in a box. The food was equally distinguished. Pheasant-Under-Glass, Quail on Toast and Filet Mignon were among the more popular dishes served and the Oriental's wine cellar caused one French visitor to call Tombstone "Little Paris." Rich oil paintings, mirrors and crystal decorations covered the walls. A miner or a visiting Wall Street tycoon could come in, spend all day loafing, take a drink and leave, without spending a nickel, for the first drink was always on the house—as well as the fifth and the eighth or ninth, depending on when the barman figured it was time for the house to spring again.

Clara Brown, a woman reporter, visited Tombstone in

1880 to inform the outside world what that ripsnortin'
little hell hole was like from a woman's point of view.
She castigated most of the town, tearing it to shreds with
her sharp pen. But she did write, "The Oriental is simply
gorgeous. The mahogany bar is a marvel of beauty, the
gaming rooms carpeted with Brussels, brilliantly lighted
and furnished with the latest reading matter and fine
writing materials for its patrons. Every evening there is
the music of a violin and a piano, and the scene is a
most gay one."

Miss Brown missed part of the entertainment by 24
hours. She didn't see Roger King call Johnny Wilson a
liar as they stood at the bar and put a .45 slug through
Wilson's forehead to prove it.

No one man was responsible for the lusty magnificence
of the Oriental. Jim Vizina had brought in the original
two wagons of whiskey and actually owned the building.
He realized it was too big for him after it passed the
canvas-tent stage, and he rented it to Mike Joyce. Joyce
decorated the main gambling hall and bar sumptuously
and hired a fellow named Haley to bring a grand piano
from Denver. Through hundreds of miles Haley brought
the majestic piano, through storms, washouts, blazing
heat and Apaches. In front of the Oriental, Haley and
his men dropped the piano from the wagon and smashed
it.

Haley made a classic understatement when he stared
down at the splintered instrument and said, "Damn,
wouldn't that burn you up?"

"Go back and get me another one," Joyce told him.

Next time around, Haley dismantled the piano and
made it successfully.

Joyce saw to it that the Oriental had everything, and
on a scale that would put Monte Carlo to shame. Roulette
wheels and tables for faro, keno, poker, blackjack and
chuck-a-luck were the finest. So were the imported crystal
chandeliers, curved staircases and deep, hand-woven car-
pets. The bar, wine cellar and kitchen were stocked in
such a manner that the thirstiest miner and most effete
San Francisco gourmet could be equally satisfied.

The patrons of the Oriental appreciated Joyce's efforts.
The first drunken cowboy who tried to ride his horse into
the bar was literally blasted out of the saddle as eight or
ten slugs tore into him simultaneously, reproving him for
his rudeness. But Joyce made one mistake. He had

worked too hard and was evidently losing his mind. He insulted Doc Holliday. Doc was in a good mood, so he simply shot Joyce through the arm and plugged an interfering barman through the foot. While Joyce was recuperating, he realized he had had enough, and he sold out to Lou Rickabaugh.

Rickabaugh was a sharpy. He knew that with the feuding guys like Johnny Ringo, Curly Bill Brocius, Charlie Storms, Johnny Tyler, Ike Clanton, Doc Holliday and Wyatt Earp around, all hell could break loose at any time and the Oriental could be damaged considerably in a free-for-all shooting match. He therefore hired Buckskin Frank Leslie as a barman and brought in Bat Masterson and Luke Short, professional gamblers who had reputations as gunmen, too. Then he played his ace in the hole and asked the Lion of Tombstone, Wyatt Earp, if he wanted a quarter-interest in the Oriental.

"How much do you want for it, Lou?" Wyatt asked.

"Not a damn cent. I just want you around."

"That's a reasonable price," Wyatt grinned.

"You'll make $1,000 a week at least," Lou said. "Sometimes that much in a day."

On a typical busy week in Tombstone before Rickabaugh took over the Oriental, there had been 14 killings reported, not counting Mexicans and Chinamen. A good half of them had occurred in, or outside of, the Oriental. Shortly before Lou put his new staff to work, Curly Bill had shot Sheriff White outside the Oriental in a little misunderstanding. Another time, Johnny Ringo had invited Louis Hancock to have a drink with him. "All right," Hancock agreed. "I'll have a beer." To which Ringo said, "No man drinks beer with me. I don't like beer." And Hancock replied, determinedly, "Well, I like beer." Ringo was just as stubborn. "I don't," he said grimly.

"Beer," Hancock said to the barman.

"Bang," said Ringo's .45, and Hancock lost the debate. They say some thoughtful citizens buried him with a bottle of beer in his hand.

Another little episode involved Jim Hickey and Billy Claiborne. Jim insisted on buying Claiborne a drink. Billy didn't want a drink. Jim's generous insistence became downright annoying, so Billy finally shut him up by shooting a sizable hole through his sociable head. In Tombstone, it was just as dangerous to be too friendly as it was to be too ornery.

273

After Rickabaugh put in his powerhouse gang at the Oriental, this sort of thing slowed down. It also divided Tombstone into two clearly defined factions. On the Oriental side were Wyatt Earp, Buckskin Frank Leslie, Bat Masterson and Luke Short. On the opposing team was most of the lawless element of Tombstone, men who enjoyed shooting when and where (and whom) they pleased, and a powerful clique under Johnny Tyler, who wanted to take over the Oriental.

Little Luke Short, who was so fearless that no one knew his reputation as a gunslinger was highly exaggerated, drew first blood. Charlie Storms, one of Tyler's top gunmen, entered the Oriental with the express desire of making trouble. He picked on Short, and started to insult the little fellow. One thing led to another and they finally began shooting in front of the swinging doors. "I'll give you first shot!" Storms yelled, going for his guns. Whether he intended to keep his promise or not will never be known. Little Luke trundled out his revolver and calmly took the first shot. Then he took two more shots just to be extra polite. Stepping over Storms' body, he went quietly back into the Oriental to deal some more faro.

Bat Masterson later shot up a couple of rowdy boys who were trying to toss up faro chips and shoot them out of the air.

Since Wyatt Earp hadn't been needed for any of the fracases so far, Johnny Tyler didn't know he was interested in the Oriental. Tyler finally brought three or four toughs in to smash up the place and scare Rickabaugh out. He sat down at a roulette table, roared that he was looking for excitement, and shot a hole through a chandelier. A second later, he was puzzled to find himself being lifted from the table by his left ear. He was even more puzzled to note that his toughs were not going for their guns and were looking as pale as ghosts. When he realized his left ear was being manhandled by Wyatt Earp, he blurted, "Hell fire! I didn't know you had anything to do with the Oriental!"

"Well I have, and I'm ready for any excitement you boys can afford me."

They allowed they couldn't afford any, and left hurriedly.

That ended the trouble for a while. In fact, things got so dull around the Oriental that Short left for other parts and Bat Masterson went to the unlikely place of New York to become successful at the unlikely profession of sports writing.

Only Earp and his brothers and his friend Doc Holliday were left. Then an ornery citizen shot and wounded Wyatt's brother Virgil as Virge was walking out of the saloon, and the consensus was that the offender was either Curly Bill or one of the Clantons or Johnny Ringo. That made the Earps mad, but when Morgan Earp was killed from ambush one night, they really boiled over. In consequence, Bill, most of the Clantons and Ringo found themselves dead shortly thereafter. But none of the shootings took place anywhere near the Oriental. Wyatt didn't want his place marked up by bullet holes.

Buckskin Frank, who had only shot one man in Tombstone proper, owed most of his reputation to his handsomely shaped wife. Once he had her stand nude in front of a large board and had used up two cases of shells shooting her voluptuous silhouette into the plank. He displayed the skillfully done outline in the Oriental and was considered a first-rate artist. Frank bucked Billy Claiborne when he threatened to shoot up the bar, and Billy promptly got himself a sawed-off shotgun and waited in front of the Oriental for Frank to come out. Some friends warned Frank of the ambush, and Frank went out the side door and came up behind Claiborne. "Hey, Billy!" he called. Claiborne whirled around, shotgun ready, and Buckskin Frank fired. Billy died with a hurt, surprised look embellishing the hole in his forehead. He always hated to be fooled.

It got so dull after that, and so many peaceful customers swarmed into the Oriental, that one old-time regular named Russian Bill went out to find some excitement. The best thing he could figure to do was steal a horse, so he swiped a scrawny old mare. But, the owners caught up to him. Since it was mealtime, they strung him up and hurried to their corned beef and cabbage while poor old Russian Bill kicked away his over-excited life.

During this peaceful time, some amusing card games took place. The boys once played a game of seven-up to see who would bury Johnny Blair. Blair had come down with smallpox and died in a cabin on the outskirts of Tombstone. The boys in the Oriental played their round of seven-up and the loser had the job of burying Johnny. It was the fastest burial in the world. The losing cowboy galloped up to the shack, lassoed Johnny by the feet, and thundered away at a dead run, dragging Johnny behind him. He jumped the deep grave they had dug, and Johnny's body flopped into it. Then he flipped his lariat into the hole and, with the help of a few brave friends, hurriedly filled the grave.

The church needed repairs, so a bunch of hard-drinking boys who had played poker all night turned over the kitty to the preacher. He wrote them a stiff note of thanks, fixed up the church nicely, and the next Sunday preached on the evils of gambling and drink.

Probably the Oriental's most vivid moment was when Wyatt Earp stepped out of its swinging doors to face singlehandedly a kill-crazed, roaring mob of 500 armed men. Johnny-Behind-The Deuce, a tinhorn gambler, had murdered an engineer, and Jack McCann had brought the gambler to the Oriental for Wyatt's protection. Wyatt, who was acting marshal, told McCann and some others to take Johnny to a bowling alley across the street. Then he grabbed a sawed-off shotgun and walked casually out onto Allen Street. The lynch-happy army boiled around the corner of Tough Nut Street and Fifth, a swarming mass of unrestrained violence. As the thundering mob surged toward Wyatt and the Oriental, he stepped toward them and called out, "Where you going, boys?"

The mob came to a halt as those in the front ranks noticed Wyatt pull back the hammers on his scatter-gun.

"We've got a necktie for Johnny-Behind-The Deuce!" someone should.

"Where is the little rat?"

"Don't try to stop us, Earp!"

"Okay!" Wyatt's voice boomed out over the mob. The Lion of Tombstone swung his shotgun at chest level along the front ranks of the lynchers. "If that's the way you want it, come and get him!"

Those in front suddenly refused to budge. Those in the rear pressed forward.

"What's the matter up there?"

"Let's get Earp!"

"Get me!" Wyatt snarled. "But the first man to shoot will get his head blown off. And a few others will go down with me."

"Kill him!"

Wyatt had done all the talking he was going to do. The tension had reached a climax. For a split second, all

276

hell was ready to explode. Then the mob leaders looked into Wyatt's cold eyes. They looked into the dark barrels of his shotgun. Neither sight was to their liking. They started to back up. In five minutes, the street was empty. Wyatt went back into the Oriental and drank a double whiskey, straight.

The fabulous saloon might have gone on making Western history and taking in thousands of dollars a day, except that a hard-working miner made the worst mistake any man ever made. Working 500 feet down in the Lucky Cuss Mine, he slashed into the rock with his pick. A tiny trickle of water crept out and dampened the pick head.

While the miner stared, the trickle grew into a tiny stream, and started pushing dirt away before it. In half an hour, it was a giant flood rushing through the mines and their joining shafts. An underground river or lake had been tapped and the mines were soon deep in water. They still are and probably always will be. There are vast fortunes in silver still lying there, unobtainable because of the underground sea that covers them.

The Oriental had grown with Tombstone. It died with it, too. The elegant gambling rooms and bar had known five years of vibrant life and violent death. Now, the Oriental died as violently as any of its patrons who had been drilled with one of Mr. Colt's revolvers. Allen Street and Fifth Street became dusty, rarely used thoroughfares. The saloon was stripped and looted as the population plummeted from 15,000 to a few hundred. The building itself fell into decay.

So did Tombstone's Boot Hill, which had derived so much of its business from the Oriental. But one marker was saved from that graveyard, and it describes in four precise, well-chosen words, the Oriental Saloon And Gambling House and the men who made it the robust, magnificent emporium that it was. In fact, that grave-marker sums up the whole wild, wonderful era. Carved into the wood are the words, *"He done his damndest."*

CLAY ALLISON
The Man Who Knew No Fear

Nothing could compare with the charge Clay got from a battle to the death with a knife or a six-gun. He fought more than twenty-five gun duels and always came out on top.

It was a rainy morning, and the ragged *Ba-room!* of the green Union firing squad half a mile down the hill was not especially cheering to the two Confederate prisoners tied back to back under the large oak tree.

"Jesus God!" the older man mumbled. "That's the third time they've cut loose. That's the last of the boys. They'll be back for us next."

Clay Allison, the younger prisoner, yawned. He was a big, bull-muscled man of 24, with thick eyebrows overhanging dark and expressive eyes. "Didn't get a damned wink of sleep all night long," he said. "You got a back like a pile of rocks."

"Should've never crossed the line in civvies," the older man grumbled. "If we'd been in uniform, they'd of had to treat us like prisoners of war, 'stead of shootin' us."

"That's one of the drawbacks to bein' a spy. Quit your

bellyachin' and give me a hand with these ropes. I got the top hitch loosened some."

"Ain't no use. We'll be dead in ten or 15 minutes. Just ain't no use to—" The older man's voice broke.

"If you're goin' to sit around cryin' all morning, at least lean out and give me some more room to work," Clay Allison said. "I got myself a lot of livin' to do yet."

When the firing squad officer, with a detail of three men, approached the oak tree, it looked as though Allison was still asleep. Holding a Colt percussion-cap .45 in his right hand, the lieutenant leaned down and shook the big man's shoulder with his left hand. It was his last move on earth. A gigantic fist whipped out and twisted the lieutenant's gun hand, so that the muzzle of his Colt was square in his own belly as his finger pulled the trigger. By the time the other three Union soldiers had whipped off quick shots with their long guns, the prisoner had the .45 in one hand and was holding the lieutenant's body tightly against him as a shield. Two slugs plowed into the officer's corpse. The third knocked down the other Confederate soldier as he struggled to get up. Aiming carefully, Clay cocked and fired his newly acquired revolver three times. At each roar of the gun, the Union Army numbered one man less.

Having eliminated the immediate opposition, Clay threw the body of the Union officer aside and dashed for a clump of trees about 100 yards away, where some horses were tethered. As he ran, bullets from the nearby Union camp began to scream all around him. Since everywhere within two miles knew he was trying to get away by now, secrecy was not important. So he waved the revolver over his head and let out a rebel yell. Judging his horse-flesh as he ran, he leaped onto a deep-chested bay mare without breaking his stride. Leaning down over her neck, he snapped the reins tied to the branch in front of her and jerked her around in a sunfishing turn that almost threw her to the muddy ground. Still crouching low over the unsaddled mount, he raced at a full gallop into a protective line of trees.

"Get that man!" a Union major shrieked over the deafening blast of small arms. "Go after him!"

Within a few seconds, two dozen cavalrymen plunged into the forest where the escaping prisoner had disappeared. But they never saw him again. The big Confederate soldier was a superb horseman. Riding at top speed, he crashed through the thickest section of the forest, then took the mare down an impossible slope that had her sitting on her haunches most of the way to the bottom. After ten minutes, he and the sweating bay had left the blue-coated soldiers far behind. An hour later, he was safe in Confederate territory once more.

Back at the Union camp, the dumbfounded major took stock of his losses. Turning to a captain at his side, he muttered with dazed, unintentional humor, "Four men. He practically executed his own firing squad!"

Clay Allison had been speaking the truth when he remarked that he had a lot of living to do yet. Moreover, he also had a lot of killing to do yet. For Clay, more than any man of his time, dearly loved a battle—and the more fatal the battle, the better. Nobody ever kept track of the killings Clay ran up in his hectic life. A safe minimum figure would be 25; maximum would probably be about twice that number. The trouble with Clay, as Bat Masterson and sundry other folks later pointed out, was that he "knew no fear."

"Holy Ned," his kid brother John once said, when six or eight hometown toughs were about to gang up on the two Allison boys, "let's get outa' here."

Clay was shocked. "What the hell's there to be scared of?" He spit on his hands and rubbed them together. "We're about to have us one mighty fine time." Whereupon to the consternation and discomfort of the toughs, he scattered them in prone positions up and down the street. Panting happily, with blood pouring from a gash across his forehead, he turned to John and said, "You puzzle me, boy. How'n hell can anybody be scared of anything that's so much plain fun?"

Born in Tennessee in 1840, Clay had mostly kept his fighting to bare knuckles, boots and an occasional good-natured battle with skinning knives up until the Civil War. But in no time at all, he decided that war was the best fun of all. Real life-and-death battles had it all over those simple, knock-down-and-drag-out brawls he had enjoyed in his youth. After his one unsuccessful stint as a spy, Clay spent the rest of the war fretting at the needless delay between military engagements. Then one sad day in April of '65, an officer read the assembled troopers the news that the war was over. Lee had surrendered to Grant at Appomattox.

"Lee can surrender if he wants to," Clay growled. "But I got a hunch we can win this here war yet. What do you boys say?" Several of the men around him agreed wholeheartedly, so Allison and a tough band of 20 or 30 guerrillas did their level best to keep the war going.

In May of '65, a detachment of 50 Yankee cavalrymen was escorting a mule train over a lonely stretch of hills in west Kentucky. The captain at the head of the line drew in his horse and held up his hand to call a halt, as a big man on a powerful, painted stallion raced down the slope before them. Reining in the paint beside the captain, the big, light-bearded man said, "I rode down to warn you. Don't know if it means anything or not, but there's a whole bunch of mean-lookin' cusses waitin' around the trail about a mile along. Might be some fellas figurin' on making trouble for you."

The captain frowned at the stranger suspiciously. He was dressed in buckskins and he wore two Colts that looked easy and at home on his hips. But his eyes were what made the captain hesitate. They were not the eyes of a man bringing news of trouble; they were those of a man playing a game he was enjoying immensely.

"Who are you to be so anxious for our safety?" the officer demanded brusquely.

"A one-time Yankee soldier like yourself, sir. Fought under Meade at Gettysburg. Cannonneer. Was on Cemetery Heights when Pickett charged us. That was one day I'll never forget if I live to be one hundred, sir. We were letting them have rounds of double canister until our guns were red hot, and then—"

"Hold on!" The captain was now certain something was wrong. There were unmistakable traces of a Southern accent in the man's voice. "You tell me the truth or I'll hang you before we move another foot. Now, why are you here?"

"The truth, sir?"

"Yes, and fast!"

"Well, now," the big man said slowly. "The real, honest-to-God truth is that I rode down here to talk to you for a little bit. That's all. The way it was, I just seen you a minute or two ago, and I guessed maybe I could talk to you long enough for my men to get in good shape around you."

The captain's eyes swung to the slopes on each side

of him, and he reached for his gun. He didn't live to see the fight. Clay's revolvers roared, and his first slug hit the officer low in the neck. A stuttering roar of gunfire raked the Union cavalrymen from both sides of the valley. They serached helplessly for targets, then fled back along the trail in swift retreat, with the terrified teamsters following on foot.

For months, Allison's tiny, compact army plagued Northern soldiers and carpetbaggers in the South. Clay was beginning to make a name for himself. And, as with most legendary characters, it was a name that meant different things to different people. To some, he was a Robin Hood. To others he was a vicious killer. But to Clay himself, he was simply doing what came naturally—fighting and having a whale of a time.

Once, in his home state, he rode past an old woman crying in a rocker on the front porch of a farmhouse. "What are you cryin' for, Grandma?" he roared from the roadway.

The old lady sobbed that a drunken Yankee soldier had, out of sheer meanness, shot a hole through her front window.

Clay rode on at a fast clip and caught up with the culprit. "Whoa, you no good window-breakin' skunk!" he shouted. "You better go for your gun!" The soldier went for his gun but got there too late. Clay leaned down in his saddle to stare icily at the still body in the road. "That'll teach you some manners," he said. "You'll never break no more poor old ladies' front windows, by God." And the Robin Hood legend was given added strength in Tennessee.

Clay's guerrillas decided about a year after Appomattox that the war really was lost, after all, and one by one, they went on to more peaceful pursuits. Clay shrugged philosophically, shoved ten or fifteen thousand dollars he had saved from looting Northerners into his saddlebags, and headed west for Texas. It was, he had heard, a big land where the citizens enjoyed lots of good fighting. He set himself up nicely on a good-sized spread in the Panhandle, hiring only the most rugged cowmen to help him work his beef.

Clay offered a standing bet that he could whip any man who worked for him, just for exercise, but a couple of fist fights and rassling matches a week got to be pretty tame, and he almost died of boredom for a time in the

Panhandle. Then a young giant named Johnson bought 2,000 acres next to Allison, and the one decent water hole in the area lay right on their boundary. This water hole, Clay immediately realized, might be the key to a genuinely worthwhile fight. He put his mind to work and came up with an idea that was to result in one of the most fantastic duels in the history of the West. The only possible flaw in his plan was the question of whether Johnson was as brave as he was big.

At the water hole, one day, Clay rode up to where Johnson had stopped to pick a stone out of his horse's shoe. "Howdy," Clay said.

"Mornin'." Johnson pried the stone out and dropped the hoof back to the ground.

"Miserable little patch of water, ain't it?" Clay said.

"Big enough."

"Wish it was. But it ain't. Just enough water here to suit my needs."

Johnson squinted up at Allison. "Meanin'?"

"I sure hate to have to tell you this, but I can't let you use this water no more for your livestock, Johnson. It's a damn shame, and I know you can't make out without this ol' mud hole, but I figure I need every drop here."

Johnson scratched the back of his neck and his huge arms swelled with rolling muscles. "You're talkin' like a man who wants to meet His Maker, Allison."

In less than five minutes, Clay had worked the giant into a killing frame of mind. He then outlined his plan, finishing with, "If, of course, you ain't too yella to do it." Johnson was mad enough to agree to anything at that moment, and once he had agreed, he couldn't back down.

The next day at straight-up noon, Clay rode out to the water hole. In the shimmering heat that welled up from the prairie floor, he could see a solitary rider coming from the other direction. That would be Johnson. Clay had a short-handled shovel hitched to his saddle and a long-bladed skinning knife stuck in his pants belt. He carried no gun. When he and Johnson came together at the edge of the water, he could see that his neighbor was carrying the same implements. "Nice day," Allison remarked as they swung down from saddle simultaneously.

"Hot," Johnson allowed.

"What about right here?" Clay etched out a crude rectangle in the dirt.

"Suits me."

Both men began shoveling. Soon the grave-sized hole was a couple of feet deep, and they paused in the broiling sun to wipe sweat from their faces. Johnson stepped out of the hole and removed his shirt. "Hotter'n hell."

"Well, one of us'll soon know," Clay chuckled.

They continued digging and Clay suddenly frowned. "Account of your bein' a fair to middlin' man," he said, "I'd like for you to know there is some truth to what I said about this water. Summer's dryin' her up at a great rate, and along about next month there wouldn't be enough water to go around."

"Yeah," Johnson grunted. "I was thinkin' the same thing."

They dug some more and then Johnson said, "Deep enough?"

"It's about right," Clay judged. "Let's hop out and have a drink. Brought me a bottle of Taos Lightning to kill our thirst."

They heaved themselves out of the grave, and Allison took a brown bottle out of a pocket in his saddlebags. He jerked the cork out with his teeth and spat it into the hole. Then he handed the bottle to Johnson. "Cheers."

Johnson took a long pull at the Lightning and passed it back. He glanced at the blue sky and saw two buzzard hawks circling high above them. "Funny how they know."

"Ain't it, though?" Clay nodded. The bottle was two-thirds gone when Clay stretched and said, "Let's get to 'er."

Johnson took his bowie knife from its scabbard and placed it between his teeth. He knelt beside the freshly dug hole and lowered himself down at one end. Clay held his skinning knife in his right hand and jumped into the other end of the hole, landing softly and ready for action like a big cat.

Johnson took the weapon from between his teeth. "When shall we go at it?"

"Any time. You make the choice."

Johnson crouched low, his back arching, the flowing muscles in his arms tensed. He whispered, "Now!" and leaped forward. Clay caught the other man's knife arm at the wrist, but not before the speeding point had sliced into his shoulder. His own hand was locked in Johnson's iron fist just under the blade of the skinning knife. The two men rocked back and forth in the shallow trench, grunting and sweating with intense effort. With a quick, deft move of his foot, Clay tripped the bigger man, but Johnson's back was only a few inches from the dirt wall behind him, and he didn't go down. Struggling fiercely, shifting his huge weight with unexpected agility, Johnson forced Clay backward until Clay's back was tight against the opposite wall of the grave. In brute strength, Clay wasn't quite equal to his mighty neighbor. The bowie knife slowly, irresistibly, began to inch toward Clay's muscle-corded throat.

When the blade touched flesh, Clay suddenly twisted his knife hand so that his own blade slashed down across Johnson's fingers, cutting them to the bone. Johnson swore and released his grip slightly. As Clay wrenched his knife hand free, the bigger man sprang back out of range, slipping to one knee as he went. Gambling everything on one, quick charge, Clay leaped after his opponent. Johnson's flashing bowie knife came up, burying itself in Allison's thigh. Clay's blade swept down and buried itself to the hilt in the other man's body, just above the collar bone. Panting hard he pulled Johnson's knife from his leg and climbed out of the grave. He tied a neckerchief around the wound to stop the bleeding, then lay down on the ground and rested. Before filling in the narrow trench, he said in a panting voice, "Damned fine fight you put up, Johnson. Wish there was more around like you." Then he went to work with his shovel, favoring the wounded leg that would cause him to limp slightly for the rest of his life.

Unfortunately for Clay, there were certain civilized souls in the Panhandle who did not take to such premeditated violence. There were also numerous friends of the departed Johnson who insisted there had been some sort of foul play at the water hole. "If they're going to make a mountain out of a molehill that way," Allison grumbled to his cowhands, "then Texas ain't the place for a man like me. I'm sellin' and movin' on to New Mexico, where I hear tell there's room to breathe and fight without everybody meddlin' in your business. Any of you boys wants to come along with me, let's go."

To a man, his cowpokes saddled up and went with him. As one of them said, "God knows he ain't the easiest man to ride for, and most of the things he does is as wrong as a striped calf, but things ain't never dull with him."

Clay and his boys took a herd of 4,000 head with them when they left the Panhandle, and a reasonable number of those steers were not marked with Clay's Circle-A brand. However, no Texans with missing livestock chased after the Allison outfit to reclaim their beef. They figured Clay's departure was cheap at almost any price, and they just heaved a sigh of relief that he was gone.

After making a long trail northwest, Clay and his men reached a spot where a massive range of mountains stretched along the distant horizon as far as the eye could see.

"Them are the Sangre de Christo mountains," a wooden-faced puncher drawled. "Means the blood of Christ."

"That's a good name," Clay decided. "I wonder if the rivers around there run red."

"Cimarron ain't far. Two, three days hard ridin' right through that pass off to the right," somebody volunteered. "It's a good, loud town, and it's wide open."

"Well, let's head on up that way." Clay rode over to a steer that was edging off too far to the left, with 50 head edging out behind him. He took off his hat, let out a mighty bellow and swatted the steer between the eyes with the Stetson, driving it back into the herd. "Come on, boys!" he yelled. "We're headin' for Cimarron!"

Clay got himself a nice spread just outside of the town of Cimarron, and he and his punchers rode into town regularly to raise hell. They would troop from the Maxwell House to the St. James to the Silver Dollar, emptying bottle after bottle of liquor and roaring for more. Clay, pushing 30 now, was getting to be as good at drinking and gambling as he was at fighting. He could belt down two bottles of rotgut and stay sober enough to play a shrewdly belligerent game of stud, blackjack or draw.

Women started coming into his life, too. It was natural to his pagan temperament that he would, from time to time, take off his boots, pants, shirt and underwear and ride "bareback," in the strictest sense of the word, through town. He would call out to his lady loves by

286

name, inviting them to join him for various obscene purposes at their earliest convenience.

"Well, look at Lady Godiva," a stranger to Cimarron once remarked, during one of Clay's spirited rides. Luckily for the tenderfoot, Clay was, of course, wearing no guns. Allison had never heard of anybody named Godiva, but the "Lady" part irked him no small measure. Riding up on the broadwalk, he leaned far down and grabbed the stranger by one ankle. He then towed the screaming and unwilling passenger through town to the great amusement of the citizens.

After some months of pleasant, riotous living in New Mexico, Clay rode into Cimarron by himself early one afternoon. His cowhands were busy branding some stock, but he didn't feel like working. He didn't know what he felt like doing, but whatever it was, it wasn't good. He was sullen and sharp to friends and barkeeps as he wandered from one saloon to the next, drinking large quantities of alcohol and muttering disgustedly to himself. For some reason, Clay felt as if life was passing him by. He hadn't done anything worth talking about since his fight with Johnson. The brawls and drinking, the gambling and wenching here in Cimarron were all right in their own limited way, but he longed for bigger and better excitement—like the time he had shot his way out of the Union camp during the war. "God damn the Union Army!" he muttered suddenly, slamming his glass down on the bar. "Fill 'er up again and leave the bottle!"

It seemed to Clay that the main purpose of the whole Yankee army was to make him miserable. Killing his Tennessee friends; taking him prisoner; breaking that poor old lady's window. And sure as shooting, it was Yankees who were taking all the good government jobs these days. Weren't the sheriff of Cimarron and that fool tax collector who had visited him last month both Yanks?

Clay smashed the bottle on the counter in indignation and walked on to the Lambert saloon, which was almost deserted. "Gimme a bottle!" he told the bartender. "Damned no good, coyote Yankees!" He was halfway through this new bottle, which gave him a grand total of nearly four bottles for the day, when five of the hated bluecoat soldiers decided to drop in for a few drinks. They were cavalrymen, hot and dusty from a long ride over the hills, and they were in no mood to be subservient.

The sergeant in charge of the group bellied up to the bar about a foot away from Clay. Allison squinted in drunken disgust at the sickening blue uniform and said emphatically, "Don't crowd me."

"Sorry." The sergeant shifted down the bar another foot. He didn't know Allison, or he would probably have shifted clear to Santa Fe.

"I said, don't crowd me, goddamn it!"

The sergeant replied, succinctly, "Go to hell," and those were the last words he ever uttered. With no warning, Clay whirled around, bringing the single Colt he wore into action. His first shot struck the sergeant squarely in the middle of the chest and sent him flying back as though he had been kicked by a horse. Whether the remaining four soldiers planned to go for their guns or run for their lives will never be known for certain. Before the sergeant had stopped rolling, Clay put two more slugs into the two cavalrymen nearest him; each shot was fatal. The fourth man was hit just over his right ear as he tried to duck behind the end of the bar. Clay's fifth bullet slammed into the fifth man as he raced out the door. It pounded into him just under the armpit and sent him crashing against the batwing doors where he sprawled in a shapeless heap.

The room was thick with smoke. Clay blew the acrid, bitter wisps from his gun barrel and slowly reloaded. Then he turned to finish his drink. "That'll teach 'em to crowd a man," he allowed. The bartender, his face shocked into a waxen mask, stood frozen behind the bar.

The people of Cimarron were too stunned by the wanton massacre to do anything. They stood in small, silent groups on the street and passed the word in strained whispers. "Five! Five men he killed in less than five seconds!" When someone took the word to the sheriff, he reacted just as the bartender had. "No point in makin' it an even half-dozen," he said, his face losing all its color. "I'll wait till he sobers up a little."

Clay polished off the rest of the bottle, set it down at the bar and wiped his mouth with the back of his sleeve. "The boys ought to have all that beef branded by now," he said amiably. "Guess I'll go back and see if they did a good job." He stepped over one body, lifted a boot delicately over the dead sergeant and went sideways through the door, so as not to disturb the corpse sprawled there. After tipping his hat to a group of people on the corner, he rode out to his ranch at a leisurely pace.

The cowpokes had not yet returned, so Clay went into the kitchen of his house and lit a fire to boil some coffee. It was just coming to a good boil when there was a loud shout from the front of the house. "Allison! Come out of there with your hands up!" Clay took the time to buckle a second gun on, then went out on the porch. A cavalry captain and eight men were sitting their horses, waiting for him. The captain, an arrogant West Pointer, felt that he would lose face by having so many men hold guns on one man, so none of the army men had a gun in his hand.

"You're my prisoner," he told Allison. "You're under arrest."

Clay relaxed, slumping into a hip-shot stance, with a hand on each hip—a hand about half an inch above each revolver handle. "Me? What for?"

"You know very well what for. For murdering five good soldiers!"

"They weren't so good, else they wouldn't have got themselves killed off so easy."

"Get your horse. You're going back to Cimarron with us."

Clay considered this at length. Finally he shrugged and smiled up at the captain. "All right. I'll be back in just a minute." He went into the house and came back with his hat and a Winchester. He put the hat on his head and tucked the rifle under his arm, so that its trigger was never far from his right index finger. "Let's go and get this over with," he said.

With Clay armed to the teeth, the procession rode back into Cimarron. Allison, sobered somewhat by now, began to think that the whole affair was uproariously funny. "Look at me!" he yelled to his friends in Cimarron. "I'm a prisoner! The army caught me fair and square and disarmed me!" At this point he raised his Winchester over his head and fired one thundering shot at the sky.

"They finally took you, huh?" his comrades called back gleefully. "Only took nine of 'em to bring you in? Hey? Just who is whose prisoner, anyway? Aw, leave 'em go, Clay!"

The horribly embarrassed captain summoned the sheriff and asked for his help in taking the "prisoner" to Taos, to stand trial. The lawman reluctantly agreed. With

Clay riding wherever he felt like riding, the 11 men moved out of Cimarron and started on the road to Taos. For a few miles, Clay exchanged jokes with the enlisted men and called the sheriff and captain unprintable but jocular names. At one point, he rode to the head of the column and held his Winchester at the captain's back. "How 'bout it, boys? Does he treat you all right, or should I blow him in half?" The soldiers snickered nervously, and the captain began to lose all interest in the trip to Taos. The sheriff had never been interested in the first place.

Finally, Clay looked at the setting sun and called the column to a halt, "Lookit here," he told the captain, "it's gettin' late and I'm tired of all this foolin'. I don't want to be your prisoner no more." Since the gaping muzzle of Allison's Winchester was on a direct line with his stomach, the officer swallowed hard and looked to the sheriff for advice. The sheriff chose to ignore the situation.

"You just write down in your report, Captain, that you turned your prisoner over to the local authorities," Clay said. "That's the sheriff here, and he won't mind. Will you, Sheriff?" The officer of the law shook his head mutely. "If you don't do that, Captain, I'll just plain have to wipe out the whole bunch of you. 'Cause I got to get back to my ranch."

Sixty seconds later, the cavalrymen were riding down the road, leaving Allison and the law behind. Clay grinned. "As for you, Sheriff, you don't really want to take me to Taos, do you?" Half a minute later, the lawman was riding away, too. He never did show up in Cimarron again, and Clay got back to his ranch in time for supper.

With Cimarron's sheriff gone, and no one else particularly eager to take over the job, the town became, for all practical purposes, Clay's personal property. He enjoyed his position as a kind of feudal baron and made it pay handsomely on the side. He sold his beef at his prices to the local merchants. If he felt like paying a debt, he did. Otherwise, he tore up the bill and handed it back to the tradesman who had presented it to him, suggesting amiably, "Let's call this paid in full."

Although nobody did anything about it, the story of the cavalry massacre was soon known throughout the West. It was followed by other startling stories. Gunmen and killers listened to the tales with intense interest. Clay now had the stature of a giant in the West, and to kill him would transfer that gigantic stature to the man bold enough to pull the trigger. Some gunmen came to town, sized Clay up quietly, and moved on rather than try their luck. Others, more confident and rash, took that last, lonely gamble with a gun.

The most formidable man who tried to cut Allison down was a tall, dark and deadly Latin named Pancho Grego. With two sidekicks named Horn and DeFellita, Grego rode into Cimarron in the early evening. He was dressed in the most colorful Mexican tradition, with fancy red-and-white embroidery thickly stitched into his short, formal jacket and skin-tight pants. His saddle was richly inlaid with silver studs and stars, and his wide, flat-topped black hat was fringed with tiny, dangling beads. Well set up on a shiny black gelding, Grego rode between his friends with the air of an amused god visiting the earth for a few laughs. DeFellita was dressed much like Grego, Horn in dusty brown homespun. They dropped off their horses at the Stanton Hostelry, then marched into the nearest saloon. After they had up-ended a few glasses, Grego asked the barman, "Where does this fellow Clay Allison do his drinking? I want to meet him."

"He generally drinks his way through all the bars in town. You got business with him?"

Grego didn't take offense at the question. "My name is Pancho Grego. In San Antone and Santa Fe, where I've been staying lately, I've heard this Allison is a man who is afraid of nothing. I want to see if it's true."

The bartender nodded wisely. Grego had won a top reputation in a series of about ten gunfights, from which he had been the only man to walk away. "Reckon Allison will be right pleased to find out you're in town."

Clay found out about the visitor in a purely accidental manner. An hour after Grego's arrival, although word had gone around immediately that he was being sought out, he had still not heard the news. Clay turned a corner sharply, on his way to the Lambert Saloon, and almost ran into three men coming the other way.

Grego stepped back, his eyes flicking over the big man with sudden suspicion. "Who are you?" he asked.

"Who am I?" Allison roared. "Who the hell are you?"

"Name's Grego. I'm looking for Clay Allison."

Clay was no fool. He saw three men, their hands itching to be filled with gun butts—and each of them had a hard, quick look that marked them as proficient gunfighters. One of them, he could take easy, two probably, but three? It was questionable. He grinned broadly, with genuine pleasure, and slapped Grego on the shoulder. "I've heard about you. I'm Allison, and there's nothin' that would give me more downright pleasure than tanglin' with you. But first I'd like to get the true of it about some of your doin's down in San Antonio. Come on into the St. James here, and I'll stand you drinks."

The four went into the bar and lined up at the rail. Once invited to brag, Grego performed admirably. He talked until a full bottle had been killed off. Then Clay said, "Say, where you fellas keepin' your cayuses?"

"Couple of blocks down. Stanton's," DeFellita volunteered.

"Damn!" Clay shook his head in disgust. "That ornery skunk Stanton's been puttin' strychnine to strange horses and callin' it alkali poisoning. Charges a sucker five dollars to cart the carcass away and gets another three for the horsehide."

Grego paled. His black gelding was worth $200, a lot of money. "Go tell that stablehand if anything happens to one of our horses we'll burn his stable down with him and Stanton in it!"

As DeFellita and Horn started for the door, Clay called after them. "We'll wait for you right here." When the two men were gone, he smiled at Grego like a tomcat smiling at a sparrow. "Just one thing I'd like to say about the talkin' you've been doin'."

"What's that?"

"Of all the men I ever heard, you are the biggest and goddamdest liar."

Grego realized he had been tricked into going it alone, and it is to his credit that he didn't back down by a hair. Stepping away from the bar, his right hand tensed for a draw, he said, "You want to die now, Allison?"

They started for their guns at the same time. Grego was fast, but he had just yanked his gun free when Clay's first slug plowed into him dead center. He pulled the trigger as he went down, and the sleeve of Clay's buckskin shirt was blackened with powder burn. Sprawled on the floor, the dying man tried to aim again, but a second slug flattened him as though he had been hit with a sledge hammer.

Allison walked to the door of the saloon and stepped out in time to see DeFellita and Horn coming quickly up the street toward the sound of the gunfight. When they saw him standing there, Horn ducked around a building and headed off in another direction. Clay Allison with a smoking .45 in his hand was hardly a cheerful picture, and the understanding citizens of Cimarron didn't blame Horn for running clean out of town.

DeFellita was made of stronger stuff. He pulled up to a sudden halt and drew his gun all in one sweeping motion. He was still skidding in the sand and dust of the street as he fired twice. One of the bullets whipped past Clay, about an inch from his left ear, and the other one whistled past his right ear. At this point, Clay shot the gunman between the eyes, and the matter was settled. Reloading over the fallen DeFellita, Clay shook his head and said softly, "For a man off balance with runnin', that was damned fine shootin', mister."

For two or three years after that, things quieted down in Cimarron. People crazy enough to challenge Clay were rare, so, except for an occasional good-natured brawl or a medium-sized, good-natured riot, town life was quiet and easy. To his surprise, Clay realized one day that he was also getting rich. This shocked and unsettled him. He was not the type to be rich. He even went so far as to pay his debts for a while, to see if this would stop his growing wealth as a rancher, but it didn't work. Finally he took to horseracing, in a further attempt to squander his substance. He and his men journeyed periodically to Colfax, Taos, Raton and other New Mexico towns to race their best ponies against the competition. It was at a small race track southwest of Raton that Clay met another one of those brave men crazy enough to fight him.

Clay was standing near the finish line on a quarter-mile track, bellowing advice to one of his punchers riding a big strawberry roan, when a well-dressed stranger elbowed him aside to get a better view. Clay kicked the man's legs out from under him, roaring, "You're in the way!" The stranger, whose name was Chunk Cooper and who had shot down nearly 20 men in his time, got up and dusted himself off. "Enjoy the races," he growled. "When they're over, you're going to be dead." Then he elbowed his way out of the crowd.

After the last race, Clay started toward a big log cabin nearby, where food was being served to the hungry sportsmen. He was pleased to note that his new-found enemy, true to his threat, was waiting for him. "Tell you what," Clay said. "I'm sick and tired of ordinary fightin'. Let's get up on a couple of these quarter horses and shoot it out runnin' straight at one another. How's that?"

"Sounds all right to me," Cooper agreed. "But waiting around for you, I've worked up a terrible hunger. Let's eat first."

They went into the chuckhouse and sat facing each other in a large room crowded with other horsemen. Word of the impending duel was passed from mouth to mouth, and the gambling men bet heavily on the outcome. Odds generally favored Clay, five to three. The meal was about finished, when, without anyone knowing quite how, Clay and Chunk had a misunderstanding. One of them made a move toward his gunbelt that the other misinterpreted. After the smoke had cleared, Chunk was lying dead on the floor, and Clay was cutting into the last piece of broiled beef on his plate as though nothing had happened. When he had finished eating, and had picked his teeth, he stood up and announced solemnly: "Boys, the contest between me and Chunk here has been called off, due to an accident to one of the aforesaid parties."

In 1875, several small ranchers and insignificant clodbusters were burned out, murdered and, in other violent ways, driven from their homes. At first, everyone in northeastern New Mexico figured it was Clay Allison amusing himself. But for once, Clay was innocent. The wealthy cattlemen in the territory had decided that there were too many small-timers settling out their way, and were taking these measures to hint that the little ranchers and farmers should move elsewhere. Although Clay was one of the richest and most powerful ranchmen around, he was not in on the deal. In fact, he was on the underdog's side. This was occasioned by the murder of the Reverend Tolby of Colfax, a friend of his who had been calling the big ranchers some unpleasant names. How a preacher and Allison came to be friendly was a puzzle to everybody, but such was the case. Two days after Tolby was found riddled with bullets near his home, two hardcase Mexicans named Manuel Cordena and Cruz Vega began bragging that they were the men who had killed the unfortunate minister. Obviously, they did not know that the dead man was mourned by Clay Allison, or they would not have boasted about it.

Clay and his boys rounded up Vega in the hills outside Colfax, and with a stiff hemp rope around his neck, he talked at length about how the ring of well-heeled cattlemen had hired him and Cordena to murder Tolby. After he had finished his nervous speech, Clay said, "All right, boys. Hang him." And they did.

Clay decided that the best way to make it publicly known who was behind Tolby's killing was to put Cordena in jail and make him stand trial. So he rounded the Mexican up and turned him over to the sheriff of Colfax County. The powerful cattlemen imported shrewd Eastern lawyers to defend man, and the trial became a farce. It took only a few minutes for the sheepish jury to bring in a verdict of "not guilty."

Cordena was freed by nightfall. As he walked happily out onto the street with several celebration-minded friends, there was a shot from the shadows across the way. A bullet went over the shoulder of one man, nicked the hat of another, sped past the nose of a third and lodged itself in Manuel Cordena's head. Although no one called him on it, it was common knowledge that Clay had reversed the decision of the jury.

With understandable indignation, the Santa Fe crowd, learning what had happened up in Colfax County, searched into Clay's past in an attempt to find some concrete evidence that they could use to brand him an outlaw. This was as easy as finding a handful of sand in New Mexico. Legal machinery was put into motion and Clay, for the first time, became a bona fide fugitive from justice, with a $1,000 price on his head. He blandly ignored the whole thing, and so did everybody else.

On a drive to Dodge City with 2,000 head of cattle and 18 of his Texas saddledusters, Clay decided to pay Wyatt Earp a cordial visit. Some say he had been paid to kill the famous marshal, but this theory leaves some pertinent questions hanging loose. Allison needed money about as much as the Wells Fargo treasury. Furthermore, Clay's peculiar but ironclad ethics would not allow him to accept pay for anything that was as personal a matter as a gunfight.

With the cattle safe in the stockyards, the Allison gang rode into Dodge to empty the town's liquor supply. At the Long Branch, after cutting the dust in his throat, Clay stated conservatively, "I would count it a privilege to run into Earp and find out once and for all how good he is with a gun." That night, Clay and Earp met. Wyatt was as steady as a rock. Clay was equally solid, except he was having more fun; it showed in his eyes. They were out on the street, and half a dozen of Allison's men were with him, their horses tied a few feet away.

"Understand you've been looking for me, Clay," Wyatt observed softly.

"That's right, Marshal." Clay stepped away from his men. As he did so, he noticed that his men were also stepping away from him. They stepped clear off the street and into a nearby bar. Then he saw why. Lounging in the shadows against the wall of a nearby dancehall was another formidable gunfighter, deputy Bat Masterson. Clay really wanted to fight Earp. But he was too smart to take on two of the West's most expert gunmen at the same time, which he figured he would have to do if he pushed this fight. Clay grunted angrily, walked to his horse, mounted and rode away. A moment later he rode back briefly and bellowed at the men in the bar, "You dirty cowards. You're supposed to back me up in a case like this!" Completely disgusted, he whirled his pony around and galloped out of town in a black rage. When he got back to New Mexico, Clay had several cases of whiskey carted out to his ranch from Cimarron, and settled down to a monstrous drinking bout.

In time, Clay reconciled himself to the Earp fiasco, and other events claimed his attention. One day he got a letter from his kid brother John in Las Animas, Colorado, which brought him up to date on his brother's activities. John had taken up gambling as a profession and was doing fair-to-middling until he got to Las Animas, where there were several uncordial fellows who did not care for the way he handled a pack of cards. They had threatened him with hanging or shooting if he didn't get out of town.

"Poor little John," Clay grumbled upon reading the letter. "He's gettin' a bad deal from them fellas up in Las Animas. And if there's anythin' I can't stand, it's bullies!"

When he explained these sentiments to his cowhands in the bunkhouse, it was all they could do to keep from laughing. But Clay was serious. He left his ranch in the hands of his ramrod, mounted a good, 16-hand buckskin and took off for Las Animas to even up the odds against his brother.

John Allison was mighty relieved to see his big brother come riding up the street. While they stabled the buckskin, John filled Clay in on what had happened. "Practically everybody in town thinks I'm a crooked gambler," he complained. "Right now, there's three tough hombres hunting for me. They've sworn to nail my hide to the wall. I've been holing up in my hotel room till you got here."

Clay heaved the saddle off his buckskin and rubbed the big horse down. "Tell me one thing, John. Have you been dealin' off the bottom of the deck?"

"Well, of course, Clay."

"Good." Clay nodded with satisfaction. "If there's one thing I can't stand, it's a man not workin' his trade for all it's worth."

"They got a place outside of town, somewhere's," John told him. "But they ride in most every evening. They'll be along come sundown, likely."

The two Allisons bucked the tiger at Lowry's place through the afternoon, had two steer-sized steaks for supper, and waited patiently for the trio to make an appearance. To kill time, Clay took John on a round of the town's numerous saloons. After a sociable drink or two, he would turn, back to the bar, and thunder out words to this effect: "My name's Clay Allison! If there's a man in the house who has a mean word for my brother John, let him step up and say it." There would be a tense pause, and then Clay would finish his short talk. "Nobody mad at him? Ain't a fairer and squarer dealer in Colorado, is there? All right. Step up to the rail, boys, the drinks are on me!"

Sheriff John Spear and a deputy paid a friendly visit to the Allisons around seven o'clock. "I hope you ain't lookin' for trouble, Mr. Allison," Spear said. "I got about 20 men standin' ready as deputies if you are."

"Why, Sheriff, I'm friends with the whole world," Clay told him. "So far, I like everybody in this town, and there ain't a man hasn't hoisted a drink or two on me."

Pleased with Clay's peaceful attitude, Spear and his deputy joined the Allisons in a few shots of whiskey, then went on about their business.

The men Clay was waiting for rode into town around 9:30. They hitched their horses and mounted the plank sidewalk to find a big, pleasant-appearing man waiting for them. A few feet behind him, looking somewhat strained, was John Allison.

"I'm Johnny's brother," Clay said. "Understand you're sore at him."

All three of the men were leather-faced, rugged six-footers who wore their guns in correct postions on their lean hips. The oldest, the leader of the three, said flatly, "Your brother is a liar and a cheat and he owes us $285. If he don't pay us back right now, we're gonna kill him."

"Think we'll kill him anyway," one of the others muttered. "Don't care for his looks, or yours either."

"Why," Clay snorted, painfully insulted, "you've got the only face I ever seen uglier than the wrong end of a mule."

There seemed to be no need for further talk. Clay and the three men confronting him hauled out their artillery. The first of the trio was down before the other two had their guns in action. Clay dropped to one knee as his first victim flew backwards off the sidewalk and into the hitching rail. Bullets were chewing up the boardwalk around him. Clay's second victim caved in as a ball of lead tore through his left lung. He fired wildly three times into the sidewalk as he folded up and fell. Clay's next shot missed the third man, who ducked to one side, running toward the horses for protection. He had almost made it when Clay's fourth and fifth slugs spun him around and knocked him to the ground.

Clay ejected the five spent shells and pried five fresh ones from his cartridge belt. Refilling the cylinder, he said, "Not a bad fight. Where the hell were you, Johnny?"

John stifled a shudder that started in his heels, ran up his back and left the hair at the base of his neck itching. "Jesus!" he breathed. "You didn't look needy for help."

"Not a bad fight at all," Clay agreed with himself. "Damned bullies. Let's tie one on, boy!"

The Allison victory celebration made history in Colorado. It lasted three or four days, and Clay later remarked modestly that there wasn't a bottle in Las Animas he had not drunk at least half of, nor a dance hall girl in Las Animas who had not succumbed to his manly charms at least three times. Toward the last of the orgy, in which John did himself proud by nearly keeping up with Clay,

298

the two brothers were talked into doing a spirited jig on a roulette table in the Crystal Dance Hall.

In the midst of this carefree gaiety, Sheriff Spear and about ten deputies, loaded with rifles, shotguns and pistols, appeared. "You damn near wrecked the town, Allison," he told Clay. "I want you both to take off your guns and quiet down."

"I got a reputation for doin' what the law tells me to do," Clay said, swaying drunkenly on the roulette table. "So I'm goin' to take off my guns." He took off the two revolvers strapped around his waist. And then, one by one, he took off all of his clothes. John, loyally following his example, also stripped bare. "Strike up the band!" Clay yelled, and the pianist sailed into *"The Yellow Rose of Texas"* with zest.

Time was running out on Clay in more ways than one. Less than a year later, he met a girl and married her. Like so many frail, slender women, she had a backbone of iron, and she wasn't a bit afraid of her big roaring mountain lion of a husband. She even convinced him that it was almost as much fun to have a family as it was to fight all the time. After meeting her, the only men Clay killed were three cattle rustlers.

After his marriage, Clay moved back to Texas and had a fine ranch near Gagsby Creek. One day he was criticizing the way a neighboring rancher was driving a team of mules that was pulling a stuck lumber wagon. "Get the hell down off that seat," he said, "and I'll show you how to get that wagon movin'." He succeeded too well. The wagon lurched forward under his expert handling of the team, and slammed into a rock. The jolt threw Clay out of the seat. He landed in front of the wagon, and before he had time to twist away, one wheel, with maybe ten tons of lumber above it, went right over his neck. He died as neatly as though he had been dropped through a scaffold trapdoor.

It was generally assumed that Clay went straight to hell—no doubt he would have been bored with all that sweetness and light in heaven—and those who knew him best would have given five to three before he was there an hour he was teaching Old Nick a few new tricks.

ONE-MAN POSSE

In forty-five seconds of blazing gunfire, the new sheriff of Apache County made frontier history.

Sheriffs were extremely popular in the tough little cow town of Holbrook, Arizona. This was due to the fact that for as long as Holbrook citizens could remember, law officers had been their chief source of entertainment. They believed there were two types of sheriff—the good-natured, friendly sort who was willing to drink with the boys and occasionally dance bullets, and the amusingly serious type who tried to serve warrants and arrest people. The former was usually shot by accident; the latter was always shot on purpose.

On the morning of September 4, 1887, bored townspeople were looking forward to the arrival of Apache County's new sheriff, who was coming from the county seat and promised to be good for a lot of laughs. Even his name, Commodore Perry Owens, was mirth-provoking.

In the saloon next to Frank Wattron's drug store, there were explosions of laughter and gruff shouts as the sheriff's name was brought into the conversation.

Old Frank was standing in front of his store at 11

o'clock when Andy Cooper passed by on his way to the saloon.

"Well, Frank," Andy said, "figure the Commodore will try anything with me when he gits to town?"

"Maybe," Frank drawled, his keen eyes narrowed under bushy brows. "I hear Commodore Perry Owens is a man to reckon with."

Andy hooked a huge thumb in his worn gun belt, smiled tightly and said, "Guess you and a few others'd be right pleased to see me git arrested. But the new sheriff's been sworn a week and ain't come after me yet. There's no man living I can't outshoot, let alone this crazy Commodore who wears his guns backwards."

Cooper walked by the druggist and swaggered into the bar where he was greeted with enthusiasm.

"You gonna sink the Commodore, Andy?" a grizzled man at the bar yelled. "Hear tell he don't mind getting wet. He takes a bath regular!"

Enjoying the raucous laughter set off by the joke, Cooper walked to the counter and ordered a drink of whiskey straight. As the bartender hurriedly poured a shot of liquor for Cooper, the grizzled man moved closer to him and threw a gold dollar on the counter in payment for Andy's drink. " 'Bout eight years now since anyone tried to jail you, ain't it?"

"What happened to the last fella that tried it?" a new-comer to Holbrook asked.

"Hell," the grizzled man snorted. "Been so long, Andy's forgot where they buried him."

"Tell you boys something that would interest the sheriff." Andy tossed off his drink. "I ran into Slim Tewksbury and one of his boys down to Pleasant Valley day before yesterday. There's two less Tewksburys to worry about now."

The newcomer glanced at Cooper nervously, taking in the firm-set, tanned face and the powerful hands that never moved far from the grim, black-butted Colt .45 hanging low on his hip. Clearing his throat and wiping his mouth nervously with the back of his sleeve, he said, "Well, what about this here 'Commodore' that's coming to town? Don't he know no better?"

"We'll soon find out," another barfly crowed, "but he's gonna have rough sailing if he ever tries to play sheriff with Andy here."

This pleasant banter went on throughout most of the

early afternoon. The gentlemen in the bar had no way of knowing that during the late afternoon they were going to witness the deadliest 45 seconds of gunfighting in the history of their state.

The quiet, solid citizens of Holbrook and the other towns in Apache County had been looking forward to the arrival of the sheriff, too, but they weren't saying much about it. Honest, law-respecting men in the territory had realized the desperate need for an outstanding man to fill the sheriff's office in Apache County. For nearly ten years there had been no law but the business end of a Colt throughout that part of Arizona. Andy Cooper had terrorized the section. Fantastically fast and accurate with a gun, he had murdered more men than most people could recall, and it was generally admitted that he could rustle cattle in broad daylight simply because no one dared to stop him.

At the same time the notorious Tewksbury-Graham feud was raging with bloody intensity throughout the area. As in all feuds, the actual reason for its beginning was no longer important. Regardless of how it had started, the feud had spread, due to marriage and senseless killing, until it involved several large families. Men on both sides shot to kill whenever they sighted anyone from the other. Andy Cooper was the most powerful figure in the bloody fight. Along with the Blevins boys of Holbrook, who were his half brothers, he was the backbone of the Graham faction in Apache County.

Those who weren't involved on either the Graham or Tewksbury side realized the murderous feud had to be stopped before it involved everyone in the territory in a good-sized civil war.

The new sheriff of Apache County would have his work cut out for him. If he wanted to wipe out rustling and lawlessness, he had to get Andy Cooper. If he wanted to win the sacred respect of every gunslinger in the county, he had to get Andy Cooper. If he wanted to stop the Tewksbury-Graham feud, he had to get Andy Cooper.

Sheriff Commodore Perry Owens wanted to do all three things. So on this early September afternoon, he was riding his bay stud through the hot Arizona sun on the trail toward Holbrook, to get Andy Cooper.

The man riding that dusty trail gave the drinking crowd in Holbrook wide range for insults and jokes. In a land famous for picturesque characters, he stood out as the most colorful personality of them all. First, there was his name, Commodore Perry Owens. There are various stories as to how he came by that monicker. One claims he had actually been a commodore in the United States Navy. Another tells how he came to a flooded river that no one could cross. The yarn goes that he lassoed logs floating in the river until he had enough for a raft, then tied them together with his lariat and crossed over. The actual way he got the name, however, was much simpler. When he was born in Tennessee on July 29, 1852, his mother gave it to him. She was a great admirer of the then national hero, and also, by coincidence, her son had been born on the anniversary of Perry's famous fight on Lake Erie. Mrs. Owens hoped her boy would live up to his namesake by joining the Navy, but the youngster preferred prairie schooners and rolling plains to fore-and-aft-rigged schooners and the rolling ocean. When he was in his middle teens, he headed west to Texas where he somehow got a good education and soon became one of the top trail drivers in the state.

Commodore's dress and habits were such that he became known throughout the Southwest as an eccentric son-of-a-gun. Although it was outdated, he stuck loyally to the old-fashioned plainsman outfit, a wide-brimmed, flat-topped prairie hat and a fringed buckskin jacket. For long rides through brush country, Commodore used a fancy, silver-studded pair of thick leather chaps instead of the rough, rawhide chivarros used by most men. He wore his hair shoulder length, and indulged in the odd practice of taking a bath every Saturday night. His bathing habits had caused many scornful words to be spoken about him—out of his hearing, of course. At that time, aside from being a sissified nuisance, such constant contact with soap and water was generally considered downright unhealthy. Clean shaven, except for a small mustache, Commodore Perry Owens had finely sculptured features and clear, keen gray eyes.

While Owens' name, dress and habits made good bar talk, the really amusing thing about him was the fact that he invariably wore his handsomely mounted revolvers backwards, butt forward at each hip. This ridiculous manner of packing his guns caused much merriment and an unknown quantity of deaths. For example, old-timers spoke wryly of a brash character who said to Commodore, 'You're as purty as a drawing I seen of

Buffalo Bill, but you size up as even a worse dude than him, from the way you're wearing your artillery. Let's see how fast you can run, mister!" Then the foolhardy gent reached for his six-shooter. Since no one knew his name, a slab was put up in a Texas boothill which simply said: "Rest In Peace."

By the time Commodore left Texas, it was a well-established fact that he could draw either of his revolvers with either hand before most talented gunslingers could unbend their elbows. His muscles, brain and calm eyes worked together as though powered by the same high explosive as his bullets. With a .44 in each hand, from 20 paces Owens could blast a rolling, bouncing, rifle cartridge case until it was nothing but a shredded, unrecognizable sliver of metal. He could shoot a rifle just as fast and accurately.

Texans especially remembered Commodore for his actions at the time a war party of wandering Mescaleros made the fatal mistake of attacking a wagon train he was leading. As they galloped down from the left, Owens pulled his left Colt with his left hand and shot three times. The surviving Indians retreated in some haste, leaving three riderless ponies behind.

When the civic leaders of Apache County heard of this invincible fighting man from Texas, they let him know they would pay him a top sheriff's salary to do some of his shooting in their behalf.

Commodore liked Arizona and was getting bored with trail driving, so he accepted their offer.

His unusual appearance, pleasant face and backward guns all spoke against him, but Apache County officials were impressed by his reputation and a certain steady sureness about his gray eyes, so they swore him in, figuring that after all the only thing they had to lose was his life.

A short while after taking the oath, Commodore visited the county clerk's office to ask about any warrants that might be on hand.

The clerk, a wiry old man named Benton, studied Commodore shrewdly and said, "There's only one warrant here that means anything, son. It's for a feller named Andy Cooper, for horse stealing, and it's been sitting here a long time."

"Why?" Commodore asked. "Has this Cooper got everyone buffaloed around here?"

304

"For good reason," Benton said dryly. "Those who aren't scared of him are dead. Except for the Tewksbury clan, which he's killing off fast."

The clerk told Owens exactly what the situation was in Apache County, winding up with the statement that if the sheriff decided to serve the warrant on Andy Cooper, he would be signing his own death warrant.

"Do you still want to take it?" he asked when he had finished.

"No," Commodore said thoughtfully. "Not now."

He turned and walked out of the office without saying another thing.

Word got around within an hour that the man behind the tin star was a coward. Andy Cooper rode into town that afternoon and insolently tied his horse in front of the sheriff's office. The next day the men who had hired Owens called him on the carpet.

"Why don't you bring in Andy Cooper?" one of them demanded irritably. "Everyone knows you can always find him over in Holbrook."

"Pick him up some time when he's out of town," another suggested. "He'll have a small army on his side in Holbrook."

"You're the sheriff. It's your duty to bring in anyone with a warrant made out for him!" the first one snapped.

"Gentlemen," Commodore said levelly, "from what I hear of Cooper, there will be shooting when I go after him. I want to be sure that his arrest is worth possible bloodshed. I'll be sheriff in my own way or not at all."

Within the next few days, Owens found that the county clerk had been right. He soon discovered that Andy Cooper was the cornerstone upon which nearly all of the lawlessness in Apache County was based. With his expert gunplay and the Blevins boys to back him up, he was still rustling openly in Pleasant Valley and was the most potent anti-Tewksbury feudist in the area.

A few days later, Owens began a routine job of presenting subpoenas to prospective jury members within the county. He visited Benton in the morning and picked up the warrant for Andy Cooper.

"I'm going through Holbrook tomorrow. Hear Cooper will be there," he said.

"You'll be killed if you try to use this," the old man repeated grimly.

Commodore folded it and put it in his jacket pocket. Outside, he swung onto his bay and rode out of town.

They say vultures carry the news of impending death. Whether buzzards whispered into the ears of Holbrook residents or not, they knew the next morning that the sheriff was on his way to visit them. Andy Cooper was instinctively discreet in his choice of places for a hangout. Fearless as he may have been, he knew he had his half-brothers there, and Holbrook was a town in which most of the menfolk just naturally enjoyed using sheriffs as targets. Its citizens were particularly anxious to meet the new sheriff who dressed in a peculiar manner, bathed regularly, wore his guns backwards and was carrying a warrant for the arrest of the town hero.

At about 3 o'clock, when Owens finally rode down the main street, he realized there might be a hundred guns shooting at him before sunset. He guided his horse at a slow walk to the combined blacksmith shop and stable. Inside, he dismounted.

Bill Gard, a cowpuncher, was in the blacksmith shop.

"Is Andy Cooper in town?" Commodore asked him.

Gard told him that Cooper had been around most of the day.

In the meantime, John Blevins, the eldest of Cooper's feuding half-brothers, hurried into the saloon where Andy and his friends were joking about possible epitaphs for the commodore.

"Andy," he called, "that sheriff just come into town. He's over to the blacksmith's."

Cooper's face hardened and his hand dropped instinctively nearer his gun. "John," he ordered, "you get me a horse and take it over to the house. I'll be along in a minute."

"Good," John said. "He tries to take you over at the house, we'll shoot him to pieces."

"I won't need help!" Cooper snarled.

"The reason I said that," John explained, "is that he don't sit his horse and look around like no tenderfoot. He sits good and sees everything without moving his head much."

"I want a horse so's if he tries to take me I can get outta the county for a while after I kill 'im," Cooper growled.

After John left, Andy said to the bunch at the bar, "If he's fool enough to come after me, give him a nice burial,

306

boys." He finished his drink and went outside to the main street.

On the south side of Holbrook's principal road, several saloons, a general store and Frank Wattron's drug store were lined up in a row. On the far side of the street there were the railroad tracks, and beyond the tracks stood the large Blevins house which Andy called home most of the time. The main street was completely deserted and shadows were stretching longer as the sun settled down in the sky. Andy looked up and down the empty street. To his left he could see the blacksmith shop several hundred feet away. As the men in the saloon gathered near the windows to watch, he walked rapidly across the street, stepped over the tracks, and a few seconds later arrived at the two-story, L-shaped building. In front of the Blevins house, he turned, his hand resting on his gun butt, scanned the street once more, then disappeared inside.

The men in the saloon saw John Blevins lead a pony up to the house and tie it a few feet from the front porch before mounting the steps to the large porch and going in after Andy.

At the blacksmith shop, Commodore finished checking his revolvers and calmly took his Winchester from its saddle holster. While he was examining the rifle, Bill Gard said, "You figuring on going after Cooper?"

"Yes."

Commodore flipped a final shell into the breech and snapped the rifle's lever into place.

Outside the blacksmith shop, he strode up the street toward Wattron's drug store. Bill Gard walked beside him. At the saloon there were scowling men standing behind the windows and crowding around the inside of the door. Commodore glanced briefly at them without changing his expression or his stride.

He entered the drug store and spoke to Wattron. "Nice place you got here, mister. Have you any idea where I can locate Andy Cooper?"

"Yeah," Wattron said. "But you better get a posse first."

"Where is he?"

Wattron gestured across the street and the railroad tracks to the Blevins house. "He's in there right now, but it'd be suicide to try and take him. No telling how many of the Blevinses are in there, plus God knows how many friends."

"Thanks." Commodore turned and started for the door.

"Listen, Owens," Gard said. "You may need some help. I'll go along with you."

"There could be a dozen men in there," Wattron added. "Whoever's in that house, you can be sure they won't let you take Andy, and they know how to use guns along with the best of 'em."

Commodore nodded to Wattron and said to young Bill Gard, "I'm the sheriff. I can take him alone."

With the Winchester under his arm, Commodore stepped out into the street and started toward the house, one man against an unknown number of hidden killers waiting in the gaunt, frame structure.

As Owens crossed the tracks, a slight wind came up that tugged at his long hair and lifted the flap of his pocket in which he carried the warrant. His eyes fixed steadily on the house, he buttoned the pocket with his free hand while he walked, studying the building before him.

There were two front doors on the porch before the house. They were about 12 feet apart and both seemed to enter into the same large living room. There were windows on the ground floor and second floor from which Commodore realized he could be conveniently shot.

Commodore passed the tethered horse and walked up the steps to the porch. Crossing the porch, he knocked softly. There was no answer. The second time, he knocked harder.

At the second knock, the door swung open a few inches and Andy Cooper, holding the doorknob with his left hand, peered coldly out. In his right hand was a .45 which was leveled straight at Commodore.

Why Andy Cooper didn't open the door shooting is best known to Andy Cooper, but once he had looked into Commodore's eyes, he was a different man.

"Cooper," Owens said quietly, ignoring the tunnel of a gun barrel staring up at him, "I have a warrant for you. Let's have no trouble."

Andy's hand wavered a moment as he glared into those calm gray eyes. "What warrant?" he finally said.

"For stealing horses." The voice was calmly matter-of-fact.

"Wait a minute. I'll see about it."

"No. You'll have to come now."

Cooper's mouth opened nervously. For the first time in his life the instinct of self-preservation warned him he was facing a more capable fighter. But a whole lifetime of being top gunslinger among dangerous men had built his ego to a point where he would almost rather be killed than back down.

In the moment of painful silence while Cooper was deciding what to do, there was a small, dry, clicking sound that made up his mind for him. The other door on the porch had opened noiselessly and one of Andy's half-brothers had made the grim clicking sound by pulling the hammer of his revolver back to cocked position.

Commodore was in an uncomfortable spot by any man's standards. There was a gun aimed point-blank at him from each door, plus an unknown number of firearms at the windows. His powerful muscles tensed for swift action.

Cooper started the history-making 45 seconds by suddenly shouting, "I won't go!" At the same time he began to simultaneously slam the door and pull the trigger of the Colt aimed at Owens.

Striking like a coiled diamondback, Commodore kicked the door in with his boot, throwing Andy's aim off, fired the Winchester from his hip, blasting Cooper dead center through the door, and leaped backwards from the porch. His incredibly fast movements threw both Andy's and John Blevins' timing off. Each of their guns roared harmlessly as bullets whined past Owens.

In mid-leap from the porch, Commodore pumped a new shell into his rifle. When his feet touched the ground he was facing the arsenal of a house ready for action. John Blevins showed himself in the second door, where he had been crouching, and threw down on Commodore. Just as he pulled the trigger, Owens' second blast knocked him spinning back into the house. His own shot went wild and struck the tethered pony in the head. The horse screamed shrilly and reared back, clawing the air violently with its hooves and breaking its reins. Whirling, it charged a hundred feet before it dropped dead.

Still holding his Winchester at his hip, Commodore's keen eyes swept over the front of the house. Cooper, a very tough scrapper, had staggered back to his feet in the front room, still holding his revolver. Commodore spotted him as he raised the six-gun to fire through the window. He blasted Andy with a second shot through the window, and this time Andy was dead before the shattered glass showered down around him.

There were shouts of enraged cursing inside the house, but no target showed itself for a few seconds. Then suddenly one of the front doors burst open and Hamp Blevins charged frantically out of the house toward the sheriff, pulling the trigger desperately as he came. Owens shot him through the chest and Hamp flipped grotesquely in the air. He sprawled to the ground and never got up again.

As Commodore fired, his attention was drawn from the house for a split second and his fighting instinct caused him to change position instantly. As he moved, another gun barked and a slug whispered viciously past his ear.

He scanned the front of the building while he snapped a fresh cartridge into his rifle, but there was nothing in sight. Then his quick eyes caught a tiny movement near one of the second-floor windows. Mose Roberts, one of the Blevins clan by marriage, was up there trying to maneuver for some more shooting. As he stuck his Colt and head out to blast again at the one-man posse, Commodore's Winchester roared for the fifth time. There was a tinkling of glass as Roberts' gun hand flew up and he smashed the window pane with his gun barrel. The action was purely involuntary, due to the Winchester slug pounding through him.

With his rifle almost out of shells, Commodore whipped his Colt from his left holster with his left hand, holding the smoking Winchester in his right. Several seconds passed while he stood waiting for whatever else the house might offer. But the fighting was over. The blazing 45 seconds that were to write frontier history were finished.

Commodore at last slipped his revolver back into his holster and turned toward the main street of Holbrook where Wattron, Gard and a few others were now crossing the tracks and coming to meet him.

"Greatest shooting I ever saw," one said breathlessly. "Damned if it wasn't!"

"Four against one," Wattron muttered as though he couldn't quite believe it himself.

"From where I stood," another said loudly, "it looked like it was lucky for them they weren't ten!"

Commodore walked by them without pausing or speaking. In front of the saloon where the outlaw sympathizers

310

were coming out into the street, their eyes filled with mixed fury, fear and shock, Commodore halted. He deliberately and slowly refilled his rifle in front of them. Then he looked them over casually with icy gray eyes. No one moved or spoke. He turned his back on them contemptuously and walked back to the blacksmith shop. A moment later he rode his bay out of town.

Rustling in Apache County dwindled to zero overnight and stayed there. The back of the Tewksbury-Graham feud was broken, and although it continued sporadically in other sections of Arizona for a short while, in Commodore's area it was stopped cold.

A day or two after the battle, Commodore walked into the county clerk's office, and put down a slip of paper and walked back out again. Benton looked after him as the long-haired sheriff strode out into the sunny street, wearing his guns, as always, backwards.

Glancing at the sheet of paper, Benton read Commodore's personal report of the incredible battle. Scrawled in a strong hand across the back of the warrant for Andy Cooper were the simple words, "Party against whom this warrant was issued was killed while resisting arrest."

It was a funny thing, but old-timers insist that within two weeks it was amazing how many men in Apache County were wearing their guns backwards. And some of them even started to take a bath every week.